THE SCORPION SANCTION

GORDON PAPE
AND TONY ASPLER

_____ **THE VIKING PRESS   NEW YORK** _____

Pape

LIBRARY OF CONGRESS CATALOGING IN PUBLICATION DATA
Pape, Gordon.
The Scorpion sanction.
I.   Aspler, Tony, joint author.   II.   Title.
PZ4.P2139Sc   1980   [PR9199.3.P33]   813′.54   79-56262
ISBN 0-670-19965-6

Printed in the United States of America
Set in Linotype Times Roman

To Kim—with love and courage,
anything is possible
G.P.

To Mike Prior—for champagne days past
and those to come
T.A.

CONTENTS

DAY ONE
SATURDAY, NOVEMBER 3

The Nile water swirled and eddied around the pontoons of Cairo's bridges like liquid camouflage. In the white morning sky, five young hawks circled on the hot air currents in lazy imitation of the water's motion below. Occasionally one of the birds would hang in the air for a moment, then drop and plunge its claws into the turbid river, only to rise again with a barely perceptible movement of its powerful wings.

Hassan Aziz, in a dirty green undershirt and gray trousers, stood in his ancient rowboat and watched the flight of the birds, protecting his eyes against the whiteness of the sun. He longed to be free, like the hawks, to soar above the Nile and glide over the stench of the city to the desert beyond the pyramids, where everything is still and clean. The sun-bleached timbers of his boat creaked as he floated downriver on the current; he could hear the constant tattoo of car horns bruising the air from both banks. The noise seemed to gather and intensify as it rolled out across the Nile.

Hassan's boat was being drawn toward El Gala'a Bridge, so he sat down and pulled on the ponderous oars. Silently, he cursed his fate. He picked up his homemade *shoka,* with its twin curved hooks bound together like the front claws of a hawk; he raked it across the water and landed another clump of Nile weed, throwing it on the mounting pile in the stern of the boat.

Hassan hated the weeds. *Ward-el-Nil,* the flowers of the Nile, had bulbous, phallic stems with thick, fleshy leaves that fouled the bridges and choked the irrigation canals. How could a handful of men in sun-bleached rowboats weed the mighty Nile? He recalled a proverb his father had taught him: Some disturb the waters; others fish them. And he was trying to farm the waters, a job designed by the Devil. But the Cairo Coast Guard paid him twelve pounds a month for his labor, and jobs were not easy to come by in a city that had doubled its population in the last ten years.

The pile of weeds had begun to rot in the heat of the sun. Hassan lit a Cleopatra cigarette. One more pass and he would head for the bank to pitch them up by the concrete retaining wall. A large clump of plants drifted slowly by; they had become entangled with a rusty oil drum used as a marker buoy. He leaned over the side of the boat and hooked the nearest tendrils. The smoke from his cigarette curled into his eyes as he pulled the mass of vegetation toward him. The weeds were heavier than they should have been and he needed both hands. As the clump came alongside, Hassan released the hooks and drove them deeper into the tangle for better leverage. He pulled upward, straining against the bow to lift the weight. His hands slipped down the wooden pole, and he sank to his knees to stop himself from falling. The lifting action had dislodged something from the weeds. Rising to the water's surface was the body of a man, the features bloated beyond recognition, the ankles roped together.

Hassan's screams were lost in the cacophony of traffic noise as Cairo went about its business, oblivious to the terror of the man on the river who had gaffed a waterlogged corpse. Overhead, the hawks continued to wheel and turn.

≅≈≅

The highway from the airport into Cairo runs arrow-straight through open desert to the wealthier suburbs on the outskirts of the city. The road is divided by a grass median planted with well-clipped ficus trees and flowering acacias. At the new industrial-bureaucratic-residential quarter called Nasr City, a major traffic circle splits the highway into several access roads leading to the city's center. Above this circle stands a massive unfinished overpass, started years ago and abandoned when the city ran out of money.

On the day that Hassan Aziz hooked a water-bloated corpse out of the Nile, an army of workmen was busy on the overpass, draping flattering portraits of the American president, H. Whitney Dunlap, over its concrete parapets. A twin portrait of the Egyptian president, Mahmoud Sayed, was still at the government printer, delayed because the subject had taken an instant dislike to the painting; the original artist was now in disgrace. A new portrait would be ready, according to the office of the minister of the interior, in good time for the U.S. presidential visit.

All along the airport road, similar gangs of workmen were stringing flags and bunting from lampposts and public buildings. The decorations would end at the traffic circle because the motorcade's route into the city was a military secret and only on the morning of the American president's arrival would flags be unfurled from windows and balconies along the street.

Ahmed Rahman, head of Egypt's Internal Security Department, ordered his driver to stop at the traffic circle. He and his aide, Ismail Ali, got out of the dust-covered Mercedes to inspect the locale. They were satisfied that up to this point a fast-moving motorcade would prove an impossible target for a potential sniper. There was little cover along the airport road, and few tall buildings with adequate sight lines.

But as the motorcade slowed down to turn onto Ramses Street (the approach favored by the Egyptian president) it would have to proceed under the overpass. Crowds of Egyptians would be on the ramp, pressing up against the barriers for a better view of the two heads of state. It would be simple for some lunatic to drop a grenade into an open car from that vantage point.

"A perfect spot for an assassination," whispered Ali.

Rahman surveyed the overpass and then concentrated on the buildings around it—a series of anonymous sand-colored high-rise structures, mainly housing government departments, some twenty-four stories tall. He pulled at the collar of his beige lightweight jacket, which was sticking to his back in the unseasonable November heat. His throat was irritated by the fine dust in the air, and he would dearly have liked to stop for a glass of sweet mint tea. But the presidential visit was a week away and the minister of the interior had requested final security plans to show to Mahmoud Sayed and, no doubt, the U.S. Secret Service.

"What are the alternate routes, Ismail?"

"From this coordinate, sir, they could come around south of the City of the Dead or take Shari Abbasia through the Old Walls and then to the city's center. But that's not the most attractive route. Neither of them is. And they're repairing the road at Al-Azhar."

Rahman shut his eyes and traveled in his mind along the two roads; both meandered through the dingiest areas of the capital—one heavily industrial, the other festering slums. Hardly a fitting image to give the leader of the United States. Rahman knew that his president would never agree to a change of route. Vanity was a stronger impulse in the man than concern for his own or anyone else's personal safety.

President Sayed had turned this diplomatic visit into a security man's nightmare, insisting as he did that he and H. Whitney Dunlap must be seen together by as many of his countrymen as could be dragooned into the streets. It was to be a massive propaganda event to strengthen his position at home and his standing among the other moderate Arab leaders.

The U.S. Secret Service had other ideas; they were anxious to keep the three-day tour as low-profile as possible. The first draft of the proposed itinerary submitted by Washington had allowed for no public appearances whatsoever. It suggested the use of closed-in, bulletproof limousines throughout the visit; the press would be told that President Dunlap suffered from mild hay fever and required air-conditioned vehicular transportation. Further, the Secret Service requested that as many ceremonial activities as possible take place away from major urban centers. When Ahmed Rahman read the draft proposals he smiled to himself. President Dunlap was an extremely cautious man, and with good reason: he had already survived one attempted assassination.

Predictably, President Sayed was angered and hurt by Washington's proposals. He summoned the American ambassador and, with all the charm and bonhomie in his armory, sought to impress upon him the importance to Egypt of his president's visit. When the ambassador asked Sayed as tactfully as he could to elucidate, the Egyptian leader waved his hand vaguely and talked of the major diplomatic benefits that would accrue to President Dunlap personally, the strengthening of the fragile alliances that made up the delicate web of Middle East politics, etc., etc. An American president must be cheered in the streets, Sayed continued; he must be seen in public in Cairo and Alexandria; he must talk to the people and touch their hands. They would expect nothing less from such a world figure. Had not the pope walked unscathed into Al-Azhar six months before to establish a historic détente with Islam?

The American ambassador conveyed the Egyptian president's reservations on the original draft proposals to the U.S. State Department, which called in the Secret Service. A suitable compromise was engineered: there would be a limited number of public appearances. But the majority of the scheduled events would take place away from potential flash points. On the question of open cars, there would be one occasion only for their use: the drive into Cairo on the president's arrival in Egypt. For Ahmed Rahman and his Internal Security forces, this hard-won concession was the most dangerous part of the itinerary. An estimated two million Egyptians would be lining the route. The flag factories were working overtime to supply them with miniature Stars and Stripes. The whole idea was crazy, Rahman said to himself, but it was his responsibility to see that both leaders arrived at the presidential palace wearing the same smiles they would exchange on the tarmac of Cairo Airport.

"All right, Ismail, we'll keep to Ramses Street. But the overpass is to be closed off."

"But sir, it was President Sayed's wish that there would be girls up there throwing rose petals."

"Rose petals?" queried Rahman, shaking his large leonine head. He smiled, showing the whiteness of his teeth below a bushy black mustache. "Girls throwing rose petals?" He began to laugh, throwing back his head and placing his hands on his hips. In this pose there was something slightly crooked about the angle of his left elbow, the result of a boyhood fracture. The village doctor in Iqlit had set the bone badly, and it took all the art of Ahmed Rahman's expensive Greek tailor to conceal it.

Ismail smiled in embarrassment, not wanting to be seen to be laughing at his president, yet as confounded by the lunacy of the idea as was his immediate superior.

"No rose petals, all right?" said Rahman suddenly. "And the girls can be on the ground in the front row, if he insists on it. And no private vehicles within a two-kilometer radius of this area for three hours prior to the motorcade. Any parked vehicles are to be towed away. I don't want a truckful of dynamite going off around here."

The aide scribbled the instructions on a pad, tore off the sheets, and handed them to a uniformed warrant officer standing nearby.

"Now, those buildings." Rahman gestured toward the high-rise government offices. "They are to be cordoned off. I don't want anyone inside. Essential staff will have to have police passes. I want our men on the roofs. Binoculars, walkie-talkies. Each building is to be thoroughly searched one hour prior to the arrival of the motorcade. There will be external surveillance of all windows and balconies thirty minutes before the motorcade arrives and until it has passed. Understood?"

"The minister of power may protest, sir. He usually brings his wife and her family to watch from his window."

"I'll speak to him." Rahman had no intention of speaking to the minister. His security plan would be rubber-stamped by the president himself, and everyone would abide by it. There were to be no exceptions. His experience had taught him that nothing must be left to chance, because there was always some determined individual who would take advantage of the smallest chink in the armor.

The system had proved effective for the visits of Presidents Nixon and Carter in 1974 and 1979—in spite of one or two anxious moments. One, which had occurred during the Nixon trip, he had witnessed himself. Minutes before Nixon and former President Sadat were due to pass, two unidentified men had suddenly appeared on an apartment balcony overlooking the motorcade route. Rahman's men were inside the apartment within three minutes. The two turned out to be Swedish TV cameramen looking for a better angle from which to film. But they could have been PLO.

The Palestine Liberation Organization and the rejectionist groups were still a force to be reckoned with; all the more so, now that their interests had been sacrificed on the altar of Middle East realpolitik. The Egypt-Israel peace treaty had given only lip service to the idea of a Palestinian state on the West Bank of the Jordan and in the Gaza

Strip, and Palestinian frustration had since found its expression in sporadic and increasingly desperate acts of violence around the world. In addition to the PLO, Rahman could expect trouble from any of the radical Arab states—those countries polarized into anti-Egyptian positions by the peace accord. Or trouble could come from newly formed terrorist groups within Egypt itself; President Sayed did not want for enemies.

Satisfied that he had covered all security contingencies at the traffic circle, Ahmed Rahman signaled to his driver. The air-conditioned comfort of the Mercedes would be a welcome relief from the blazing sun. Once inside, he settled back and loosened his shirt collar. He was about to instruct the driver to proceed, when he was disturbed by a tapping on his side window. A scruffy-looking old man with a brass oval disk pinned to his jacket demanded baksheesh as the official parking-lot attendant, even though he had been nowhere to be seen when Rahman's driver had stopped. Rahman wound down the window and held out a ten-piaster coin, the smallest he had. The man kissed the money and called down a blessing from the Prophet upon him.

The Mercedes bulldozed its way into the line of heavy traffic to a barrage of instruction from the old man. It was eleven a.m., and another of Cairo's traffic jams was being spawned with the sudden ferocity of a desert sandstorm.

"You know, Ismail," Rahman remarked, "in Cairo the first circle of Hell is reserved for motorists. And the second for telephone users."

The car inched toward an intersection where a lone policeman nonchalantly waved cars through, ignoring the red light above his head. The incessant car horns added to the confusion as traffic came to a dead halt. The policeman wandered through the heating metal, mindless of the turmoil, wearing an expression of benign resignation, as if Allah had willed it and nothing he could do would alter what had been ordained.

The Mercedes was caught behind a crumpled bus whose side panels threatened to come away under the weight of passengers clinging to it. The bus had no doors or windows, and the inside was black with the crush of bodies. A plume of dark, oily smoke belched from its exhaust pipe and hung over the stationary traffic like a shroud. The

Mercedes's air-conditioning system began to suck in the foul air, causing the occupants to cough. A small boy weaved through the line of cars, selling boxes of colored tissues.

"Shall I turn on the siren, sir?" asked the driver.

"And add to the noise? No, we'll walk. Follow us if you can; otherwise, I'll see you back at the office." Rahman and Ali got out of the car once more, and the heat hit them like an explosion.

"All these side streets are to be barricaded off, Ismail," said Rahman as they picked their way down Ramses Street through the milling pedestrians. They passed the Pont Limoun Station and the statue of Ramses II. At its base an old woman dressed in black sat on a page of newspaper; in her lap she balanced a metal bowl brimming with fava beans. With great deliberation she picked out the discolored beans and flicked them into the traffic.

Apart from the hazards of oncoming pedestrians, there was the broken sidewalk to be negotiated. Over the years the paving stones had fractured into piles of rubble, exposing the sand beneath. There were holes and jagged edges to be avoided. The sight of the sidewalks reminded Ahmed Rahman of the purpose of President Dunlap's visit: to sign a long-term military and economic agreement with Egypt, and to open the door for much-needed American investment. Without a massive injection of capital, Cairo would collapse within two years; the city would become unworkable. The projections were for a population of twenty-two million by the year 2000 at the present birthrate.

Rahman smiled to himself; in what other country would the head of the Internal Security Department of the General Intelligence Directorate be expected to fight his way through rush-hour crowds to conduct a top-priority inspection? But this was Cairo and he'd been through worse.

To the black-robed women, the pajama-clad children, and the business-suited merchants who choked the narrow sidewalks, the elegant man in the well-pressed beige suit was remarkable for his height and size. Ahmed Rahman towered over them all, and his heavily lined face and drooping mustache drew more than a passing glance from men and women alike. But no one recognized him. The elite of Egyptian intelligence remain in power as long as they preserve their anonymity.

"We will need crush barriers along this stretch of road, Ismail," said Rahman, ducking under the suspended carcasses of sheep that dangled from poles outside a butcher's shop. The meat was painted with livid red stripes identical to the markings on the wool of the live sheep that nuzzled the dusty sidewalk outside the shop. The emaciated animals, ten in all, shivered in the heat as if they were aware they had the mark of death on their backs. In six days it would be *eid-il-adha,* the feast of the slaughtered sheep, one of the most sacred celebrations in the Islamic calendar. *Eid-il-adha* was the festival of sacrifices, when those with money purchased a sheep and slaughtered it after morning prayers, in commemoration of Abraham's sacrifice. Two thirds of the meat was distributed among the poor, the balance eaten by the family.

It was no accident that the arrival of President Dunlap on Egyptian soil had been timed to coincide with the festival. President Sayed wanted the visit to take place when the country was on holiday and in a festive mood. There would be more people in their best clothes to line the streets, more color, more excitement.

Rahman paused to watch the wretched sheep huddle together, buffeted by the passersby. Soon the butcher's knife would end their misery.

"That reminds me," he said, turning back to Ismail. "Crowd control is vital in this area. I want troops shoulder to shoulder through here—facing the crowd, not the street. They, too, are to be our eyes. Make a note. Plainclothesmen to mix with the crowds. Armed, of course. The drivers are to be instructed to move at a good pace past here. There're too many windows. I know the president wants a show, but he'll be a sitting duck if the motorcade slows down. Another thing. No one except uniformed police and military to be in the street itself."

Rahman and Ismail were opposite the Red Crescent Hospital when their driver came running up to them.

"Why have you left the car?" demanded Rahman.

"An urgent call on the radio, sir. You're asked to come immediately."

"Where? To the office?"

"No, sir. To the morgue."

≈≈≈

Ever since Henry Kissinger's step-by-step diplomacy had pressured the Israelis to pull back in the Sinai, the Egyptian government had concentrated on developing the country's tourist potential in anticipation of a full Middle East peace. While Cairo now had its necessary quota of first-class hotels—this had been accomplished with the reconstruction of the Semiramis by the Intercontinental chain and the addition of a second Hilton hotel—the minister of tourism had invited international businessmen to suggest projects for other areas of the country. First in the field had been an aggressive, Hong Kong–based development company, Venture International. In 1977 the company president, William H. Leamington III, had made a presentation to the minister for not one but three hotel projects of such flamboyance and originality that even that dull civil servant's imagination had been kindled by dreams of pleasure domes that rivaled those of the *Thousand and One Nights.*

Currently near completion was the first of Leamington's extravaganzas: the Oasis Hotel, set among the dunes of the Western Desert between Giza and El Faiyum, equidistant from Highway 22 and the Nile itself. The hotel complex could be reached only by helicopter—to protect the privacy of those wealthy and privileged enough to enjoy its amenities. The main building had been executed in traditional Moorish style, a creamy confection of arches, columns, and pinnacles. Lapis lazuli and gold mosaic decorated the walls; the floors were of Italian marble and covered with enough Oriental carpets and runners to keep the nomads of Iran, Turkey, and Afghanistan employed for generations. The carpets had been selected by Bill Leamington himself. The dining rooms, with their carved stucco ceilings, were divided by tall *mushrabiya* screens inlaid with mother-of-pearl, and hung with gigantic handcrafted brass chandeliers. Outside, a three-tiered swimming pool had been sculpted to resemble a series of lagoons descending by means of waterfall slides from the roof of the building to the ground. Each lagoon was fringed with lush growths of papyrus, bamboo, and bulrushes. For entertainment, a nightly cabaret promised the most sensuous (and slimmest) belly dancers in Egypt, and for those jaded by music and champagne there was a casino to rival any in Las Vegas.

Bill Leamington had planned the complex with extreme care, mindful that the daytime activities in his contemporary fleshpot had to be as irresistible as the nocturnal adventures. So, intrepid tourists might join camel safaris through the desert to the Pyramid of El Lisht, ride

Arabian stallions across the dunes, indulge in the kingly sport of fal-
conry, or hunt desert foxes and wolves from Land-Rovers. For more
traditional guests he had added tennis courts, a nine-hole pitch-and-putt
golf course, yoga lessons, and lectures on Egyptology.

"I'm building you a fantasy," Leamington had told the minister,
"where businessmen can pretend they're Arab princes and their women
can be as pampered as harem girls." The minister, who had a penchant
for London's gaming clubs, had been impressed.

But between the dream and the reality, Leamington had experienced
all the frustrations of bureaucratic Egypt. His deadline for completion
of the Oasis Hotel project was a week away, when President Dunlap
was scheduled to break a bottle of champagne on the molded copper
doors and declare the newest playground of the superrich officially open.
The U.S. president was to be the first guest. Leamington was dumb-
founded when the minister of tourism broke the news to him. The
publicity value alone would be worth millions.

Dunlap's consent to the visit was based on two circumstances: the
Secret Service's insistence that he spend as little time as possible in
the overpopulated cities of Cairo and Alexandria, and the diplomatic
overtures of the Egyptians, who were eager to let American tourists
know not only that they and their hard currency were welcome but also
that Egyptian tourist facilities were unparalleled anywhere. The request had come from the office of President Sayed, who let Washington know that his government's share of the joint venture was being
financed by long-term, low-interest loans from the United States. After
some hesitation—the Oasis was so opulent that the president's Middle
America constituency might find it degenerate—the White House had
finally agreed. Now it was up to Leamington to make sure his extravagant watering hole was ready on time.

This Saturday morning he was seated in his office on the ground
floor of the hotel, gazing out of the window at the workmen who were
raking the ground outside in preparation for the laying of the sod. His
assistant, Nicole Honeyworth, tore a sheet of paper out of her electric
typewriter and brought it to him.

"Your entry for the *International Business Who's Who*. Will you
check it over, Bill?"

Leamington smiled at her. He watched her as she moved away and began to arrange a posy of desert flowers she had collected before breakfast. He looked down at the paper.

LEAMINGTON, WILLIAM HAWES III, financial and development execu-tive; *b.* Boston, Mass., U.S.A., 17 Dec. 1941; *s.* William Hawes II and Margaret-Ann (Schofield) L.; *educ.:* Charles Sch. for Boys; Ridgeway Military Academy; Harvard Univ., B.A. 1962, M.B.A. 1964; London Sch. of Economics, Ph.D. 1965; *m. 1st.* Katherine Francis, *d.* Shamus O'Reilly, Dublin, Ire., 1965; *2nd.* Anesta Wildewoode, *d.* Buchanan Buckler Wharton, Greenwich, Conn., U.S.A., 1969; president, Ven-ture International (Hong Kong) Ltd., since 1976; served in U.S. Army, Vietnam, 1966–67; senior aide to Gen. H. M. G. Wilson, chrmn. Joint Chiefs of Staff, 1967–69; resigned commission with rank of major 1969; vice-pres., planning, Florida Holdings Inc. 1969–71; exec. vice-pres. Western Developments of America 1972–76; Protestant; *rec-reations:* trapshooting, sailing, Oriental carpet collecting; *clubs:* Hong Kong, Washington Military; *home:* Pacific Towers, Hong Kong; *office:* Venture House, Hong Kong.

He dropped the paper on his desk and began toying with the scale model of the Oasis Hotel.

"My life in a couple of inches," he said.

"A lot of people don't even make that," replied Nicole. "If it makes you feel any better, Egyptian intelligence has probably got a file that thick on you." She held her thumb and forefinger two inches apart.

"Did you have to put in all that stuff about my ex-wives?"

"I thought you were a great supporter of the institution."

"Very funny. Why not go whole hog and tell the world who I'm sleeping with now. *'Current mistress:* Nicole Honeyworth.' "

Nicole's face turned as red as her hair. "Another remark like that and you can find another name to insert. You're not funny."

"I'm sorry, honey. You're absolutely right. This thing's getting to me. The president's due in seven days and we still haven't finished the landscaping. The shower faucets for the third floor haven't arrived from Cairo, and those assholes haven't finished the frescoes in the bar."

"At least the pools are filled. Don't worry, Bill, it'll be ready on time. Sit down a minute." Leamington sat at his leather-topped desk. Nicole crossed behind him and placed her thumbs at the base of his neck. Slowly she began to massage the tension away.

"This is the biggest damn thing Venture's ever done. We've got millions of dollars tied up in it. The future of the company's riding on it."

Nicole knew Leamington was not exaggerating; Venture International of Hong Kong had been involved in large development projects in India, Kuwait, and Iran (the company's interests here had been nationalized soon after the revolution), but none of them approached the Egyptian schemes in size, imagination, or cost. The total investment in the three hotels was close to two hundred million dollars, half of which was Venture's own capital.

For that reason Leamington had decided to supervise all phases of the project personally, a decision motivated as much by his inability to delegate authority as by his love of the exotic. When word came from Cairo that Venture's scheme had been accepted, he knew he could not sit half a world away while someone else built his hotels for him. Over the objections of his board he left the day-to-day operations of the Hong Kong office in the hands of his senior vice-president and headed off to Cairo with a small support staff, a case of bourbon, *Fodor's Egypt,* and Nicole.

His initial elation over the project had begun to evaporate in the heat of the Cairo day as he charged headlong through the corridors of the Egyptian civil service. Like so many Western entrepreneurs before him, whose digestions had been ruined by too many ritual Turkish coffees, he was to experience the frustrations of the damned in his endless passage from one functionary to the next. Ground down by a mixture of Levantine charm and inertia, he had learned—at the cost of a stomach ulcer—that patience was also a weapon; and he vented his annoyance on his own staff rather than on those government inspectors who, for all their warm assurances, seemed bent on sabotaging his entire operation.

Nicole Honeyworth, in her dual role as executive assistant and lover, did much to ease Leamington's moods of despair, but even she occasionally bore the brunt of his sudden outbursts. As she massaged the back of his neck, she could feel his muscles relaxing.

"I know you've got a lot on your mind, Bill, but did you remember to have Tohamy's office in Cairo send down a copy of *Students' Flora of Egypt*?"

Leamington had forgotten, even though Nicole had reminded him delicately on a couple of occasions. The muscles in his neck tightened again. Nicole could feel his exasperation under her fingers. She wished she had not spoken. Leamington broke away from her and stood up.

"Jesus Christ, Nicky! A damned botany book. I'm going to see what's going on around here."

Outside, the sun was dazzling after the cool, shaded rooms of the hotel. Leamington paused for a moment to check that the ice machine had been installed in the bar by the ground-level pool, the largest of the three. At the main entrance he stood and watched the workmen placing rolls of sod on the incline up to the front door.

"I must have been mad to insist on real grass. The bill to keep it green will pay off their national debt," he said.

"At least I found you the best grass to lay—*Imperata cylindrica*," replied Nicole.

But Leamington wasn't listening. His attention had been distracted by the sudden appearance of two battered buses. They emerged out of a cloud of dust on the unpaved construction road that ran east from the hotel site to the Nile. The buses stopped, and the workers watched as the passengers tumbled out, shouting, chanting, and waving painted placards.

"What the hell's happening?" yelled Leamington.

The foreman in charge of the landscaping picked up the hem of his galabia and came running over to him.

"It's a demonstration, sir. They're making a protest."

"Protest! What the hell are they protesting about?"

"I don't know, sir."

The group of some sixty demonstrators shook their placards at the grinning workmen and began chanting in a hoarse, throaty rhythm, moving their feet in the dust.

"What do those signs say?" shouted Leamington, whose Arabic was limited to "thank you" and "no."

"They say they don't want the hotel, sir. That one there"—he pointed to a large poster with red lettering—"that one says: 'Egyptians are not waiters and bellboys.' The one next to it says: 'Egypt is not a—' " The foreman looked at Nicole and flashed a gold-toothed smile.

"A what?" demanded Leamington.

"Sir, it says: 'Egypt is not a whorehouse for the West.' "

Nicole giggled and whispered, "That's about the only service you haven't provided for, Bill."

The demonstrators spread out in a line at the perimeter of the hotel property and kept up their hypnotic chant. While Leamington could not understand the words, their import was clear enough. He had heard it before in Asia: Yankee go home.

He scanned the moving line to see who was leading the demonstration. A thin-faced man with a pointed black beard ran along behind the ranks of the demonstrators, exhorting them forward. Even from a distance of a hundred meters Leamington could see the man's face clearly. It was lined with hatred. A pink scar ran along the left cheek and terminated in an empty eye socket, a disability that forced the man to present a half profile to the world.

Meanwhile, the Arab laborers were leaning on their tools, watching the demonstrators with amused interest, as if the spectacle had been provided by a thoughtful management for their entertainment.

"Get those men back to work," ordered Leamington. The foreman shouted at his workmen, but just at that moment someone threw a construction brick and hit a demonstrator. The injured man's howl of pain acted as a signal for his colleagues to rush threateningly at the group of men on the lawn. Suddenly frightened, the workers retaliated with a hail of bricks. The demonstrators retreated, only to regroup and rush again, using their placards as shields.

"Bill! For God's sake, do something before someone gets killed," screamed Nicole.

The one-eyed man stood leaning against a bus, like a general surveying his troops. Leamington told Nicole to get back inside the hotel while he edged his way around the skirmishing men, some of whom were now bleeding profusely. He ran toward the leader of the demonstrators.

"Now, look here, you," he yelled. "I don't know who the hell you are or what you want, but you call your men off and get the hell back to where you came from."

At six feet two, Leamington stood head and shoulders over the puny figure of the one-eyed man, but his threatening presence did not seem to move the bearded interloper. Up close, Leamington found him even more repulsive, with the grinning scar on his cheek and the watery red eye socket like a fresh wound. When the man spoke, his purplish lips pulled back to reveal teeth yellowed by nicotine. At his waist he wore a curved ceremonial dagger.

"My name is Saraj al-Rahid."

"You're trespassing!" roared Leamington. "Get the hell off my property and take those animals with you."

"They are disciples of Wind of the Desert," replied al-Rahid. So saying, he turned and yelled an order. Immediately, his followers disengaged themselves from the battle and began to fall back. They clambered aboard the buses as if nothing had happened.

"You and your kind are tools of the Devil," al-Rahid hissed at Leamington. "You have been sent to destroy Egypt. You are not wanted here." The engines started, and at the last moment the one-eyed man leaped onto the steps of the first bus. His head was now on a level with Leamington's, and as the bus began to pull away, he leaned forward and spat full in the American's face. Both buses roared off, and before Leamington could react they had disappeared down the construction road. The only evidence of their passage was a ruined lawn, a few broken bones, and a column of dust that spiraled toward the horizon.

≈≈≈

Although Ahmed Rahman was only two kilometers away from the Cairo morgue, it took his driver nearly an hour to nose through the noonday traffic. When the Mercedes finally pulled up in front of the building, Rahman noted with satisfaction that someone had had the presence of mind to post guards at the door. A young police lieutenant was pacing the steps outside. He saluted smartly as Rahman stepped out of the car.

"Colonel Rahman? Please come with me, sir. Captain Mamdouh is waiting to brief you."

The lieutenant led the way through the dingy reception area. Dark-green paint was peeling off the walls, which seemed to exude the reek of formaldehyde. In a tiny high-ceilinged office Captain Khaled Mamdouh shuffled his papers impatiently as Rahman entered. He rose and began talking at once. Rahman noted that he failed to salute.

"We were called in by the city coroner at eleven-thirty this morning, sir. Two of his men became ill and began vomiting two hours after cleaning an unidentified corpse found in the Nile. The men were taken to the hospital for tests."

"I'd like to speak to the coroner, Captain," said Rahman.

"I took notes of our conversation, sir. He told me—"

"Would you kindly send for the coroner?" interrupted Rahman.

"Yes, sir." Captain Mamdouh shook his hand angrily at the young lieutenant, who immediately went in search of the coroner.

Rahman sat down on the edge of the desk.

"Sir, the hospital sent a messenger with the preliminary findings." Mamdouh handed Rahman a piece of paper, but before the colonel could finish reading it, he added, "The two men exhibited symptoms of radiation poisoning."

Rahman looked up in irritation. "Radiation poisoning, Captain?"

"Yes, sir. Apparently, vomiting can start within two hours if the dose is high enough. The examining doctor says the men were exposed to over three hundred rads."

"What does that mean?"

"A rad, sir, is a measure of radiation density," replied the captain with a smugness that bordered on insolence. "It says so in the report."

"Then perhaps you'll be kind enough to let me read it for myself." Rahman scanned the document and then turned back to Mamdouh. "It says nothing here about how the men came to be contaminated."

"We assumed it must have happened here at the morgue, sir. They live in different parts of the city."

"Have you checked it out?"

"Yes, sir." Mamdouh seemed to puff up with self-congratulation. "I ordered two Geiger counters and had the building swept. The radiation source has been isolated. It was, as I suspected, the body found in the Nile."

Before Rahman could reply, the lieutenant had returned with the coroner, a slight little man whose natural pallor, heightened by his white lab coat, suggested a morbid affinity to the cadavers with which he associated daily.

"This is Colonel Rahman, head of Internal Security," said the captain. "You are to answer his questions."

The coroner blinked and looked expectantly at the large man who seemed to block out the dust-stained windows behind him.

"Thank you, Captain Mamdouh," Rahman said. "Now I want you to trace everyone who came in contact with the body—whoever pulled it out of the river, ambulance crews, everyone. I want full statements from them. And they are all to have immediate medical examinations."

"Yes, sir. It was my intention, as soon as you arrived—"

"Good. Well, get on with it."

Captain Mamdouh reddened and half turned on his heel. As an afterthought he saluted and, pushing the young lieutenant before him, marched swiftly out of the room.

Rahman called after him, "And I want your report on my desk this afternoon." He turned back to the coroner. "Tell me, Doctor, have you had any dealings with radiation sickness?"

"No, Colonel, but I've studied it. I've kept up with the journals," replied the little man proudly.

"Am I right in thinking that a body with radiation poisoning is not necessarily a hazard to people who come in contact with it?"

"That all depends. It could contaminate on contact if there were particles of radioactive matter lodged on the body—in the hair or on the clothing, perhaps."

"Which could have happened to the coroner's men?"

"Yes."

"A figure of three hundred rads has been mentioned."

"Yes, that would be more than sufficient to induce radiation sickness."

"Where is the body now?"

"It is waiting to be transferred to the university hospital."

"Have you inspected it personally?"

"No, Colonel. I was waiting for the two lead-lined suits I ordered from Dar el Shifa Hospital. I was going to have a peep at it, when you sent for me. Clinical curiosity, you might say. I've never actually seen a radiation death before. Would you care to join me?"

Rahman hesitated for a moment. "There's no danger?"

"Not with the protective clothing."

Rahman nodded and smiled, extended his hand as an invitation for the lugubrious doctor to lead the way.

They walked down a long, dark corridor to a locker room hung with rubber aprons. Rows of Wellington boots lined the walls. The lead-lined suits and visored helmets were laid out on a table. The coroner handed Rahman a pair of surgical gloves and indicated the larger of the two suits. They changed in silence, Rahman wondering whether his suit would be big enough to fit him.

When they were dressed, the coroner checked Rahman to see that he was adequately protected. The two men then donned thick white rubber boots and clumped into the corridor leading to the morgue.

The bluish light of phosphorescent tubes reflected off the white-tiled floor. On three sides of the room, reaching almost to the ceiling, were banks of wooden lockers, numbered with ceramic disks. In the middle of the cement floor, which had recently been hosed down, were a number of marble slabs. They were all empty except for one that was covered with a plastic sheet. The coroner, with the air of a magician unsure of his final trick, gingerly unveiled the body.

Rahman leaned forward and then recoiled in horror. He had seen death on the battlefield and death in the street, but his stomach was not prepared for the sight of the half-dressed corpse in front of him. The skin was white and bloated, the nose and lips distorted out of all recognition. Patches of hair were missing from the scalp, and the pearly skull was exposed from the forehead to the left ear. One eye was closed; the other bulged unnaturally in its socket. Bones protruded through the skin at the elbows and knees.

Rahman reminded himself that the body had been in the Nile for some time. The breaks in the skin would be consistent with repeated collisions against bridge pilings as it floated on the fast-moving water.

The colonel moved around to the dead man's feet. The ankles were bound—clearly, someone had weighted the body down before disposing of it in the river. Carefully he lifted the pants leg to inspect the rope. Cheap and frayed. Small wonder the corpse had refused to stay at the bottom of the Nile. On the instep of the left foot was a white mark, almost like a brand. But it was impossible to make out what it was.

The coroner was busy forcing the jaws apart and peering into the mouth. Rahman motioned him aside and looked for himself. Two teeth were missing, and there was evidence of expensive dental work in the gold crowns on the upper right molars. He closed the mouth and studied the swollen face. A slight discoloration above the lips suggested the man had once had a mustache. The nose was exceptionally large, as were the ears, which protruded comically from the head. Something about the ears struck a chord in Rahman's memory. He shut his eyes and mentally skimmed through his files of wanted men. Suddenly he clapped his hands and then almost lifted the coroner out of the room.

As soon as they had taken off their helmets, Rahman requested that the dead man's clothes be sent to his office when they had been decontaminated. He then asked for a telephone. Furious at being unable to complete his call, he ran out to the parked Mercedes and had Ismail radio the minister of the interior.

"Get hold of him, wherever he is," he ordered. "I don't care what he's doing. And call the president's office. I have to see him this afternoon."

"Yes, sir. But if the minister asks me why, what shall I tell him?"

"Tell him nothing, Ismail." Ahmed Rahman was not about to inform the whole of Cairo that the radioactive body in the morgue was the last remains of Juan Herrara, the Argentinian terrorist who for the past three and a half years had been the explosives courier of the Popular Front for the Liberation of Palestine.

"And Ismail, I want a list of every dentist in Buenos Aires."

≅≅≅

Like Anwar el-Sadat, his predecessor as head of state, Mahmoud Sayed preferred to conduct the nation's business from the comfort of his home rather than from the drafty, overly ornate presidential palace. Accordingly, on taking power, Sayed had had an extension built onto his private villa. The annex included an office large enough to house his extensive collection of first editions, as well as a conference room where he presided over meetings of the cabinet and the National Security Committee. The nineteenth-century Qubbah Palace, a vast structure with four hundred rooms, a swimming pool, and even its own railway station and engine shed, was now used for ceremonial occasions, such as the upcoming visit of President Dunlap.

Ahmed Rahman, in his capacity as head of Egypt's Internal Security Department, was required to report to the president at least once a week. Sayed had many enemies, ranging from Communists on the far left to fanatical Muslims on the far right, none of whom would rest until he had been deposed.

To the head of Internal Security fell the responsibility of protecting the president from these dangerous elements, a task made all the more difficult by Sayed's decision to work at home. The villa stood in its own grounds one block east of the busy Corniche road, which runs along the Nile embankment; the rear of the building was clearly visible from that road. The side streets around the sandstone mansion had been barricaded off, but nothing could be done to neutralize the threat from the Corniche without further disrupting Cairo's tortuous traffic flow. It was Rahman's waking nightmare that a rocket attack from the Corniche would kill the president in his bed. He had repeatedly urged Sayed to move his residence to a more remote part of the city, where he could be more effectively guarded. But Sayed had laughed away the suggestion: "If anyone wants to kill me, my dear Ahmed, the best security in the world won't save me. In the meantime, I shall stay where my people can see me."

Given these limitations, Rahman had provided an all but impenetrable cordon around the president. All visitors to the house had to pass through three checkpoints: one at the front gate, where the caller's appointment was verified by telephone with the duty officer; a second in the parking area, at an inner, electrified fence, where briefcases were X-rayed and visitors frisked; and a third at the front door, where the caller was identified visually before being admitted through the bullet-proof door to the presidential antechamber. No one, not even the president's most trusted advisers, was exempt from this procedure. When Sayed protested at the stringency of the security checks—ministers' wives objected to having their handbags searched—Rahman reminded him that most Middle East coups and assassinations were plotted by those closest to the victim. The most dangerous threat to Sadat's regime had come in 1971, when Egypt's top intelligence officers had joined forces with the minister of the interior, Sharawi Gum'ah, in an attempt to overthrow the president. Thanks to the alertness of Ahmed Rahman, then a junior officer in Internal Security, the plot had come to light. A grateful president had rewarded him with a major promotion, and he had been in favor ever since.

President Sayed was waiting for Rahman in his book-lined office. He sat behind an enormous Louis Quinze desk, his back square to the window. Rahman groaned inwardly, seeing what an easy target he presented to a resolute sniper. Opposite the president sat Maher Nagib, the dour, slow-moving minister of the interior, a plodding, loyal man elevated to ministerial rank on the downfall of his mercurial predecessor. Technically, Rahman reported to Nagib through his own immediate superior, the head of the Mokhabarat, as Egypt's Directorate of General Intelligence is commonly known. But that man had been down with hepatitis for some time and Nagib would be somewhat slow to grasp the significance of Rahman's disclosures. As a result, the Internal Security chief had decided to go directly to the president.

"Come in, Ahmed, and sit down here by me," said the ebullient Sayed. "You'll want tea, of course."

"Thank you, Excellency. If I may make a suggestion, I wish you would have the furniture rearranged so that you don't sit with your back to the window."

"What else would you have me do? Pull the blinds and work in darkness? Come, sit down. What is so urgent that you would have me cancel an interview with the editor of the Los Angeles *Times*? We need all the American goodwill we can get right now."

With a sigh, Rahman proceeded to brief the two men on the events of the morning. The body in the Nile. The sudden illness of the morgue attendants. The confirmation of radiation poisoning. And finally his tentative identification of the corpse, which would be verified by checking the dental records as soon as they were received from Buenos Aires.

The president leaned back in his chair, frowning. "Where did this radioactive material come from?"

"Well, sir, there have been no reported thefts of radioactive material from any of our nuclear establishments. And there is no record of the Argentinian Juan Herrara entering Egypt. There is no whisper from any of our usual sources that he's been operating within our boundaries."

"So, at this point you have no idea what he was doing here, how he got into the country, how he came to be contaminated, or who disposed of his body in the Nile?" the president asked.

"Is there any chance you might be mistaken in your identification?" It was the first time Nagib had spoken since Rahman had entered the room.

"It is possible, but I know I've seen the man before. I'm almost positive it's Herrara."

"Ahmed's memory is a legend in the force." The president smiled as he made his point. "Do you know that he memorized the entire Koran while he was still at the *kuttab* in—where was it, Ahmed?"

"Iqlit, in Upper Egypt."

"Ah, yes. Iqlit." Nagib raised his eyebrows and nodded his head in polite acknowledgment of his subordinate's youthful accomplishment.

"Now, how long will it take you to find the answers to these questions?" The president's tone had hardened.

Rahman's reply was interrupted by the arrival of tea. The servant, wearing a black suit and white gloves, placed a small tray on a marble-top table next to him. He waited until the man had left the room.

"I'm afraid I cannot answer that, sir. Two days, perhaps. But it could be two weeks."

"President Dunlap arrives here in seven days," Nagib interjected.

"Yes, Minister, I'm aware of that. I can only assume that we have stumbled onto a plot to kill the American president. And perhaps you, too, sir." Rahman let the import of his words sink in before he added, "And that's why I must recommend to you that the visit be postponed until we have the answers."

"Excellency, I am inclined to agree with Rahman. We cannot afford to take any chances. Should an American president fall victim to an assassin's bullet on Egyptian soil—" Nagib enjoyed the drama of his words, heightening their effect by leaving the sentence unfinished.

President Sayed swiveled his chair around ninety degrees and gazed at the wall of books. He began to weigh the alternatives in his mind. As Dunlap's host he had both a moral and a political obligation to

ensure the American leader's safety; Nagib was right about the consequences of an assassination—or even an attempt at one—while the
American was in Egypt. The political face of the Middle East had
changed beyond all recognition since the Egyptian-Israeli peace treaty
and the forging of what an editorial in *Al-Ahram* referred to as the
new "Cairo–Tel Aviv axis."

The region had been polarized. Egypt and her uneasy ally, Israel, had
been isolated by the other Arab states; the radicals and moderates of
the Islamic world had banded together in rejection of the peace treaty.
Egypt was the pariah of the Middle East and had been subjected to
economic and political sanctions to force her to repudiate the hard-
won accord. Most aggressive among the rejectionists were the leaders
of Iraq, Libya, Syria, and the PLO, many of whom had vowed to
bring about the assassination of Anwar el-Sadat, and later, when Sadat
retired, of his handpicked successor, Mahmoud Sayed. The United
States had also been castigated repeatedly for its crucial role in forcing
a peace settlement. President Carter had been on the death list of
several of the more desperate offshoots of the PLO, and President
Dunlap had fared no better as a result of his strong pressures to push
Egypt and Israel toward closer economic ties. A successful attack on
the American head of state during his Egyptian visit would serve the
interests of the radicals well, plunging the entire Middle East into
turmoil.

Sayed now swung back in his chair to face Rahman. "You speak
of assassination attempts. Why? At the moment, all we have is a
radioactive corpse."

"We must assume the worst, Excellency. The PFLP has sworn to
eliminate you and to wreck the peace settlement. Herrara had known
PFLP connections."

"But—I'm not clear what you are implying, Ahmed." Although
Sayed thought he knew what Rahman's answer would be, he could
not yet accept the horror of its implications.

"Excellency, we have the body of a known Palestinian terrorist. It
is found in the Nile a week before the American president is to visit.
The body is radioactive and has been weighted down. For years there
has been speculation that a terrorist organization would eventually get

hold of atomic weaponry and use it for purposes of international black-mail—or worse. Some experts in the field have stated publicly that the PLO has had the expertise and the access to nuclear materials for some time, but has chosen for its own reasons not to go nuclear—until now."

"Ahmed, you cannot be serious. Are you suggesting that terrorists are going to use an atomic device to attempt to assassinate President Dunlap and me, or to hold us for ransom?"

"I'm suggesting nothing at this point, except that we have a serious situation to which there are no immediate answers. Until we get them, I am recommending we postpone Dunlap's visit."

Sayed could feel his face flushing; the warning Rahman was sounding appalled and terrified him. Across the room, Nagid sat silently in his chair, his brow furrowed.

"Ahmed, this is impossible. Anyone experimenting with atomic devices would be threatening the lives of millions of people. They would run the risk of unleashing a third world war. There has to be some other explanation. Perhaps this Herrara became contaminated while spying—maybe at the site of our research reactor."

"Of course, that is possible. As are any of a dozen other explanations. But I repeat, Excellency, we are running a risk in allowing the American president to come at this time. A very grave risk."

Sayed swung his chair away again. Postponing Dunlap's visit would undo months of intensive diplomatic activity. The trip had been timed to extract the greatest political capital for the Egyptian leader. First, as an American signal to Moscow of strong U.S. support for Egypt and, by association, for the other pro-Western countries in the area, it would serve as a subtle warning to the Soviets not to let their Middle East surrogates get out of hand. But even more important, the visit was to be the occasion for the signing of a major agreement between the two countries. By the terms of the accord, Egypt would receive massive arms shipments and a wide-ranging program of American technological and economic aid. The total package would result in an annual infusion into the Egyptian economy of fifteen billion dollars.

"Gentlemen, unless this agreement is signed next week, we'll have serious street riots in Cairo within a year," said the president after two minutes of silence. "The signing of the peace treaty with Israel raised expectations in the hearts of Egyptians that we cannot fulfill. Our economy is virtually bankrupt. We simply can't afford to maintain food subsidies at their present level much longer. You remember what happened in January 1977 when Sadat tried to eliminate the subsidies to placate the International Monetary Fund."

Maher Nagib shifted uneasily in his seat. After the two days of street riots, finally quelled by the reluctant army, a shaken government had restored the subsidies, and it was the then minister of the interior who had been sacked as a scapegoat.

"We have not been able to give our people the edible fruits of peace. It is only natural that they have become restless," continued the president. "Another rise in food prices could easily ignite the powder keg."

"May I respectfully suggest, Excellency, that you go to Washington to sign the agreement."

"If I have to change the arrangements now, Ahmed, the Americans will be asking themselves questions about the stability of my government. They will find an excuse to delay signing to see what happens. We cannot afford that. No, I'm afraid Dunlap's visit must go ahead as planned."

"But I can't guarantee your—"

Before Rahman could finish the sentence, the president had cut him short. "The visit is to proceed. But nothing—nothing—must happen. There will be no incidents. I want you to round up every known militant. If you have any terrorist groups under surveillance, lock them up until the American president is safely home. You have my authority to do anything you have to."

Rahman lifted the porcelain cup to his lips. The tea tasted bitter. "If those are your orders, Excellency, they will be carried out."

"What about this Herrara, the Argentinian?" interjected Nagib.

"He has worked for various international terror groups. Baader-Meinhof, the Red Brigades, the Tupamaros, and lately the PFLP. But we've no proof that's his connection now. That's what my people must find."

"Let us assume for a moment, Ahmed, that your Señor Herrara had maintained his links with Dr. Habash. The PFLP doesn't move these days without first consulting Baghdad. That would suggest an Iraqi connection."

"We have had one of their cells under surveillance here, Excellency. We've managed to infiltrate their group, so it's in our interest to keep it alive. From information fed back to us, it seems the PFLP has limited its activities to putting out propaganda sheets denouncing the peace treaty."

"And that is the only Palestinian cell operating in Egypt?" the president asked incredulously.

"To our knowledge, yes, since we closed down the Voice of Palestine."

"May I make a suggestion?" Nagib had been sitting in silence, listening to the exchange. "You say, Rahman, that the key to the problem is the link between this dead terrorist and an unknown group, possibly the PFLP. If we *are* dealing with some lunatic Palestinian terror organization, then why don't we ask for help?"

"Who from?" asked Rahman. "The CIA?"

Nagib directed his answer to the president.

"No. The Israelis. The Mossad knows the operations of the PLO and every other splinter group better than anyone else. After all, they've been fighting them long enough."

"I hardly think we need help from the Jews when it comes to our internal security," exclaimed Rahman, rising furiously from his chair.

"Now, just a minute, Ahmed. Sit down, please. Maher, would you mind explaining what is behind your thinking?"

The ironic edge to the president's voice and the waves of hostility he felt from Rahman made Nagib choose his words extremely carefully. "Israeli intelligence has been cooperating with us covertly for some time now. That cooperation bore fruit when they acquainted my predecessor as to the probability of an attempt on the life of Sadat in 1977. That piece of intelligence came from Jerusalem. They have a man there—no, I believe he has retired now—a man who is said to know more about the Palestinian guerrillas than Arafat himself. His name is—uh—"

"Uri Bar-Zeev." Rahman spat out the name. He could feel the anger welling in his stomach.

"Bar-Zeev, yes," said Nagib. "I understand he has an impressive record of uncovering PLO cells within Israel and planning attacks on their operations abroad. But Rahman would know more about that than I."

"You give him too much credit, Minister. The Mossad has all the resources of the CIA behind it, as well as British intelligence and the French when it suits their purposes."

"Ahmed, please." The president's voice was stern.

Sensing that he had captured Sayed's interest, and secretly enjoying the discomfiture of his subordinate, Nagib continued to salt the wound. "May I suggest, Excellency, that you put through a formal request to the Israeli prime minister for the services of Bar-Zeev on a matter of the highest priority. Explain to him frankly what the problem is and that no word of it must leak back to the Americans. It wouldn't be in Israel's interest either if Dunlap were to be assassinated here. They have almost as much at stake as we do."

The president nodded in agreement. Rahman felt as if he were on the top of a huge mountain of sand that was shifting and sliding under his feet. "Excellency, I must protest. Have you so little faith in our own security service that you would bring in outsiders? Bar-Zeev would be more of a hindrance than a help. How could this man know more about the PLO than we do? Is he an Arab? No, he's a Jew. An immigrant at that. He wasn't even born in Israel." Rahman began to perspire. Dark circles formed under the arms of his beige jacket. He was losing face before the president's eyes.

"And another thing about Bar-Zeev"—Nagib went on as if Rahman had never spoken—"if memory serves me correctly, he has an extensive knowledge of radiation and nuclear devices. I believe he was chief of security at the Dimona nuclear plant on the Dead Sea in the early 1960s. I think he has some academic background in nuclear physics. Am I right, Rahman?"

Ahmed Rahman could not resist the temptation to parade his phenomenal memory, even though by confirming the minister's conjectures he was damning his own case. The president noted how Nagib had played on Rahman's weakness.

"He studied electrical engineering at the Technion in Haifa from 1940 to 1942. In 1943 the Jewish Agency sent him to the United States to study physics at MIT. He returned in 1947, when he was seconded to the Weizmann Institute for nuclear research, and in 1954 he was appointed deputy director of the industrial branch of the Committee of Atomic Energy. He worked in the laboratories of Nahal Sorek, close to Dimona." Rahman was reading the image of the page he saw in his mind's eye, detailing the background of one of Israel's most accomplished intelligence agents. His voice was sullen and expressionless.

"Very good, Ahmed. You see, Maher, Allah bestows His gifts on those He favors. I hardly need the file in front of me, but I would appreciate it if you could have it delivered to me personally. And I want to see everything in it. Do I make myself clear, Ahmed?"

"Yes, Excellency."

"Good. Thank you, Maher. I shall send a message to the Israeli prime minister, asking for Bar-Zeev. In a consultative capacity."

Sayed saw the tears of frustration forming in Rahman's eyes. His security chief was loyal and competent. Sayed knew that the mere idea of bringing in an Israeli was a humiliating gesture toward him, especially since Rahman had no love for the Jews—having been their guest as a prisoner of war after the 1956 Sinai war. And Ahmed Rahman had his own private reservations about the peace settlement.

"I would like a word with Rahman alone if you don't mind, Maher. Good day."

"Good day, Excellency."

Rahman waited until the minister had left the room. "If you would like my resignation, Excellency . . ."

"Resignation, my dear Ahmed? On the contrary. Please, you must not interpret my decision as doubting your competence to perform your duties. I have the utmost confidence in you. You are a first-rate officer, but desperate times demand desperate measures. There is too much in the balance; it's not only your future and mine. We must not live in the past. We have only one week to resolve this problem, so we must use all the resources available to us. Is that not sensible?"

The president rose from behind his desk, walked to where Ahmed Rahman stood, and put an arm around his shoulder. "This is still your operation. You are in charge. And I can promise you that my gratitude will take a very tangible form if you and Bar-Zeev solve this puzzle for me."

Using a gentle pressure, Sayed guided Rahman to the door. "You know, Ahmed, there are decisions a president has to make that are painful for him, but he must follow them through for the sake of his people. If you could see matters from behind my desk, you would do the same thing I must do. You know the proverb: He who makes a bridge of himself must bear the treading. That is the lot of a president."

"Am I free to leave, Excellency?"

"Yes," the President's attempts to mollify Rahman had failed. He changed his tone once more. "Have the Bar-Zeev file on my desk within the hour. I will advise you as to what arrangements will be made."

Rahman made his way out of the president's villa and through the checkpoints. The pulse in his forehead throbbed painfully, and he saw the soldiers on duty through a film of tears. His face had been blackened by his president. He felt dishonored and degraded, like an officer stripped of his rank—and all because of an Israeli. He clenched his fists and called down a curse on the head of Uri Bar-Zeev.

DAY TWO
SUNDAY, NOVEMBER 4

Kibbutz Lev Hasharon is situated, as its name implies, at the heart of the Plain of Sharon. If Israel has a geographic center, the honor of occupying it goes to Lev Hasharon, a kibbutz of the Hashomer Hatzair movement, built by Czech settlers in 1938 on the apex of a gently sloping hill that overlooks the entire valley. The sandy soil bears witness to the dunes that stood there from biblical times until the Czechs arrived, six months before the outbreak of World War II. The new immigrants, mainly professional men and their families, ran the Royal Navy's blockade in the eastern Mediterranean and beached their leaky tramp steamer north of Tel Aviv. Once ashore, they joyously lit fires of driftwood and danced through the night in the sands of the Promised Land.

Today, the kibbutz created by these pioneers at the navel of Israel stands protected by a ring of sycamore and jacaranda trees. The slopes leading up to the settlement from the old Tel Aviv–Haifa coast road are luxuriant with cotton and alfalfa; behind, looking south toward the Jordanian town of Tulkarem (now part of the occupied West Bank), lie extensive citrus groves, vineyards, and melon fields.

Although Lev Hasharon stands a mere ninety feet above sea level, it commands the only high ground in the area, and its location at Israel's narrowest point—it is only thirteen kilometers from the Mediterranean to the 1948 Jordanian border—gives it great strategic importance: a surprise thrust here by the Arab Legion in any of the Arab-Israeli wars could have severed the country at its waist. So Kibbutz Lev Hasharon is well fortified with concrete bunkers, air-raid shelters, and a network of trenches discreetly hidden behind rosebushes and gladiolus beds.

Uri Bar-Zeev had been a member of the kibbutz since his parents helped to found it over forty years before. He was fourteen then, small for his age, with a large head and blazing eyes. While the years had tempered his impetuosity and the wars had blunted his personal ambitions, he remained as dedicated to the Zionist dream as on that first night when he danced with his father in the sand by firelight. Today, as he went about his kibbutz duties—he worked in the orange groves, and each season had its special demands—his thoughts turned to those early years in Israel while his hands pruned the trees, sprayed them, and picked their fruit. Uri Bar-Zeev had fought in four wars; he had lost a brother and a son. He had given everything but his own life for the State of Israel, and now, because he refused to accept the conditions of peace with Egypt, they were saying he had turned his back on his country and retired, like Achilles, to sulk in his tent. He was the first casualty of the Cairo–Tel Aviv axis, the new politicoeconomic reality in the Middle East. But Bar-Zeev would have none of it and was content to give up matters of state in favor of oranges.

Men who make a habit of secrecy, who have been conditioned to do so, develop certain unconscious mannerisms: Bar-Zeev kept his hands in his pockets as if to protect the secrets he carried about with him. The other kibbutzniks all knew that this withdrawn, thickset little man who didn't suffer fools was a high-ranking intelligence officer, but they were tactful enough not to press him on the subject, even when military cars drew up behind the communal dining room and unsmiling men with briefcases asked for Lieutenant Colonel Bar-Zeev. On such occasions he could be seen walking through the melon fields with the visitors, listening intently to what they had to say. Once, when curiosity got the better of Aviva Lowenthal, the head laundress, and she asked Bar-Zeev what they discussed on those walks, he merely winked, thrust his hands deep into his pockets, and replied, "Men's talk."

While Kibbutz Lev Hasharon was fiercely democratic—everyone had to take a turn at the kitchen sink—there were some members who were

treated more democratically than others, and when Bar-Zeev returned
to the kibbutz and told the secretary that he was now a full-time member again and would be available for work, he was invited to choose
the job he would like to do. Bar-Zeev opted for the orange groves
because he could be alone there and would not have to make conversation with the *haverim* who picked the melons or tended the vines. If
he had chosen the plastics factory, as the secretary had secretly hoped,
he would have had to make continuous small talk with his colleagues
above the throbbing machinery. Another factor that determined his
choice of work was the knowledge that he was being watched. He did
not know exactly who was watching him, but it was routine operational
procedure in the Mossad that when a senior officer resigned, a close
surveillance was kept on him, both for his own safety and for the
protection of the knowledge he had acquired. By working in the *pardes*
among the newly planted orange trees, Bar-Zeev felt most secure, as
he could tell who was approaching at a great distance.

Intellectually, he understood the Mossad's need to have him watched
—he himself had ordered the surveillance of two ministers of the
Mapam party after their visit to the nuclear power station at Dimona—
but it rankled nonetheless. He wondered if it was the kibbutz secretary
who reported his movements back to Jerusalem. Or perhaps Shlomo,
who was in charge of the citrus operation. He had quarrelled with
Shlomo over the method of irrigating the young trees. The new *pardes*
had been planted in a field that sloped badly. This meant that the runoff water collected at the bottom, causing the roots of the last three
rows of year-old saplings to rot. Bar-Zeev had suggested that they
irrigate the first fifteen rows intensively and leave the others unwatered.
The runoff would do the rest. He had even conducted his own ex-
periments on the absorption rate of the soil and had calculated the
volume of water needed to ensure that the bottom half of the grove
received the same amount of water as the top. But Shlomo was adamant:
they would stick to the tried and trusted methods.

Bar-Zeev had also quarreled recently with the secretary, over the
continuing use of Arab labor on the kibbutz. Before the 1967 war, six
Arabs from the local village had worked in the fields, taken their meals
in the dining hall, and occasionally spent the night in the guesthouses.
For the cotton and citrus harvests extra outside labor had been hired.

While many of the kibbutzniks abominated the idea of paid labor—
and Arab labor at that—the majority had realized that the extra
hands were a necessary if uncomfortable fact of life. During the debate
in 1964 when the kibbutz first decided to hire local Arab help, Bar-Zeev
had spoken passionately against the idea, but faced with the presence
of Arab workers he not only accepted them but singled out the extrovert
Abdul for instruction in conversational Arabic, a study he furthered
from textbooks at night in his bungalow while his wife played Mozart
and Chopin on their wind-up gramophone. After the 1967 war, the
kibbutz had compromised: Arab laborers, while they could still be
hired, were not allowed to live on the kibbutz premises, for reasons of
security.

When Bar-Zeev returned to Lev Hasharon following the peace accord
with Egypt, he found that Abdul was still there, the only remaining Arab
worker. Abdul gave him his toothy smile and welcomed him home in
Arabic. Bar-Zeev turned his back on him and walked away. The image
of his son, Yuval, rose up before him: Abdul smiling and holding up the
boy so that he could pick pomegranates from the tree outside their
bungalow. Lieutenant Yuval Bar-Zeev had been blown up by an anti-
personnel mine at El Arish in 1973. His father blamed all Arabs for
his death.

Wouldn't it be ironic, Bar-Zeev thought, as he connected the irrigation pipes and turned on the water supply, if the Mossad had assigned
Abdul as his shadow. It's just the sort of thing they'd do, he mused.
The tiny jets of water arched over the saplings like blooms of lavender.
He looked along the geometrical rows of trees. The sun caught the
water droplets, which fragmented its light into dozens of tiny rainbows.
Lizards flitted from under the slender branches, startled by the sudden
shower. Bar-Zeev smiled with satisfaction and ran a muscular forearm
across his eyes, pushing the sweat up into his iron-gray hair. This was
the time he liked best—when he was alone with the young trees, the
sun high and a regiment of rainbows dancing over the sandy earth. In
the distance he could hear the sound of a tractor.

He stood at the top of the grove and cast a practiced eye over the
disposition of the aluminum irrigation pipes, each five meters long,
set half a meter away from the line of trees to allow the jets to douse
the entire root area. Then he sat down on a pile of pipes that should

have been in position along rows sixteen to twenty-four had he followed Shlomo's express instructions. He breathed in the warm, sweet air and reached into his shirt pocket for a cigarette, part of his weekly issue from the kibbutz store. He lighted it and waited for the match to cool. He put the burned match back into his pocket—a habit acquired during his military service—and closed his eyes. Behind him, obscuring the view of the buildings of Lev Hasharon, was the old *pardes,* the mature orange groves now heavy with green fruit. In a month it would be time to pick them. In the center of this grove was the kibbutz cemetery. The bodies of his parents, his brother, Asher, and the remains of his son, Yuval, were buried there. And the only thing that softened these painful memories was the beauty of the orange trees, their scent in April and their fruit in December. His family was surrounded by growing things.

The death of loved ones in war, the death of compatriots, and even the death of enemy soldiers had filled Bar-Zeev with an aching sadness. Memories of the wars he had fought haunted him, and his nights were tormented by dreams of desert carnage in which he relived every bloody engagement. These nightmares exhausted him more than the years of Spartan pioneering. His accomplishments in the intelligence service and his contribution to Israel's nuclear advancement—once a source of pride and satisfaction—were now merely a vain memory. Yet, that part of him not singed by war or blunted by the machinations of politicians still hankered to be at the center of things—a sentiment he could ascribe only to a kind of professional curiosity.

When he resigned from the Mossad, they had accused him of betraying his country, of acting treacherously at a time when all citizens must stand shoulder to shoulder. But for Bar-Zeev the terms of the peace were the real betrayal because they could only hasten yet another and more terrible conflict, one in which Israel would be forced to use her nuclear capability.

The sound of the tractor grew louder, droning away like a drunken fly. Bar-Zeev saw it as it turned into the *pardes* at the far corner below him. At first he thought it was Eli, come to take him back to the *hader ochal* for lunch, but shielding his eyes from the sun, he made out two people on the tractor. He squeezed his eyes to focus on its approach. The driver wore a blue kibbutznik hat—probably Eli—but his passenger wore khaki and was standing in the style of a tank commander. Bar-Zeev waited until the tractor was fifteen meters away before he rose and pinched the coal out of his cigarette. Instinctively he shredded the butt, scattered the remaining tobacco, and rolled the paper into a tight ball. Then he put his hands in his pockets.

"*Shalom,* Eli. Lunchtime, is it?" Bar-Zeev had moved so that the sun was in the stranger's eyes. The man wore the uniform of an army captain, he noted.

"Uri, this is Captain David Goan. He's come to see you," the boy remarked unnecessarily.

"Colonel Bar-Zeev," said the officer by way of salute.

"Do you know anything about oranges, Goan?" Bar-Zeev asked pleasantly.

"No. I've come on another matter," the captain replied, looking significantly at Eli.

"Eli, would you mind checking the pipes on row fifteen? I think there may be a leak. The captain and I will wait here for you."

Captain Goan jumped clear of the tractor as Eli turned it sharply and throttled noisily off downhill.

"I hope he doesn't handle the M-sixty-four like that when his time comes," Bar-Zeev remarked.

Captain Goan waited until the boy was out of earshot. "I have an urgent message from the *memuneh.*"

"Ah," murmured Bar-Zeev, "the boss of bosses."

"He wants to see you immediately in Jerusalem."

"He knows where I am. In fact, he knows everything about me. One of his boys is my constant companion." A thought flashed through his mind: Maybe it's Eli.

"Colonel Bar-Zeev. My instructions are to escort you back to Jerusalem. It is a matter of national importance."

"Then you know why he wants to see me?"

"No, I have been told only that it is a matter of national importance and I am to accompany you to Jerusalem. There is a car back at the kibbutz."

Bar-Zeev looked him over quickly to see if he was carrying a weapon. There was nothing in the outline of his clothing to suggest he was. "Well, then, we mustn't disappoint the *memuneh.*" He signaled to Eli, and soon the three of them were heading back to the kibbutz, the two men standing on the footplate behind the young driver, the wind bringing tears to their eyes.

≅≅≅

It was too hot to play squash, but Oliver Simpson, first secretary at the British embassy in Cairo, did not want to give offense to Professor Rashad Munir by suggesting they cancel their game. And Professor Munir did not want to lose face by backing out, since his partner might consider it weakness on his part if he did. So the British diplomat and the professor of Islamic studies at Al-Azhar University were the only ones using the courts at the Ghezira Sporting Club this morning. The thermometer read thirty-one degrees centigrade, and Simpson was sweating profusely. Munir, by contrast, looked immaculately cool, although he was losing.

The condition of its squash courts exemplified the slow decay of what was once the most exclusive club in Egypt. The walls were black with the marks of countless balls, the glass roof was cracked and weatherstained, and the doors did not fit properly. The Ghezira Sporting Club had once been the bastion of the British Raj in Egypt, where wealthy Cairenes aped the aristocracy with their strings of polo ponies and their silver-handled croquet mallets. The rot had set in after the exile of the lubricious King Farouk. Although Nasser suffered the club's continuing existence after the July 1952 revolution—on the pretext that the foreign diplomatic corps had to have someplace to meet the Egyptian elite—it had never been the same again. The flat and uninteresting golf course had gone to seed, and the clubhouse, built by the British in 1935 in Neo-Palladian style, had the air of an abandoned railway station. In Ghezira's heyday, children who spoke above whispers in the locker rooms had been asked to leave; now they could be heard singing popular songs in the showers. Anyone who could afford the exorbitant membership fee was allowed in.

Oliver Simpson lamented the club's decline whenever he and the ambassador drank their iceless whiskey and sodas by the pool. ("Reminds me of my wife's relatives in Chichester," the ambassador once remarked. "Shabby-genteel.") But they both recognized the fact that there was really nowhere else to go, especially if one wanted a game of squash to keep in shape. A creature of habit, Simpson had for years played every Sunday at the same time with the Canadian commercial attaché, but then his partner had been warned by his doctor to find a less vigorous pastime. Simpson had been waiting outside the court as usual when a runner brought him a message of apology from the Canadian. His first emotion was annoyance at having been let down, and in his anger he forgot to tip the boy. When he was approached by the overcourteous Professor Munir as he walked back to the locker room, he agreed to a game. Simpson was pleased when he beat the aggressive and volatile Egyptian with his disguised dropshots and lobs—all the more since defeat seemed to make the academic seethe visibly.

"You must let me take my revenge," Munir had said after their first encounter.

"Any time, old boy," Simpson had replied, and he had found himself playing the energetic professor every Sunday thereafter.

Oliver Simpson belonged to the "wogs-begin-at-Calais" school of British civil servants. The right schools and army connections (he passed an undistinguished war in the Eighth Army and carried his rank of captain into civilian life) secured him a position in the Foreign Office when he was demobilized. After a series of dull postings in cold climates, Simpson was eventually sent to Egypt on the strength of his time spent "with Monty at Alamein." While he lamented to friends that he missed his club (Boodle's), racing at Goodwood, and the Henley regatta, he had no real desire for a desk job in London. Cairo offered him endless scope for his love of intrigue and his penchant for gossip. Here he felt at the center of things, and his only regret was that the Americans were running the show now—unlike the good old days of Farouk.

To his closest friend, a fellow officer and Lloyd's underwriter, he observed in one of his letters that he had been born too late; he would have made a "not half bad" colonial administrator. But he was "bound and determined to use what little influence Britain still has in this part of the world to propagate the notions of fair play and honor, even if such old-fashioned virtues are beyond the comprehension of my American colleagues here."

Simpson played squash in much the same style as he conducted his life: he appeared to treat the game with an exaggerated indifference, yet all his shots were cunningly disguised to ensure the least possible energy expended on his part and the maximum discomfiture inflicted upon his opponent—a strategy that had in his youth won him a Half Blue at Oxford. When asked by the ambassador why he continued to play against Munir, Simpson replied that such social contact with a leading Egyptian academic could have its uses. To the trained diplomat a chance remark could be most revealing, and secretly Simpson enjoyed the game of espionage as much as he enjoyed squash. On more than one occasion he had passed on information to the Mokhabarat that had been well received. And although he would not admit it to the ambassador, Simpson relished the sight of Munir racing terrierlike around the court while he himself commanded the center T.

"You have much inner reserve for a man of your years," remarked Munir as they walked into the locker room after their most recent encounter.

"Yes," drawled Simpson, not knowing whether there was an implied insult, as he was not much older than Munir. "But then I learned the game at Harrow."

Munir drew his lips into a tight smile. Simpson seemed to bait him constantly with reminders of the British colonial past.

The two men sat on the wooden bench under the slow-moving fans and unlaced their sneakers. Physically they seemed to embody the spiritual health of their respective nations: the one, puffy, choleric, the color of raw meat; the other, sinewy and smooth, with a bronzed and cunning face. Munir reminded Simpson of a fox; the Egyptian would not insult the animal kingdom by choosing a correlative for the British diplomat. Neither spoke until a white-suited attendant brought them towels and cakes of soap.

"Can I buy you a drink, old boy?"

"Mr. Simpson, you know I do not drink. It is against my belief. I think I have mentioned this to you before."

"Yes, yes, of course. It's just the damned heat. My apologies."

"But I will sit with you and take a little water." Munir watched Simpson drop his sweat-stained shorts to the floor and then slide his jockstrap over his protruding stomach. He saw the uncircumcised penis and looked away in disgust. He picked up his towel and walked along the coconut matting to the shower stalls. He lingered in the shower until Simpson had finished washing and had dried himself.

Outside on the patio, the hot midday air was redolent of the scent of jasmine. They sat down under a faded orange umbrella by the croquet lawn. Oliver Simpson ordered a large pink gin; normally it would have been a small one, but he was damned if he was going to be intimidated by the fellow's religious scruples. Munir asked the waiter for a bottle of Perrier water. They watched four men playing croquet.

"You should have known this place in the old days, Professor. Shame it's gone to the dogs so." Munir sipped his Perrier water. "When I first arrived in Cairo in 'forty-two, that lawn was as good as the wicket at Lord's."

"I suppose you're extremely busy now with the visit of the American president," said Munir, steering the conversation away from the diplomat's idle reminiscences.

"Not really, it's an American show. By Jove, look at that! Good shot. Really seen him off, hasn't he."

One of the croquet players had knocked an opponent's ball diagonally across the lawn. It came to rest near their table.

"Surely there will be social events surrounding the visit. That is the way the diplomatic corps functions, or so I believe."

"Oh yes, we'll probably get hand-delivered invitations as an afterthought."

The player whose ball had been struck was now lining up to get back in the game. He was a middle-aged Egyptian businessman.

"When the British were in control here," said Simpson in a whisper that seemed to carry across the patio and echo around the building, "if you didn't wear white you'd be thrown off the lawn."

"Perhaps you would let me buy you a drink."

"My dear chap, delighted."

Munir nodded toward the waiter, who wore a blue galabia. "You were saying about the president's visit . . ."

"Was I?"

"Yes, you see I have a nephew who has set his heart upon meeting the American president. I told him I had friends who might—well, shall we say who might be able to arrange an invitation. An embassy party, perhaps."

"Ah, I don't know, old boy. It's all very hush-hush."

The waiter arrived with the drinks and placed them on the plastic tabletop. An undernourished cat rubbed itself against Simpson's leg; he kicked it away, and it skulked off behind the hibiscus bushes.

"Hush-hush?"

"It means secret. Security, you know." The combination of the gin and the hot midday sun was beginning to take its toll of the British diplomat. His words started to slur.

"So you don't think it's possible for my nephew to shake the president's hand?"

"Press the flesh, they call it. Know that?"

"Well, perhaps he can watch the motorcade, if nothing else. Do you know which way they'll be traveling?"

"Uh-uh." Simpson smiled, muzzily shaking a finger at Munir. "That's strictly confidential information. Not even my ambassador knows that."

"Well, at least you probably know where he's going. I know he has to sign an economic agreement with our president in Aswan. Where else is he traveling?"

"Your nephew going to follow him around, old boy?"

"It's not every day the president of the United States comes to our country, Mr. Simpson. Naturally, the boy is most interested. As I am."

"Frankly, between you and me, the whole thing's a big pain in the neck. It's not like flying from Washington to Chicago. We even had the CIA and your security people knocking on our door to inspect the roof of our building."

"You live in Zamalek?"

"No. We've a flat on Shari Ismail Pasha."

So, the motorcade will be passing El Tahrir Bridge, past the British embassy, to the president's private residence, thought Munir. He sipped his Perrier water and sat back in his plastic chair. He listened to the *pock* of croquet mallets striking the colored balls and the players' cries of triumph and frustration. He glanced at the sweating profile of Oliver Simpson, who had once again returned to the theme of the Ghezira Sporting Club's former grandeur under the British Raj. How infinite was the wisdom of the Prophet when he ordained that his followers should abstain from alcohol, Munir mused. He recalled the verse from the Koran: "The harm is far greater than the benefit."

≅≅≅

Captain David Goan drove steadily south from the kibbutz through the Plain of Sharon. Beside him, Uri Bar-Zeev sat in contemplative silence. They passed through Petah Tikvah and the old Arab town of Lod, and into the Valley of Ayalon, where the Lord made the sun stand still for Joshua. The sun was high in the midday sky now, glancing off the wheat stubble in the fields on either side of them.

"The road to Jerusalem" was a phrase that resonated with memories both tragic and triumphant for Bar-Zeev, as it did for all Israelis. An ancient camel route, the road rises more than eight hundred meters above sea level over a distance of only seventy-two kilometers. Hebrews, Roman legionaries, Crusaders, Saracens, Turks, and pilgrims of three faiths have traveled that route, and many have died there in the Judaean Hills. To the memory of those who fell stand the ageless pines, like sentinels, above the rocky escarpments.

At the end of the valley, terraced vineyards lead up by gigantic steps to the Monastery of the Seven Agonies of Latrun, which houses a silent order of Trappist monks who make wine and honey. The red tiles of the monastery roof stand out in sharp contrast to the encircling pines. Bab el Wad, "the Gate of the Valley," eight kilometers east, marks the mouth of a sheer, granite gorge, its sides thick with evergreens. In the first Arab-Israeli war, of 1948–1949, when Jerusalem was under siege, this road was the supply line for the 100,000 Jews who defended the city. Convoys from Tel Aviv had to run the thirty-two-kilometer gauntlet of ferocious Arab ambushes to feed the embattled defenders. Rusting trucks have been left in roadside ditches as memorials to those who gave their lives to keep Jerusalem from falling to the Arab Legion.

Bar-Zeev's elder brother, Asher, had been killed by a sniper on this road, just before his truck reached the top of the gorge, under the Arab town of Kastel—before he could reach the safety of Kibbutz Kiryat Anavim, some six kilometers from the outskirts of Jerusalem. He had died two days before his thirtieth birthday.

"This is where my brother was killed in 'forty-eight," Bar-Zeev said as they passed a brass plaque set in a stone at the roadside. It was the only conversation he had offered so far.

Captain Goan nodded. "Would you like to stop for a moment?"

"No," replied Bar-Zeev. "He's not buried there."

The car labored up the steep highway, and as it rounded a bend, Bar-Zeev could see the honey-colored buildings of Jerusalem. *"Yerushalayim Shel Zahav,"* "Jerusalem the Golden." That song, which captured the Jews' love and longing for the city, had inspired the Israelis during the 1967 war. It *was* a golden city, shimmering in the November sunshine. Bar-Zeev could never approach Jerusalem without experiencing a surge of exultation and excitement. When the Old City was reunited with the New in the Six Day War, he had shared the extraordinary feeling of coming home at last after twenty years.

Although he was not a religious man, he was moved to tears the first time he saw the Western Wall—the granite remains of Solomon's Temple. But his euphoria was tempered by a revulsion for the Arabs who had desecrated the Jewish graveyard on the Mount of Olives. Not a stone stood in place; the cemetery had been used as a public latrine. And the Arabs of Jerusalem had stabled their donkeys in the synagogues of the city's ancient Jewish Quarter.

They drove down Jaffa Street and skirted the Old City Walls. At Herod's Gate they turned left into the American Colony. Captain Goan brought the car to a halt outside a small, modern apartment building. Ber-Zeev recognized it as one of the Mossad's training centers. They climbed the stairs to the second floor and paused outside a door marked with the innocent legend ZICHRON TEXTILE COMPANY. Captain Goan rang the bell. The door was opened by a young man in an open-neck shirt. Once inside the room, Bar-Zeev raised his arms wearily, waiting to be frisked.

"It's not necessary, Colonel. The *memuneh* is expecting you." The young man unlocked an inner door and led Bar-Zeev and Goan down the hall to a small office that looked out on Mount Scopus. Seated at the desk was a bald man with glasses.

"Uri!" said the man, rising from his seat. "It's been too long."

"Hello, Yakov. And how do you like my desk?"

"Fine, fine. Sit down, please. Thank you, Captain. Will you wait outside, Danny? I'll call you if I need you." Bar-Zeev waited until the two Mossad operatives had left the room.

"Have you had lunch?" inquired Yakov.

Bar-Zeev smiled. "No. Your man seemed to think you are more important than my stomach."

"Can I get you something?"

"No, thanks. I'm not hungry. Just curious."

Yakov studied his fingernails for a moment. "Uri, you know that none of us ever leaves the Mossad, don't you."

"I left."

"Yes, you had a difference of opinion, but not with us. We don't make policy. We have to take the long view. Policies change. Our job doesn't."

"Come on, Yakov, I don't need lectures. Why did you send for me?"

"Ever since you stepped down I've made it my business to keep you briefed on developments in your field."

"The only field I have now is the *pardes*."

"You were the best man we had. You are a national resource, Uri."

"Yakov, will you get to the point?"

"All right. The peace treaty has opened many avenues between ourselves and the Egyptians. You know that even when a state of war existed between our two countries, the Mossad was in contact with Egyptian intelligence on matters of mutual concern. Since the peace, that contact has been strengthened. Now the Egyptians have a problem, and it's become our problem, too. As you're aware, the American president arrives in Cairo next week for a three-day state visit. Your old department has had word that he could be a target. Also President Sayed. This has now been confirmed by Egyptian intelligence. I don't have to tell you what this means."

"Do you know where the threat comes from?"

"Not exactly. Nor do the Egyptians. They've asked us to help."

"Well, you've helped them before."

"Yes. But this time they want more than an exchange of information. President Sayed himself phoned the prime minister yesterday afternoon and made a specific request. The prime minister called me in with the defense minister. It was agreed that we would acquiesce in Sayed's request."

"Well? What does he want?"

"He wants us to send him our best operative, a man whose knowledge of international terrorist activities is unparalleled anywhere. In a word, he wants you."

Bar-Zeev began to laugh. "You're out of your mind, Yakov. You brought me up here without any lunch to tell me that you and those brass hats have decided to bundle me off to Cairo to play spies with the *Arabush*?"

The *memuneh* smiled politely. "Yes, Uri, that is exactly what we have decided."

"Well, you can tell the cabinet and whoever the hell else you like that I've left the service and if anyone wants to shoot Sayed he has my blessing."

Yakov opened the drawer of his desk and took out a file. He opened it and began to leaf through the papers. "Looking over your record, I see that the State of Israel has been good to you. You were educated at the taxpayers' expense. You have been out of the country on many occasions, lecturing at military academies around the world, again on the taxpayers. Don't you think you owe the country something?"

"You son of a bitch! I've fought in four wars. I've lost a brother. A son. Both killed by Arabs. I've seen my friends blown up around me. My own sergeant was killed at Qantara in 'sixty-seven. You know how? He gave a drink of water to a wounded Arab soldier, and as he held it for him, the bastard pulled a knife and slit his throat. That's the Arabs for you. Don't give me this bullshit about what the state has done for me, Yakov."

"All right. But you can't live in the past the rest of your life. This isn't your personal vendetta. The security of Israel is tied in with the security of Egypt now, whether you like it or not. We have agreed that you will help Egyptian intelligence. They've asked for you and we're sending you."

"And what if I refuse to go?"

"I see that your reserve military training is due. I can bring it forward; once you're in uniform, it will be an order. If you disobey an order while under army command, you will be court-martialed."

"I know where the bodies are hidden, Yakov. You don't scare me. The press would have a field day with what I could tell them about some of the Mossad's less savory exploits."

The *memuneh* sighed and closed the file. He put it back in his desk and locked it with a key chained to his belt. "Will you excuse me for a moment, Uri? I'll have a sandwich sent in for you." He rose and began to leave the room.

"Am I a prisoner here, or what?" demanded Bar-Zeev.

"No, I'll be back in a minute."

The sandwich arrived before the *memuneh,* but Bar-Zeev left it untouched. He was trembling with anger and disbelief. The door opened finally.

"Uri, come along with me," said Yakov, like a prefect inviting a troublesome schoolboy to the headmaster's office.

"Where to?"

"The prime minister has asked to see you."

Although Bar-Zeev was hostile to the government's acceptance of the peace terms with Egypt, he still admired the man who had negotiated them behind the scenes on Israel's behalf, and who had eventually been rewarded with the prime ministership. Avri Ra'anan was a scholar and historian, a quiet-spoken man whose study of history had taught him that there were no such things as traditional enemies, only temporal needs. He lived in a modest stone house surrounded by fir trees, two kilometers from the Knesset, a distance he walked every day to the despair of his bodyguards.

The prime minister liked Bar-Zeev; he respected his accomplishments and his integrity, even if the man's right-wing views offended his own, less hawkish principles.

"I was sorry to lose you," he began when Bar-Zeev and Yakov were seated in his study. His face was paternal and concerned behind explosions of pipe smoke. "Not everyone agrees with the terms we accepted. But there are other considerations, Uri. International considerations."

"Mr. Prime Minister, I can't bring myself to accept this."

"Avri, please. We're among friends here. We are friends, aren't we, Uri, even if we don't always see eye to eye?"

"You know we are."

"Good. I understand your reservations. I was as taken aback as you must have been when President Sayed asked me to send you. But we must show good faith. I have seen four wars between our countries. I don't want to see a fifth. We must do everything in our power to prevent the deaths of our young people. Because next time it won't be twenty-five hundred of our people, as it was in 1973. We will be counting corpses in the tens of thousands. The more we make Egypt dependent upon us for technological know-how, for investment, for trade and tourism, the less likely they are to renege on their agreements with us. If we don't accede to their request to send you to Cairo, then we are not showing good faith."

"Why does it have to be me? There are any number of operatives who could do it. I could brief them if you want."

"They have asked for you," said the prime minister. "It's a question of diplomacy. To send anyone else would be tantamount to downgrading the importance of the issue."

"But what if it's a trick? I have information in my head that could be invaluable to them."

"Yes, we've thought of that. Yakov, perhaps you would like to reassure Uri."

"We have drawn up contingency plans to pull you out if necessary. I'm not going to tell you what those are until you have accepted the assignment."

"You would be a one-man Entebbe," said the prime minister, in a smiling reference to the rescue of 104 Israeli hostages held by Palestinian terrorists at the Ugandan airport in 1976.

Bar-Zeev smiled, too, because he was one of the team that had planned the operation.

"You need have no worries on that score. Our people will be watching you," said Yakov.

Bar-Zeev sighed. He knew in his heart that he could not refuse the prime minister. Though he found the whole enterprise distasteful, he recognized that his refusal to go could damage relations between the two countries, and the Mossad had a way of making life difficult for those who did not readily subscribe to their scheme of things.

"When do you want me to leave?"

Yakov looked at his watch. "You are booked on the three-thirty flight this afternoon."

≈≈≈

Even before the ink was dry on the peace treaty, enterprising travel agents in Tel Aviv had arranged package tours of Egypt for Israelis interested in seeing the land of the Nile in slightly more comfort than from the turret of a tank. As one of the codicils to the treaty, a commercial air link had been established between the two capitals, and both state-owned airlines had found the route profitable enough to schedule three flights a week.

Uri Bar-Zeev had been booked on an El Al flight by the Mossad. He had been briefed by Yakov and given certain code words and contacts in Cairo in case of emergency. Finally, he was handed a new passport which gave him an assumed name, and listed his occupation as "hydro engineer."

"You are an Israeli engineer spending a week in Cairo and Aswan to discuss hydroelectric projects," Yakov told him. "You will be met at the airport by Ahmed Rahman, the head of Egyptian Internal Security."

Bar-Zeev knew the name from his files.

The *memuneh* even came to see him off at Ben-Gurion International Airport, a singular honor since Yakov had sent out his operatives on missions, when there was considerably less likelihood of their returning, without so much as a handshake in his office.

"I just wanted to assure myself that you weren't foolish enough to take along a firearm for comfort," the *memuneh* said as he wished the reluctant Bar-Zeev a pleasant stay in Africa.

Bar-Zeev was driven straight from the prime minister's office to the airport. When he protested that he wanted time to pack, to say good-bye to his wife and tell the secretary of the kibbutz of his enforced absence, Yakov told him that it had all been taken care of. A Mossad agent had helped his wife to pack clothes for a week; the suitcase was in the trunk of the car.

As the El Al jet banked west after takeoff, Bar-Zeev sat back in his seat and drew the blind against the afternoon sun. In forty minutes his plane would be touching down over the sand hills at the southern end of Cairo's runway 05-23. What the hell am I doing here? he asked himself. He had washed his hands of the whole business eighteen months before. The mind-set of twenty years does not alter with the stroke of a pen. Just because the enemy has taken off their battledress, it doesn't mean they have suddenly learned to love the Jews.

As an officer in the Mossad he had monitored and analyzed the serpentine twists of Egyptian domestic and foreign policy from Nasser to Sadat to Sayed; and with each radical change of direction, the Egyptian cabinet, the opposition leaders, and the editor of *Al-Ahram* had been summarily dismissed to make way for a new group of ministers and propagandists resilient enough to accept and articulate the regime's new thinking.

For Bar-Zeev there was too much blood in the sand to forget or forgive the Egyptians or their allies the Syrians, who for nineteen years had manned a twenty-one-kilometer-long military outpost on the western slope of the Golan Heights. The Syrians had constantly bombed the kibbutzim in the Jordan Valley below with 122-millimeter mortars and long-range Russian artillery. Until 1967 there were children in the Galil who had been born in air-raid shelters, who had never slept a night above ground. The Syrians had a special trick: they would build three walls of a house, drive a tank inside, and then brick up the fourth wall and roof it. Then they would fire on the settlements in the valley. When the source of the shellfire had been pinpointed, the Israeli Mirage jets would be ordered in to knock out the house; the Syrians would then go whining to the UN, accusing Israel of firing on civilian housing.

The heat rose off the desert and pressed up against the belly of the aircraft. Beneath him Bar-Zeev could see a low range of razor-back granite mountains, the color of dried blood. The sand, which stretched to the Mediterranean coast, looked like snow, piled in undulating drifts. The black thread of a tarmac road ran straight across the empty desert. And we have fought four wars over this inhospitable land, he thought. The Yom Kippur War of 1973 had been a *michdal,* a fuckup. Behind the Bar-Lev Line, the Defense Forces did not believe the Egyptians would attack; that was "the concept" held by the army brass and by the prime minister herself. The officers in the front line knew, and so did the Mossad. Bar-Zeev had tried to convince the chief of staff, David Elazar, but an order for full mobilization in May had cost the country four and a half million Israeli pounds on a false alarm. Another such mistake would have been a crippling blow to the economy. But Egypt did attack, and the Bar-Lev Line, like every other "impregnable" line of defense in history, had been overrun. Within two weeks Israel had lost half her armor and a quarter of her air force. A new era of warfare had arrived: put a guided missile like the Sagger into the hands of an Egyptian farmer and with a minimum of training he can knock out a five-hundred-thousand-dollar tank. Egypt's mobile surface-to-air missiles, the SA-6 and SA-7, accounted for heavy Israeli losses in the air. Israel would have lost the 1973 war had it not been for General Arik Sharon's bold thrust across the Suez Canal, north of the Great Bitter Lake, at the Chinese Farm. Sharon's main tank force cut south and encircled the Egyptian Third Army, cutting it off from its sources of supply. It was only the enforced cease-fire engineered by the Americans and the Russians that saved the Egyptians from annihilation. Sharon had pressed for a total victory, but the politicians held him back. A man after my own heart, thought Bar-Zeev.

"We are about to land at Cairo Airport. Kindly extinguish all smoking material and return your seats to the upright position." Bar-Zeev was startled from his reverie by the announcement over the loudspeaker.

He experienced a feeling of morbid excitement as he filed down the steps with the other passengers and walked the short distance across the tarmac into the terminal building. The sun was low in the sky, and a cool wind off the desert made him shiver. Mosquitoes buzzed around his head, and the air was heavy with the smell of jet exhaust. He held his briefcase with both hands across his chest and hurried past the two uniformed soldiers who stood at the door, rifles slung carelessly across their shoulders, bayonets fixed.

The young immigration officer in a blue uniform sat in a glass booth, methodically reading the contents of Bar-Zeev's passport. He looked at the photograph and then back at the glowering figure who stood in front of him, almost challenging him to find fault with it. He stamped it three times and handed it back. "Welcome to Cairo, Mr. Bar-Zeev. Have a pleasant stay," he said in perfect English. Bar-Zeev nodded, noting the officer had identified him immediately, despite the false passport. He, picked up his briefcase and carried it to the baggage area. He could feel his heart beating as he waited for his suitcase in a drab room hung with dusty posters of Luxor and Karnak. He did not speak to his fellow Israelis, who inspected their surroundings with voluble curiosity. A tour group, he said to himself with distaste. He wondered how much they knew of war and the perfidy of the Egyptians who now carried their suitcases instead of guns. He looked around for his contact, but no one approached him.

Two porters dragged in a dolly stacked high with luggage. The passengers swarmed around it, pulling off the pieces to reach their own. He waited until his was visible and then shouldered his way through the crowd to retrieve it. As he did so, one of the porters said something to him in Arabic that he didn't grasp. He shook his head and began to move toward the customs area. The porter caught his sleeve and held out his hand. Bar-Zeev brushed past him, swearing to himself.

At the customs benches a group of uniformed men stood chatting and smoking. They could have spared me this indignity, he thought. But then he was supposed to be just another Israeli businessman, and as such he could not expect preferential treatment. He put his luggage and briefcase on the bench and waited, his hands deep in his pockets. One of the customs men looked at him and then at his suitcase and waved him on.

He followed the signs to the main terminal, looking around expectantly for Ahmed Rahman. In the long, shedlike hall the noise of the passengers bounced off the ceiling, augmented by the unintelligible announcements of the public address system. Groups of Bedouin squatted on the floor next to shopping bags and bundles of their belongings tied up like dirty laundry. Elderly European tourists sat glumly on orange plastic seats waiting for transportation. Young men, arm in arm, jostled their way through the throng with transistor radios pressed to their ears. Helmeted soldiers and police leaned against the railings that divided the check-in desks from the waiting area, and lazily scrutinized the crush of people through half-closed eyes. The noise, the dirt, and the smell of bodies appalled Bar-Zeev. Everything looked soiled and squalid under the harsh neon lights, like a scene by Hieronymous Bosch. The Israeli was homesick already for the tranquillity and freshness of the orange groves.

A man in a dirty galabia pointed to his luggage and offered to get him a taxi. Bar-Zeev shook his head. No sooner had the Egyptian shuffled off to find a more receptive tourist than Bar-Zeev was approached by a second man.

"You want alabaster head of Nefertiti?" He reached down the front of his filthy garment and produced the proffered artifact.

"No, thank you," said Bar-Zeev sternly.

"You want scarab from the tomb of Seti the First?" Again the object was produced.

"I don't want anything."

"Hand-rolled Egyptian cotton handkerchiefs? Perfume essence? American cigarettes?" The voice caressed Bar-Zeev in a pleading singsong. Each article was conjured out of the depths of the peddler's robe as the litany of delights proceeded.

Bar-Zeev moved away; his nerves were frayed and he did not want to lose his temper.

But the man was not to be shaken off so easily. He insinuated himself before Bar-Zeev again, his hands full of his dubious wares.

"I have antique amber beads. Earrings for the ladies in gold."

Bar-Zeev looked desperately around. Turning on the man, he whispered through clenched teeth, "If you don't disappear I'm going to shove that junk down your throat, understand?"

Ahmed Rahman had been watching Bar-Zeev from the moment he entered the hall. He wanted to get the measure of the man before he introduced himself. He was disappointed in what he saw; he was expecting a more commanding presence. A man with Bar-Zeev's reputation should have been bigger; he should have had the look of a leader. Rahman felt no threat at all from this mannikin; in fact, the only emotion he had was a vague feeling of contempt for the little Israeli. The head seemed too large for the body. The face, though instantly recognizable from the slightly blurred photograph in the Mokhabarat's file, was more lined than Rahman remembered. The frosty blue eyes darted about under the shelter of bushy eyebrows and a prominent forehead. He had the color of a man who spends his time out-of-doors. The lines about the eyes had been etched deep by wind and sun. The hands, which protruded from a shapeless suit, were large and powerful, a farmer's hands. He wore a white shirt, the collar spreading flat across his jacket to reveal the graying hairs of his chest. He looks like the father of daughters, said Rahman scornfully to himself.

It was only his innate sense of hospitality that overrode Rahman's antipathy toward the Israeli. The idea of Bar-Zeev's coming to Cairo had been repugnant enough, but faced with the physical fact of the man himself, Rahman experienced a sensation he had felt only in war: the awakening of an ancient hatred so deep and dark it could be satisfied only by blood. The Arabs may fight among themselves, but underneath they are all brothers, protected by Allah. "I and my brother against my cousin," goes the old saying, but "I and my cousin against the stranger." And the stranger stood before Rahman now, a stranger who symbolized his own personal humiliation.

He forced himself to remember that in welcoming Bar-Zeev he was acting not on his own volition but at the express orders of his president, who believed the Israeli operative might just provide some useful information about current PLO activities. He determined he would not give Bar-Zeev the satisfaction of knowing how much his presence troubled him. He fixed a smile on his face and moved forward to make contact, although he regretted having to bring to an end the spectacle of the persistent peddler's importuning of Israel's top intelligence expert.

At the approach of the large and smiling Rahman, the peddler melted away into the crowd, much to the relief of the exasperated Bar-Zeev. From a safe distance he watched as the big man smiled down at the tourist and extended a welcoming hand. Then he headed for a side exit and made a note of the time that Colonel Uri Bar-Zeev had met Colonel Ahmed Rahman. The Mossad are meticulous in their record-keeping.

"My name is Ahmed Rahman. Welcome to Cairo, Mr. Bar-Zeev."

The two men looked into each other's eyes and shook hands.

"May I see your identification, Mr. Rahman?"

"You speak Arabic. I speak only a little *Ivrit*. I learned it in one of your camps," said Rahman, still smiling, as he pulled his wallet from the breast pocket of his seersucker suit. Bar-Zeev looked at the photo in the folded green plastic case. He nodded and handed it back.

"Shall we go? My car is outside. Let me take your bag."

"No, thank you, I'll carry it if you don't mind."

"As you wish."

They edged their way through the milling crowd, past the souvenir counter selling copies of the Koran, silver jewelry, and leather wallets stamped with pictures of the Sphinx. Rahman waved away the taxi drivers. It was almost dark outside. Cars and buses, disgorging their passengers, parked where they could, throwing the approach to the terminal into a honking pandemonium of metal. Rahman signaled to the Mercedes, which drew out into the road and parked three-deep from the curb, effectively blocking any movement until the two intelligence men had threaded their way through the horn-happy congestion.

"Ismail, this is Colonel Bar-Zeev of Israeli intelligence," said Rahman, once they were inside the car. Ismail turned around in the driver's seat and shook Bar-Zeev's hand.

"Ismail is my aide-de-camp. He will be your driver for the duration of your stay."

The Mercedes turned off the airport access road onto the highway. Bar-Zeev looked out the window; all he could see was desert.

"We have arranged for you to stay at Shepheard's Hotel," said Rahman. "You will have a splendid view of the Nile. I understand that you will not require kosher food."

"I'm not an observant man," replied Bar-Zeev quietly. "In the religious sense."

"Of course."

The car sped along the highway, changing lanes with little regard to the proximity of other vehicles. Bar-Zeev gripped the seat in front. They're worse than Israeli drivers, he thought.

"Perhaps you might begin briefing me," he suggested. "I know only what my people have told me."

"All in good time, my dear Colonel. Are you not interested in the sights of Cairo?"

"I am here to work, at the request of your government," replied Bar-Zeev coldly. Rahman pretended he had not heard the remark.

"On your left is the new Sheraton Heliopolis Hotel. One of our latest five-star hotels."

"Yes, I know," said Bar-Zeev without even glancing in its direction.

"In a moment we will be passing the Technical Military Academy. There we train all of our technical officers."

"I know. Including your missile controllers. Other prominent buildings along this route are the National Computing Center, the Ministry of Planning, the Nasr City sports complex, the old military barracks left to you by your friends the British, the Ministry of Power, and Al-Botrossia Coptic Church."

Rahman turned toward him with amused surprise. "When were you last in Cairo, Colonel?"

"I've never been here. I have made it my business to find out. I know the topography of your city as well as I know Tel Aviv. I could walk your streets blindfolded. I've studied maps and aerial photos for years."

"You hear that, Ismail? The colonel will have no need of your talents as a guide." The two Egyptians exchanged ironic smiles in the rearview mirror, a moment of collusion not lost on Bar-Zeev.

"Geography is not my only suit. I prefer people. Let me think. Colonel Ahmed Rahman. Head of Internal Security. Close to the president. A rising star. Born in Iqlit, Upper Egypt, in 1932. Father, a farmer. Military background, infantry. Fought against us in Sinai in 1956. Rank of sergeant major. Taken prisoner and repatriated in an exchange. Decorated. Transferred to military intelligence in 1957. Coordinated the Israeli branch of the research division for a time. Served in various attaché capacities in London, Athens, Paris, and Zurich. Became assistant to the deputy director of military intelligence in 1968. Nasser liked you. You warned Sadat of a plot to overthrow him in 1971. Promoted to present position in 1972. Shall I keep going?"

Rahman lit a cigarette. "I have done my homework, too." And he began to list the contents of the Mokhabarat file on Bar-Zeev that now lay locked in President Sayed's desk.

The Israeli listened impassively to his life story. He had known that the Egyptians would have a psychological profile on him, just as his department had on all prominent military and political personalities in Egypt. He was surprised, however, by its accuracy and detail.

"And my favorite color is blue," added Bar-Zeev when Rahman had finished.

"So you see, my dear Colonel, we are professionals, too."

"My memory is perhaps not as good as yours, Rahman, but there's one incident I left out. In 1969, when you were military attaché in London, you had a liaison with a young Arab student at the London School of Economics. She was studying social anthropology. I don't think I'm giving anything away now if I tell you that she was one of ours."

Rahman's face darkened. He tried to cover his anger and confusion by slapping Bar-Zeev playfully on the thigh. He glanced furtively into the rearview mirror to see if Ismail had heard the conversation. His aide kept his eyes diplomatically on the road ahead.

"I'm glad you have a sense of humor," Rahman replied finally, laughing more loudly than he had intended.

The two men fell silent for the rest of the journey, each lost in his own thoughts.

≈≈≈

"I told you, you should never accept ice cubes unless you know the water's been boiled first," Nicole admonished Bill Leamington. "No wonder you're feeling queasy."

Leamington had experienced a wave of nausea as soon as he stepped out into the spectacular chaos of Cairo traffic. Kasr el Nil, once the pride of the capital and the most fashionable shopping street in the Middle East, was now cracking under the weight of the crowds that daily thronged its sand-strewn sidewalks. The stench of gas fumes made his stomach revolt. The exhausts of countless badly tuned cars hung in the air above the shop fronts, blackening the laundry left to dry on apartment balconies above.

"And I was so careful, Nicky." Leamington was feeling sorry for himself. "When I ran out of bottled water this morning, I brushed my teeth in bourbon."

"Bourbon! And you wonder why you've got Tut's revenge?"

Bill groaned as his stomach turned over again.

"We'll get straight back to the Hilton and you can lie down and rest." Nicole was all solicitude and amused concern.

There was no point in driving the kilometer between the offices of Tohamy Brothers Limited, Architects and Interior Designers, and the Nile Hilton. It would take half the time to walk the distance. They picked their way, hand in hand, through the afternoon crowds. Merchants on stools outside their shops hissed at them like geese as they passed: "Change money? Give you a good rate." A small boy dressed in striped pajamas ducked past them; on his head he held a rush basket piled high with flat cakes of bread. He tripped on a broken flagstone in front of them, spilling the entire contents of the basket under the feet of the passersby. The boy, no more than eleven years old, burst into tears where he fell. Concerned strangers scrambled in the sand, retrieved the bread, dusted it on sleeves, and placed it reverently back in the basket. Bread in Egypt is sacred; they call it *aish,* meaning "life."

"Jesus Christ," marveled Leamington, and his stomach went through another convulsion. His load restored, the boy picked himself up, stuck the basket on his head once more, and continued on his way.

"Poor kid," said Nicole. "I hope they don't punish him."

Men in a sidewalk coffeehouse followed Nicole with their eyes while they lazily smoked *shisha* pipes or popped *lib* nuts—dried watermelon seeds—into their mouths. She felt their stares and wondered if it was her red hair that drew their attention. She patted it automatically. She had seen belly dancers do this; the hair was the only part of themselves they actually touched while they danced.

In every store window, large posters of President Sayed smiled down on them. He was dressed in full ceremonial uniform as the commander in chief of the armed forces, replete with medals and a marshal's baton.

As they waited for the lights to change at Talat Harb Square, Bill's face contorted with pain. Nicole held his arm and suggested that they sit for a while in Groppi's, across the street. Menaced by cars that ignored the light favoring pedestrians, she supported him across and into the once-famous ice cream parlor with its mosaic facade and Art Nouveau grilles. They passed through the high-ceilinged room hung with wrought-iron chandeliers and slow-moving fans. Trays of candied fruit, chocolates, pastries, and exotic jams were set out invitingly on glass counters. At the back of the shop, up a small flight of stairs, was the *salon de thé,* where dignified Nubians in long gray robes and red fezzes glided about, carrying trays of beer, tea, and ice cream at shoulder level. Nicole and Bill sat down at a white-topped table, happy to be off the streets. The plaster was coming away from the wall behind them, and there was a tear in their red vinyl bench. Groppi's had seen better days.

"The problems of this city are beyond human solutions," said Bill wearily.

"Would you like something?" asked Nicole, placing her hand on his. "Tea or a beer?"

"I don't think I could keep anything down. You have something."

"Perhaps I'll have a Stella. My throat is full of dust. Are you feeling any better?"

"A little. I'm sorry about this. It's a stupid thing. I've always had a lousy stomach, ever since I was a kid. And now this ulcer. Maybe I'll have a Perrier water. Waiter!"

At the next table two men were playing backgammon and eating plates of *fool*—fava beans cooked in spices.

"By the way, Bill, did you get in touch with the police about the demonstration yesterday at the Oasis?"

"What's the point? They'd only come snooping around and questioning the workers, and waste more time. It was just a bunch of fanatics. They won't be back."

"Maybe, but you should have called."

"I tried, but you know the phones."

"You could have used the radio." All Venture's projects were equipped with shortwave transmitters.

"That reminds me. It's broken. Be sure to have it repaired before the president arrives."

The waiter arrived with the quart bottle of beer and the Perrier water. Leamington inspected the glass and wiped the rim with his handkerchief before pouring his mineral water.

"What do you think of the brothers Tohamy? Are you happy with what they've done?" asked Nicole. Part of the contract signed with the Egyptian government called for the use of local companies to carry out certain work. This ensured that a percentage of hard currency remained in the country and that the Egyptian professional class, as well as the labor force, benefited from foreign-investment projects.

"They're okay but not very imaginative. A New York interior decorator could have done the job in a third of the time. It's a pity Hoda Chafik has swanned off to Zurich when we need her."

"I can handle it if you let me," said Nicole frostily.

Hoda Chafik was a wealthy Cairene in her early forties who knew everyone worth knowing in the Middle East. Leamington had taken her in as a business partner because of her connections and her ability to pick her way through the impenetrable maze of the Egyptian bureaucracy. It was in Venture's interest to have a sleeping partner since, under Egyptian law, foreign companies enjoyed a preferential tax status if a resident Egyptian had a stake in the investment project. As far as the wealthy and elegant Hoda Chafik was concerned, Nicole suspected that for Leamington the title of sleeping partner was no longer a mere figure of speech.

"How do we stand on the Red Sea project?" asked Bill, changing the subject.

"You must be feeling better; you're beginning to sound bossy. It would be easier to show you on the models back at the hotel."

"All right, shall we go?" Leamington threw a pound note on the table; the tip would be more than the check.

Venture International had rented two adjoining suites on the fifth floor of the Hilton, facing the Nile. For the sake of decorum, and not to give offense to the women who cleaned the rooms, Bill and Nicole slept in separate bedrooms. The living room of Nicole's suite had been turned into an office, while Bill's was used to entertain his Egyptian contacts. Here they could drink champagne and bourbon in happy violation of the Prophet's injunction against alcohol.

When he first moved in, Bill had the hotel staff unscrew everything mounted on the walls so that he could surround himself with objets d'art of his own choosing: Oriental rugs from his extensive collection. Costly Heriz Dozars and Bokaras, purchased at the Cairo souk after time-consuming rounds of haggling and endless cups of Turkish coffee, now graced the room, hiding the dust-defined squares made by nondescript pharaonic wall hangings and prints of Upper Egypt. The standard green-and-blue heavy-duty hotel floor covering was barely visible for Afghan, Shiraz, and Tabriz carpets, with pride of place going to an old Shirvan rug executed in lustrous blues, reds, and white. By the huge plate-glass window that ran the width of the room was a small silk Qum.

A sliding glass door gave access to the balcony, furnished with wicker chairs and footstools. As the sun went down, Nicole and Bill would take their drinks out onto the balcony and watch twilight fall over the city, washing it in a faint purplish haze. Directly across the river, on Ghezira Island, stood the Cairo Tower, the tallest structure in the city, built by Nasser to his own greater glory and financed, so the rumor went, by a few million dollars slipped to him for his own private use by a hopeful CIA.

Venture International paid $150 a day for each suite, a long-term rate Leamington had negotiated with the management. Not a substantial reduction, since the Nile Hilton was full every month of the year, but it satisfied the businessman in him to know he was paying less than the amount written on the card hanging on the inside of the door.

"Can I get you anything for your stomach?" Nicole inquired as they entered Bill's living room.

"Maybe a glass of champagne. The French swear by its medicinal properties."

"They're probably right. Those champagne widows live as long as Russian peasants." Nicole took a half bottle of Pommery & Greno '71 from the fridge and uncorked it with the panache of a sommelier. She poured two glasses and handed one to Bill. "You wanted to know about the Red Sea project. Come over here by the models."

In one corner of the room stood a green-baize table supporting balsa-wood models of Venture's three hotel projects in Egypt. Next to the Oasis stood a miniature replica of a hotel in Aswan to be built overlooking the newly raised Temple of Philae. Next to that was the Red Sea project—the most ambitious of the three. This hotel would offer tourists a unique feature: underwater dining rooms and bars whose windows looked out on the coral and marine life ten meters below the Red Sea waters. Essential to the construction of these rooms was a super-strength glass capable of withstanding tremendous water pressure. It had been developed in Germany, and without its immediate delivery, work on the project could not proceed.

"The work on the foundation is finished," said Nicole, pointing at the beautifully crafted model with a pencil. "The cofferdam is in place, and the seawater's been drained. The engineer says they've managed to plug the leak. So they're ready to lower the first room module in place. The second one is on site. This means that unless we get immediate delivery of the glass, we're going to run into delays."

"Our critical path calls for the glass to go in next Friday, for God's sake." The Red Sea project had been undertaken at the specific request of the minister of tourism, whose dream it was to turn that coast into an African Riviera. Tourism in Egypt had dropped from an average stay of nineteen days to six, and the minister's future depended on his improving these statistics. The Sheraton chain had been first in the field, with a one-hundred-room hotel at Hurghada. But the whole area was ripe for development. Farther south, where uninterrupted stretches of white sandy beach had been protected for thirty years by land mines, the climate allowed for year-round bathing.

The minister had waxed lyrical on the subject when Leamington met him at an international conference on tourism in Acapulco. "The water is so clear and blue, Mr. Leamington, you can see the pink coral fifteen meters below the surface. And the fish, they are like the rainbow in motion. It's a tourists' paradise."

"Aren't there sharks in the Red Sea?" asked Leamington.

"Sharks? Maybe one or two. Occasionally they set off the floating mines, before we had them cleared. They are no problem."

"We could drop control nets around the swimming area, I guess."

"I rely on you, Mr. Leamington, to make it work. Europeans and Americans will flock there for winter sunshine."

"I believe you," Bill replied. The next day, he cabled his office in Hong Kong and the Red Sea project was added to Venture's list. The minister ensured that Venture's bid was accepted over that of other developers—that is, after Hoda Chafik had informed him of her participation in the scheme.

Venture's contract with the Egyptian government contained a bonus clause if the work was completed ahead of schedule. Leamington was determined his company would get the money. There were also expensive penalty clauses if the completion dates were not met. Having had experience of construction work in Africa and the Far East, Leamington extracted written guarantees from the government negotiators that he would be free of labor disputes and bureaucratic interference.

"Damn it all, what's the problem with the glass?" he complained to Nicole.

"The customs people in Alexandria won't release the shipment. The bills of lading are fine; the trucks are there, ready to transport it, but now customs is demanding a twenty-five percent duty."

"That's crazy! Our contract specifically exempts us from import charges on all structural materials."

"It seems that some humorist in Alex thinks that heavy-duty glass for watching fish doesn't qualify. He marked it down as aquarium glass. I told you we should have shipped it to a Red Sea port, Bill."

"It wouldn't have made any difference. Anyway, there were no freighters available. I'm going to see the development minister and hold him to the contract. Can you set up an appointment for eight a.m. tomorrow?"

"Try eleven a.m. You're more likely to find him there."

Nicole slid open the balcony door and stepped outside. She loved to watch the sun go down over the Nile; it seemed to slide out of the sky like a huge copper tray. Across the river, on the opposite bank, a group of men and boys were swimming in the river, splashing and laughing in the mud-colored water. They wore no trunks; when they stood up, they covered their genitals with both hands. She studied their glistening, wet bodies, bronzed by the last rays of the sun. She felt curiously excited by them, hoping that one might forget his modesty and take his hands away. A cool breeze stirred her hair, exposing the whiteness of her neck. She had never considered herself a classic beauty —her face was too plump and square, her nose too small—but she knew men found her attractive, and this gave her confidence. She had a wide, generous mouth that spread into a spontaneously warm and inviting smile. Her full red lips suggested the voluptuousness of her body. Her hips, thighs, and breasts were rounded, like a 1950s cover girl's. Her red hair and large blue eyes were her best facial features, she knew, and she distracted attention from the chubbiness of her face by wearing large glasses—which she needed in any case, being near-sighted.

Bill Leamington watched her for a moment, fascinated by the movement of her hair in the wind and the way it pressed her light summer dress to her legs. He joined her on the balcony and stooped to kiss the back of her neck. She leaned against him, still watching the naked swimmers cavorting in the Nile like sporting dolphins. He followed her gaze and gently began to massage her shoulders. She caught a glimpse of black pubic hair and flashes of tight, muscular buttocks. She could feel her nipples hardening against the fabric of her dress.

"Make love to me, Bill," she whispered. His hands closed around her breasts and squeezed her nipples to hard, jutting points. She held onto the iron railing and pressed herself back against him, feeling the warmth of his body. His hands moved downward over her hips and thighs to the hem of her dress. She felt his fingers moving upward. She enjoyed the way he touched her, the way he made her want him more than she had wanted any other man.

"Don't stop," she said. His hand slid under her panties, and his fingers explored the moist, warm hair of her mound, sliding down the opening petals of her lips, unlocking the center of her desire.

She turned quickly, breaking away from him; she was breathing heavily. "Let's go inside. No, don't pull the curtains. I want to see the sunset."

She pulled him down to the floor and began to unbutton his shirt. She kissed his chest as his hands cupped her buttocks. It aroused him to run his fingers over her skin and feel the silkiness of her panties on the backs of his hands. He reached around and unzipped her dress; she shook it free of her shoulders. He struggled briefly with the clasp of her brassiere, long enough for her to sit up with an exasperated chuckle and undo it herself. Her large round breasts bounced out of the gauzy material. Leamington raised himself up on his elbows and kissed her nipples. She took off her dress and panties and then began to undress him. He lifted his back off the floor like a wrestler as she slid his trousers off, and then he pulled her down beside him and rolled on top of her. Nicole guided him into her with a sigh of pleasure. As he moved she could feel the silky caress of the Qum rug under her buttocks. She felt as if she were wrapped in silk as her lover slid over her with deep, powerful thrusts that filled her body with a pleasure so close to pain she wanted to cry out. She dug her nails into his back and suddenly twisted under him; she rolled over, pressing herself to him so that he was still inside her. Leamington lay where she had been and watched her face as she rotated her hips, bringing herself to a gasping, back-arching climax.

Nicole paused momentarily and lay against him, a thin film of perspiration drying on their bodies. Then she began to move again, slowly and rhythmically, willing him to his orgasm. With a groan he exploded inside her. She smiled down at him and relaxed. They lay together on the floor, side by side, holding hands, drowsily watching the sun sink below Ghezira Island; then they fell asleep.

It was dark when Nicole awakened. Outside, the Cairo Tower was illuminated and the lights of El Tahrir Bridge twinkled on the water. She got up quietly so as not to disturb Leamington. It was almost seven o'clock. She went into the bedroom and put on his robe, then mixed herself a drink and sat on the sofa. She studied the sleeping form of the man she loved. His mouth was open and as he breathed his stomach rose and fell like a sleeping puppy's.

It had been three years since her first meeting with Bill Leamington in Hong Kong. She had lived in countries around the world most of her life because her father was a career army officer. The family had moved virtually every three years to a new posting, a peripatetic life-style that had given her a taste for travel. After graduating from Sarah Lawrence with a major in botany and biology, she decided to take a year off before settling down. She chose Hong Kong, a previous posting of her father's, because she loved the city.

Nicole first saw Leamington in an antiques shop. He was examining a Persian rug, expertly separating the pile and scrutinizing the knots. She had been immediately attracted to the tall Bostonian. She watched him bargaining good-naturedly with the shop owner, a tiny Cantonese with skin the color of parchment. When a price was fixed, Leamington asked the merchant to have the rug delivered to him at Pacific Towers. He wrote out a check, handed the man a business card, and walked out without even looking at her.

Nicole strolled over to the cash desk and casually glanced at the card.

"Excuse me," she said to the owner as he rolled up the rug. "That's a beautiful piece. Where does it come from?"

"It's a Shiraz, very old, very fine," replied the man, smiling.

That night she went to Pacific Towers, hoping to bump into Leamington. She waited in the bar, fending off the advances of lonesome Japanese businessmen, but he did not appear. She spent the next three nights in the hotel bar and lobby, and on the fourth night she saw him again. She summoned up her courage and approached him as he handed his key to the receptionist.

"Excuse me, Mr. Leamington?" When he turned inquisitively toward her, she almost forgot her prepared speech.

"Yes?"

"The Shiraz rug you bought on Tuesday. I think you paid too much for it."

Bill looked at her for a moment and frowned. "Do you work for Mr. Cheng?"

"No, no. I just happened to be in the shop at the time. My name's Nicole Honeyworth." She extended her hand, not knowing what else to do. Leamington shook it and smiled.

"Well, Miss Honeyworth, you may be right. Let's discuss it over a drink." And he ushered an extremely relieved Nicole toward the bar.

Bill told her later that it was her aggressiveness and enterprise that attracted him to her originally, a comment she found less than flattering. But the manner of her approach suited Leamington very well. He was not successful with women. In theory, he had all the credentials of a campus hero—good looks, athletic ability, academic prowess, an aristocratic Bostonian background—but he was afraid of women. He was awkward in their company, and he disguised the fact by either treating them with locker-room contempt or placing them on pedestals.

A Freudian psychiatrist might have ascribed this attitude to his parents' divorce when he was seven. At that age he had been placed in high-priced boarding schools by the mutual agreement of both parents, who were sensible enough not to use the child as a pawn in their battle. The result was that William Leamington III grew up without the company of women; they were aliens in his world, and he was at a loss as to how to deal with them. Recognizing this lack in himself, he channeled his student energies into sports and the pursuit of knowledge. When he graduated from the Harvard Business School, money and power became his substitutes for female companionship.

Nicole put it down to the Puritan New England ethos. She recognized that she fulfilled a need in him for a woman who could take the initiative without undermining his sense of manhood. Throughout their three-year relationship she had remained completely feminine, knowing when to lead him, when to follow. Their lives, both public and private, had become inextricably bound together; yet he had never once suggested that they get married. Nicole wanted desperately to be his wife and the mother of his children. She knew she could make him happy, but his two previous marriages, contracted more from motives of conventional requirement than from feelings of love and friendship, had left deep scars. A chance pregnancy led to the first—to an Irish air hostess. His sense of honor dictated matrimony. The child was stillborn, and the marriage ended in disaster. The second was to a cool New England beauty, daughter of a leading Boston family related to both the Cabots and the Lodges. She turned out to be an alcoholic. Leamington was defensive about both, as if it were his fault that his two attempts at marriage had failed.

Nicole finished her drink. She would let him sleep a little longer. She would slip back to her room, shower, and change for dinner. She put her dress on and covered him with the robe, still warm from her body. In the corridor she remembered he was out of cigarettes. He'd reach for one as soon as he woke up. She headed for the elevators. As the door opened she stepped into a solemn tableau of Egyptian women in long white dresses, holding trays of white and pink sugared almonds. She smiled at them but they did not respond. In the lobby the women suddenly became animated as they joined a wedding procession that was filing past, led by young men beating a loud, intoxicating rhythm on *tablas,* small goatskin drums, which produced a high, thudding sound that seemed to pulsate in Nicole's stomach. Small girls in floor-length white dresses with pink ribbons in their hair carried long white candles with a grave air of self-importance. Older girls followed, scattering rose petals in the path of the bride. The air was heavy with the sweet, musky smell of incense.

The bridal party wound its way up the staircase to the mezzanine ballroom, where the entertainment would continue well into the night. Nicole had seen it all before. The bride and groom would sit together on a raised stage. There would be music, singers, exotic dancers, and, at midnight, a lavish buffet of the finest Egyptian delicacies. Not until the early hours of the morning would the bridal couple be permitted to slip away.

In a village, the groom would be expected to present the bride's father with a bloodstained handkerchief the next morning as proof of his daughter's virginity, a badge of honor for the whole family. They would sing songs to the young bride "who has covered the white silk with her own blood." How many chickens, Nicole wondered, had been slaughtered in the dead of night, sacrificed on the altar of a bride's good name—the old traditions were dying out in Egypt. As the dark-eyed young bride passed her, fussed over by female friends, Nicole felt a twinge of envy. She sighed and crossed the lobby to the cigarette stand. Thinking of the handkerchief ritual, she realized she desperately wanted a shower. She had made a dinner reservation for nine o'clock and it was getting late.

≈≈≈

The picturesque driving habits of Cairenes and the dearth of spare parts have combined to make the automobile-repair business a most lucrative option for the aspiring Egyptian entrepreneur. Cairo is replete with auto body shops, which seem to cluster together, vulturelike, around major intersections in eager anticipation of trade. Such a cloning of garage premises is to be found off Muhammad Ibrahim Helmy Street, convenient to the daily traffic rampage through the city's center. The street resembles a car graveyard, since none of the shops, however large —and they range from single bays to buildings of warehouse proportions—can possibly house the number of vehicles towed in for repair.

During the day the street resounds with a symphony of clanging metal, hissing acetylene torches, throbbing generators, and the shouts of workmen as they hammer out dented doors and fenders. The unfortunate apartment dwellers who live above the shops have had to come to terms with the din. The housing shortage being what it is in Cairo, they have little hope of finding alternative accommodation. (When they petitioned the governor of Cairo for relief, he replied with a gesture of world-weary resignation, "It would be easier to build nests for the birds of the air than to house Cairo's homeless.") Such is the demand for car-repair work that business goes on late into the evening; but mercifully the shops close down at night and a deafening silence falls over the rusting skeletons of cannibalized wrecks. So the street was deserted just before midnight when a cream-colored Peugeot drew up outside a garage bearing a faded sign in Arabic and French: ATELIER MÉCHANIQUE, ABDUL SAMY. In the driver's seat was Professor Rashad Munir of Al-Azhar University. He was angrily berating his passenger, Saraj al-Rahid, who stared back at him with his one good eye. "I am not interested in excuses. You had no authority for the demonstration. Did you have my permission? You did not."

"If the American did not like it, he can drink from the sea," replied the truculent al-Rahid.

"Son of a donkey, do you not think at all?" Munir turned off the ignition but made no move to get out of the car.

Stung by the insult, al-Rahid refused to be silent. "I would remind you that only five months ago you encouraged such demonstrations. You said they would mobilize public opinion against the Western intruders."

"So they did. But that was before this project became so critical. I thought I made it clear to you that all other activity must be suspended."

"You issued no such directive."

"Your ears have calluses, my dear Rahid. But that is water from the pump now. It is fortunate for you the American did not call the police. I want no more demonstrations. Nothing that will call attention to our movement. Do I make myself clear?"

Al-Rahid nodded sulkily.

"Then we will go in."

They left the car and walked to the garage. Munir unlocked a small wooden door, and the two men crouched to enter the body shop. A twenty-five-watt bulb had been left burning, and its feeble orange light illuminated two rows of cars in various states of repair. They squeezed sideways along the workbenches to the end of the bay, where several stacks of tires, piled almost three meters high, concealed a small office, which the manager occupied during business hours. Once inside, Munir locked the door behind them and then switched on the desk light. The room was painted dark green. Three of its walls were decorated with dusty posters of European car models. The fourth was covered from floor to ceiling with an oil-stained blanket woven from sheep's wool. Al-Rahid pulled it aside, revealing a second door. Munir produced another key, and a moment later they were in a brightly lit corridor. At the end, a man sat at a desk reading a newspaper. Hearing their footsteps, he drew a revolver from his belt.

"It is all right, Jabir," said the professor softly. The man put down the gun and took Munir's hand, pressing it to his forehead.

"Unlock the door, please." Jabir did as he was ordered, pulling the heavy steel door wide enough to allow Munir and al-Rahid to pass. Inside was a sterile, white-walled laboratory, without windows. The steel door swung shut behind them.

"Professor! Welcome." A middle-aged man with a graying beard, wearing a white coat and rubber gloves, rose from behind two stainless-steel vats. "It's some time since you honored us with your presence." From another room could be heard the intermittent sound of a welder's torch punctuated by the scraping of a file on metal.

"Greetings, Dr. Nasif. May Allah protect you," said Munir coolly. "How is your work progressing?"

"If Allah wills, we shall be ready on time," Nasif replied in the same formal rhythm.

"You are certain?"

"There is no question now."

"Now?"

"There was a problem. . . ."

"You are referring to Herrara, our courier?"

"Yes. You have heard?"

"I have heard. But more important, so, too, have the police. His body was taken from the Nile yesterday."

"But the body was weighted down! It should not have been found." Dr. Nasif ran his tongue nervously over his lips.

"Apparently the rope was frayed. They have also discovered that Herrara was radioactive. The alarm has gone right to the president. They have even sent for help from the Israelis." Munir's tone brought beads of perspiration to Nasif's forehead.

"Surely you do not blame me, Professor? The men had to dispose of the body as quickly as possible."

"I blame no one. It is Allah's will," Munir said. "It is unfortunate, but it cannot be helped. Now explain to me where we stand. We have only one week left."

Dr. Nasif, unctuous in the role of technocrat, extended his hand in a courtly invitation for Munir to follow him. His beard was wet with perspiration, and he wheezed as he moved on short, heavy legs.

"We are fortunate that Herrara completed enough successful trips before his death. The accident took place during his final delivery. He lost some material, but we already had enough uranium stockpiled to complete the device." The sound of the welder's torch intensified as they moved toward the end of the room.

"If you will stand here one moment, I will show you what is happening." He opened a door, revealing two white-coated technicians wearing goggles. They were bent over a vise that held a shining metal ball twenty-five centimeters in diameter. "They are working on the steel casing," explained Nasif, shouting over the roar of the torch. A shower of brilliant orange sparks arced over the steel surface and sputtered on the cement floor.

"There are three such casings in the device: one coated with beryllium to contain the plutonium, one to surround the detonating explosive, and an outer shell."

"And the plutonium?" Munir inquired.

Nasif shut the door. "If you will follow me." He waddled over to what appeared to be a small well in one corner of the laboratory. Professional enthusiasm had dissipated his earlier nervousness, and he spoke more quickly now.

"When Herrara took delivery of the spent uranium fuel rods, they were still in their zirconium-alloy sheaths. They were put in lead containers to shield against radiation. When he delivered them to us, they were stored here in this well until we were ready to handle them. Water is one of the most effective radiation shields, provided you put enough of it between you and the source."

The three men stared down into the water. From the bottom of the well came an eerie bluish light. "That's Cherenkov radiation," Nasif explained. "It's caused by the gamma rays emitting from the fuel bundles."

"How did Herrara carry them? Are they heavy?" asked Munir.

"Not particularly. A bundle weighs about fourteen kilos. It's all right; you have nothing to fear." The remark was addressed to al-Rahid, who was backing away from the lip of the well. "There are five meters of water down there. At the bottom is the last of the fuel bundles. Herrara could carry three at a time."

The play of the neon lights on the black surface of the water fascinated Munir.

"We've been able to refine out of the uranium rods one and a half kilos of weapons-grade plutonium two-thirty-nine, which will go critical if we can compress it sufficiently," continued Dr. Nasif.

"Is that enough plutonium?"

"Professor, you asked for a device to do a specific job. This one will do it. You will have a bomb as powerful as the one the Americans dropped on Nagasaki. The larger the bomb, the heavier it is. Too much plutonium and it could blow up in our faces."

"How much will this one weigh?" asked al-Rahid.

"Approximately nintey kilos. It can be lifted by two strong men."

"How did you refine the plutonium, Dr. Nasif?" asked Munir.

"That is the most crucial and dangerous part of the whole operation," beamed the bearded doctor. "I did it myself, with the assistance of my daughter."

"Your daughter?" Both men looked at him—Munir in surprise, al-Rahid with a disdainful smile.

"Yes, my daughter. She has a degree in chemistry from Cairo University. I taught her the process myself. Leila, come here."

There was movement from behind the two stainless-steel vats, and a tall, olive-skinned woman emerged. Munir noted with satisfaction that in keeping with the dictates of the Koran her arms were covered and her hair was completely hidden by a white headcloth that framed the oval of her face. She looked at them briefly and then lowered her eyes.

"This is my daughter, gentlemen. She is now preparing the explosive that will trigger the device. You need not worry. It is perfectly safe."

"Your daughter is a credit to you, Dr. Nasif. You are doing fine work, Leila. You may return to it." The girl's face was devoid of expression as she accepted the compliment from Munir and moved away.

"In the separation process," continued Dr. Nasif, confident in the jargon of his calling, "we first extract the plutonium rods from their sheaths. We are, of course, protected by lead shields against both alpha and gamma radiation. It was the gamma rays that killed Herrara."

"And cost us a key man," interjected al-Rahid.

Nasif ignored him and spoke directly to Munir. "To obtain enriched plutonium we dissolve its impurities chemically, first with nitric acid. Then we pipette off the rest. The result is plutonium two-thirty-nine."

"Spare me the technical details, Doctor. Is the plutonium dangerous now?" asked Munir.

"It is not dangerous in the radioactive sense. We can handle it with normal laboratory equipment. But it is a highly toxic and cumulative poison. If you inhaled it or got some in a skin abrasion or scratch, it could kill you eventually."

"Then I have your assurances that all will be ready when the time comes?"

"Without question. My daughter and I were at risk in speeding up the chemical process by using a highly concentrated acid, but we took all the necessary precautions. All that remains is the final assembly of the device. It will be ready when you require it."

"And the smaller one?"

"I am pleased to inform you, Professor, that it is already finished." Dr. Nasif fairly levitated with pleasure as he gestured toward a wooden crate in one corner of the room. "It awaits your command. As we all do."

"Excellent, excellent. Allah will reward you, Doctor."

Nasif bowed and led the way back to the door. "I am sorry about the South American. I pray his loss will not create difficulties for you."

"He will have to be replaced, and quickly," Munir said. "His role went beyond delivering the material. But our plans will not be changed. What has been ordained will be."

DAY THREE
MONDAY, NOVEMBER 5

Ahmed Rahman was awake before the sun had climbed the Mukkatam Hills. He had not slept well; wrapped in his troubled thoughts, he sat on his balcony with a glass of sweet tea to watch the sunrise. Six stories below him the river traffic had already started: a tug pulled a stately line of six feluccas downriver, their triangular sails furled and roped to their decks. A four-man racing shell, taking advantage of the vacant river, skimmed over the water like a giant insect, feathered its oars, and glided to the dock of the Cairo Rowing Club. On a floating jetty, knots of workmen waited for the water taxi to ferry them across to the eastern bank. The city was quiet at this hour; only the sound of the riverboats and the ringing hooves of a horse-drawn trailer rose to where Rahman sat in a black silk dressing gown.

In the blue haze of morning he could see the ridge of sheer cliffs rising like a great brown cowl over the eastern part of the city. The graceful minarets and the breast-shaped dome of the Muhammad Ali Mosque softened the harsh lines of the encircling hills. The mosque formed part of the Citadel, originally built in the twelfth century by Saladin to command the whole Nile Valley. The crumbling fortress had been reconstructed by Muhammad Ali, the nineteenth-century pasha who, until his death in 1849, single-handedly attempted to modernize Egypt, and who added to the Citadel the mosque that bears his name.

Today, the ancient fort and the house of worship still dominate all views of Cairo to the east.

As the first pale rays of the sun appeared over the hills, the voices of the muezzins drifted out from minarets around the city, calling the faithful to *salat-es-subh,* the first prayers of the day. Rahman finished his tea and went inside to dress.

His apartment house on Shari el Nil had once been considered fashionable. Dokki was still a desirable residential area, and former President Sadat had had his private villa nearby. But Rahman's 1930s stucco building, with its bowed windows and rounded balconies, had been allowed to fall into disrepair by a neglectful landlord. Paint was peeling off the gray slatted shutters, and rust had eaten away at the awning rods, discoloring the orange canvas. For Rahman, the woeful condition of the building was offset by its proximity to the Lebanese embassy; he was fond of using this fact when giving directions. "You'll find me adjacent to the Lebanese embassy," he would say. "Not bad for a village boy from Iqlit."

As he carefully knotted his tie, his thoughts went back to Uri Bar-Zeev. Their first meeting had not gone well, and Rahman was frankly worried. What had started out as a briefing had degenerated into a heated argument between the two men over the terms of the peace treaty. Rahman had argued that Israel's intransigence had heavily weighted the terms in her favor; the accord had completely failed to come to grips with the Palestinian question, which was the heart of the Middle East problem.

Bar-Zeev had exploded with anger. "I'm sick of hearing about the Palestinians," he had shouted. "They're your problem. You could have housed them in 1948. Instead, you stuck them in camps in Gaza. They weren't the only refugees. You seem to forget that seven hundred and fifty thousand Jews were expelled from Arab countries with only the clothes on their backs. We absorbed our people. Why couldn't you?"

"Now you try to absorb the Palestinians with napalm," Rahman had countered.

"Because they bomb our children!"

"Let us not argue, Colonel. We have an assignment."

But Bar-Zeev would not let the subject drop. He had accused Rahman—as if *he* had formulated the terms of the treaty—of using the bogus peace to erode Israel's defense lines. The Arabs were merely marking time, rearming with American weapons for the final all-out war to annihilate the Jewish state.

Stung by this insult, Rahman had angrily lectured the Israeli on the Egyptian sense of honor and the pride his countrymen took in living up to their promises.

"You speak of Arabs. I would remind you we are descended from pharaohs. We are a people with ancient traditions and values, and among those things we revere most are honesty and integrity. Self-respect, both individual and collective, is central to our system of ethics. We Egyptians respect our obligations; we do not betray our word. We will stand by our treaty unless you break it."

On that acrimonious note the meeting had ended, and Rahman had driven Bar-Zeev back to Shepheard's Hotel in silence.

Rahman went to the kitchen and poured himself another glass of tea. The lack of progress on the case made him irritable. He was no nearer discovering how the South American had ended up a radioactive corpse in the Nile. President Dunlap's visit was only five days away, and Sayed was pressing him for results. The Israeli might be able to help, or he might not. Rahman understood only too well that if anything were to happen to the American president, it would be he, and not Bar-Zeev, who would suffer the consequences. Much as he disliked the arrogant Israeli, Rahman recognized that it was in his own best interests to make use of him now that he was in Cairo.

Downstairs, Ismail was waiting for him, parked outside the building.

"Any news?" Rahman asked as Ismail opened the door of the Mercedes for him.

"No, I'm sorry, Colonel."

"Where is the front license plate?"

Ismail looked quizzically at Rahman and then trotted around to the front of the car. He stood staring down at the empty housing. "Stolen?" he exclaimed in disbelief.

"Is nothing sacred?" groaned Rahman, and with a look of disgust at his aide he walked away, signaling Ismail to follow him in the car. A donkey cart laden with fresh vegetables passed him as he crossed the street to the embankment. At the entrance to the water-bus station, a vendor was selling nuts from a brightly painted box. Rahman purchased a paper cone of sunflower seeds and munched them as he walked toward El Gama'a Bridge. A crestfallen Ismail hugged the curb at a respectful distance behind him.

Ahmed Rahman had met few Jews in his life, and he wondered whether they were all like Bar-Zeev. He found the Israeli a most unsettling person to be with. There seemed to be no warmth or humor about the man, as if the gray of his hair had tainted his soul. He reacted like a machine: everything was calculated, devoid of emotion. Rahman was sensitive to the man's enmity toward Egyptians and his distaste for the cheerful chaos of Cairo—a distaste he hardly bothered to conceal. His very tone of voice was patronizing, especially when he talked about the Mokhabarat, which, in his view, was clearly a second-rate intelligence operation.

Rahman turned onto Shari el Giza and passed the Sheraton Hotel. A group of Saudis wearing red-and-white kaffiyehs and spotless white robes were getting out of a limousine. The Sheration was their favorite watering place in Cairo, and to Rahman's department fell the responsibility of providing round-the-clock security for the visiting princes and oil sheikhs.

On El Gama'a Bridge he looked down on the rotting hulks of paddle steamers moored in hopeless abandon under the embankment. They symbolized the old, decadent order, and their very decay afforded him a grim satisfaction. For all its faults he had come to love his adopted city, and he worked out his thoughts on endless walks through its streets.

He had no anterior hatred of Jews. When he was a village boy in Upper Egypt, Jews existed only as an alien people who played politics to usurp Palestinian land. His father had taught him to hate no man and to love those who labored with their hands. His father, Omar, was a chick-pea farmer who scratched a barely adequate living from three feddans of land. Ahmed shared a single room with two older sisters and a younger brother. They lived on peas, onions, and fava beans; as a special treat his mother would favor them with an occasional dish of treacle mixed with curdled milk. They knew that, according to custom, the land would be divided between Ahmed's brother and himself on their father's death, but Omar Rahman was an unusually enlightened man who wished something more for his talented eldest son.

The old man (he always appeared old to Ahmed, although he was only forty-eight when he died) frequently showed the boy the stump of his right index finger, which had been cut off at the first joint. "Your grandfather, may Allah protect him, did this to me," he would say. "He was a fine man, but he wanted to keep me at home to help him in the fields. I was his only son. His greatest fear was that the army would take me. When I was seven he led me to the back of the house and did this," he would say, holding up the stump. "The trigger finger, Ahmed. A man without a trigger finger is no good to the army. So I stayed here. I do not expect you to do the same."

Once, when a larger boy teased Ahmed about his father's mutilated finger, he threw himself at the bully. In the ensuing fight, the boy pinned him with his face in the dirt, pressing his arm up his back and demanding that he beg for mercy. Ahmed would not give in, in spite of the pain. The bully kept pushing until with a sickening crack he broke Ahmed's arm. When the splints came off, Ahmed found he could not straighten his elbow, and he cursed Allah because the army would not take cripples.

But when, encouraged by his father, he applied for military service at the age of sixteen, the examining doctor did not even mention the deformity in his report. The armed forces needed all the men they could get, even if they lied about their age.

The blaring of a car horn broke into Rahman's concentration. He found himself on Ghezira Island. A Fiat had stalled in the center lane, and the drivers behind were giving vent to their impatience. He thought about flagging down his car, as the sun was prickling the back of his neck. But his thoughts were beginning to take a coherent shape, so he decided to continue walking. He passed the exhibition grounds on his left and, to his right, El Tahrir Gardens—once one of the most sequestered spots in Cairo, but now used as a military depot. Khaki-painted trucks were lined up in brutish rows among the cypress and acacia trees.

Trucks like those had carried him to his first war, the 1956 Sinai Campaign. He still remembered the jolting nighttime ride across freezing desert to the front at El Arish, the few brief moments of combat, and the swift, humiliating capture by the Israelis. The war was typical of the persistent conflicts between Egypt and Israel: the Jews, bent on conquering Arab land, had attacked first and without warning—and they called themselves the Israeli *Defense* Forces.

It was as a prisoner of war that he first experienced a genuine hatred of the Israelis. Dishonored by defeat, he and his brother Egyptians were subjected to further degradation at the hands of their captors. Israeli guards strutted among them, treating them as less than human. Rahman never forgot that deep personal wound, and during his three months' confinement in Israel his desire for revenge found expression in committing to memory details of strategic importance that he later recorded for Egyptian intelligence when he was repatriated. In one session he was able to reconstruct the entire layout of the port of Ashdod, seen from a truck en route home. His amazing capacity to retain such information so impressed the debriefing officer that he requested Rahman's immediate transfer to military intelligence.

In the course of this work he learned more about the Israelis, and the more he learned the less he trusted them. Their treatment of the Palestinians whose lands and homes they appropriated in the name of a Jewish state was a crime against humanity. Even if the Palestinians were not the most attractive of Arab peoples, they were Muslims like Rahman himself. "The believers are a band of brothers," says the Koran, and Ahmed Rahman made the Palestinian cause his own.

Even more traumatic to the self-respect of a patriotic Egyptian was the Israeli seizure of the Sinai Peninsula in 1967. Each grain of sand was sacred to Rahman, and the most momentous day in his life had been October 7, 1973, when, with special permission from Anwar el-Sadat, he had been allowed to cross the Suez Canal with the advancing Third Army to witness the liberation of Egyptian territory.

As Rahman approached El Tahrir Bridge he noted that the soldier on duty was sloppily dressed. Two buttons of his tunic were undone. Military pride is soon forgotten, Rahman thought. Discipline is becoming lax. Peace has made us flabby. At the other side of the bridge stood Shepheard's Hotel. Bar-Zeev would be waiting for him in the lobby. He knew the Israeli had lost two close relatives in the wars with Egypt, but so, too, had thousands of families on both sides. Surely the Jew must realize that those who raise up the sword are responsible for the havoc it wreaks.

Rahman shook his head sadly. He had to work alongside this man.

They must submerge their differences in a time of truce. The job at hand was the priority, and there was little time left to them. Leaving the bridge, he turned right and dodged through the traffic toward the hotel. He would meet Bar-Zeev and drive the rest of the way to his office. This morning there would be no talk of politics between them. The briefing would concentrate on the presidential visit. He would make sure of that.

≅≅≅

The black Mercedes bumped over the railroad tracks that bisect Shari Sheikh Rihan. On this tree-lined street are several architecturally uninspired government buildings, including the Ministry of the Interior, where Ahmed Rahman had his office. A complex of yellow-and-brown high-rise structures surround a large courtyard that serves as a parking lot. Armed guards wearing steel helmets and carrying submachine guns patrol the sidewalks, in sober contrast to the crowds of children who pass them every morning on their way to the school a block west.

Rahman's car arrived at the ministry's double-gated entrance just after eight a.m. The guard on duty bent down and glanced at the occupants. He saluted as he recognized Rahman, and waved them through. Once they were inside the building, Rahman ushered Bar-Zeev into the elevator. The door opened on the top floor, and the Egyptian led the way to his office. During the drive the two men had exchanged only the most cursory of small talk. Bar-Zeev seemed restless, as if he, too, had had a bad night.

The Internal Security head's office was as anonymous as his calling. The walls were painted a dove-gray; the only decoration was a framed photo of President Sayed that hung next to the Egyptian flag. Rahman's chipped wooden desk was piled high with files; in front of it stood two matching chairs that would have been equally at home in a dentist's reception area. Bar-Zeev took in the office at a glance, his gaze lingering momentarily on the worn carpet and the overstuffed sofa at the far end of the room. All the ashtrays were filled with cigarette butts.

"It is probably not so well appointed as the Mossad offices," said Rahman in mock apology, "but I am hardly ever here."

"There's no need to apologize. One question: do I have your assurance that our conversation is not being recorded?"

Rahman raised his eyebrows. "My dear Colonel. We expelled the Russians from Egypt in 1972. That is not our way."

"Are you going to give me a proper briefing this morning or not?" Bar-Zeev cut in, ignoring the irony in Rahman's voice.

"I am prepared to do so, Colonel."

"Good. To start with, I need full details of President Dunlap's itinerary. Times, places—everything. Nothing held back. You either trust me or you do not."

Rahman studied his fingers before replying. Were you not a guest under my roof, I would tell you, my dear Colonel, that I do not trust you, he thought. But he said nothing and merely nodded his head.

"Then I want a rundown on all the security measures you will be instituting. How many men will be available, deployment, support staff, weaponry, communication plans. Everything I should know if I am to be of use to you."

A fleeting look of pain crossed Rahman's features at the idea of revealing such sensitive information to an Israeli. Bar-Zeev caught the expression, and before Rahman could reply, he quickly added, "Don't worry. I promise you I will have an instant attack of amnesia as soon as I leave Egyptian soil." It was the nearest he had come to a friendly response since his arrival, thought Rahman.

As if to catch himself for such a human error, Bar-Zeev thrust his hands into his pockets and continued, "If you want my help, I must be completely in the picture."

"Colonel, you were invited to Cairo to identify the current connections of Juan Herrara, not to take over the organization of presidential security," Rahman reminded him coldly.

"That is not my intention, Colonel Rahman. But if I am to be of use to you, I must know exactly what is happening. Otherwise, I'll take the next plane back to Israel and explain the situation to my prime minister."

A tray of tea arrived; Rahman waited until they had both been served and the secretary had departed before agreeing to Bar-Zeev's demand. He unfolded maps and pulled down wall charts to give the Israeli chapter and verse on the presidential visit. The first day would be spent in Cairo; there would be the drive from the airport, lunch with President Sayed, discussions after lunch, a brief public appearance, and then a helicopter trip to an oasis in the Western Desert where the American president would officiate at the opening ceremony of a new hotel. The presidential party would stay the night there. The second day would feature a visit to Alexandria, including a tour of new harbor facilities built with American aid money (and soon to be made available to the U.S. Sixth Fleet) and a visit to a hospital. On the third and final day of Dunlap's visit, he would fly to Aswan, where formal discussions and the signing of the aid agreement would take place aboard the luxury cruiser *Osiris* during a brief excursion on the Nile. The president would then board *Air Force One* at Aswan Airport for the return flight to Andrews Air Force Base.

Bar-Zeev listened without interrupting. When Rahman had finished, the Israeli stood up and began pacing the room. "If we were talking about an ordinary assassination attempt, the situation would be clear. The main danger points would be Cairo and Alexandria, with the motorcade the event of most concern. The only danger to the *Osiris* might be from mines or rocket attacks, and we could head off those possibilities effectively. But the circumstances here are hardly ordinary. We can take nothing for granted. An attack could come anywhere, at any time."

"Colonel, would you mind sitting down? The carpet is worn enough."

"I'm sorry. I think better on my feet." Bar-Zeev perched on the edge of his chair. "With your permission, I should like to inspect the planned route of the itinerary in all three cities. To familiarize myself with the terrain at first hand."

"I have tours of inspection in Cairo and Alexandria arranged. By all means, you may accompany me. Aswan is another matter. To go there would mean the loss of an entire day. I don't feel we can afford it at this stage. Why don't we plan to fly down the evening before the presidents are due to arrive there? That will give us several hours to inspect the area and to arrange for any changes in the security arrangements that seem appropriate."

"All right. What about Herrara? Have you confirmed his identity?"

"Yes. The report came in last night. Forensic tests and dental charts from Buenos Aires prove beyond a doubt it is he."

"Where's he been recently?"

"According to our files he dropped out of sight about six months ago. We know nothing of his movements since then."

Bar-Zeev picked up an ashtray and emptied the contents into a wastepaper basket. He took out a cigarette and lit it. "I would like to check with my people. I'd be surprised if they don't have more recent data. Could you have a message sent to Jerusalem?"

"The lines of communication have been established," said Rahman with stiff formality. The idea that the Mossad might have information unknown to his own agency rankled him.

Bar-Zeev scribbled a short note on a piece of paper and handed it to him. Rahman did not even glance at it. He pushed a button on his desk and handed the paper to an aide. "I want this relayed to Jerusalem through the usual channels," he said.

When they were alone again, he turned to Bar-Zeev. "You have studied nuclear physics, Colonel. I am a simple man. The army has been my university. Tell me, what do you make of this radioactivity? Surely they are not planning to assassinate the presidents with an atomic bomb? I cannot see how even the most desperate of men could resort to such a terrible act. It would mean the deaths of tens of thousands of people. Yet, with the facts available to us, what other interpretation is there?"

Bar-Zeev inhaled the acrid smoke from his kibbutz-issue cigarette. The taste reminded him of home, and it comforted him. "I've been thinking about that. An assassination doesn't make any sense. There are many scientists in the world who could put together a nuclear device if the price were right. And there's enough missing uranium to build a hundred clandestine bombs. But not for an assassination; it's too unselective. Why would anyone think of blowing up Cairo or Alexandria or Aswan to kill two men, when there are much simpler ways?"

"You are answering my question with a question, Colonel."

"I am saying that I find the assassination theory untenable. Blackmail, that's another matter. Threaten to detonate a bomb in Cairo during the visit unless some outrageous demands are met. That seems more logical."

"Among rational men, yes. But I would remind you, Colonel Bar-Zeev, that logic has not been the strong suit of some of these terrorist organizations. Even some of our governments have operated on the fringes of nuclear lunacy in recent years. Does the name Plumbat ring a bell?"

Rahman could not resist the jibe. In 1968 a quantity of uranium sufficient to manufacture twelve nuclear bombs had been shipped out of Antwerp on the freighter *Scheersberg A*. The vessel arrived at a Turkish port sometime later, minus its cargo. Subsequent investigations by Euratom were inconclusive, but it was widely believed the uranium had ended up in Israel. The incident became known as "the Plumbat Affair."

"Plumbat?" repeated Bar-Zeev. "I'm not familiar with the name. But if you want to talk about nuclear irresponsibility, I would remind you that our unlamented friend in Libya, Colonel Qaddafi, tried unsuccessfully for years to purchase an atomic bomb from China to use against Israel. That madman would have dropped it, too, if the Chinese had needed his billion dollars. Thank God he's gone."

"Don't be too thankful. Our reports suggest the new man, Jalil, is even more of a megalomaniac than Qaddafi was. Our Libyan neighbors are as angry at us as they are at you. Jalil has no love for the Jews, my friend."

"I'm not too familiar with him. But we're getting sidetracked. At the moment, Herrara's body is the only clue we have."

There was a subdued knock at the door. Rahman got out of his chair to answer it, and found Ismail, who beckoned him outside.

"What is it?"

"The pathologist's report you asked for, sir. About the mark on the instep."

"Yes?"

"He asked me to tell you that it was difficult to identify due to the advanced state of decomposition."

"Is that all?"

"No, sir. He said he would not swear to it, but he believes the mark is some kind of brand."

"A brand?"

"Yes, sir. The doctor thinks it might have been a scorpion."

"You mean a scorpion's sting mark?"

"No, sir. The image of a scorpion. Branded on Herrara's foot."

Rahman whistled softly. "Thank you, Ismail. That information is classified. Do you understand?"

Bar-Zeev was at the window, looking down on the compound, as Rahman reentered the office. For the time being, at least, the Egyptian decided, this was one piece of news that he would keep to himself.

≅≅≅

Al-Azhar is the oldest university in the world. Its history of continuous instruction in the teachings of Islam stretches back a thousand years. As the font of Islamic thought, Al-Azhar has, over the centuries, produced the scholars and missionaries who have spread the faith of the Prophet and kept his message alive in times of defeat and subjugation. It is the sacred trust of these men, the ulema, to protect and pass on the faith and to train new generations of teachers. While Al-Azhar's fortunes have waxed and waned down the years, it is the epicenter of Muslim orthodoxy today, even if its authority is constantly challenged by secular elements in Egyptian society. More than forty thousand students of all ages currently attend its classes, and it enjoys generous financial support not only from the Egyptian government but from other Muslim states, particularly Saudi Arabia.

Although the university comprises some forty buildings in the Mouski area of Cairo, its spiritual heart remains the soaring, elegant Al-Azhar Mosque, dating back to the tenth century and considered to be one of the finest examples of Islamic architecture in the world. Worshipers leave the clamor of a street market and enter the mosque through a small archway. They entrust their shoes to the crippled doorman and pass through a corridor into a vast open-air courtyard of blinding white marble. Around the four sides of the quadrangle runs a pillared colonnade, where students pace their steps to the rhythm of their recitations. Along the north side of the courtyard stands the mosque itself. Its whitewashed ceiling is supported by huge wooden beams resting on symmetrical rows of squat, square pillars. The floor is covered with red carpets. On the eastern wall shines a green neon sign fashioned in classical Arabic script, which reads: GOD IS THE LIGHT OF THE EARTH AND SKY. Students sit cross-legged around the pillars in small groups or doze against the walls. Some kneel in prayer, touching the ground with their foreheads.

Originally, all classes at Al-Azhar took place within the mosque. But as the university expanded and added nonreligious studies to its curriculum, the traditional facilities were outgrown. Today, only courses in Koranic studies are given in the mosque.

One such course was taught by Professor Rashad Munir, a highly respected and senior member of the Al-Azhar faculty. On the morning that Ahmed Rahman and Uri Bar-Zeev were agonizing over the mystery of the radioactive corpse, Munir, who carried the religious title of sheikh, was unraveling the finer points of Islamic thought for a small group of advanced students. They sat in a semicircle around him as he stood at a portable blackboard, wearing the *abaya,* the traditional robe of the teacher, and the *ima,* a red, four-cornered hat bound with white linen.

"What you must realize, my children, is the fundamental importance of Egypt to the whole future of Islam." Munir swayed slightly as he talked in the melodious, arcane cadences of classical Arabic. "Allah has blessed us as the most ancient and most influential nation in the Muslim world. If our faith is degraded here and our people allow it to fall into disuse, it cannot hope to survive elsewhere. It is our sacred trust to defend it. We are its champions. It is our holy obligation to set an example that others may follow if Islam is to thrive and spread its message throughout the world."

He paused and looked around at the students. Their eyes were fixed on him. Behind him a man was lazily sweeping the carpets with a long palm frond. The dust motes, thick as a cloud of mosquitoes, rose and danced in the stale air.

" 'Truth,' said the Prophet, 'is holy, and the words of truth echo louder than the cannons of our enemies.' From your studies you are familiar with the history of our creed. You are also aware of the flowering of interest in Islam today, not only in our own country but around the world. There are good and valid reasons for this. In times of rapid change, the spirit of man turns to those ideas which are as immutable as the rock from which Muhammad ascended into Heaven. In such times as these, religion exerts a powerful call, the call of the heart to God. But perhaps more important, our faith has for generations been subjected to the pressures of the foreign powers who have ruled Egypt until now. As masters of our own destiny is it not natural for us to abandon the imposed values of our former colonial masters and turn back to the one true faith?"

There was a murmur of approval from the students at his feet. Munir moved to the blackboard and sketched a pyramid. At the apex he wrote *Egypt,* and at the base, *the world.*

"If there is to be a return to the true principles of Islam, it must begin here in Egypt. It is from here that all teachings must radiate." He tapped the chalk emphatically on the board. "But we cannot begin to return to the purity of Islamic thought until we have rid ourselves of the last vestiges of decadent, foreign influences. We must begin with ourselves and our families. There can be no national awakening unless there is a rekindling of faith in the heart of each one of us. We must turn our backs on material things and reexamine our spiritual roots. We must return, as individuals and as a nation, to the Sharia, the legal and moral code given to us by Allah, blessed be He, in the Koran."

He looked up at the carved plaster of the arch above his head, with its frieze of inscriptions from the holy book.

"We must reject the influence of nonbelievers who would impose their cultural values upon us. The Western way of life has much to commend it; its science and technology have helped our people. It respects the freedom of the individual, as does the Koran. It respects the rights of workers, as does the Koran. It upholds the principles of justice and equality, as does the Koran. But Western culture has chosen the sensual path of materialism and thereby weakened its resolve, its moral fiber. The West has carried individual freedom to excess and slid into the swamps of moral turpitude and degeneracy. It has allowed democracy to deteriorate into unbridled capitalism, spawning the vicious monster of usury, which is forbidden by the Koran.

"So we have nothing to learn from the West; it is a bankrupt civilization. Yet many of our people stretch out their arms to embrace the false god of materialism of this corrupt society. By so doing, they abandon the teachings of the one true religion. When you leave these sacred walls, look around you. You will see the images of materialism: advertisements for American goods and frivolous entertainments. See the shoddy Western goods in our shops, exciting unquenchable desires among our people. Look at your television sets and witness the programs glorifying American values. These are the cultural influences that erode our will and threaten our religion. These people who would offer you such dross have come among us to take what we have to offer—our natural resources, our labor—and they offer nothing in return, save trinkets. And they have implanted their own agent on our doorstep: a Jewish state, snatched from our Palestinian brothers, through which they seek to conquer us again with their economic hegemony—and after us, all the lands of Islam. . . .

"But I stray into politics, and that is, of course, forbidden."

The students smiled knowingly. Professor Munir put down his chalk and dusted his fingers.

"I shall take up this subject again in my next lecture with a discussion of the Sharia and its application to the life of today. That is all, my children. May Allah be with you."

The students rose, bowed to Munir in silence, and filed out of the mosque into the dazzling whiteness of the courtyard. Munir cleaned the blackboard and replaced his notes in his briefcase. As he prepared to kneel in prayer, he noticed that one of the students had remained behind. The boy stood waiting, self-consciously fingering the material of his robe.

The youth was not unknown to Munir; his name was Mustafa Habib. A second-year student with a pale, undernourished look about him, Habib had come to Al-Azhar from a small town in the Delta and appeared to be devoutly religious. The boy had first attracted Munir's attention the year before when he had displayed a painful eagerness to grasp the philosophical implications of the professor's lectures. Munir had found him attentive, quite bright, and eager to ingratiate himself with his teachers. Over a period of months he had warmed to the boy, spending time with him in intellectual discussions as they sat cross-legged together on the carpeted floor of the mosque. On a number of occasions he had asked Habib to run errands or act as a courier for Wind of the Desert, and the young man had shown himself willing and reliable. Equally important, his moral instincts appeared sound.

"Yes, Mustafa?" Munir's voice was soft and encouraging; he had developed a fondness for the shy student.

"May I speak with you a moment, Sheikh?"

"You are doing so. What do you wish?"

"Your lecture, sir. It set me thinking." The young man seemed unsure of himself under the unwavering gaze of his professor.

"In what way?"

"The things you said about Islam and the need for a spiritual re-awakening."

"Yes?"

"Well, sir, it seems to me—and I mean no disrespect—but it seems to me that if there is to be a return to the spirit of the Koran, it should begin right here at Al-Azhar."

"Was that not the theme of my lecture?" Munir was intrigued by the boy's struggle to articulate his thoughts. "Let us sit down." They squatted on the carpet, facing one another, as they had so often done before.

"Sir, you have been a teacher for many years. You understand these things. But I am confused. With respect, I wonder if this school has not forfeited its right to lead the world in Islamic thought. So much has changed in recent years. We now have women in our classes."

"Islam does not proscribe education for women so long as they dress according to its tenets and acknowledge that their basic responsibility is to home and family."

"But many do not. I have heard them talk. They don't want the old ways. They want careers. And many of them go about with head and arms uncovered."

"I have seen it, too. Go on."

"I have heard other talk. There are those who say that Al-Azhar teaches only the Islam of the dead past. That it's irrelevant to Egypt to-day. That its sheikhs—forgive me, sir, I don't mean you personally—that its sheikhs are more concerned with student recitations than with showing how meaningful the Koran can be for our people now. They say the ulema no longer have the will to speak out against the influence of nonbelievers. I repeat only what I have heard. Al-Azhar, because it is weak, has weakened the force of Islam in Egypt."

Rashad Munir stroked his chin and studied the frowning young man before him. He had never been close to any of his students, but increasingly he found himself talking with Habib as he might with a son. The boy was only twenty-three, hardly mature enough for such profound thoughts. Yet he constantly tested his teacher with the logic of his observations. Munir decided to pursue the matter further.

"Tell me, Mustafa. Where have you heard such things? Have you been talking with the Muslim Brothers? They subscribe to such views and have been outspoken in their criticism of Al-Azhar."

"The Muslim Brotherhood has been outlawed, Sheikh."

"Nevertheless, it continues to flourish and attract new members. They have successfully infiltrated student organizations at Cairo University and in Alexandria. Come, Mustafa, we men of God are not naive. Ours is an age of politics."

Habib averted his eyes. "Yes, sir, I have talked with them. But I have also formed my own thoughts."

"And what are they?"

"Many of the things the Muslim Brothers say are true. They are the same things you talked about today. That's why I'm confused." He began to rise. "I have spoken out of turn. May Allah forgive me."

With a click of his tongue Munir motioned him to sit down again. "I have not dismissed you. Nor have you offended me. To wrestle with such thoughts is the duty of an inquiring mind. I only wished to know who has been influencing your thoughts."

For the next hour, Rashad Munir probed the mind of the young student with the skill of an inquisitor. He questioned Habib about Islam and its values, about Egypt past and future. At the end of the hour, Munir, apparently satisfied, rose to signal the end of their discussion.

"I am glad you came once again to talk with me, Mustafa. For a teacher the highest reward is that his words fall like seed on fallow ground. If you would like to talk more, you may come to my home tomorrow evening for tea."

"You do me honor, Sheikh."

Munir took a card from his briefcase and handed it to the young man. "That is the address. I live in Zamalek. Here is twenty-five piasters for your taxi fare."

Habib accepted the crumpled banknote and bowed.

"Come at nine o'clock. There will be food and refreshments."

"Thank you, sir. May Allah increase your well-being."

Munir watched until Habib disappeared across the courtyard. The invitation he had just issued was unprecedented; never before had he invited a student to his home. But he had had positive feelings about young Habib for some time and the student had passed every test of

devotion and intellect Munir had presented thus far. During their conversation, Munir had suddenly been seized with the inspiration that Habib might be ready to fill an urgent need within his organization. But
only if the boy could demonstrate that his faith was built upon true
courage.

Thoughtfully, Munir snapped his briefcase shut and knelt to pray.

≈ ≈ ≈

Bill Leamington lit his third cigarette in a row and shifted uncomfortably in his chair. His appointment with the minister of development had
been confirmed for eleven a.m. The clock above his head showed
eleven-fifty-five. He half rose as the door opened, and then collapsed
back in the chair when he realized it was the minister's secretary bringing in the ritual Turkish coffee and glass of tap water, which she set
down on the table in front of him.

After the unpainted concrete corridors of the ministry building in
Nasr City, the anteroom where he now sat boasted some semblance of
ministerial elegance: wood-paneled walls, yards of bookshelves (mostly
bare), and a polished conference table that reflected the pulse of a
faulty neon light. Its flickering made him all the more impatient, but he
knew from experience that in Egypt appointments began, not necessarily
at the scheduled time, but when both parties happened to find themselves together in the same room.

Fearing for his stomach, he left the coffee untouched on the table.
Instead, he thought about the hotel projects and their importance to
Venture. President Dunlap's agreement to open the Oasis Hotel would
set the seal of international approval on the whole Egyptian enterprise. If he could complete the other hotels with the minimum of difficulty, Venture would become the most-sought-after development company in the world.

When Leamington assumed the presidency of Venture International,
the company was regarded merely as a competent builder of Hong
Kong apartment houses. Residential construction was a prosperous
business, of course—Hong Kong apartment blocks usually returned the
full investment within five years. But the owners of Venture were ambitious. Leamington was reluctant at first to move from Santa Monica;

he had an enviable record of successful enterprises there as vice-president of Western Developments, including a retirement community in the Arizona desert, two new casinos in Las Vegas, an award-winning ski lodge in Aspen, and his biggest coup: the planning and execution of the Space World Fantasy Park in Florida. But Bradford Hallman, Venture's chairman of the board, had dangled the carrot of virtually unlimited financial backing to lure him to Hong Kong. Leamington would have complete independence in his choice of projects, as well as a generous financial stake in the company. The board asked only one thing of him: that he build Venture into a major multinational development firm. A month later when he walked into the apartment in Hong Kong provided for him by his new employers, Leamington was the new president of the firm.

The folding doors at the end of the room swung open, and an explosion of sunlight heralded the arrival of the minister of development. Leamington stubbed out his cigarette and glanced back at the clock. It was twelve-thirty.

Hassan Riyal's greeting was cool. The habitual smile had gone, and his tone was perfunctory. He led the way to a pair of leather chairs away from the window.

"I'm glad you called for an appointment, Mr. Leamington. It saved me the trouble of summoning you." The lofty manner of the minister put Leamington immediately on his guard.

"Oh? What did you want to see me about, Minister?"

"I will not beat about the bush. We are both busy men. My department tells me that you have not been honoring the terms of your contract with my government." The minister had no discernible eyebrows, the absence of which gave his face an expression of perpetual surprise.

"I don't understand." Leamington had expected to take the initiative, but the wily minister had thrown him on the defensive.

"You will recall that under our arrangement your company contracted to purchase not less than thirty-five percent of all building materials from Egyptian firms. My report says less than twenty percent has been purchased locally. The rest has been imported from Europe and the United States."

"I don't have the figures at my fingertips, Minister. But I assure you we've done everything possible to comply with the contract. Our problem is delivery dates. I've been quoted up to two years by some firms, in particular the state-owned companies. With the penalty clauses in the contract and the deadlines set by your government, we simply can't operate on that basis. Sure, we've had to go abroad for some materials —porcelain fittings, for example. We were going to get them here, but they just couldn't supply the quantity in time."

Riyal picked up a file from the coffee table in front of him. "I understand the problem. We lack the capacity to meet current demand in certain areas of production. But according to my report you have been importing such materials as cement, glass, and steel—all of which are produced in quantity in this country."

Leamington realized that he could not impress the minister of development with dreams of grandeur, as he had his more flamboyant colleague at the Ministry of Tourism. It was true Egypt could produce all the steel Venture needed. The integrated plant at Helwan had an annual capacity of one and a half million tons. But the price was well above world levels, owing to high production costs. It was far cheaper to import it, especially with the company's tariff exemption on construction materials.

"I shall have to reexamine our policy regarding steel, Minister. I assure you it'll be done. Regarding cement, we imported very little, and that was a special grade not available in this country. The same is true of glass. All standard glass has been purchased here; however, we've had to order some special high-pressure glass abroad. In fact, that's why I wanted to meet with you this morning."

"Oh?"

Leamington explained the difficulty he was having with customs in Alexandria and outlined the urgency of the matter. The development minister listened, interrupting once or twice with a question. When Leamington had finished, Riyal leaned back in his chair a few moments before speaking.

"Mr. Leamington, I don't know if you're aware of the economic priorities of this country. Perhaps it might be worthwhile if I took a few moments to explain them."

"Minister, I don't see—"

"Be patient, please. I will come to the point. Now, my first priority as minister is to ensure that our people have sufficient food. This will be achieved by increasing the amount of arable land and by improving the agricultural efficiency of the land already in use. If a farmer grows sugar beets instead of cane, for instance, he gets two crops a year instead of one. In that way, his plot of land delivers a higher yield and the national efficiency is improved."

"But how—"

"Your company is not in that business. So your problem does not rank as a top economic priority.

"Our second priority is infrastructure. Putting into place the basic elements of a modern society, such as adequate roads, sewage systems, telephones—you know how dreadful the current phone system is."

Leamington nodded. Everyone who did business in Egypt knew the frustration of spending hours trying to complete a single call.

"Housing, bridges, water systems, rural electrification, new population centers," the minister continued. "All of these things must be accomplished and at a pace compatible with our population growth. One million new Egyptians are born every year. Now, your company is not engaged in assisting our needs in this area, either. In fact, you are making things more difficult, because your hotels require services that we have had to provide under our contract with you. But we respected the contract."

Leamington could see what was coming. But the minister went on.

"Our third priority is Sinai. It has tremendous potential, and we believe much of our surplus population can be accommodated there. Now that it has been returned to us, we must work rapidly to develop its agricultural and mineral potential. But your company isn't involved there, either. Industrial development comes next. This is a country of high unemployment, and we need more job-creating industries. But your hotels don't really fall into this category, either."

"We will be providing jobs—several hundred, in fact."

"True. But nonproductive, low-paying jobs. And under the contract, which we will of course respect, you are permitted to fill up to fifty percent of the managerial positions with foreigners during the first five years of operation." Riyal glanced again at the file. "In fact, I believe you're in the process of negotiating a contract with a Swiss-based hotel-management firm. Correct?"

"Correct."

"So. Where are we? Your operation, although it undoubtedly has benefits for Egypt in the long term, does not rank among our top four economic priorities. Your contract—very generous, I may say—permits you to export all profits in hard currency in the first five years of operation, to bring in outsiders to manage the hotels, to have tariff-free access to imported construction materials. It also requires you to meet certain commitments regarding the purchase of Egyptian goods, which could provide some direct benefit to us. But by your own admission, you haven't lived up to this part of the agreement. Now you come to me seeking my intervention to assist you in importing still more foreign-made material."

"Minister, with great respect I would remind you that President Sayed has taken a personal interest in Venture's hotels and that President Dunlap will be opening the Oasis Hotel in a few days."

"I'm aware of all that. I'm also aware of the fact that our president does not know of your failure to meet your local-purchase commitments. If he should learn of it, he might find some urgent reason to request that President Dunlap be elsewhere on the evening he is scheduled to be at your hotel."

The minister softened his tone. "Bill, I do not wish to make things hard for you. But you must understand that you have made my position very difficult by not living up to your commitments to buy Egyptian goods. The government attaches a great deal of importance to such matters. I must ask you in the strongest possible terms to rectify this situation."

"And what about my glass?"

Riyal rose, a signal that the meeting was terminated. "In the present circumstances, I cannot help you. My intervention to assist in further importation of foreign materials when you have already exceeded your quota could be misinterpreted later." He put a hand on Leamington's shoulder and steered him toward the door. "I will, however, do nothing to hinder you, as I understand your need for the glass to continue construction. But you will have to make your own peace with the department in Alexandria. I wish you luck in that. In the meantime, I trust you will treat our discussion today seriously and take appropriate measures."

"Yes, Minister. Of course. Thank you."

Bill Leamington suddenly found himself back in the outer office. A feeling of impotent rage boiled inside him. He knew that if he did not pick his way more carefully through the minefield of Egyptian bureaucracy, the entire project could be in jeopardy.

≅≅≅

The office provided for Uri Bar-Zeev in the Ministry of the Interior was small and bleak and even less prepossessing than Rahman's. A desk, two chairs, and the ubiquitous portrait of President Sayed in all his military feathers were the only objects in a room that had obviously been hastily emptied of old filing cabinets. But Bar-Zeev would have considered anything beyond the purely functional as frivolous; he worked best in a Spartan environment.

Before sitting down at the desk, which was stacked with files, the Israeli ran an exploratory finger around the furniture and checked the desk drawers. He unscrewed the telephone receiver and inspected the mouthpiece. There was no evidenc of a planted microphone. Although there was little reason for his hosts to bug the office—he would hardly talk to himself about Israel's security secrets—he wanted to see if the Mokhabarat trusted him.

He returned to the desk and began studying the files Rahman had given him. They included precise details of the presidential visit and the measures planned for its security. There was, as well, the autopsy report on Herrara, and a file on the South American, which he put to one side for later study. Finally, there was a capsule summary of all known terrorist groups currently operating inside Egypt. Bar-Zeev knew at a glance that a couple were missing; he wondered whether the omissions were deliberate. As he read through the material, he made notes on a large yellow pad in a small, spiky hand.

The lab report on Herrara intrigued him: it said the Argentinian had died from a "sizable" dose of gamma radiation. As Bar-Zeev thought about this, there was a knock at the door. A junior officer entered, saluted, and handed him a telex. Bar-Zeev waited until he withdrew, then read it, noting with amusement that it had been written in Yiddish. A Mossad joke to confuse the Arabs.

The telex was almost a meter long, and it wasn't until he reached the penultimate paragraph that he found the information he needed. He reread the paragraph twice, slid the yellow pad into the desk drawer, and headed down the corridor to Ahmed Rahman's office.

The Egyptian was in the middle of a planning session with two of his senior aides when Bar-Zeev burst in, unannounced. Rahman looked up in annoyance.

"This just arrived from my company," the Israeli said, waving the document. It was the first time Rahman had seen him excited since he arrived in Cairo. "I thought we had something on him. Herrara and those lost six months. You know where he's been?"

"Colonel Bar-Zeev, I'm in the middle of a meeting."

"Libya."

"Libya!" the three Egyptians exclaimed in unison.

"He's been spotted in Tripoli on at least four occasions in the last six months. I have the details here." Tripoli. The name was etched into Bar-Zeev's memory. Five of the Palestinian terrorists who had gunned down the Israeli athletes at the 1972 Munich Olympics had traveled there from Libya's largest city.

"Tripoli," murmured Rahman to himself. "Of course. It fits."

"That can only mean Jalil is involved in it somehow. From what you said earlier, there's little that goes on in Libya that he doesn't know about."

The mere mention of the Libyan dictator's name galvanized Rahman to action. "Get me all the current information we have on Libyan operations against us," he snapped at the two aides. "Also on any group in Egypt with Libyan contacts. Also reports of all border incursions."

The aides hurried off to the basement vaults, and Rahman turned back to Bar-Zeev; their shared excitement made him forget momentarily the animosity between them. " 'Patience demolishes mountains,' Colonel. A proverb of my father's. Let us sit and talk."

The rest of the day was spent in Rahman's office as the two intelligence men pored over maps, studied aerial photographs, and tossed theories back and forth as to what the Libyan involvement might be. They were so intent on their work they did not notice the passage of the lunch hour.

"If we could only establish where and how Herrara got his lethal dose of radiation. That's the key, I'm positive," said Bar-Zeev.

"To determine that, we must reconstruct his movements," Rahman replied. "First we must discover how he got into Egypt. He could not have used a commercial airline. My men would have spotted him even if he had been in disguise. And our radar would have picked up a private plane."

"What about the ports?"

"We monitor them closely, too. I doubt it."

Bar-Zeev looked at a map and traced the border between Egypt and Libya with his finger. "Could he have come overland?"

"I would say that is extremely unlikely. Our relations with Libya are, shall we say, not the friendliest, as you know. We have military concentrations in the area, and the border is routinely patrolled."

"Don't be modest, Colonel," said Bar-Zeev. "You have a standing army of one full division and four armored brigades in that sector."

Rahman allowed his flash of annoyance to pass before he spoke. "Whatever we may or may not have in the area, Colonel, is not the point. The fact is that it would be virtually impossible for a vehicle to slip across the border undetected. And not even a madman would cross the desert on foot."

"What about the Bedouin? Camels?"

"Too slow. We inspect everyone coming across that border—Bedouin, Libyan, and Egyptian."

"Well, the only alternative—if he came directly from Libya— is the sea."

The two men bent over the map again. From the Libyan border, Egypt's Mediterranean coastline stretches five hundred kilometers to Alexandria, on the western edge of the Nile Delta. The coastal plain is sparsely populated, and there are no more than a half-dozen towns of any consequence. Rahman knew the area well; his brother had married a girl whose family lived in Matruh—a town small enough that a stranger passing through provides gossip for a week. The coastal road was not heavily traveled, and there were five police checkpoints along the route.

"If Herrara did come by sea, then he would have entered the country through Alexandria," said Rahman unequivocally. "The only other place could be Abukir, but it is a sensitive military area and well guarded. If a man wanted to slip ashore undetected, it would have to be at Alexandria. There are always foreign seaman there all year round."

"That sounds plausible."

"I suggest we make a trip to Alexandria in the morning," said Rahman, leaning back in his chair. "You expressed a desire to inspect the presidential route there, I believe."

"Why don't we go now?"

"We should see it in daylight. I can arrange an early-morning flight. Besides, you have seen only the inside of these offices. I would be a neglectful host if I did not show you my city at night. We have some most entertaining spots," Rahman said, smiling.

"I don't need nightclubs," growled Bar-Zeev.

"You will find the experience most diverting, Colonel, I assure you. Be gracious enough to accept my invitation. I will drive you back to your hotel. You can change, and I shall return for you at half past eight."

The grudging respect Uri Bar-Zeev had begun to feel for Rahman's professionalism was suddenly expunged by this butterfly change of direction and purpose. They just can't concentrate on anything, he said to himself. Doesn't he appreciate how serious this is?

≅≅≅

As the Mercedes roared along the Giza plateau, Uri Bar-Zeev saw the massive outlines of the pyramids looming out of the darkness. The vainglorious monuments of stone, symbols of man's futile quest for immortality, obliterated the night sky. Cheops, Chephren, and Mycerinus . . . how many slaves had perished to satisfy this craving of the pharaohs? he thought. How many Jews had felt the lash of their Egyptian taskmasters? He studied the silhouettes in silence. They said you could build a two-foot wall around France with the stones. Perhaps that might not be a bad idea. The French, with their usual cynicism, had abandoned Israel to assure themselves an uninterrupted flow of Arab oil.

"How much farther?" he inquired of Rahman.

"Not far."

Bar-Zeev felt as if he were on an unstoppable roller-coaster ride. Rahman had whisked him from one drinking spot to another. The evening had begun in the Caravan bar of Shepheard's Hotel, where the Israeli ordered orange juice and Rahman left him at the table to spend about twenty minutes laughing and joking with the bartender. The same thing happened at the Champs de Mars Tavern in the Hilton, the After 8 Disco off Kasr el Nil, and the Cellar at the President Hotel in Zamalek, and now they were heading across the desert west of Cairo to yet another nightclub. The road dipped down past the pyramids, and Bar-Zeev could see nothing in the headlights but rolling hills of sand. Suddenly, in the distance, he noticed a ranch-style archway straddling the road, its neon lights inviting them to SAHARA CITY. Five hundred meters beyond the sign stood a vast circus tent.

"Sahara City, Colonel," announced Rahman, beaming, as he parked the car. "Have you ever seen belly-dancing?" He handed the attendant a ten-piaster coin and ushered the reluctant Bar-Zeev into the tent. The air inside was damp and filled with smoke. The blood-red canvas walls, blown by the wind off the desert, heaved in and out like a bellows. The Israeli had the unpleasant sensation of standing inside a gigantic lung.

The tent was supported by steel poles, painted red, which defined the inner rectangle of the stage area, raised one meter off the coconut matting floor. Few Egyptians patronize Sahara City; they consider it a tourist trap for wealthy foreigners, particularly the Saudis and Kuwaitis who come to Cairo to escape the rigorous injunctions against alcohol and dancing girls in their own countries.

A waiter in a blue galabia seated the two men at a circular brass table. Bar-Zeev felt a cat brush against his leg. He kicked it away in disgust: he was allergic to cats. While Rahman, clearly in his element, ordered food for them, the Israeli watched a group of dancers with illuminated candelabra on their heads gyrating around the stage. At the next table a group of Saudi businessmen held glasses of Scotch in the air and shouted *"Asal! Asal!"* ("Honey! Honey!") to the girls, who balanced their flaming headgear with athletic poise. At the end of their act, the dancers wandered haphazardly offstage to wild applause.

A family of whirling dervishes followed, spinning like human tops over the checkered floor of the stage, their skirts and capes swirling dizzily around their bodies as the drummer increased his tempo. The audience clapped to the rhythm as it became more frenzied, but Bar-Zeev had to look away.

"You could stay here till dawn," Rahman shouted to him over the noise, "and you would not see the same act twice."

Bar-Zeev nodded glumly. There were animal acts to follow, jugglers, comedians, and, of course, the dancing girls again. When the food arrived, Rahman excused himself and left the Israeli to contemplate the tray of roast pigeon, salad, and *tahina*. A roar from the crowd, followed by the nasal whine of a reed pipe, introduced the next act: a statuesque, auburn-haired belly dancer. She stood for a moment in the center of the stage and then slowly began to undulate her pelvis, to the delirium of the drunken Saudis behind him. He could not understand their excitement. The girl was attractive enough, and exotic dancing was forbidden by the Koran; but the whole affair was somewhat chaste by Western standards. He had seen more eroticism in Mandy's discotheque in Tel Aviv. The girl's breasts were completely covered, and there was only a suggestion of her legs visible through the sheer pink gauze of her harem pants, which were tied with a sash to accentuate the bulge of her stomach. A flesh-colored body stocking hid her midriff. Yet, the Saudis were bouncing on their seats with delight and dashing up to the stage, proffering ten-pound notes; the girl held them in her hand as she danced.

Another cat insinuated itself under his table, drawn by the smell of food. Bar-Zeev nearly upset the tray in his efforts to expel it. Where was Rahman? The whole evening had been a waste of precious time. He tore a piece of bread from the flat, round *pitta* and dipped it into the *tahina* sauce. The girl finished her act, to a crescendo of applause and whistles. Then she skipped lightly down the stairs, dodging from table to table while a photographer recorded souvenir pictures. Before he knew it, the girl was behind him, her hands on his shoulders, smiling into the camera. Bar-Zeev could smell her sweet, musky perfume.

"No photos!" he shouted and raised his hands in front of his face as the flash went off. When he opened his eyes the girl was already at the Saudis' table, dodging, posing, and smiling as the photographer moved inexorably through the audience. The cat took advantage of his inattention to leap onto the table, snatch a portion of roast pigeon from the tray, and run off to demolish it under a nearby banquette. Bar-Zeev, too stunned to react, watched the animal disappear.

"Don't look so upset. It's only a pigeon." Rahman stood at his side, laughing. "You of all people should appreciate that maneuver. It's what you might call a surprise tactical strike."

The Israeli smiled in spite of himself. "Damn cats, the place is crawling with them," he growled.

"Would you rather it was crawling with rats? It's a question of priorities," said Rahman, sitting down.

"Talking about priorities, what's the point of all this? Why are you dragging me to every nightclub in Cairo? It's no pleasure for me, and I consider it a waste of valuable time."

"Since you are obviously not a cat-lover, I have an English expression you will appreciate. There is more than one way to skin a cat, Colonel. Surely you are aware that our friend Herrara had the reputation of being a ladies' man. He liked drinking and nightclubs. He was not your usual ascetic terrorist; he enjoyed the bright lights. It was all in the file I left on your desk."

Bar-Zeev said nothing. This piece of intelligence was not in the Mossad message, and he hadn't gotten around to the Herrara file before the telex arrived from Jerusalem.

"Did you seriously believe I was chasing around Cairo's nightclubs for the good of my health—or yours? I have been trying to find someone who might have seen him—a waiter, perhaps, or a barman, a regular customer."

"Well, did you turn up anything?"

"Perhaps. I showed Herrara's picture to the cashier. He thinks he might have seen him here, maybe six weeks ago. Apparently he was alone. I want to check the parking attendant outside. He might remember what kind of car he came in."

"But why did you bring me along? You don't need me for that."

"My dear Colonel. We could hardly have the Mossad's master spy wandering loose in Cairo, unchaperoned. Only Allah knows what might happen to him," said Rahman with a grin that showed the whiteness of his teeth.

Bar-Zeev grunted and looked away at the stage, where a corpulent tenor in a silver lamé jacket intoned the praises of King Khalid of Saudi Arabia while the royal gentleman's inebriated subjects cheered and sent up more money.

DAY FOUR
TUESDAY, NOVEMBER 6

Alexandria is the world's only city of four million inhabitants that does not have its own airport. An airfield—Al-Nuzha—does exist, but it was commandeered by President Nasser as a military base and has yet to be given back to the people. The fact that there is no commercial air service is a source of constant irritation to Egypt's second largest city—especially to its business community, whose frequent petitions to the government have so far gone unheeded. Studies of the problem have been promised, but it is still necessary to travel 225 kilometers by rail or road to catch a plane.

The driver approaching Alexandria has a choice of two routes. One runs through the Nile Delta; the other, through the Western Desert, is marginally longer but free of the donkey carts and caravans that make the more scenic of the two roads a hazardous experience. Because he was in a hurry, Bill Leamington had chosen the road through the desert —against the unspoken wishes of his chauffeur, Amer, who had hoped to stop at his cousin's in Benha to collect a box of dates.

"But Mr. Leamington, sir, on the agricultural road you will see the real Egypt," the chauffeur had protested.

"I don't have time to see the real Egypt, Amer. Just get us to Alexandria in one piece."

The thwarted chauffeur, thinking only of his dates, took Leamington at his word and drove like a man possessed. He had tied a miniature pair of baby shoes to the rearview mirror for luck; the charm bounced noisily against the windshield as the Cadillac Seville roared across the desert. Even the threat of dismissal would not make him take down this talisman.

"How can you read with those damn shoes clicking?" Leamington said irritably to Nicole, who was deeply engrossed in a copy of *Students' Flora of Egypt,* a volume she had finally managed to secure at the Anglo-Egyptian Bookstore in Cairo.

"Shoes?" she replied vaguely, looking around her, and then returned to the mysteries of *Portulaca oleracea* ("Leaves obovate to spathulate, obtuse. Flowers, small yellow, sessile in clusters . . .").

Leamington, who had few interests outside of Venture, treated Nicole's hobby with a mixture of tolerant amusement and mild resentment. Absorbed in her reading, Nicole seemed lost to him; this obsessive interest in botany was an area of her life that excluded him, and in a childish way he was jealous of her for pursuing it, although he had encouraged her initially lest she become too reliant upon his company for entertainment.

Nicole recognized his impatience whenever the subject came up, and she had tried to involve him by having him ask his Egyptian acquaintances the names of particular trees or flowers. The usual response was: "That? That is a tree," or, "It is a pink flower."

"Egyptians know nothing about the vegetation of their own country," she had once lamented to Bill. "And they have such wonderful varieties."

"They probably just don't know the English for it," he had replied tersely, and for him the matter was closed.

Leamington felt slightly nauseous watching the tarmac rushing up at him, so he looked out of the side window at the endless horizon of desert. A rusting metal signpost flashed by. It warned in English: FOREIGNERS ARE FORBIDDEN TO LEAVE MAIN ROAD. The route skirted a military area. He could see an occasional concrete missile silo or radar post set low in the sand dunes.

Everything in that desolate landscape was hard-edged. The blue sky and the camel-colored sand were separated only by a razor's line. And the black road divided the desert in two. It pleased Leamington's sense of order that the landscape was so definite, so geometric. But the sand itself had infinite shades and textures: there were dunes like folds of silk, beaches of shale the color of cinnamon, and murrains of rotting sand as black as a widow's robes. The sun picked out a palette of reds and golds and browns to relieve the monotony of the vista. In places the desert was stippled with anemic scrub, fodder for the wild camels and other luckless herbivores whose lot it was to inhabit this wasteland. Nicole had told him once that when it rained the desert bloomed with a thousand wild flowers that lived only as long as butterflies. But he soon became impatient with the view.

"What's the program, then?" he said, turning back to Nicole.

With a sigh she closed the book. "I tried to get you an appointment with the chief customs inspector, but we couldn't get a phone connection. I left word at the hotel to try to get a message through, but we may arrive unannounced."

"Half past seven," he said, looking at his watch. "The way Amer's going we should be at his office by ten."

"Then the fun begins." Nicole smiled, placing her hand on his. "If he likes you, we could be out of there in ten minutes. If not, maybe I should book a hotel in Alex. But promise me, Bill, you won't lose your temper."

Leamington groaned. Dealing with the Egyptian bureaucracy was a task to make Sisyphus blanch. Usually Hoda Chafik worked her magic on civil servants; with her away, he had no option but to deal with the matter himself. He had to get the glass. He knew he should have left Nicole in Cairo to handle the myriad problems that arose every day, but it was a long drive to Alexandria with only the churlish Amer for company.

"I've got a file of papers here if you feel like doing some work," suggested Nicole.

"No," he said, "you go back to your weeds."

Nicole opened her book again, and Leamington studied her as she squinted through her glasses at the page. He had never met a woman like her. She was intelligent, remarkably efficient, attractive, and desirable—a combination of qualities he had never encountered in a woman until she intruded into his life. He closed his eyes and summoned up the image of her in a black silk nightgown: Nicole bending over him, exploring his body with her lips; Nicole, her red hair like fire across the pillow, smiling up at him, pressing her nails into his back while he drove furiously into her. He could feel a stirring in his groin, and he crossed his legs, wondering if she had noticed.

Leamington had never cared so deeply for a woman before. Although the affair with his first wife had been passionate, he had married her out of a sense of duty. Their union, founded on sex, foundered without it. Through the latter stages of her pregnancy the obstetrician warned there would be complications. His wife had an extremely nervous disposition, the doctor said, and any undue excitement or stimulation could cause a miscarriage. He suggested they refrain from lovemaking until after the birth of the child. Without sex they soon discovered they had nothing in common save a shared concern for the baby's safety. When the child was stillborn, that bond evaporated. The marriage limped on for another six months and then fell apart.

Leamington's second marriage had, if anything, been more traumatic, lacking as it did even the sexual attraction of the first. Anesta Wildewoode Wharton was considered by both New England families an ideal match for the major who had performed so brilliantly as senior aide to the chairman of the Joint Chiefs of Staff and who clearly had an outstanding career ahead of him either in the military or in industry. A well-connected wife was an appendange that Leamington felt he needed, and he agreed to the merger, to the well-mannered gratification of the two families. But Anesta, it turned out, abhorred physical contact. After the first month of marriage she demanded her own bedroom, and when he appealed to her to see a psychiatrist, she retreated farther from him, finding solace in alcohol. Frequently drunk, she taunted him by playing with herself mechanically on the sofa, shouting obscenities at him whenever he approached her. In the end, there had been no alternative but to commit her to an institution where she remained to that day.

He blamed himself for her collapse, lying awake at night for months afterward, reliving their life together. It was two years before he could bring himself to petition for divorce.

Bill Leamington could not live with failure; it was anathema to him. His driving sense of ambition steered him subconsciously away from activities in which he could not excel. His two broken marriages disturbed him deeply, since he considered that the failure to make them work was his. Much as he loved Nicole, his self-esteem would not allow him to risk a third marriage. He knew that if she were to force the issue he would have to choose a life without her.

Yet their relationship was a marriage in all but name. Leamington was devoted to Nicole and faithful to her—in spite of her suspicions regarding the dazzling Hoda Chafik. While he sought to reassure Nicole, he secretly enjoyed her flashes of jealousy, although her possessiveness alarmed him and foreboded anxiety in the future.

The Cadillac began to slow down as they neared Wadi el Natrun, the halfway house to Alexandria. There, an arcade of small shops offered wine, raisins, soft drinks, and olive oil. A busload of tourists was busy buying oranges, nuts, and jars of honey. Amer pulled into the parking lot and asked Leamington if he could say a prayer at the mosque. Leamington looked angrily at his watch before agreeing.

"Bill, you must respect his faith," said Nicole gently as they watched the chauffeur amble over to what looked like a small garage. Amer took off his shoes and socks and washed his feet under a tap before disappearing inside the building.

"Okay, let's get something accomplished today," he said. "Where's that file?"

Nicole handed him the folder and watched him as he bent over it, his forehead puckering in a frown of concentration. She noticed the silkiness of the hairs on his arm and the strength of his fingers. She knew the pressures he had been subjected to, and was willing to forgive his sudden outbursts of temper. If only he would show her some of his old warmth, some concern for her needs, which went beyond the mere act of lovemaking . . .

Over the past weeks Nicole had sensed that she was approaching a crisis in her relationship with Leamington. The affair seemed to be marking time; it had lost its dynamic. She knew that Bill loved her, but theirs was still an affair that would end one day, if only for lack of progress. She desperately wanted to marry him, and this one desire had become all-absorbing, although she knew that she could destroy the tenuous bond between them by any attempt to strengthen it.

This need to become Bill Leamington's wife was an ache that had tormented her of late, a feeling not unlike the urge to make love to him that had overwhelmed her that first day in the Hong Kong antiques shop. When she introduced herself at the Pacific Towers, she had come prepared to spend the night with him. But although Bill passed many of his subsequent evenings and weekends with her, they did not make love until some two months later. Bill seemed eager for her company, but not her body. She even wondered whether he was gay when he failed to respond to her signals, which became more and more overt, falling just short of an engraved invitation.

Seducing Leamington became a project to which she applied herself with all the resources and strategy of the daughter of an army man. She realized that, in the best tradition of warfare, the general chooses the battleground and, where possible, attempts to capitalize on the element of surprise. To this end, she invited Leamington for dinner one night at her apartment. She lived in two rooms overlooking Kowloon Harbor, within walking distance of the office where she worked as a secretary in an English import-export business. The other girl in the office had mentioned that the local Chinese used an aphrodisiac called ginseng, whose medicinal properties included stimulation of the sexual appetite. Nicole had pretended to take no interest in this intelligence, since the girl in question was well known around the colony for having round heels. But faced with the recalcitrant Bill Leamington, any weapon was fair.

Nicole bought a ginseng root from a dealer in the market and determined to grate it over the salad, knowing that Bill enjoyed fresh vegetables. The question was when to serve the salad? Before the beef Wellington or after it? She could not bring herself to discuss with the Chinese grocer how long the venereal effects of the drug lasted and in what quantity it should be administered for the most dramatic results.

While the doctored salad was the main assault weapon, a bottle of Chambertin 1959 was the tactical decoy. ("Napoleon's favorite burgundy," the wine merchant told her, "and the last bottle commercially available on the island.") The skirmish was to start with smoked salmon and Chablis, followed by the major engagement of beef Wellington and Chambertin, with a final commitment of strawberries and champagne as reserves. The timing of the salad was crucial, and even up to Leamington's arrival Nicole dithered about whether to serve it first (on an empty stomach) or after the beef.

Leamington arrived twenty minutes late, with a basket of orchids. He admired her new suit—a lime-green shantung silk creation that had cost her two weeks' wages—and proceeded to talk nonstop about a Venture project in Egypt. He was very excited about it, and the first course remained untouched on the table while they drank the chilled Chablis. When they had emptied the bottle, Nicole suggested that they sit at the table and eat.

"Good idea," said Bill.

She decided to open the champagne, acknowledging her father's dictum that a wise commander will improvise on the plan of attack in the field to suit changing circumstances. Instead of the smoked salmon she brought out the salad. She lit a fat orange candle in the middle of the table, indicated his seat, and asked if she could serve him some salad.

"By all means," said Bill, whose mind and conversation were still on the Egyptian project. She poured him a flute of champagne and heaped a portion of salad on his plate, making sure that he got a megadose of ginseng. Bill continued his monologue, oblivious to the food in front of him. Nicole crossed her legs and shifted in her chair, smiling at him and looking down at his plate as if willing him to eat.

"Do start, please, Bill." She gave a sigh of relief when he finally plunged his fork into the salad.

"More?" she inquired when he had finished the plate.

"No, thanks. It was delicious."

At the end of the meal, during which Leamington returned to the subject of his new Egyptian projects, Nicole stacked the dishes in the sink and suggested they look at the view over the harbor from her balcony. Even the sight of lantern-lit junks could not deflect Leamington from his single-minded concentration on the multimillion-dollar hotel scheme.

Nicole changed her tactics; if he was interested only in talking of his business, then she would go along with him.

"Isn't it rather risky, investing in the Middle East?" she asked innocently.

"The bigger the risk, the higher the profits. There's going to be a boom in Egypt as soon as a peace treaty is signed. It just takes a little faith to commit ourselves now. Before a lot of international capital starts flowing in."

"Bill, did I tell you I read palms? I do. I'm very good at it. Let me read yours. I'll see if your project is going to be successful. Let's sit inside."

She led him to the sofa.

"You sit there," she said, as she took the candle from the dinner table and placed it on the coffee table. She sat down next to him and took his right hand in hers. With her fingertips she lightly traced the lines of his hand.

"You have a very strong hand. Look at the length of that life line."

She moved her head nearer to him so that he could smell her perfume.

"Your heart line breaks in two places. You see where these other lines cut across it? That means some interruption in your love life."

"You know about that already. Some fortune-teller you are."

"No, it's in your hand. Even if I didn't know, I could tell."

"What about Venture? Is it going to be successful?"

"I see continuing success for you in anything you attempt." She cradled his hand in her lap and stroked it gently, looking into his eyes. Her knees touched his.

"Nicky," said Bill softly.

She closed her eyes and waited for him to kiss her. She could feel him moving toward her; she lay back against the pillows and drew his hand forward. Suddenly there was a crack as Leamington's knee struck the coffee table, toppling the orange candle and spattering its hot molten wax over Nicole's silk suit.

"Jesus Christ Almighty!" he shouted as Nicole shot to her feet, stung by the hot wax, which instantly congealed and hardened into the fabric of her skirt. She ran to the kitchen, closed the door behind her, and began to sob uncontrollably over the sink.

Leamington sat dejectedly on the sofa, holding his head. He set the candle upright and picked at the tallow on the velvet material. Then he stood up and walked into the kitchen.

"I'm sorry about the suit, Nicky. Tell me where I can get you another one," he said, which only made her sob the louder. He approached her shaking back and put his hands on her shoulders, turning her toward him. "I'm not usually this clumsy."

Nicole leaned against his chest. "It's my own fault," she said in a tired voice. "I was trying too hard."

"Trying what?"

"To seduce you, you fool."

"Is that why you put ginseng in the salad?"

She looked up at him in surprise and then laughed, wiping the tears from her eyes. "You knew?"

"Of course. I guess I *am* a fool. What if I were to tell you that it really works?"

"I'd lock the door so you couldn't get out," she replied, leading him to the bedroom, where she took off her tallow-spotted suit.

Their lovemaking was not an unqualified success; the interaction of two unfamiliar bodies needs more than a mutual desire to achieve the highest pleasure spontaneously. But it proved to Nicole that Leamington enjoyed sex and could be encouraged to explore his preferences.

One evening several weeks later, she finally plucked up the courage to ask him why he had hesitated for so long before making love to her.

"It's not that I didn't want to, Nicky. It's difficult to admit, I guess. In every other department of my life I have unbounded confidence in my own abilities. But with women I'm never sure of my ground. If you had pushed me away, I would have got so mad I might have hurt you."

"That might have been fun," Nicole answered, laughing, but his confession made her realize that he had unconsciously shifted the responsibility for their lovemaking to her; from then on, she would have to take the lead.

The next night in bed at Leamington's hotel, he asked her to come to work for him. He needed a senior assistant whom he could trust. She deliberated for several weeks before finally accepting. Leamington had told her that he would have to spend at least a year in Egypt on the hotel project. If things didn't work out between them, she thought, she could use his leaving Hong Kong as an excuse for breaking off with him. But of course she hadn't needed an excuse after all.

It seemed that the very day she went to work for Venture International, her relationship with Leamington had settled down into a stable and comfortable arrangement. True, there had been occasional arguments, mostly about the business, and their sexual activity had diminished from the intensity and regularity of the early months. But, looking back, Nicole knew those three years had been good ones, with more excitement and laughter coupled with more hard work than at any other time in her life.

Now, as she sat in the limousine with Bill—who was, as always, absorbed in his business—she wasn't sure why she felt they had reached some kind of emotional watershed. Maybe for her it was a simple need for some stability after a childhood spent in a dozen countries and the feeling of living out of a suitcase ever since. Besides, there was something about Egypt that unsettled her: the timelessness of its cities juxtaposed with the constant flux of people and events was disturbing. For the first time in her nomadic life she felt herself an alien and had begun to think more and more of her home in Bloomington, Indiana.

Nicole knew that if she ever forced the issue with Bill she could lose him; but then she could lose him by silence, too, if he should tire of her. Just as her nature had compelled her to seduce him in Hong Kong, so now she was being driven against her better judgment to offer him an ultimatum. She had no strategy for that maneuver, only a heavy heart and the dispiriting feeling that she already knew what his answer would be.

≈≈≈

While Nicole pondered her relationship with Bill Leamington, Ahmed Rahman and Uri Bar-Zeev were strapping themselves into the seats of a military jet at an air base east of Cairo. Their destination was the same as Leamington's, but they would be landing at Alexandria's Al-Nuzha field. They sat alone in the forward compartment while Ismail and the junior officers from Internal Security waited for takeoff in the rear section.

The jet turned onto the runway, revved its engines, and waited for instructions from the control tower. A moment later, the plane was airborne. In his window seat, Bar-Zeev looked down on the sprawling capital with its polluted mantle hanging over it like a curse. Rahman read the implied criticism in his face.

"That's our new secret weapon. We hide Cairo under a blanket of smog so your Israeli bombers can't find it." Rahman chuckled at his own joke.

Am I that transparent? thought Bar-Zeev. I mustn't relax. He was beginning to feel at ease in the company of the large Egyptian, but he told himself he must remain vigilant at all times. He must give nothing away. "I take it we've exhausted all leads on Herrara," he said, more by way of a statement than a question.

"Yes, there was a faint possibility he might have visited Jackie's Discotheque at the Hilton, but no positive identification. We are back to where we started, my friend," said Rahman with a sigh. He opened his briefcase and withdrew a thick file. "I have made a schedule for today. I suggest we concentrate on how Herrara got into the country. We can inspect the presidents' route later. First we will go to the docks. There are people there who will be of help if they know anything. Are we agreed that Herrara came in from Libya?"

"In our business we can be sure of nothing. He was spotted in Tripoli on several occasions. We must assume he came from there."

"Certainly that would make sense. Abd Jalil is no friend of our president. He's been infected by Qaddafi's craziness. He sees himself as leader of the entire Arab world."

Bar-Zeev nodded. He knew little of the thirty-four-year-old air force major who had ousted Muammar al-Qaddafi, the Middle East's most mercurial leader. The Mossad's political intelligence suggested that Jalil was tarred with the same brush and had already embarked upon dangerous and self-aggrandizing foreign adventures. At home Jalil had demonstrated himself to be in full sympathy with the reactionary reforms of his predecessor.

As a Muslim fundamentalist Qaddafi had reimposed the Sharia, the ancient Islamic legal code, and had decreed a total prohibition against alcohol throughout Libya. He had eradicated most European influences, expelled the Americans in 1971, and given lavish support to revolutionary movements around the world, from the PLO to the IRA. Libya was one of the few countries whose borders remained open to fugitive terrorists.

But Qaddafi had never realized his ultimate dream: to be hailed as a latter-day Muhammad in the Arab world. Astute enough to recognize that the key to his ambition lay in Egypt, he had stated on numerous occasions that he was a leader without a country, while Egypt was a country without a leader. Until his fall he continued to cast covetous eyes eastward, even after his attempt at political union with Egypt in 1972 had been summarily rebuffed by Sadat. To the end, conservative Arab leaders regarded him with fear and suspicion as a fanatic; radicals saw him as a clever but unstable man.

The collapse of his efforts to achieve union with Egypt had resulted in a rapid deterioration in relations between the two countries. Qaddafi never tired of proclaiming that his country was the only reliable ally in the fight against Zionism; and he seized every opportunity to fulminate against Sadat, accusing him of betraying the Arab cause. After the Yom Kippur War of 1973, Sadat's heightened stature on the international scene and his moves toward peace with Israel had isolated Qaddafi, and the Libyan leader had seen his dream of a pan-Arab state diminish.

Since 1974 the two countries had existed in a state of semiwar, each trying to undermine the government of the other. Cairo offered political sanctuary to Libyan exiles, including Major Umar al-Mahaishy, one of Qaddafi's former colleagues. Mahaishy had used Egypt as a base from which to launch broadcasts and written attacks against the Libyan colonel. Qaddafi had responded by aiding and financing terrorists seeking to overthrow the Sadat regime.

Uncovering Qaddafi's operatives had been one of Ahmed Rahman's main preoccupations in recent years. He had been instrumental in foiling an attempt by a Libyan Secret Service operative to blow up Sadat's summer house at Mersa Matruh. (The information had come from the Mossad, via the CIA. A grateful Sadat had used his remaining influence over the Libyan leader to dissuade him from a scheme to torpedo a liner carrying Jewish tourists to Israel.) In April 1974, Rahman's department received a tip that fanatical Qaddafi supporters were about to storm the Technical Military Academy at Heliopolis. The information had come too late to prevent the attack, and thirteen people were killed. But the second phase of the operation, which involved seizing weapons at the academy and taking over the offices of the central committee of the Arab Socialist Union, where Sadat was to speak that day, was foiled. Egyptian intelligence also arrested a Libyan operative sent to assassinate a prominent Cairo journalist.

The years that followed had seen more of the same: in 1975, a Libyan plot to annex part of Egypt's Western Desert; in 1976, bombs at Alexandria railroad station, apparently planted by Libyan operatives;

the arrest of more than forty Libyan agents on charges of planning to assassinate former members of the Libyan Revolutionary Council who had fled to Cairo for political asylum.

Relations between the two countries reached their nadir in 1977 during the acrimonious border conflict. Qaddafi had made massive purchases of Soviet arms, including the highly advanced MiG-25s. He had stationed squadrons of fighter bombers, backed by Soviet SAM 6 and 7 missile batteries, along the border with Egypt. The same threatening stance was repeated along the southeastern border with Sudan, as part of a plot to overthrow that country's moderate government and put further pressure on Egypt. Mossad agents got wind of the plan, and after much deliberation, Jerusalem decided to alert Egyptian intelligence. Sadat reacted immediately by ordering in his warplanes against two Libyan positions near the border town of Salum and the Oases of Kufra. The desert battles raged for four days in the eastern Maghrib before other Arab leaders were called in to mediate a cease-fire. The border had remained tense ever since, and the Soviets continued to aggravate the situation by pouring new equipment into Libya along with Russian "advisers" to operate it. When the peace treaty with Israel was effected, Egyptian military leaders declared openly that the main threat to peace and stability in the area now lay to the west.

Qaddafi's downfall would have been a cause for rejoicing in the more moderate capitals of the Middle East had his successor not quickly shown himself to be of the same stripe. There was something ominously disturbing about the little-known Major Abd Jalil. He had maintained a low profile since his coup, but reports out of Tripoli suggested that he was an empire-building hawk who nurtured a deep resentment of the Israeli-Egyptian peace treaty. (The personality report in the Mossad's files stated that Jalil suffered from migraine headaches and was not seen at cabinet meetings for days on end.) Where Qaddafi had been capricious, Jalil was described as highly organized and systematic —his bloodless coup had certainly been a masterpiece of planning and execution. Foreign observers had noted no letup in the influx of Soviet arms and advisers into Libya since the takeover. One European diplomat who had succeeded in gaining a private audience with Jalil shortly after he seized power reported that the new Libyan leader, who was slight in stature, had referred to himself at one point as "the Napoleon of the Middle East."

All in all, the portents were not good.

"Do you think Jalil is insane enough to play with nuclear weapons?" asked Rahman, breaking the silence between them.

"I really don't know," replied Bar-Zeev. "Since my retirement I haven't had access to the Mossad's confidential files, so I haven't been able to study the man's psychological profile. But men with delusions of power like to have powerful toys. Nuclear weapons tempted Qaddafi. They tempted Pakistan and India. And even the PLO flirted with them."

"Your country, too, has not been above temptation, Colonel."

Before Bar-Zeev could reply, the navigator approached their seats and requested they fasten their seat belts for landing.

"Let's put ourselves in the mind of Abd Jalil for a moment," continued Bar-Zeev. "He's a new and inexperienced dictator whose country is virtually immune from outside pressures. He has his own mad dreams of conquest. He's a man of violence who knows no other means to accomplish his ends. He's suspicious and fanatical. He has the money to buy what he wants. And he desperately wants to leave his mark on history, but has little time to do it. What better way than holding the rest of the world to ransom with nuclear weapons? Your aspiring leader of Islam is a threat to us all, my friend."

The pilot throttled back and began the descent into Alexandria.

≈≈≈

"Let me explain it again. I'm obviously not making myself clear to you." Bill Leamington was leaning over the desk of the customs official in Alexandria, fighting to keep his temper. "The glass I'm importing is for use in the construction of a large hotel on the Red Sea. The dining room and two bars will be under water, get it? So guests can see the beauty of the reefs without putting on scuba gear. Understand?"

"Wonderful," said the sad-faced official. "You are a lucky man."

"Thank you. Now, it's a special type of glass I need. A heavy-duty glass to withstand the water pressure. It is *not* for aquariums."

The customs man scratched his ear with a pencil and studied the bill of lading again. "You are welcome in my country," he said solemnly, and nodded at Nicole to include her in the greeting. "But it is written here 'aquarium glass.' "

"It is not aquarium glass! I am not building aquariums! I am not a zookeeper!"

Nicole put a restraining hand on Leamington's arm. "What Mr. Leamington means," she said, smiling winningly, "is that obviously there has been some mistake."

"No, there has been no mistake." The little man shook his head forlornly and held up the bill of lading showing the words "aquarium glass" handwritten in ink. "It is here for all to read."

"Yes, I see that," replied Nicole sweetly, "but whoever wrote it made a mistake."

"But that cannot be. It is written here. I have shown you."

"Just because something is written on a piece of paper, that doesn't make it Holy Writ." Leamington's fuse was rapidly running out. The hissing irony in his voice was a danger signal.

"Bill, please. Remember your ulcer. Perhaps I can persuade this gentleman. Why don't you walk along the dock for a few minutes." Nicole could feel that he was shaking with anger and frustration as she ushered him toward the door.

"Don't you realize this material is urgently needed for a project President Sayed has taken a personal interest in?" shouted Leamington from the door as a parting shot.

"You are doing good work. Sayed is a fine man. You are welcome."

Bill sat on the harbor wall and watched the fishing boats bobbing gently on the light swell. Behind the customs office, a small stone building shared by the harbor master, stood Fort Kait Bey, the fifteenth-century fortress constructed on the site of the Pharos lighthouse, which was one of the seven wonders of the ancient world. Inside the dusty office Nicole was tilting at the windmills of bureaucracy with her own weapons.

Leamington took a deep breath to slow his pounding heart. The air smelled of fish and diesel oil. Along the seawall boys and old men fished with long bamboo poles. Beyond the fishing fleet was the Yacht Club, and next to that the Shooting Club, where members held competitions on the number of pigeons they could bag. The dead birds fell into the harbor, and the fishermen supplemented their income by collecting them and selling them to the local shopkeepers, two for thirty piasters. From where he sat, Leamington could see the fishermen mending their nets along the sidewalk of the Corniche.

After five minutes he returned to the customs inspector's office, in time to hear the man say to an exasperated Nicole, "—but you are welcome in my country."

"It's no good, Bill. We're going to have to pay the duty."

"Like hell we are. We have a contract with the government that allows us the tariff-free importation of construction materials. I've shown it to you," he said to the official. "You have seen it. It is written, right?"

"Yes, Mr. Leamington. But it says on this form that you are importing aquarium glass. This is not classified as construction material. I cannot release it without the payment of duty." The man's features had degenerated into an advanced state of melancholia.

"Dammit, man, your paper is wrong. Can't I get that into your head? Whoever wrote 'aquarium glass' didn't know what the hell he was talking about."

"I assure you there is no mistake. 'Aquarium glass' is not listed under the heading of construction materials."

"Do we have to go through all that again? It is not aquarium glass!"

"It is marked here as aquarium glass." The customs man's voice did not falter. He spoke to them as if they were willful children who could be made to see their error if he was patient enough with them.

Leamington felt as if he were on a Kafkaesque merry-go-round. Hoda Chafik was worth every cent she would make from the project if only to take this kind of burden off his hands.

"Suppose you just crossed out 'aquarium.' You don't really like fish, do you? Then it'll just be 'glass.' Plain glass. We'll all be happy."

"You are welcome."

"You keep saying that, but what about my glass? Can I have it or not?"

"I will be happy to release it when you have paid the duty."

"What is it you want?" Bill was shouting now, and Nicole was too exhausted to stop him. "Baksheesh? Is that what you want? Tell me

what you want. Go on. Just to forget the word 'aquarium.' How much?"
The customs man shook his head in sorrow.

≋ ≋ ≋

A car was waiting on the tarmac of the military airport at Alexandria
to take Uri Bar-Zeev and Ahmed Rahman directly to the harbor
master's office. Rahman wanted to determine if any unusual shipping
movements had been brought to the harbor master's attention, and if
not, to have his men begin systematic questioning of dockworkers and
seamen. He would also check with the local agent for Lloyd's of London, who made routine reports on all maritime traffic in and out of
the port.

As soon as he landed in Alexandria, Bar-Zeev felt an immediate
affinity with the place. Free from the noise and chaos of the capital, the
air was clean and still. The manic traffic of Cairo seemed far away, and
the drive along the Corniche to the harbor master's office afforded him
a view of the sweeping Mediterranean coast that reminded him of
Tel Aviv.

"There is a beach at Natanya where my family used to take their
holidays," he said to Rahman. "The sand is like this."

"One day I'd like to see it," Rahman replied. Then they passed the
Tomb of the Unknown Soldier, and the Egyptian fell momentarily
silent.

Rahman and Bar-Zeev arrived at the harbor master's office at the
same time that Bill Leamington was shouting his offer of a bribe to the
customs inspector across the hall. Rahman paused, listened for a moment to the strident voice coming through the door, and motioned to
Bar-Zeev to wait for him. Without knocking, he walked straight into
the customs office.

Leamington, unaware of Rahman's presence, had taken out his wallet
and was riffling his thumb over the bills, demanding to know how much
the man wanted. Rahman absorbed the tableau quickly: the sad-faced
customs man, the ebullient American flashing his wallet, and the attractive red-haired woman sitting nervously beside him.

"Excuse me, please."

Everyone turned in his direction.

"Who the hell are you?" Leamington demanded.

"My name is Muhammad Ahmed Rahman, head of Egyptian Internal Security. And your name, please?"

"William Leamington. I'm an American. This is my assistant, Miss Honeyworth."

Leamington. In an instant Rahman's mind had found the file. *Developer, Venture International of Hong Kong. Government contracts. Well connected with the minister of tourism and the delightful Hoda Chafik.* Rahman also knew that Sayed was interested in the American's work. The Egyptian leader would not want a scandal on the eve of the presidential visit.

"Perhaps you do not realize it, Mr. Leamington, but I have just witnessed you in the act of committing a felony. Attempting to bribe an Egyptian official."

Leamington blushed. "There's been a misunderstanding." He smiled, affecting an insouciant air.

"I'm sure there has, and it appears to be on your part, Mr. Leamington. I know this man. He is a conscientious and loyal servant of the government. By attempting to bribe him you have not only insulted him personally, you have cast aspersions on his professional conduct. Your money has no influence here."

"You don't undersand." Leamington had regained his old self-confidence. "Mr. Rahman, you're a man of the world. This is a top-priority construction project. President Sayed is fully behind it. There are materials in port that must be released immediately."

Rahman turned to the customs man, whose expression of sorrow had turned to one of incipient bereavement. He asked him a couple of questions in Arabic. Leamington heard the word "aquarium" mentioned three times, and winced as if he'd been punched.

"My colleague says there is duty payable, Mr. Leamington. Why not pay it? It will be little more than the bribe you were about to offer. You Americans are a generous people. By paying the duty you will restore the self-respect of this good man and you will have your glass. I shall not lay charges against you this time. As a visitor you must be presumed not to know our ways. But it must not happen again."

"Thank you," replied Bill, "for making me welcome in your country."

Rahman smiled and bowed toward Nicole. He closed the door behind him and apologized to Bar-Zeev for keeping him waiting. The Israeli, who had witnessed the scene from the corridor, smiled up at him. "They should have made you a diplomat," he said. "Your talents are wasted as a spook."

≅≅≅

A blood-orange sun was sliding into the Mediterranean when the two intelligence men finally stopped for a meal. They had not eaten since breakfast in Cairo, and soon it would be dark. After an abortive day of interviews around the harbor area they were no nearer the answer of Herrara's route into Egypt than when they first arrived in Alexandria.

Bar-Zeev sat, tired and disconsolate, under the weathered canvas canopy of the Monsignor Restaurant-Casino. Hands deep in his pockets, and feet resting on the chain separating the sidewalk café from the pedestrians, he rocked back and forth in his wicker chair, listening to its noise as he gazed out on the turquoise waters of the East Harbor. The indefatigable Rahman had left him in order to talk with the restaurant owner on the off-chance he might be able to recognize the South American from a photograph.

Directly in the line of Bar-Zeev's vision was a sign on the lamppost in the middle of the divided highway; it read, in both Arabic and English: 26TH OF JULY AVENUE. The date of the 1952 revolution, when a decadent monarchy was overthrown in favor of a pack of power-hungry colonels, thought Bar-Zeev. July 26, 1952. Where was I when I heard the news on the radio? I was with Yuval Ne'eman at the Weizmann Institute in Tel Aviv. Ne'eman eventually wound up in Aman, the espionage section of military intelligence. One of the most brilliant men I've ever met. It was Ne'eman who convinced me to come to Nahal Sorek on the nuclear program. We used to call him "the Brain." When Ne'eman heard the news he turned to me and said, "Uri, we will find these republicans even more implacable than the royalists." And that was three wars ago.

A soft salt wind blew off the sea, causing the masts of the fishing boats to move like metronomes. Beyond the stone breakwaters that defined the harbor, the sea grew rougher and broke against the rocks at the harbor mouth, sending sheets of water, pinkened by the sun, over the encircling walls. It's the same sunset they're admiring in Tel Aviv, he told himself.

The harbor master and the Lloyd's agent both had had nothing to report, and when they toured the West Harbor, Alexandria's commercial shipping terminal, Bar-Zeev had been surprised by the strictness of the security. No one, sailor or dockworker, could get through the iron gates without a thorough check by armed guards. It would have been virtually impossible for Juan Herrara to enter Alexandria undetected if he were aboard a commercial vessel.

After a fruitless three hours at the West Harbor, Rahman had turned his attention to the streets leading away from the dock gates. As in all port cities, Alexandria's bars and brothels are within staggering distance of the ships, and in between the visitor runs a gauntlet of peddlers and pickpockets, sleazy bazaars and cheap souvenir stalls, all vying for the sailor's pay. The two intelligence men had pressed their way through the crowds, brushing aside cheap dresses and flimsy leather cases hung over the sidewalks at eye level. The air was rank with the smell of sheep's blood, overripe guavas, and roasting nuts. Rahman stopped here and there to ask questions. He would dart into a dark shop front, flash Herrara's photograph, and then move on. His energy seemed boundless. Bar-Zeev was beginning to feel his age.

"Perhaps we should eat something," he suggested finally, not because he was hungry, but because he needed to sit down and rest.

"Yes, but I do not advise that we eat here. Let us drive back to a more salubrious part of town."

Bar-Zeev caught the disparaging innuendo. The Egyptian was something of a snob—another expression of his dandyism, perhaps. But Bar-Zeev was glad to get back into the car and to the Monsignor Restaurant-Casino, where he could relax at last.

He followed the sweep of the bay from his left, where brightly painted fishing boats had been dragged out of the water and onto the sidewalk; along past Fort Kait Bey, with antiaircraft nests set in its battlements; to the stone breakwater's end. The mouth of the harbor was marked on this side by a small hexagonal lighthouse; on the other, fixed to a rock base, was a five-meter metal tower with a light on top.

His eye traveled along the other arm of the seawall and lingered on the concrete missile silos and radar installations overlooking the East Harbor.

As darkness fell, the red and green lamps of small fishing vessels began to appear at the harbor mouth. The wind had freshened, and the fleet had come to seek the sanctuary of the port for the night. Bar-Zeev watched one tiny boat buffet its way through the heaving swell outside the breakwater; as soon as it had been swallowed into the tranquil waters of the East Harbor, the Israeli leaped up out of his chair.

"Of course!" he shouted at the wind. "How could I have been so stupid?"

He ran into the restaurant to find Rahman. "Our man had to use a fishing boat. He would have come in here, into the East Harbor."

Rahman looked outside and nodded. "I think you are right, my dear Colonel."

Five minutes later, their car had deposited them at the entrance to the fishing dock. Under the shadow of a mosque built on the jetty for the convenience of departing sailors, fishermen were frantically unloading their catch in great rush baskets: mullet, squid, eel, shrimp, crab, sea bass—all thrown in together to be sorted into crates under the light of hurricane lamps for instant sale at the street market outside.

The men shouted and swore as they handled the slippery fish, and any attempts by Rahman and his men to interrupt their work with questions were brushed aside. A storm was brewing, and the fishermen's first instinct was to get their merchandise to market, their boats safely battened down, and themselves home to bed.

Bar-Zeev watched the frenzied activity, which seemed to draw every undernourished cat in the city with its alluring odors. He put his hands in his pockets and pressed his elbows to his sides. He knew he was right; he could feel it, as he could feel the coming storm. Herrara had to have come in this way. Everyone's attention was focused on the catch; even the guard at the entrance to the quay was away from his post, gingerly picking up crabs for close inspection. A stranger could have wandered through the area naked without raising an alarm. Or, simpler still, he could have been rowed to the small beach below the seawall and then sneaked up to the road through the boats trestled for careening above the sand.

"Tell me," said Bar-Zeev when Rahman had finished questioning a reluctant fisherman. "Are these boats inspected at all when they come in here?"

"They have to check in with a Coast Guard boat outside the harbor entrance. All incoming vessels are searched, mainly for hashish," replied Rahman.

"Every vessel?"

Rahman called the departing fisherman back and questioned him further. The man looked at the intelligence officer and laughed. Rahman looked serious for a moment and then dismissed the man with a good-natured chuckle.

"He says the patrols are mainly concerned with strange boats. They rarely check the ones they know."

"What was so funny, then?" asked Bar-Zeev.

"There is a tradition, it seems. The fishermen throw up a fish to the patrol boat when they return with a catch. We have an expression in Arabic that means 'It's for your mother.' The fish is a guarantee the boats won't be held up for inspection. A little harmless corruption," added Rahman defensively.

"Can you get your hands on some Geiger counters?"

"Yes. The military would have them," replied Rahman.

"Herrara was radioactive. If he was smuggled in on a fishing boat, it might still have traces of radiation," said Bar-Zeev.

Rahman looked out at the dozens of boats lying at anchor, and then, impulsively, he put his good arm around the Israeli's shoulders and gave him an appreciative squeeze. Bar-Zeev stiffened. Rahman released him quickly and turned toward the car. He radioed the army base, and within an hour Alexandria's East Harbor had been transformed into a restricted military area.

Portable searchlights set along the esplanade illuminated the entire bay. Armed troops formed a cordon around the dock entrance, restraining angry fishermen who were fearful that their boats were about to be seized. Patrol launches moved from vessel to vessel, standing by each craft while a two-man team clambered on board with a Geiger counter to sweep the cabin and holds.

Rahman and Bar-Zeev sat on the seawall drinking coffee and waiting. The army had been able to supply four Geiger counters, and a thorough inspection of each fishing boat took about ten minutes. Bar-Zeev counted seventy-eight vessels at anchor, which meant that it would take about three hours to check them all.

"In our business, Colonel, patience is the bread of triumph. The Koran says: 'Allah is the guardian of the faithful.' "

"I'm not a religious man. I believe in intellect and hard work. That's how we get results. No problems are insolvable. Tell me, Rahman, what would you say if future scientists looked back on our times and equated your belief in God with your ancestors' worship of the sun or the crocodile?"

"I would say, my dear Colonel, that to live without faith is your loss, not mine."

"In our work we deal with the doings of men. I don't see much redemption there. You just have to look to history to see the oceans of blood spilled to convince people of the superiority of one godhead over another."

"I believe in the perfectability of mankind. If we can learn to live together in peace, that is a start."

"Yes. And that will require the amnesia of three generations of people in both our countries."

"You are a cynic, Colonel."

"On the contrary, I'm a realist."

The searchlights danced on the inky water, catching the momentary apparition of the waves as they broke over the stone arms of the harbor walls. A necklace of pearly lights delineated the voluptuous curve of the bay, and behind them, the Moorish facades of the buildings, eaten away by the salt wind, slept in shadows.

Bar-Zeev watched the nearest patrol launch nudge up to a white, two-masted trawler. Its superstructure was painted yellow, and its prow bore the Arabic name *Halewan el Gadid,* surrounded with flowers. A uniformed sergeant pulled himself aboard; his colleague handed him a Geiger counter and then joined him. The two men disappeared into the cabin. Two minutes later they emerged on deck, shouting and waving their arms.

Bar-Zeev jumped off the wall and ran to the nearest searchlight to direct its beam at the vessel. "They've found it! By God, Rahman, they've found it!"

≋≋≋

Zamalek, Cairo's most prosperous residential district, protects the exclusivity of its sequestered villas and sumptuous apartment blocks by making it all but impossible for the less fortunate to find their way through the labyrinth of its streets. The occasional road signs, barely decipherable by day, are completely obscured at night. The dim streetlights are tastefully hidden from view by the luxuriant foliage of untrimmed trees, giving Zamalek the air of a suburb that goes to sleep on its wealth after dark.

Taxi drivers have been known to refuse fares if they cannot give precise directions to their destinations there.

Mustafa Habib had only Professor Munir's address, and his driver had circled the area in voluble frustration for twenty minutes, trying to find the house. The student looked nervously at his watch. He was half an hour late already. "There's a guard outside that embassy over there," he said, leaning forward toward the driver. "Ask him."

But the soldier merely shrugged his shoulders and shook his head at the shouted request for directions. The driver swore at him for his pains. "I'll try turning right here. This is the only road we haven't tried," he said bitterly.

After two more turns, the driver drew up with a smile of accomplishment in front of a square stone house with shuttered windows, which was set back in its own walled grounds. Elegant palm trees fanned their fronds above its tiled roof.

"Your friend must be very rich," he said, in expectation of a handsome tip. "That house must cost a million pounds." The meter showed twenty piasters. Habib handed him the twenty-five-piaster note Munir had given him. The driver grunted in disgust as the student hurried out of the taxi.

Habib fumbled with the catch on the wrought-iron gate and dashed up the drive, arriving panting at the door. After a moment the door was opened—not, to the young man's surprise, by a servant, but by Munir himself, wearing a white robe. His head was covered.

"Ah, Mustafa. You are welcome to my house. Come in. Come in."

Munir took the student by the arm and guided him over marble floors to a sitting room elegantly furnished with *mushrabiya* chairs and screens. A copy of the Koran stood open on a small wooden lectern. The walls were hung with old lithographs of Egyptian scenes. On a wooden sideboard were two trays of food, encircled by loaves of bread. The floor was covered by an enormous carpet; at the center was a glass coffee table, through which could be seen an illuminated display of pharaonic artifacts: shards of pottery, amulets, oil lamps, and shining scarabs. Munir noted Habib's immediate interest in the collection.

"A hobby of mine, Mustafa. I like to surround myself with reminders of our glorious heritage. Our people are artists and craftsmen. We have been so for seven thousand years. Come, I have tea for you."

Munir could see the astonishment in the boy's eyes as he looked about the richly appointed room. He read in his expression an implied rebuke: how could one of the ulema, who preached against materialism, live in such luxury?

"This house belonged to my father's older brother," said Munir, as he poured a glass of tea. "Please, help yourself to some food. My uncle was a doctor who came to Cairo many years ago from Aswan, where I was born. He was personal physician to Egypt's first president, Muhammad Naguib. He never married, and when he died he bequeathed this" —Munir made a dismissive gesture with his hand—"residence to me. It is far from Al-Azhar but it is ideal for contemplation. And convenient to the Sporting Club."

Habib could not imagine his professor indulging in any kind of sport.

"You have no family, Sheikh?"

"The Egyptian people are my family, Mustafa. Come, sit. I have been thinking a great deal about the questions you asked me at my last seminar." Munir placed his glass on a small inlaid table and leaned back against the embroidered cushions. "The answer to your questions lies on that table. In those artifacts fashioned by our forefathers. The reign of the pharaohs ended when Alexander the Great conquered Egypt. Since that time, our people have been under the heel of foreign powers down the centuries. The Greeks, the Romans, the Mamelukes, the Turks, the French, the British, the Russians, and now, it would appear, the Americans. We have been masters of our own destiny only for very brief periods in our history, most notably in the time of Saladin, whose faith in the strength of Islam made Egypt a great power again. Only when we were our own masters did Egypt flourish. Under foreign domination we languished as a third-rate nation. Do you understand that?"

"Yes, Sheikh." Habib was once more the student sitting cross-legged at the feet of his teacher.

"Good. Then follow my thinking. During the periods when our country was free from foreign oppression, our own cultural and spiritual values were allowed to flourish. After the coming of the Prophet, the spirit of Islam permeated all facets of our life. It provided us with our moral and ethical codes, with our inspiration, with our sustaining power, with our philosophy, with our laws, with all those values which are woven together to create the glorious tapestry of our civilization.

"Foreign domination, especially when our rulers were nonbelievers, corrupted this purity of culture and religion. Our masters imposed their own values upon ours and led us into a period of stagnation from which we have yet to recover. Have you ever stopped to consider, Mustafa, why Egypt and the Arab peoples once ruled the known world and then fell into a state of decline? Because of foreign domination and the desire to make of us a subject race. More tea?"

"No, thank you."

"Only now are we beginning to understand the true significance of all this," Munir said, the light of conviction shining in his eyes. "Look what happened in Iran recently. Is it not ironic that a non-Arab country should lead the way back to religious purity? Allah is wise in His ways. Our Iranian brothers understood what was happening to their land, how their ways were being destroyed by petrodollars and the influence of the Americans. We must come to a similar understanding here, before the light of Islam is extinguished. The warning is clear in the Koran: 'If you yield to the infidels, they will drag you back to unbelief and you will return headlong to perdition.'

"Think what the influence of outsiders has done to our country, Mustafa. Many of our elite have abandoned their proud heritage in an effort to ape the ways of the foreigners. They refuse to acknowledge their birthright. They speak French instead of Arabic among themselves. They are more interested in social gossip from Saint Moritz than in political events in Cairo. They fill their homes with European artworks. Their lives revolve around a world that is not real. The so-called Christian countries accuse us of rigidity and lack of purpose. But they have moved too quickly to wild excess. European civilization is like a fermenting drink that breaks the vessel that holds it.

"Think of our women, corrupted by foreign influence, no longer living the chaste lives prescribed in the Koran. You see them on the street, their arms and legs bare, encouraging any foreigner who looks at them. Many are no longer virgins when they marry. The sanctity of the family, which is the base of our social structure, is being dangerously eroded. Why? Because our women are being exposed to corrupting influences. Public dancing. Lewd Western music on the radio. Dirty films in the cinema and on television. Alcohol, which weakens their moral resolve. Nightclubs, where their senses are stimulated to the point where they can no longer resist the blandishments of unscrupulous men. And all of this because the Europeans do it, the Americans do it, and we would be like them." His voice rose and fell with the cadence of his words, as if he were chanting.

"Think of our commerce. Our economic and financial affairs are controlled by outsiders. We cannot even make internal changes in our tax laws and subsidy payments without permission from the World Bank, which is dominated by the United States. And now Israel is beginning to insinuate its way into our economic life, and there are those among our people who are actually welcoming the Jews, who tell us we should imitate their progressiveness. I cannot believe this is happening.

"Think of our armies. Instead of being the Sword of Islam, they have now become a tool to be used by the Americans in their colonial squabbles with the godless Soviets.

"It goes on and on, Mustafa. Everywhere you look. Unless action is taken, our country will be ruined. We will differ from the West only in that we will be poorer, speak Arabic, and practice a greatly weakened Islam as our religion. And all other Arab states will be so affected."

"But what is to be done, Sheikh?"

Munir looked at the student for several minutes, as if he were deliberating whether to continue. Habib sat unflinching under his gaze.

"There is only one road to national salvation," Munir said. "It lies in the reestablishment of a truly Islamic society. Without the inspiration and guidance of Islam, the future holds barren prospects for the Muslim world."

"What do you mean?"

"I mean we must precipitate our own revolution, a new revolution, if Egypt is to survive."

"A spiritual revolution?"

"Spiritual and secular. There can be no true Muslim state unless the government, the rulers, are permeated with the spirit of Allah."

"What you say is similar to what I have heard from the Muslim Brothers."

"We do not differ in our objectives. Only in the means."

"What are the means, Sheikh?"

"Let me tell you a story. When I was eight years old my father sent me to live with a Bedouin family. He told me the experience would mold my spirit and make a man of me. Do you know the ways of the Bedouin?"

"No, Sheikh."

"Too few of our young people do. Yet it is in the Bedouin that we find preserved the best of our values and traditions. A strong sense of honor. Generosity and hospitality to the stranger, even if that person is a sworn enemy. Self-respect. And, above all, courage, for a man's courage is the measure of his commitment and his worth.

"For a year I traveled the desert with the Bedouin. Sometimes we had nothing to eat but dates and sour camel's milk. My bed was a tent floor. There was no formal school. But I learned much, as my father said I would. I learned to ride. I learned the ways of the desert. I learned about livestock. But, most important, I learned *who* I was. For the Bedouin remain pure, untainted by outsiders. They live their lives according to the teachings of the Koran. They are patient in the face of tribulation and adversity. Their women adhere to the code of sexual morality laid down by Allah. The men are strong, not just in a physical sense but inwardly—there is a nobility about them that has been lost in the cities. Wealth, poverty—these things are unimportant when set beside man's honor, dignity, piety, and bravery. We all have much to learn from a people so many regard as primitive."

Munir paused and looked at Habib. The student was sitting on the edge of his chair, absorbing his every word.

"What do you think of all this, Mustafa?"

"I think you are a great man, Sheikh," Habib said softly. "You have much to teach us all. I wish my own father had been as wise as yours, that he had sent me to the desert, too."

"It is a hard life, Mustafa. Young boys are sometimes lashed or burned as a test of their courage. Even though the pain can sometimes be terrible, they are expected not to cry out or even to show any sign of anguish in their faces. If they pass the test, it proves their manhood, but failure means disgrace."

"Were you subjected to such a test, Sheikh?"

"I was. I was accepted into manhood during my year with the Bedouin."

"Did you feel the pain?"

"Yes. But my desire to prove my worthiness conquered the pain. And when I had successfully endured it, I felt purified. I knew in my soul I could endure anything. That is the true meaning of the test."

"Then it did something important for you?"

"Yes. I have forgotten the pain, but I have never forgotten the exaltation."

"I would be like you, Sheikh."

"You would endure the test?"

"I would."

Munir sat back in his chair and reflected. He had not intended to initiate young Habib into Wind of the Desert just yet, but Herrara's death had created a certain urgency. The boy had already proved himself in a dozen small ways. He was physically strong. His basic instincts seemed sound. A check of the boy's record had revealed nothing that would militate against his membership in the organization. Most important, Munir felt a personal fondness toward Habib that suggested to him the lad could be trusted. He looked at Habib again. The boy's eyes were large and sincere, his expression open. He was quite handsome in an unformed sort of way. His hair was neat and close-cropped. Munir made his decision.

"Tell me, Mustafa, what do you think of the matters we have discussed tonight?"

"I think you have put into words all the thoughts that have been troubling me. I think I would like to learn much more from you."

"Would you like to work with me, Mustafa? To help regenerate the spirit of the Prophet in our country?"

"You do me great honor, Sheikh." Habib bowed his head. "Nothing would please me more."

"You would have to pass a test, Mustafa."

"A test?"

"Yes. A proof of your courage and commitment. Would you be prepared to do that?"

"What kind of test?"

"A Bedouin test. Come."

Munir led the way through the house to the kitchen at the back. He motioned Habib to take a chair. From his pocket he took a key, which he used to unlock a wooden cabinet. From it he withdrew a thin metal device that Habib recognized with horror as a branding iron. Without looking at Habib, Munir turned on a gas jet and placed the iron in the flame. Habib felt his heart start to pound, and the sweat began to pour from his body; he realized Munir intended to apply the iron to his body—this was to be the test. He squirmed in the chair and looked toward the door.

"Remove your left shoe and sock, and roll up your trouser leg," Munir commanded over his shoulder.

In a panic of indecision, Habib watched the iron turn red over the blue circle of flames. He seemed hypnotized by the singing of the metal as it grew brighter and somehow larger. His head began to swim, and he thought that he was going to pass out. He bent over, and the blood returned to his head. Slowly he began to unlace his shoe.

Munir lifted the iron from the stove. He held it close to his cheek to feel its heat; the glowing orange of its tip reflected in the blackness of his eyes. His lips began to move, but no sound came out. He moved closer to the student.

"Do you believe, Mustafa? Can you conquer yourself?" Munir moved the iron slowly across his body, as if he were conducting a celestial orchestra that only he could hear. The iron had turned a grayish-red. Habib could feel the heat emanating from the metal. He pulled his leg back involuntarily. Munir hurled the iron into the sink, where it lay hissing in protest, sending up a cloud of steam.

"You are not man enough. You are still a boy. Go. Leave my house," shouted Munir.

Habib gripped the chair and willed himself to stay. "No, Sheikh. You are unfair. In the desert, boys are given time to prepare themselves, are they not?"

Munir turned back to him. "Yes, that is correct."

"With respect, you gave me no time. I can pass the test. I can conquer pain."

"Very well. Prepare your mind and your body." Munir took the iron from the sink, placed it back into the gas jet, and then left the kitchen.

Habib fought the urge to vomit and tried to compose himself. What Munir wanted to do was insane. But there seemed to be no other way to win the man's confidence. He breathed deeply to calm his nerves. He wondered how much it would hurt and whether he could withstand the ordeal without crying out or grimacing, as demanded by the Bedouin code.

He looked once more at the iron glowing menacingly on the stove, and then he called out, "All right, I am ready."

Munir returned and without a word lifted the iron from the flames. Habib extended his left foot, tightened the muscles in his leg, and gripped the sides of his chair until his knuckles turned white. Munir stood over him, his face illuminated by a beatific smile. He knelt down in front of the trembling student. Habib shut his eyes. Suddenly he felt the jolting pain of an electric shock shoot up his leg and through his body. His teeth sank into the inside of his lip, and tears of pain formed at the corners of his eyes. He could smell the smoke of his own charred flesh. The instep of his left foot throbbed unbearably. His head began to swim again, and he fought to remain conscious.

Munir withdrew the iron and looked down at the semiconscious boy in front of him. He hadn't managed to hide his pain, but at least he had not screamed like a woman. He would do. Munir set the iron down on the stove and returned to the cabinet. In a moment he was kneeling again in front of Habib, applying a cooling salve to the wound and preparing to bandage it.

The pain continued, but Habib's mind was clear now. He saw the figure of Munir bent before him, treating the burn.

"You have done well, Mustafa. You have shown your courage. You have passed the test." Munir smeared a butterlike substance over Habib's instep and bound his foot lightly with a thin bandage.

"Thank you, Sheikh." Habib's voice was hoarse and dry.

"I will now tell you the last part of the story. When I was with the Bedouin, I was tending their sheep one day. It was hot, and as children will do, I removed my sandals. One of the ewes wandered away from the flock, and I ran after it. It was a foolish thing to do in the desert. I kicked over a stone, and underneath it was a particularly large scorpion. It stung me on the instep of my left foot.

"Everyone was certain I would die. There were no doctors in the desert. The Bedouin had their own cures, but I became feverish and fell into a coma. I was laid in the tent of the head family, and everyone gathered to await my death.

"In my delirium during the night, when my fever was at its height, I had a vision of the Prophet Muhammad. He came close to me. He wiped my forehead with his cloak, and he commanded me to become well and to devote my life to Allah. In the morning I awoke and the fever was gone."

Munir, who had been kneeling before Habib while he told his story, now rose to his feet. He went to the sink and began to wash his hands.

"When your bandage is removed, you will see that your own foot now bears the mark of the scorpion. It is a badge of courage, a sign of your personal bond with Allah, blessed be He. You are now a member of a small group of men who have passed this test. We have dedicated ourselves to the task of reestablishing the primacy of Allah's rule on this earth. We call ourselves Wind of the Desert."

"Wind of the Desert," repeated Habib.

Munir offered him a glass of water. "Drink this. Then rest awhile. For a day or two, you will find it difficult to walk, but the wound will heal quickly. When you have rested I will take you to a place where you can spend the night with friends." Munir smiled down on the student, who gingerly flexed his foot to see if he could move it.

≈≈≈

According to the register of shipping in the harbor master's office, the radioactive trawler, the *Halewan el Gadid,* was jointly owned by one

Hosny Ashraf and his son, Taher. The address showed that they lived in a slum area of Alexandria within walking distance of the fish market.

It was shortly before midnight when Rahman and Bar-Zeev located the four-story building in a street of multicolored tenements with cracking walls and missing windows. A platoon of troops sealed off the area as the two intelligence men, accompanied by three armed guards, climbed the urine-scented staircase to the third floor. The Ashrafs' two-room flat was tucked away at the end of a dark, damp corridor. Rahman stationed one of the guards at the top of the stairs and motioned for the other two to follow him.

"Perhaps you should wait downstairs," Rahman whispered to Bar-Zeev. "They may be armed." But the Israeli dismissed the suggestion with a snort. "Very well"—Rahman shrugged—"but please keep behind me. I do not need a diplomatic incident on my hands."

As they moved stealthily toward the door, they could hear the sound of a radio playing popular music. The two guards leveled their sub-machine guns at the ill-fitting door. Pale-yellow light filtered under a large crack along the floor.

Rahman turned on a flashlight. Taped to the splintering woodwork was a bunch of plastic flowers. He looked back at the guards, nodded to them, and then knocked authoritatively. He waited and was about to knock again when the door opened a few inches to reveal the anxious, deeply lined face of a middle-aged woman dressed in black. The woman's eyes registered a mixture of fear and anxiety at the sight of the looming figure of Rahman.

"Is this the house of Hosny Ashraf?"

"Yes, but it is late," replied the woman in a strained, tired voice.

"My name is Muhammad Ahmed Rahman. I am with the police. I want to speak to Hosny Ashraf."

"The police! He had done nothing!" The woman's eyes opened wide, showing their bloodshot rims.

Rahman applied a gentle pressure to the door and stepped inside, followed by Bar-Zeev. The smell of rancid olive oil assailed their nostrils.

"My husband is sick. And my son. I do not think you should disturb them. Tomorrow, come tomorrow."

"I'm afraid I must insist," said Rahman gently.

The room was lit by a naked bulb whose dim light cast shadows over the sparse furnishings. Under a window covered with a blanket stood a frayed, lumpy couch. In the center of the room was a plastic-topped table set with four chairs. On a shelf in a corner were a primus stove and a few metal pots. Dominating the wall opposite the door was a large family portrait, hand-colored by the photographer. The rush matting on the floor creaked as they moved across it.

"Where is your husband?" asked Bar-Zeev.

The woman wrung her hands and pointed to a room at the back. "He is very sick," she protested.

"What is wrong with him? asked Rahman.

"He burns with heat and he shivers. He cannot eat. I feed him but he can keep nothing down."

"How long has he been like this?"

"Three days, sir."

"And your son?"

"Like his father."

"He's in there, too?" asked Bar-Zeev.

The woman nodded, and tears welled up in her eyes.

"It sounds like radiation sickness," murmured Bar-Zeev to Rahman.

"Is there any danger?" asked Rahman.

"It depends if they have any traces of the material on them. Don't touch them, whatever you do."

Rahman ordered one of the guards to bring up the Geiger counter from the car. A sweep of the room revealed no indication of gamma rays. Rahman gestured for the door of the bedroom to be opened. The feeble flame of an oil lamp illuminated a large bed in which father and son appeared to be sleeping. Rahman could tell at a glance that both men were seriously ill: the older man was shaking violently, and both bodies were bathed in sweat. He motioned to the guard to check the room with the Geiger counter. Again it registered nothing.

"Fine," said Bar-Zeev. "There's no danger."

At the sound of voices, the son began to stir. He raised himself painfully on his elbows and called to his mother. Seeing two strangers in the room, he fell back moaning on the bed and pulled the sheet up to cover his nose. His eyes flicked about in terror.

"Don't be afraid, Taher. We are here to help you," said Rahman softly. "We want to ask you a few questions, and then we are going to send you and your father to a hospital, where the doctors will look after you."

"Questions?" The boy's voice was weak.

"Is he delirious?" asked Bar-Zeev, turning to Rahman.

"What day is it, Taher?"

"Tuesday," replied the boy, shutting his eyes.

"Fine," said Rahman. "Now we want you to tell us about your fishing boat. You've been using it for something else besides fishing recently, haven't you? We want you to tell us all about it."

"Please, sir, my son is tired. He will talk to you tomorrow," pleaded the woman.

"Take the lady into the other room, please," said Rahman to one of the guards. The woman let out a high-pitched keening sound as she was ushered from the bedroom, and her son immediately burst into tears. He began to shake uncontrollably and beat his fists on the mattress. The old man next to him groaned in his sleep.

Bar-Zeev pinned Taher's shoulders to the bed. "Get a grip on yourself. You're a man, not a boy," he said tersely in Arabic.

Taher gasped and stared wildly at Bar-Zeev. His body relaxed, and the shaking stopped. He coughed and looked down at his father.

"He can't help you," said Bar-Zeev. "He's too sick. You must tell us what happened."

Taher Ashraf began to talk in a slow monotone. The story that emerged from his wandering narrative was very much along the lines of the intelligence men's own hypothesis.

Two months before, Hosny Ashraf had been approached by a man who spoke Arabic with a pronounced foreign accent. He had offered father and son one hundred Egyptian pounds if they would carry him into Alexandria's East Harbor from a rendezvous point fifty kilometers offshore. The man gave no explanation as to the purpose of the trip, and Taher had opposed the idea, warning his father that they would get into trouble. But fishing had not been good at the Delta. Since the construction of the Aswan High Dam, artificial control of the Nile had destroyed the feeding cycle of the sardine and the fish had moved to more hospitable waters. Money was scarce, and there were payments on the boat to keep up; so Hosny Ashraf had agreed to the stranger's proposition, overriding his son's objections.

At the appointed hour they had dropped their sea anchor at the rendezvous and watched an unmarked cutter approach from the west. The man was aboard, wearing fisherman's clothes and carrying a large canvas duffel bag. The bag appeared to be heavy, but he allowed no one to touch it. During the run into Alexandria he sat with the bag in the trawler's small cabin, reading the Koran. He never spoke, and left the bag only to use the toilet.

When the trawler was in sight of the East Harbor, the man went below into the hold, taking the duffel bag with him, and stayed there until the boat cleared the cursory inspection procedures. He remained below until Taher dropped anchor and the harbor area was deserted. Then Taher rowed him ashore to a small beach below the seawall, where the man handed the boy an envelope full of money and gave him the date and time for the next trip. He swore him to secrecy, indicating with a hand across his throat that if Taher valued his life he would tell no one. Then the man disappeared into the night.

Two days after each inbound trip, the man would reappear on the beach at four a.m. to be taken back to the rendezvous, where the cutter would be waiting.

"How many trips did you make?" asked Rahman.

The boy thought for a moment. "Eight, ten, I can't remember."

"When was the last one?"

"Five nights ago."

"Did anything special happen on that trip?"

"Please, sir, I'm not feeling well."

"You'll get help soon enough. Did anything unusual happen on that trip?"

"The weather was bad. We had trouble reaching the meeting point, and when we did, we couldn't see the cutter."

"Were you taking him out?"

"No, we were meeting him to bring him in."

"Go on," prompted Bar-Zeev.

"We were about to return to the harbor when the cutter appeared. We managed to come alongside in spite of the heavy sea. It was very dangerous. The boats were pitching against each other, and we couldn't see for the spray. He managed to get aboard with his duffel bag, and the cutter left as usual. I've been going to sea with my father since I was seven, but I've never seen a storm like that. I even got seasick."

"What about the man?"

"He just sat in the cabin as usual, clutching his bag."

"He didn't speak to you?"

"He never spoke. We were about halfway back when we were hit broadside by a wave as tall as our masts. The boat heeled over so far the gunwales were under water. I thought we were going to capsize. Everything not tied down was thrown across the cabin. The man was not used to the sea. He was no sailor. He was thrown against the wall and struck his head. The boat righted herself and then heeled over the other way. My father and I were holding on, and we couldn't help him. He was knocked unconscious and thrown back again. Luckily, the cabin door jammed, or he would have been swept overboard."

"What happened then?" asked Rahman, as the boy began to tire.

"It's hard to remember. It happened so quickly. We struggled to get the door open, and we could see the man scrambling about on his knees looking for his bag. It must have split open when it hit the bulkhead. There were three metal cases with great rubber seals on them. One of the seals had been broken and he was trying to fix it."

"Sounds like he was carrying radioactive fuel—spent fuel rods, perhaps," Bar-Zeev whispered to Rahman. "Under the impact, the rods must have broken."

"Go on, Taher," said Rahman. "What happened then?"

"We got the door open, and the man shouted at us to go away. Then he grabbed the broken case and stumbled out on deck and threw it into the sea. He took off a scarf and began scrubbing at the cabin floor with it. He looked crazy. Then he threw the scarf into the sea."

"Did he tell you what it was all about?" asked Bar-Zeev.

"No, he just locked himself in the toilet and didn't come out for a long time."

Rahman turned to Bar-Zeev. "What do you think?"

"It could be Herrara got some of the material on his body. He junked the stuff overboard and tried to decontaminate himself. But he wouldn't have had the proper chemicals for the job. There were still radioactive particles on his body."

"The laboratory report showed ceramic fragments in his hair and clothes."

"Nuclear fuel bundles contain ceramic rods of spent uranium fuel. When the zirconium sheath got broken, one of the rods must have shattered. Herrara was being thrown about the cabin. He was probably rolling around in the stuff. No wonder he couldn't get it off."

"But why was he radioactive when these two aren't?" asked Rahman, gesturing at the fishermen.

"Herrara still had radioactive particles on him. These two were merely exposed to a high dose of radiation. That is why they're sick but not radioactive themselves."

Rahman turned back to the boy, who had slumped down in the bed again. "Were you carrying any fish?"

Taher Ashraf nodded. "We were told always to complete the day's catch before the rendezvous. If we came back empty, it would create suspicion."

"What happened to the fish?"

"We sold them as usual."

Rahman and Bar-Zeev looked at each other.

"You two, get in here immediately," Rahman shouted at the guards. "I want you to advise the local police to try to track down a consignment of fish from the *Halewan el Gadid*. It would have been sold five nights ago. It's probably too late to do anything, but some people may end up poisoned. And make sure the dock area is quarantined."

Further interrogation of the boy revealed nothing more. The Ashrafs knew nothing about the man, where he came from or whom he worked for. Rahman was satisfied that their involvement ended when they dropped off the man and his duffel bag in Alexandria.

"All right," Rahman said finally. "Call in the woman."

Taher's mother crept into the room, dabbing at her eyes with a handkerchief.

"I am calling an ambulance to take your husband and your son to a hospital for treatment. There is nothing to worry about. They will be in good hands."

The woman nodded in resignation and moved to the bed, where she stroked her son's forehead.

Rahman and Bar-Zeev groped their way out of the building and sat in the car, discussing what they had learned. Herrara had been a courier, bringing in radioactive material, probably from Libya. He had made perhaps ten trips. This meant that there was a sizable stockpile of uranium somewhere in Egypt. Presumably, the material had been transported to Cairo, since Herrara's body had been found in the Nile there. But who had taken delivery of it? And for what purpose? The young fisherman had merely confirmed what they already knew; they were no nearer to the heart of the matter than before.

≋≋≋

The scorpion brand on Mustafa Habib's left foot continued to throb, but the motion of the car made him drowsy in spite of the pain. Professor Munir, who was driving, had let him sleep for an hour in the sitting room and then had shaken him awake. Habib paid little attention to where he was being taken. When they left the professor's house, the slightest pressure on Habib's foot had made his leg buckle under him, and Munir had had to support him to the car. But Habib had said nothing, knowing Munir would interpret any complaint as a sign of weakness.

"I would be pleased to have you as a guest in my house, Mustafa," the professor had said, "but the servants come at six in the morning and a stranger would be a cause of gossip among them. Our members must remain as invisible as the wind of the desert—the hot, cleansing wind of the desert."

"Why can't I go back to my room?" Habib had asked.

"There would be questions about your foot. It is better to rest in a safe place for a day or two. I have applied a special salve. You will be surprised how quickly your foot heals."

Munir had driven across the 26th of July Bridge, skirting the commercial center of Cairo. Late at night the traffic melted miraculously away, and he was able to move quickly through the city. Habib dozed briefly.

"You must wake up now, Mustafa. We are almost there," said Munir.

Habib opened his eyes and looked out the window. He recognized the plain stone facade of Al-Azhar University; directly ahead stood the remains of the Old Wall of Cairo.

"Are we going to Al-Azhar?"

"No. A little farther."

Munir drove up the hill, through the wall, over Salah Salem Avenue, one of the roads into Cairo from the airport, and onto a dirt road. Mustafa Habib suddenly realized Munir was driving into the City of the Dead.

The giant necropolis that stretches for eight kilometers along the southeastern perimeter of Cairo has been the city's burial ground since the thirteenth century, when the Mamelukes first interred their dead under the shadow of the Citadel. Muslims are never buried in the earth; instead, they are laid to rest in tombs aboveground or in underground sepulchers. The City of the Dead is more than a graveyard of a hundred thousand tombs; it has the appearance of a well-planned town. Its walls of stone and plaster stretch as far as the eye can see along straight, dusty roads. The monotony of the one-story structures is broken by brown mosques with bulbous domes and spindlelike minarets that tower over the network of walls and buildings. The predominant colors are rose, pink, and lemon—pastel shades that lend a macabre air to the vast cemetery where the living share quarters with the dead. There are an estimated quarter of a million living squatters who call the necropolis home, and more come each year as Cairo's housing shortage becomes increasingly critical. As for the dead, no one knows how many are buried there or how many bodies have been snatched from their resting places to be sold to teaching hospitals for research.

Mustafa Habib knew the City of the Dead well. He knew it as a place to be avoided.

"We will stop here and walk the rest of the way," said Munir. "I will help you."

Leaning on Munir's arm for support, Habib hobbled along beside the professor as they made their way deeper into the city. The impacted sand road under their feet was strewn with rubble. In the darkness, rats scratched over broken bricks, chased by thin, half-wild dogs. Cats pawed at piles of garbage to dislodge anything edible. The air was fetid and rank with the smell of fried garlic, urine, and hashish, and even the wind that swirled the dust along the open streets could not carry the stench away.

All the stories Habib had been told of the City of the Dead came flooding back: the ghosts that could be seen floating over the necropolis at night; the hashish smugglers who stored their forbidden supplies in the mouths of corpses; the body snatchers; and the cripple-maker, a demented doctor who lived somewhere in the bowels of the city—a man who, for a price, would extract an eye, cut off a hand, or create an appalling deformity, the better to help the begging community. And, it was said, there were those who had found themselves under the cripple-maker's knife against their will.

"We turn down here. It is not far, Mustafa. Courage."

"I'm fine, Sheikh. Just tired."

The road ahead was deserted, but Habib knew that behind the line of walls on both sides there were men, women, and children sleeping in sepulchers or lying under blankets in small courtyards, oblivious to the cadavers around them. Some families had lived in the necropolis for two or three generations and would probably never escape. The government tolerated their presence because there was no other place for them to go; it even pumped water and electricity into parts of the necropolis.

"Here," hissed Munir. They stopped in front of a small mausoleum that appeared to be no different from any of the others along the road. The professor looked around to see if there was anyone else on the street. When he was satisfied they were not being observed, he knocked softly on the wooden door of the tomb. Habib could hear the sound of bare feet on stone, and then the door opened, its hinges complaining. A man peered at them through the darkness, and Habib felt his stomach tighten when he saw a gaping hole where the left eye should have been. Visions of the cripple-maker rose before him.

"We have a new recruit," whispered Munir. "His foot is still in pain. You will take care of him." With that, he disappeared back down the road, leaving the student to the tender ministrations of Saraj al-Rahid.

DAY FIVE
WEDNESDAY, NOVEMBER 7

"If it's not one damn thing, it's another." Bill Leamington put his feet up on the coffee table and his hands behind his head. "Sometimes I wish I hadn't started this whole damn business." Nicole, still in her bathrobe, was standing by the window of the hotel room, looking down on the changing patterns of the Nile water.

"Well, at least you got your glass, even if you did have to pay for it, so that's one problem less."

"Yeah, and all we need is for some idiot to plow into the trucks and smash the whole load before it gets to the Red Sea."

"Don't be such a pessimist, Bill."

"I don't mind my share of troubles. God knows, you expect them on this kind of project. But not every ten minutes. I don't know what the hell we're going to do about Aswan. The government surveyors guaranteed the rock face would support one hundred pounds per square inch. If we can't sink those girders, we'll have to redesign the whole damn project."

Venture's third hotel, to be built overlooking the newly raised Temple of Philae behind the old Aswan Dam, called for huge reinforced concrete beams to support a patio extending out over the sheer sandstone rocks around the artificial lake.

"Call Aswan, Nicky, and tell them I'll fly down there as soon as the

Oasis is opened. The president arrives in three days, and that means I could be down there on Sunday afternoon."

"Okay. Now, how about some champagne to cheer you up? I had a boyfriend once who gave me champagne and kippers for breakfast. It's great."

"Hold the kippers and I accept."

While Nicole opened the half bottle of Pommery & Greno, Leamington gazed at the Avshar Zaronim on the wall opposite him. He had bought it at a Parke-Bernet auction in New York and was especially fond of it, with its impressive Serabend motif and diamond-shaped medallions. He stared into the rug as if it were a fire whose constant changes of color and mood had hypnotized him. Each time he looked at it he discovered details he had not seen before. And the fact that such beauty had become priced out of the range of all but the superrich appealed to his collector's instinct. The art of hand-knotting and the manufacture of natural dyes would soon be a thing of the past. Certainly, no more rugs like it would come out of Iran.

"The nomads who made that wove their lives into it," he said moodily. "They probably couldn't read or write, but look what they did. Sometimes I'd like to trade it all, just to be able to do something like that."

"I can just see you sitting cross-legged in the desert, knotting away," Nicole answered, laughing, as she handed him a glass of champagne.

"Maybe you ought to get onto my insurance broker in New York and have him up the value fifteen percent on this one. And while you're at it, have them add Hoda's rug to the list."

Hoda Chafik's rug had been something of a bone of contention between them. The small silk Qum of silvery blue that now lay near the sliding door to the balcony had until recently graced Hoda's lavish apartment in Zamalek. When Leamington took her in on the hotel projects as a business partner, she threw a dinner party for twenty guests of impeccable social credentials to celebrate the association. The German ambassador and his wife, the minister of tourism and his wife, and the governor of the Bank of Egypt and his wife were among the rich and powerful who never turned down an invitation to Hoda's table. Her hospitality was legendary among a people renowned for the warmth of their welcome; but Hoda had the money and the style to dazzle even the jaded sensibilities of European career diplomats.

Hoda's apartment had reminded Nicole of Versailles in miniature; the brocade curtains, the hand-painted rococo scenes on the walls, the embroidered Louis Quinze chairs, the fountainlike crystal chandeliers, and the massive gilt mirrors overwhelmed the guests, much as the hostess did herself with her penchant for Yves St. Laurent black dresses and Gucci accessories. She could hardly lift her wrist for gold bangles, whose value could go no small way toward defraying Egypt's balance-of-payments deficit. Vulgar, thought Nicole, and she was furious with Leamington when he admired a silk rug by the alabaster fireplace.

Dinner—dozens of quail freshly caught in Alexandria and presented on a bed of rice and stuffed vine leaves—had been served by tarbooshed waiters from silver platters. The wine was Gruard Larose 1961 (a gift from an admirer at the French embassy). Nicole had hardly spoken throughout the meal, since the conversation seemed to revolve around the latest Cairo gossip. Was it true that President Sayed's wife had a controlling interest in a new state taxi company? Did the minister of housing really get one million pounds for that run-down summer place of his near Rosetta? And have you heard about the American ambassador's daughter's affair with that actor? And my dear, how can we expect to keep our servants when the Saudis come in and offer them four times the wages?

At the end of the meal the social lodestone had exerted its influence over the gathering, physically repelling the sexes into two mutually exclusive groups. While the ladies withdrew to the drawing room with their coffee, the men remained at the table, serviced with brandy and Cuban cigars at the merest nod of the hostess to her staff.

Nicole would have preferred to stay with Bill, but etiquette demanded that she accompany the ladies. Her silence during dinner had not gone unnoticed by Hoda Chafik, who had taken her arm as the ladies left the dining room, saying, "My dear, you were so quiet. I hope we haven't bored you."

"I'm sorry. I'm really enjoying myself," replied Nicole. "I've been listening. It's all so fascinating."

"And how are you enjoying Cairo?"

"Oh, I love Cairo. So does Bill."

"Good. You are always welcome here. He is a very fine man, Mr. Leamington."

"Yes," said Nicole, a touch more frostily than she had intended.

"Come, sit next to me here," Hoda said, patting the moss-green velvet of a love seat. "Did you know I read fortunes? I'm very good at it. I'll read yours in a minute. When you've finished your coffee, turn your cup upside down in the saucer and let the grounds settle—that's it."

A fat, jolly Cairene—the wife of the man who held the Mercedes concession for the entire country—bounced over to her hostess and perched on the arm of a chair nearby.

"Hoda, did I tell you about the teacher who rented our winter house in Luxor? She went down with her husband to try for a reconciliation. She left her nine-year-old daughter with her mother. While she was away the grandmother found out that the girl had not been fixed by the *ghagarieh*. So the old woman did it herself!" She dissolved into flesh-shaking spasms of laughter while Hoda smiled politely.

"My guest has not understood, Nevine."

"Oh, it doesn't matter," said Nicole.

"But I think you might be interested. My friend Nevine is telling me that a grandmother circumcised her nine-year-old granddaughter because the child's mother refused to have it done."

"What do you mean?" Nicole asked.

"The operation is called a clitoridectomy. It is still widely practiced in Muslim countries. Not so much in the cities but certainly in the villages. I doubt if you would find a woman over fifty in my country who has not had it done."

"Had what done?" Nicole's curiosity had been aroused.

Hoda sighed and folded her hands in her lap. "It is traditional for Muslim boys to be circumcised. Until recently, young girls, too, have been circumcised, not for reasons of piety but as a guarantee of a woman's chastity before marriage. It reduces sexual desire and so, the villagers say, eliminates promiscuity."

"How is it done?" asked Nicole, her eyes wide with morbid fascination behind her glasses.

"In the villages a Gypsy woman, a *ghagarieh,* performs the ceremony. The girl sits on her mother or grandmother's lap. Her legs are held apart by other female members of her family, and the clitoris is removed with a razor blade. In the Sudan they cut out the labia as well."

"Oh, my God, that's barbaric," gasped Nicole.

"Yes. There are many folk remedies to stop the bleeding. But it is painful. In the villages they call it 'cutting the cockscomb.' You see, it is believed that a girl will not be pleasing to a man if it has not been done. It is said that the operation is to achieve a tightness that is pleasing to the male."

"That's horrible."

The fat Nevine shrugged her shoulders at Nicole's remark and waddled off to pass on her story to a more receptive audience.

"Look around you, my dear. I would hazard a guess that every Egyptian woman in this room has been so treated."

Nicole gazed around her in shocked disbelief. Finally her eyes settled on Hoda Chafik's face. Her hostess smiled and nodded her head affirmatively.

"You, too?"

"Yes. But mine was done clinically and only the tip of the clitoris was removed. After a few years it regenerated. You find it strange, don't you? My mother was a highly educated woman, but the tradition is strong. She did what she thought was right."

"How has it—er—affected you?"

"Oh, I can enjoy sex, my dear. It takes practice to have an orgasm after a clitoridectomy, but I have mastered the art. And I enjoyed finding out how."

She smiled warmly at Nicole, who suddenly found herself blushing.

"A high color becomes you, my dear," said Hoda. "Here, let me see that coffee cup." She took the cup from the flustered Nicole and turned it upright again. The fine coffee grounds had stuck to the porcelain surface. Hoda stared into the muddy image. She turned the cup around in her fingers.

"Most interesting," she murmured. "I see large buildings—but then I would, wouldn't I," she added, laughing. "Water," she continued. "I see water. Beware of water."

"I never drink it," replied Nicole.

Hoda laughed again delightedly and put the coffee cup down. "Oh, you Americans are so sensible. So free of our ancient superstitions. Now

I think it is time to reclaim our menfolk before they solve the problems of the world and leave themselves with nothing to occupy their minds."

When Leamington and Nicole left, around two a.m., Hoda handed Bill a brown paper parcel—the rolled-up Qum rug.

"This is a gift of friendship to seal our association," she said, and she stood on tiptoe to kiss him on the cheek. "It is the rug you admired."

Bill protested that he could not accept it, but Hoda was adamant. He opened the parcel in the taxi on the way back to the Hilton and ran his fingers over the silken fabric.

"I can't get over it," he kept repeating. "I'm going to have to get her something. Would you pick out a piece of jewelry and have it sent to her? Something really nice. Something she'd like."

"Sure," Nicole said, staring purposefully out of the window. "What about a diamond-studded razor blade?"

"What?"

"Oh, forget it."

≋≋≋

The first glimmer of the sun over the City of the Dead awoke the roosters, whose morning alarm set off the geese and dogs of the neighborhood. The living began to stir for a new day, which would be the same as those that had gone before it and those still to come. The belching chimneys of the iron foundry to the east of the city had already blackened the sky with a massive shroud that hung like doom over the pastel-colored monuments to Cairo's dead.

Mustafa Habib tried to block out the morning chorus and return to sleep, but the marble floor and the stabbing pain in his foot made it impossible. He pulled the evil-smelling blanket over his head and kept his eyes closed. He needed time to collect his thoughts. He could hear the irregular breathing of others in the room. Lifting the corner of the blanket, he looked about him. He recognized the one-eyed man snoring softly in the corner. Next to him were two younger men, about his own age.

They had been asleep when he had arrived at the tomb the previous night. Al-Rahid had given him a blanket and ordered him to bed, making no mention of them. The room was located to the left of the entrance to the tomb. It was small and bare, with whitewashed walls and a small window giving out onto a courtyard. There would be another like it on the other side of the entrance passage, Habib knew. These rooms were used by the families visiting the graves of their relatives: one for the men, the other for the women.

He could hear children moving about outside, and the sound of a primus stove being pumped into flame. We must be sharing the tomb with a family of squatters, he decided. As he lay feigning sleep, there was a knock on the wooden door of the mausoleum. Al-Rahid stirred and sat up. Coughing, he left the room. Habib strained to hear his conversation, but in vain. A few minutes later, al-Rahid returned, put on his shoes, and hurried out again. The noise had awakened the other two sleeping figures, who rose, stared at Habib curiously, muttered something to each other, and then went outside to relieve themselves.

Habib knew he could pretend to sleep no longer. He raised himself painfully to his knees and stretched. One of the young men came back into the room; he had two glasses of tea in his hands, and in his teeth he held the hem of his galabia. He smiled at Habib and placed the tea on the marble floor.

"So, the newcomer awakes," he said in a friendly tone. "You are welcome. My name is Salah Kader."

"Mustafa Habib."

"May Allah give you peace."

"May Allah increase your well-being."

"You are a student of Sheikh Munir?"

"Yes."

"Here, a glass of tea for you."

Habib took the glass and sipped at the scalding liquid.

"The sheikh is a great man," Kader remarked. "We are blessed to have him at this time of need."

"May Allah protect him," replied Habib.

The second man entered, and Kader introduced him as Gabal Marwan. He, too, offered the ritual greeting. Habib glanced quickly at their bare feet; both men bore the white mark of the scorpion. In a display of camaraderie, Habib slid his foot from under the blanket and inspected the bandage.

"When did you have the test?" asked Kader.

"Last night."

"It is painful for the first day, but tomorrow you will not notice it. Here, lean on me," said Kader, as Habib put his weight on his good leg to rise.

"The women are preparing food," said Marwan. Through the open door, Habib could see two old women, dressed in black, hovering like witches over a steaming pot on the primus. Three pajama-clad youngsters stared solemnly at the food with large, round eyes. The smell of stale olive oil wafted into the room.

"We pay them money, and they tell others we are of their family," explained Kader. "We are safe here."

"How can they live this way, surrounded by the dead?" asked Habib.

"They must live somewhere, Mustafa," said Kader seriously. "There are many buildings here to protect them from the sun and the cold. The Koran says: 'It shall be no offense for you to seek shelter in empty dwellings.' "

Outside, in the walled courtyard, chickens and geese pecked in the dirt. In the shade of a newly limed wall stood an amphora of water under a cascade of flaming bougainvillea. A young girl in a shapeless floral dress was hanging wet clothes on a line, her back to the blinding sun. Habib noticed that her head was covered with a tight-fitting black cloth and she wore scruffy white gloves.

In the center of the courtyard was a low slab of marble surrounded by a single chain, looping between squat white posts. In front of it a flight of whitewashed stairs descended into the burial vault. As a child, Habib had visited such crypts, small cells with barrel-vaulted roofs and sandy floors. The men were buried in plastered-up niches along the right-hand wall, the women along the left. Even in death the sexes were segregated.

One of the women in black shuffled across the courtyard with three tin plates of fava beans and three round, flat *pitta* loaves. She grinned at the men, displaying brown gums. Kader and Marwan began shoveling down the beans with the aid of pieces of bread.

"What is it, Mustafa? You are not hungry?" asked Kader, his mouth full.

"No."

"Then I will eat yours," said Marwan, sliding Habib's plate toward

him. Habib noticed the size of the man's shoulders and hands; he had
the build of a wrestler.

"Never mind," said Kader. "We shall be leaving here soon."

"When?" asked Habib, immediately alert.

"Oh, in a day or two. Al-Rahid does not tell us much, does he,
Gabal?" The other man shook his head.

"Where are we going?" asked Habib.

"We will know soon enough. We are to wait. That is all al-Rahid has
told us. When he is ready we will know." Something in Kader's tone
suggested that Habib should not be too inquisitive.

"I am from Cairo. I am studying to become a qari. If Allah wills it,"
said Habib, hoping to draw out the two men. Marwan stood up and
went to fetch himself a glass of tea.

"Where are you from, Salah?"

"It is better we know nothing of each other," replied Kader. "Then
we cannot tell others."

"But I am one of you now. I have passed the test."

"What did Sheikh Munir tell you of Wind of the Desert?"

"That we are a select band of brothers working together in the service of Allah to reestablish His rule on earth."

Kader nodded.

"How many are there of us?" Habib asked.

"We are everywhere. We are like the wind. You do not see us, but
we are there."

"But how many, Salah? We have been chosen for a divine mission.
Surely there are more than just us."

"Be patient, Mustafa."

Habib studied the faint white mark on Kader's foot. "You have been
a member of the movement for some time, Salah. Surely you have not
lived here from the beginning."

"I have been many months in a training camp."

"With Palestinians? In Lebanon?"

Kader laughed. "You have the curiosity of a woman, Mustafa. I was
in Libya."

"Will they send me there?"

Marwan returned with his glass of tea and sat down without a word.

"He wants to know about our training, Gabal. He would go himself."

Marwan scratched his hair and grunted by way of response.

"Did you learn to kill Zionists?" Habib went on.

"We learned about weapons and explosives and how to behave under interrogation," answered Kader.

"Is that all?" pressed Habib.

"We learned how to handle a boat, how to dive under water. Gabal nearly drowned, didn't you, my friend?" Gabal merely scowled. "But most of all, we learned how to conquer ourselves for the glory of our cause."

Habib studied him in silence. Kader was tall and thin and moved with a muscular grace; he exuded a friendly warmth, a quality the recruit had not noticed in his other new companions.

"Are we allowed out of here?" he asked as the two men went back to their food.

"We must get the permission of al-Rahid. He must know where we are at all times."

"Where is he now?"

"He will return."

Habib finished his tea. An argument had developed between the two women. Their high-pitched screeches echoed off the walls of the mausoleum. Marwan bellowed at them, and their voices trailed away in a chorus of mutual complaint.

"Who is al-Rahid? He is not Egyptian." Habib was determined to keep the conversation going.

"He is Libyan. He was one of our instructors."

"He can kill a man with one hand." Marwan added, smiling.

"How did he lose his eye?"

"There are many stories. He never talks about it himself. It is said he lost it in a knife fight," said Kader.

"He carries the genitals of the man who did it in a leather pouch under his galabia," added Marwan with obvious relish.

"Is that true?" asked Habib, turning to Kader.

"He has not favored me with a sight of them," replied Kader, with the hint of a smile. "But I believe it. He is terrible in anger."

Habib leaned back against the cool stone wall, reflecting on what he had learned. A small boy with a runny nose and matted hair came and collected the dishes. "Cigarette?" he inquired hopefully. Marwan pushed him away with his foot.

Salah Kader took out a cheap cardboard backgammon set and methodically placed the red and white counters in position. "A game, Gabal, to pass the time?"

While the two men concentrated on the board, Habib repeated to himself the details of the conversation, much as he would as a Koranic student pacing the Al-Azhar courtyard, to memorize every detail. It was clear that he had been recruited into a terrorist cell; for what purpose he did not know. The men around him had been trained for some job. Since he was a virtual prisoner in the tomb, he had no option but to wait.

The sweet, prickling smell of hashish suddenly filled the air, masking all other odors. Marwan had lit a cigarette and was inhaling deeply as the game proceeded. Habib closed his eyes, listening to the click of the counters on the board and the fall of the dice. He breathed in deeply; the smell of the drug seemed to dull the ache in his foot.

≈≈≈

The sun is still behind the Mukattam Hills when classes begin at Al-Azhar, a concession to the heat of the Egyptian day. By nine a.m. Professor Rashad Munir had already dismissed his first group of students, seven young men studying for the diploma that qualifies one to be a *qari,* a reciter of the Koran. The *qari* is held in great esteem by his coreligionists, since the successful candidate must combine a deep reverence for Allah with the intellectual capacity to interpret His word; naturally, he must also be blessed with a fine speaking voice. Of all his students, Munir treated these seven young men with something more than his usual diffidence, since the grueling course ended in a rigorous viva voce examination before a five-man committee of senior tutors. The students would be required to prove their ability to recite the entire Koran by heart, without hesitation and with sufficient music to touch the hearts of their listeners.

Munir remembered his own examination as a young man—sitting cross-legged on a hard chair in front of his tutors and reciting on request random passages of the Koran for twenty minutes at a time. There was no knowing which verses the examiners would choose, and although they tried to put the nervous student at ease, their standards were exacting. Munir had been one of only five successful candidates in his class of twenty-six.

Since the role of *qari* was central to the religious life of the country, Munir's messianic fervor compelled him to devote all his efforts to preparing his students fully for their end-of-the-year ordeal. If they passed the exam they would leave Al-Azhar as dedicated missionaries, equipped to recite in the mosque as well as at religious ceremonies outside it. They would tour the villages, visiting families in their homes to bring the Koran to the illiterate, receiving food for their holy work. It would be these students who would keep the flame of Islam burning in the hearts of the people, reasoned Munir. Although the true role they were to play was unknown to them, these students and others like them were to be the intellectual arm of their professor's revolutionary crusade.

The verses of the Koran that Munir had assigned the young men to learn for their next meeting dealt with Mary and the birth of Jesus, a great prophet like Moses, Isaac, and Jacob who had preceded Muhammad, the last of Allah's messengers. The aspiring *qaris* would spend the next few hours committing the passage to memory, measuring their steps across the great courtyard of Al-Azhar to the rhythm of the Prophet's words, reciting the lines over and over.

Munir had no more classes for another two hours, and he had been asked to meet with the rector to discuss the merits of a new training program for muezzins in Port Said. As he was about to leave the mosque he heard a hissing sound coming from the side door. Partially concealed by a pillar, Saraj al-Rahid was motioning to him.

With quiet deliberation Munir gathered up his papers and filed them neatly in his briefcase. He glanced around him and then moved slowly toward the door. His face was a mask of fury; he had given al-Rahid explicit instructions never to contact him at Al-Azhar. If the two of them were seen together and al-Rahid were identified, the plan he had so painstakingly formulated would be completely destroyed.

Al-Rahid was as close to being apologetic as his truculent personality would allow. "I know I'm not supposed to come here, but it's an emergency," he whispered as Munir pulled him into the shadows.

"What is it that could not have waited until tonight?" growled Munir.

"They have found the fishermen in Alexandria."

"Who has?"

"The Mokhabarat. The pig Rahman and his people. They questioned them last night."

"Then we have to assume they know how Herrara got into the country and where he was coming from," said Munir.

Al-Rahid uttered a curse.

"Remember where you are!" Munir raised his arm as if to strike the one-eyed man.

Al-Rahid took a step backward. "How could they have found out so fast?"

"It was probably the Jew," muttered Munir. "Was he there?"

"Our information is that he is at Rahman's side wherever he goes."

"Did the fishermen know anything that would link Herrara with us?"

"They knew nothing."

"Good. We are so close. We need only a few more days. We cannot afford to have them find out anything more."

"Perhaps it is time to eliminate that damned Jew."

"Is that your answer to everything, Rahid?"

"We cannot be squeamish, Professor. If the fishermen had joined Herrara in the Nile, as I suggested, we would not have this problem now."

Munir thought for a moment. Perhaps there was merit in directing al-Rahid's psychotic tendencies. Since the arrival of the Israeli intelligence man, the Mokhabarat had moved more swiftly than might otherwise be expected of them. Rahman was clearly getting closer. The plan could be seriously jeopardized if he were to establish where Herrara had been taking the material. With Bar-Zeev and the Mossad involved, that piece of information might come to light too soon. But if Bar-Zeev were to meet with a sudden accident, the Mokhabarat's investigations would be thrown into turmoil. Not only would Bar-Zeev's death give Wind of the Desert more time, it would afford an added bonus: the possible rupture of Egyptian-Israeli relations. Jerusalem would hold Cairo responsible for the demise of their top agent—an admirable solution. The problem was how to lure the Israeli away from under Rahman's protective wing.

"Yes, I think you are right. It is time to strike another blow against Zionism."

Al-Rahid smiled. "When?"

"The sooner the better. Today. There must be no mistakes, no evidence."

Al-Rahid nodded.

Munir reached inside his briefcase and took out a black-and-white photograph. He handed it to al-Rahid. "This is Colonel Uri Bar-Zeev of Israeli intelligence." The photo showed the unmistakable grizzled head of Bar-Zeev caught in the act of holding a hand, palm extended, to the camera. Behind him, her hands on his shoulders, her mouth set in a plastic smile, stood the belly dancer at the Sahara City nightclub.

"He must be isolated, flushed out from his cover, Rahid."

Munir preferred not to know how such a skillful assassin as al-Rahid went about his business. He turned away and walked toward the main door of the mosque. He looked back, and the one-eyed man had vanished.

≋≋≋

When Ahmed Rahman and Uri Bar-Zeev arrived back at the Ministry of the Interior, there was a message from the Mossad awaiting them— a message that resolved for the Israeli a nagging discrepancy in the known behavior of the South American terrorist Juan Herrara. The young fisherman in Alexandria had told them that Herrara spent most of his time on board the trawler reading the Koran. Yet the personality profile in the Mokhabarat's files suggested that Herrara enjoyed the hedonistic pursuits of the playboy, a life-style incompatible with a student of Islam. The Mossad had provided more information on the missing six months in the dead man's life, clarifying the apparent contradiction. Bar-Zeev whistled as he read the telexed report.

"It appears our man spent some time at a Libyan training camp out-side Benghazi, Colonel. While he was there, he converted to Islam. Have you got the autopsy report there?"

Rahman shuffled through a stack of files on his desk to find it. "Does it say he was circumcised?"

Rahman scanned the report. "Yes. He was. It's possible the operation was performed at the camp, then."

"Up until the time he hooked up with the PFLP, Herrara operated mainly in Europe. He was the armorer for the Japanese Red Army, the Basques, and a couple of terrorist organizations in Italy. A busy boy. Then he joined the Palestinians, and now he turns up in Libya, a convert. What does that suggest to you?"

"He has turned to the one true faith, my dear Colonel," said Rahman, smiling.

"It suggests to me that Herrara tried to legitimize his fanaticism. By becoming a Muslim he embraced the radical Palestinian cause with all the zeal of a convert. They are the most dangerous kind."

Rahman took off his jacket and hung it carefully on a hanger. He ran his fingers over his crooked elbow, which pained him when he was tired. "Herrara is dead now, though."

"His might not be the only death unless we can establish a link between his trips to Egypt and the known terrorist groups operating here. Instead of doing the rounds of the nightclubs we should be chasing down the Muslim Brotherhood."

"We have every known sympathizer under interrogation, Colonel. My people have had all leave canceled," replied Rahman irritably.

The two men had had little sleep since their return from Alexandria, and the lack of progress had made them both edgy.

Bar-Zeev began to crack his knuckles loudly. "We're still in the dark. Whoever Herrara was bringing in that stuff for has managed to cover his tracks completely."

"Do you mind not doing that, Colonel? It is extremely disconcerting."

Bar-Zeev got up and strode over to the window, where he stared down on the rooftops of Cairo. "What about that rope that was used to tie the weight to the body? Did anything come of that?"

"Nothing," said Rahman, tilting back in his chair. "It can be bought in any one of a thousand shops around the city."

"Is this city never clear of smog?" Bar-Zeev grumbled. Looking down on Cairo from the fifteenth floor of the ministry building, he saw the city through a uniform haze of brown. Even the bright afternoon sun could not penetrate the gauzy film of dust and pollution that hung over its buildings and domes. Even the trees looked brown, as if the sand of the desert had returned to claim the capital and would bury it forever. By contrast, Tel Aviv, Haifa, and Jerusalem were clean and alive with color.

On the flat rooftops of the apartment houses below him, Bar-Zeev could see whole communities of jerry-built shacks. Old men lay indolently in the sun, sharing the space with chickens and dogs.

"What's that?" he asked, turning to Rahman.

Rahman joined him at the window. "What?"

"There, on the roofs."

"They're squatters. You'll see them all over Cairo."

"On the rooftops?"

"Yes. They build those places themselves. Cairo is too small for its population. People live where they can. Those people probably work in that building: janitors, cleaners, watchmen. The owners allow them to build their shacks up there and live rent-free."

Bar-Zeev looked back to the aerial slum across the road. Garbage was piled against a wall; a torn mattress had been hung over a line to air. Two barefoot boys kicked at a soccer ball fashioned from old socks. An old woman in black poured a basin of water onto the asphalt.

"Do they have any facilities?"

"You mean electricity and plumbing? Not usually. Most building owners regard squatters as a temporary necessity. They don't want to encourage them to become too comfortable."

"My God, Rahman, what kind of a city is this? Does the government not look after these people? How can they be allowed to live in such squalor? I've seen enough poverty and human misery since I've been here to last me a lifetime."

"You see only what you want to see, my friend," said Rahman bitterly. "You are a stranger here. You came expecting to find poverty and disease, and that is all you see. Yes, we are poor. Our people live on a knife edge, scratching a living where they can. We are hopelessly overcrowded, and our buildings are crumbling like brown sugar for lack of attention. Why? Why does the government not do anything about it, you ask? Well, I will tell you. Because the state is bankrupt. All our money has gone to defend our people. What is the point of building if we are threatened with bombs? If we tried to build homes for nine million people, it would take the entire gross national product for the next twenty years. That is why our people live on rooftops or in graveyards. It does not mean we are indifferent to their plight."

"I'm sorry," said Bar-Zeev. "I meant no offense."

"You know, Colonel, we had a delegation of city planners from London come to advise us recently on how to deal with our problems. After a week they threw up their hands and told us Cairo cannot survive as a city. They offered no solutions because there were none. They said it would be easier to build a brand-new capital in the desert than to make our city habitable again. A new city in the desert, of concrete and glass. But it would never be Cairo. You see, Cairo is more than just a capital. It is a city for all Arabs; it is Islam. I have lived in Paris, London, and other European capitals, but there is nowhere like Cairo. I was not born here—you know that from your Mossad researchers. But Cairo is my adopted city. *Al-Qahirah,* 'the Victorious.' It was founded in the seventh century as the seat of Islam. It is the largest city in Africa, and it no longer works.

"To understand it, you have to live here. You must feel the history in its cracking walls and the vitality of its people. All you see is dirt and decay. You Israelis, like the people of the West, are in love with progress because you think that progress alone elevates mankind. But we Egyptians are nourished by deeper things. Look at the crowds down there. What do you know of them? With all the scraps of information you feed into your computers, do you really understand anything about them? Do you know that they would share their last loaf of bread with you if you knocked on their door? You, a stranger. Do you know that they have more laughter in them, more love of life, than any of your dedicated kibbutzniks? Do you know the reverence they have for family, or their moral values? Their respect for tradition? Their love of Allah? With such things does it matter how they live? If you cannot see that, you can understand nothing of Cairo.

"You say you know this city, that you could walk blindfolded through its streets. Well, my friend, that is exactly what you are doing. In the Middle Ages they called this city 'Grand Cairo.' And that is what it is still. Have you any idea what is going on down there? Books are being written. Movies are being made. Students are learning. Our people are building hotels and factories, not as efficiently perhaps as your people are doing it, but the job is being done nevertheless. Political decisions are being taken that will affect the course of history. Plots and conspiracies are being hatched, and someone may even be making an atomic bomb! This city is alive, Bar-Zeev, bubbling like a caldron.

"Do you understand what it all means? Try to break out of your Israeli fortress for a moment. Think about it. Cairo is the crucible in which all the value systems of the modern world are being tested—Christianity, Communism, capitalism, Islam, and anarchy. This is the battleground. Traditional values are pitted against every modern ideology, and the outcome could shake the world. There are those who would drag us into the twentieth century and those who would have us retreat back into the age of feudalism. Cairo is a city in ferment. I am no seer; I cannot tell how these forces will resolve themselves. They may tear Egypt apart. But I cannot imagine a more stimulating place to be, at this point in history. The world is no longer run from Washington or London or Moscow. The future is here, and I am proud to have a small role to play in shaping the course of history."

Rahman fell silent. The two men gazed down on the incessant movement below them.

"I had no idea you were so eloquent, Colonel," said Bar-Zeev quietly.

The mood was broken by a knock at the door. Rahman turned away abruptly. "Come in."

Ismail Ali appeared at the door. "May I see you for a moment, please, sir?"

"Excuse me," said Rahman to Bar-Zeev and left the room, shutting the door behind him.

"What is it, Ismail?" he said, once they were in the corridor.

"An envelope has just been handed to security at the main gate. It's addressed to Colonel Bar-Zeev."

"Let me see it."

Ismail led Rahman to his office down the hall. "I haven't opened it, sir."

Rahman picked up the envelope and ran his fingers over it to ensure it did not contain an explosive device. He held it up to the light and studied the handwritten address.

"I've put it through the machine. It's only paper."

Rahman took a letter opener from the desk and slit the flap. He took out a single sheet of paper and unfolded it. "It's in Hebrew. Fetch me an interpreter and somebody who can copy this handwriting."

While Ismail was out of the room, Rahman took a photocopy of the short note. The aide returned with an interpreter, who studied the text for a couple of moments.

"Well?" demanded Rahman.

"It purports to be a letter from an Israeli agent operating in Cairo. He has requested an urgent meeting with Colonel Bar-Zeev. He says he has information concerning Juan Herrara that he will pass on. It says Bar-Zeev must come alone. If he is accompanied by Egyptian intelligence, the writer says his usefulness to the Mossad would be finished."

"Does it say where and when?"

The interpreter returned to the note. "At the Khan el Khalili souk, five o'clock. In the Street of Gold."

"Is that all? Nothing more specific?"

"It repeats that he must come alone and he will be contacted. That is all."

"Ismail, I want this letter resealed in a plain envelope. It is to be addressed in the same handwriting. Quickly. Have my secretary hand it personally to Bar-Zeev. If he leaves the building, I want him followed. And I want two men, our best, in the Street of Gold."

"Why would an Israeli operative risk sending such a message here?" asked Ismail.

"Either he is desperate or we are closer to our friends than we thought," mused Rahman.

≅≅≅

The spirit of healthy skepticism that pervades the lives of intelligence men caused Uri Bar-Zeev to be as suspicious of the handwritten letter as Ahmed Rahman had been. Yet the Israeli realized there were no other avenues of inquiry left open to him now. Nor was there time to check back covertly with Mossad headquarters in Jerusalem to authenticate the message. Whatever the consequences, he determined to keep the rendezvous. He scribbled a hasty note for Rahman, explaining that he had gone back to his hotel for a rest. Then he opened the office door and, seeing the corridor empty, walked swiftly to the emergency stairs. It took him five minutes to reach the ground, and, without looking back, he crossed the parking lot and exited through the main gate. Almost immediately an anonymous-looking man in a grubby galabia was on his trail.

Bar-Zeev turned left out of the gate and walked resolutely down Shari Sheikh Rihan toward Shepheard's Hotel. He was certain he would be followed, and he wanted to give himself ample opportunity to shake the tail that Rahman had set on him. As he approached the railroad tracks, a ringing warning bell and flashing red light signaled the arrival of a train. Bar-Zeev stood at the open level crossing and looked around him. The man in the galabia lounged against a wall, the only person in sight not moving. A pair of shiny shoes protruded from the hem of his garment. Bar-Zeev waited until the train pulled slowly into sight. The carriages had open doors, and there was no glass in the windows. Nonpaying passengers clung to the sides like barnacles wherever there was a toehold. Bar-Zeev waited until the engine approached the crossing, then, judging the distance carefully, he leaped across its path. The engineer did not even brake as the train moved inexorably forward, cutting him off from sight.

Now that the advantage was his, the Israeli turned right immediately onto Shari el Falaki and headed north in the direction of El Tahrir Square. The central bus depot and the confluence of several major arteries made it an ideal spot to melt into the hordes of home-going Cairenes.

Buses, oblivious to the waves of pedestrians, plowed their way through the traffic, challenging oncoming cars for the right-of-way. The air was thick with carbon monoxide and the shouted curses of drivers and pedestrians alike. And, above all, the constant tattoo of car horns battered the flaking facades of the encompassing office buildings. Bar-Zeev was experienced enough to know that while he might have lost one tail, that did not mean he was not still being followed. To flush out any more of Rahman's men, he climbed the steps of the enormous walkway that runs in a circle eight meters above the square, built to offer some protection for those on foot from the dueling metal below them.

He allowed himself to be borne along on the tide of humanity, marching, it seemed, endlessly around the circle as if doomed to expiate some primeval sin. He recalled what Rahman had said about the people of Cairo; he could see little joy in their faces now as they elbowed their way around the circle. He ducked down the next staircase and into the roadway again, weaving through the slow-moving traffic until he found an empty taxi. He jumped into the backseat and instructed the driver in Arabic to take him to the Street of Gold at Khan el Kahlili.

The taxi turned east, and Bar-Zeev felt secure at last. He checked his watch: it was four-thirty-five. The traffic was dense along the main road, slowed to a crawl by the herds of Bairam sheep spilling off the sidewalks in giddy anticipation of their imminent slaughter. The carcasses of their newly dispatched brethren, thick with flies, dangled from poles outside butchers' shops. The scene from Bar-Zeev's window was an ever-changing kaleidoscope of movement and color. Greengrocers piled fruits and vegetables in delicately arranged patterns to attract the eye of women shoppers, who balanced plastic baskets on their heads. Bakers hauled panniers of bread, still steaming from the oven, onto the sidewalk. Newspaper boys, loaded down with the late edition, shouted on street corners. Old men sat on blankets beside boxes of cotton handkerchiefs, shoelaces, and toothpaste, waiting for customers. Shopkeepers turned on their lights to dispel the soft purple twilight that had begun to envelop the city.

Bar-Zeev recognized Cairo police headquarters as the taxi eased past the eight-story stone building; its door was flanked by two slovenly guards in grimy white uniforms and black berets. He wondered what Rahman would be thinking now, and what he would do if he were in the Egyptian's shoes. It occurred to him that Rahman's prolonged absence from the office might in some way be connected with the delivery of the letter. Perhaps the Egyptian knew its contents and that was why it had been so easy for him to leave the ministry building unchallenged. Was he being set up for some design of the Mokhabarat? He read the letter again. Both the calligraphy and the style suggested that the writer was not a native *Ivrit* speaker; but the Mossad had many Arab operatives on its payroll. The informer had given no definite meeting point, which meant that he would be watching for Bar-Zeev's arrival and would follow him to a place of his own choosing. Bar-Zeev determined to stay in the open at all times until certain of the man's intentions.

The taxi pulled up on Shari Gohar el Qaid at the corner of the Street of Gold. Bar-Zeev paid the driver and scanned the road behind him with a practiced eye. At the entrance to the market a small boy sold American and British cigarettes from a rickety table. Bar-Zeev bought a pack of Rothmans and lit one before stepping into the dirt road. On both sides, stretching for several hundred yards, were rows of cramped single-story shops whose windows were stuffed with a variety of gold jewelry and trinkets. The merchants sat outside, fingering their prayer beads and importuning the passing tourists. Every shop appeared to have the identical merchandise on display: gold rings, cartouches, bangles, necklaces, charms, and intricately wrought earrings, artfully arranged to reflect the light of hurricane lamps and naked bulbs. On one corner sat the government gold inspector, a fat man whose haunches hung over his small stool. In front of him was a brass scale in a glass case; all purchases had to be weighed by him to guarantee the price of the object was based fairly on the weight of the metal.

Bar-Zeev watched the man lift the weights with his fingers and place them on the scale. The Israeli smiled to himself. The natural oils of the inspector's skin would make the weights heavier than they ought to be— another example of innocent corruption to be noted for his files. A boy carrying a small tray of coffee suspended from a chain pushed past him. The body contact made him alert once more. Behind him a donkey cart laden with bolts of material came creaking over the rutted road. An old man perched aloft shouted at the women to clear a path. Dogs as thin as greyhounds scuttled to safety, whining and growling at the smell of sheep blood in the air. From the depths of the market the sound of piped Arabic music rose like an invitation to unspeakable pleasures in blind alleys and curtained-off rooms. The sights and smells and the sense of incipient danger reminded Bar-Zeev of the Old City of Jerusalem immediately after the Six Day War—before it had been cleaned up and made safe for the American tourists.

He allowed the donkey cart to pass him and then moved in behind it, looking around for any sign of his potential informant. The cart suddenly turned off the Street of Gold, and Bar-Zeev found himself alone at a crossroads. In front of him was a crumbling mosque; around its broad stone steps were stalls offering cheap tin kitchenware. On the corner opposite the mosque stood a perfume shop. Dozens of brightly painted bottles of perfume essence and khol were arranged on mirrored shelves. A blue ceramic tile set in the wall above the wooden awning read: MOUSKI STREET. A crowd of women had gathered around the half door of the shop and were holding out money to the owner, who was endeavoring to shut his premises.

Bar-Zeev realized that he had come too far. The Street of Gold ended at this point. He had turned around and begun to walk slowly back, when his eyes were drawn to the figure of a blind man coming toward him, swinging a thin white stick in a wide arc around his feet. He was dressed in a gray galabia and wore a cheap pair of plastic sunglasses. The man moved with a slow confidence, as if he were more than a mere beggar, and the crowd parted respectfully for him. He held his free hand across his stomach, lost in the folds of his robe. Something in the set of his shoulders and the way he carried his free arm inti-mated to Bar-Zeev that the man was sighted. His head was erect and moved slightly from side to side as he walked; his face was weasel-thin, its length accentuated by a pointed black beard, which made the plastic glasses all the more incongruous.

Bar-Zeev stood with his hands in his pockets, waiting for the blind man to draw level with him. He could feel the beat of his heart as the white cane swept nearer. He waited until the man was three paces away from him and then stepped back against a stone wall. He took his hands from his pockets and struck a match on the wall. The man seemed to check momentarily in his stride at the sound.

"Bar-Zeev," whispered the Israeli. The noise of the women clamoring outside the perfume shop rose to a crescendo. The blind man stopped and turned to face him. There was a livid scar down the length of one cheek. Bar-Zeev shook out the match and flicked it at the man's eyes. Involuntarily, the man moved his head sideways. Bar-Zeev grabbed him by the arm, but the man twisted away and pulled a thin dagger from his galabia. The Israeli saw the flash of the blade and lunged forward, raising his arms to ward off the attack. The man swung the dagger upward and drove it in under Bar-Zeev's rib cage. With a groan the Israeli collided with his assailant, and his momentum threw them both to the ground. As they fell he brought up his knee sharply into his at-tacker's groin. The two men sprawled in the dust. Passersby detoured around them, staring in mild curiosity. The fall had dislodged the man's glasses; tears of pain trickled down from his empty eye socket.

"Filthy Jew," hissed al-Rahid as he doubled up in agony. Bar-Zeev gasped for breath, raising himself to his knees. His head began to swim as he pulled himself to his feet, clutching his wounded side with both hands. He began to stumble away, blood flowing out over his fingers. His instinct was to lose himself in the souk to evade his attacker, who was still writhing in pain on the dirt street.

Even as his consciousness began to ebb, Bar-Zeev experienced a certain clarity, as if his will for survival had summoned up new strength. The black specters of the people he passed were etched in light, and the nasal whine of the Arabic music seemed to emanate from inside his own head. As he ran he pulled out a handkerchief and pressed it against the wound. The golden trinkets in the shops winked mockingly at him as he hobbled by. He gulped for breath and felt a wave of nausea churning in his stomach. He stopped momentarily, leaning against a stone plinth at the entrance to an alleyway. Down the street he could see the gray-robed figure of his assailant running toward him, like an apparition. He turned blindly into the darkened alley, supporting himself with one hand on the walls. All the paraphernalia of the market seemed to loom up at him to impede his passage; camel-leather suitcases and beaten-brass trays, water pipes and woven wall hangings—all went cascading in his wake across the cobblestones as he crashed deeper into the alley. Shop owners ran shouting from their counters, blocking the path of the oncoming al-Rahid, who shouldered them aside in his single-minded pursuit of the Israeli.

Bar-Zeev reached the top of the alley, which ended in a T-junction. He hesitated, wondering which way to go. Behind him he could hear the slap of sandal leather on the worn stones as al-Rahid raced to catch him. He looked to left and right, desperate now as his strength oozed away with his blood. He felt dizzy, and his legs could hardly support him. He turned right and then left in an effort to lose his pursuer, plunging up a slight gradient past carpet-menders and beadmakers sitting at their hand-operated lathes. He wanted to cry out for help, but no sound came. He could no longer move in a straight line; he began to weave drunkenly, bouncing against walls and staggering to maintain his balance. He could hear the sound of running footsteps ringing down the alley behind him.

Bar-Zeev turned right again and found himself in a lane of small shops. In front of him a large stone arch framed an imposing mosque in the distance, its spindlelike minaret soaring into the graying sky. The amplified voice of the muezzin was calling the faithful to *salat-al-magrib,* the sunset prayers. If he could only make the sanctuary of the mosque, he could escape.

The lane opened out onto a small square, to the right of which was an open-air coffeehouse. Groups of men moved from its tables toward the mosque across the street. Bar-Zeev ducked in among them, bent over to conceal his bloodstained jacket. Along the outside wall of the mosque was a line of stalls where prayer beads, leather wallets, and copies of the Koran were being sold. He hid behind one of the stalls to see if his attacker was still giving chase. The black-bearded man in the gray galabia was standing in the middle of the square, peering around. Bar-Zeev crouched down and took off his shoes. His hands were sticky with blood, and he thought he was going to faint. He waited for a group of men to pass in front of him. When he was shielded from sight, he staggered around the corner and slipped through the open door of the mosque. The worshipers knelt in rows on the carpets, responding to the recitation in a low, rumbling sound. The Israeli sank to his knees and followed the actions of those around him. His wound had begun to bleed again, and he had to fight for breath.

The rhythm of the prayers rose and fell like soothing waves around him. In the dimly lit mosque he looked around for a means of escape. To his right was another door surmounted by a green neon sign in Arabic. If he could reach the door before he passed out . . . He caught sight of the gray-robed man standing behind a pillar, scrutinizing the lines of praying Muslims. Bar-Zeev turned his face away and prostrated himself on the carpet. It smelled of dust and the imprint of countless feet. Slowly he edged his way to his right. One thought pounded deliriously in his head: his survival depended on not disturbing the faithful at prayer. Superimposed on the features of those around him he saw images of war—charred bodies hanging out of tanks and lacerated hands bristling from the sand. When he had reached the line of pillars nearest the door, he pulled himself to his feet and looked back toward his assailant. For an instant their gaze locked, hunter and hunted, and the chase was resumed. With his remaining strength Bar-Zeev launched himself off the pillar and through the side door. Al-Rahid moved like a ghost around the periphery of the mosque, closing quickly on the stumbling figure of the Israeli as he tripped on the stairs and sank to the flagstoned square outside the mosque. Al-Rahid's hand slipped inside his robe as he flattened himself against the wall of the mosque for a final, catlike assault.

Suddenly, two pairs of hands grabbed the Israeli, and he felt himself being lifted and dragged. He dimly heard a voice shouting, "Get him! The one with the scar!" Bar-Zeev struggled, trying to break the grip of his captors, but he was too weak. He was carried to a car, where he was helped gently into the backseat. The door was closed, and he lost consciousness.

DAY SIX
THURSDAY, NOVEMBER 8

It wasn't a dream, because there was no movement; only a picture, frozen like one frame of a film. A large room, filled with people sitting in rows. In front, a table draped with the blue-and-white flag of Israel. In the center a soldier's helmet, holding a pot of roses, next to a single white candle in a silver candlestick. Also on the table, a red beret, a commando knife, a regimental badge, and a black-and-white photograph of a young man with a high forehead, looking straight at the camera, a half-smile on his lips. In front of the photograph, a pile of envelopes tied together with a blue ribbon.

A young girl lights the candle, and a boy plays a piece by Fauré on the flute—a haunting, wistful melody whose sweet, painful notes betray the communal loss—while the crickets sing outside the hall. The secretary rises and delivers the eulogy and asks the congregation to stand. He tells them how the boy died, fighting for his country. He speaks of the future, of the boy's contribution to their lives. He does not mention God, and there are no prayers. The mourners leave the hall; some of them are crying.

Uri Bar-Zeev had blocked the scene from his mind. The death of his son had been too painful to endure. Now, as he hovered on the cusp of consciousness, the memories of the heart played themselves back in his mind. His eyes were wet when he opened them to stare at the ceiling of his hotel room. He became aware of the wound in his left side. He ran tentative fingers over the bandage. He remembered the thrust of the knife and the black-bearded man pursuing him through the alleys of the souk. He raised himself painfully on his elbows. The faint bluish light of morning seeped in around the drawn curtains. In a chair by the window Ahmed Rahman sat sleeping, his large head resting on his chest, fingers locked across his stomach. Bar-Zeev could hear him breathing. He must have been there all night, Bar-Zeev thought as he reached for a glass of water on the side table. The movement caused Rahman to stir.

"You are awake, my friend," said Rahman, smiling at the Israeli. "How are you feeling?"

"I have felt better. What time is it?"

"Ten to six. Are you in pain?"

"Only when I breathe."

"Good. A man who has a sense of humor is indestructible. I am sorry, Uri. This should not have happened."

"It's my own fault. I forgot the first rule of our business: Never commit yourself unless you've got the advantage."

"I should never have let you go."

"It was my decision. There was nothing else to do."

"The doctor says that you were very lucky. A bit higher and you would have been a dead Zionist."

"Ah, the doctor is a politician, too."

Rahman stood up and rubbed his eyes. "If you had not shaken off our man, it would not have happened. He would have contacted my agents, who were waiting for you. I blame myself; I should have trusted you."

"It doesn't matter. Did you get him?"

"No. Unfortunately, he escaped. But we have a description."

"A man with one eye and a scar down his left cheek?"

"Yes. He is unknown to us, but we will find him. We are closing in, Uri. Whoever they are, they are frightened now. They are getting desperate."

"What does the doctor say?"

"It is merely a flesh wound. You have lost a lot of blood. You were given transfusions last night. Perhaps you shouldn't tell the Mossad that you now have three pints of Egyptian blood in your veins."

Bar-Zeev lay back on the pillow and laughed. "Maybe I'll be able to understand you better now, Ahmed."

"If only I had blanketed the area with our people," said Rahman.

"It would only have frightened him off. At least we are one step nearer them."

Rahman nodded. "Uri, I have to suggest that you return to Israel. You have done enough. We cannot allow you to risk your life further."

Bar-Zeev winced as he sat up. "I'm not leaving, Ahmed. I take my orders from the Mossad, and I haven't been relieved of this assignment."

"It would be a great embarrassment to my government if anything were to happen to you."

"I thought something *had* happened."

"If you were to be killed."

"The Mossad doesn't know about this, do they? You haven't told them?"

"No, unless one of their agents happened to be in the Street of Gold."

"Then there is no reason for them to know. Besides, why should you get all the glory?"

Rahman approached the bed and placed a large hand on Bar-Zeev's shoulder. "Rest, my friend. You have been under sedation. We will talk later. The doctor will be by to check you over. He says there's no reason for you to stay in bed, as long as you are careful about the stitches. He's a very good man. He's the president's personal physician."

"As long as he doesn't ask me to stay in bed," replied Bar-Zeev.

"Just rest until he comes. And you might reflect on the goodness of Allah. If you had not sought shelter in His house, we would not be talking now. May Allah continue to protect you, Uri."

≈≈≈

Under the umbrella of a giant fig tree at the end of his walled garden, Rashad Munir sat across from Saraj al-Rahid at an ornamental wrought-iron table. The ancient tree, four meters around at its base, hid the two men from the view of servants inside the house, and their conversation was lost in the hum of Cairo's morning traffic. Had any one of the six male servants seen the expression on their employer's face, they would have found any excuse to absent themselves from his presence. For the anger of Sheikh Munir was as ferocious as a desert storm, and as sudden.

"Escaped! Do my ears play tricks on me, Rahid? You say he escaped? You interrupt my breakfast to tell me you have failed?"

"It was not my fault. The Jew had many friends with him. They were everywhere. He moved faster than an old man should." Al-Rahid made extravagant gestures with his arms.

"Of course he did. He is disciplined. He has had a lifetime of training. You made the classic mistake, Rahid. You underestimated the enemy. Now he is twice as dangerous to us."

"He may be dead. The wound was deep. He lost much blood."

"Revolutions are not made on 'maybe' and 'perhaps.' Results are what matter. You have failed to eliminate Bar-Zeev; that is a fact."

"If I could not do it, no one could have done it," riposted the Libyan.

"Of course, of course, Rahid. You are death's own harbinger. Your reputation is well known," said Munir acidly. "But you have failed, and I am tired of excuses."

"He who carries the waterskin is the one who gets wet," muttered al-Rahid with a sneer.

"You are incredibly stupid. That you are alive today is a measure of the blessing of Allah for our mission, not for *your* ability to control events. We are all in His hands. Do not forget that."

Al-Rahid shivered like a whipped dog. His sense of his own manhood had been impugned by the neat little professor with hands like a woman's who sat opposite him; the intensity of those black eyes boring into him made him unsure of himself and acquiescent.

"It is clear we cannot undertake any more such adventures," said Munir finally. "Our attempt to rid ourselves of the Israeli was a calculated risk, and Allah willed it was not to be. Very well. We will imitate the action of the foxes of the desert. We shall go to ground. We must not be diverted from our main objective. Bar-Zeev has seen your face and will be able to identify you. Since you are not exactly of an unforgettable appearance, you are to stay out of sight until all is ready. You will return to the City of the Dead, and you will not leave its walls until it is time. You must tell your men nothing. If you or any one of them is captured, the police must not find the car-repair shop. Is that understood?"

"Yes, but Allah will deliver the Jew to me yet."

"You will concentrate on the business at hand, Rahid. Since the police know who you are, it is up to me to find out what the Mokhabarat know about us. As far as the plan is concerned, assume that everything proceeds on schedule unless you hear from me to the contrary. Have faith, Rahid, we will be rewarded in the end, when Allah crowns our enterprise with success."

≈≈≈

In his efforts to trace the movements of Juan Herrara within Egypt, Ahmed Rahman had the support of one of the most sophisticated and best organized intelligence networks in the Middle East. While not as efficient as the Mossad on an international level, Egypt's Mokhabarat was highly effective inside the boundaries of its own state. The systems had been set up by the British, who had instructed their Egyptian civil servants in the black arts of intelligence and, ironically, had become their first victims.

During the 1950s and 1960s the main target of Mokhabarat operations had been Israel. Agents inside the Jewish state had fed back a constant stream of seemingly irrelevant information, but the accretion of detail provided Egyptian analysts with a total picture of the vicissitudes of the enemy government, its relations with foreign states, development of new military hardware, troop movements, national morale, international fund-raising efforts, and the key friends of Israel abroad. No fact was too insignificant to be documented.

As radical forces in other Arab countries began to threaten the internal security of Egypt, its intelligence service began to pay more attention to the goings-on in the countries of technically "friendly" neighbors. The political situations in such states as Syria, Jordan, Saudi Arabia, Iraq, and Libya were minutely studied and constantly updated. But it was inside Egypt that the Mokhabarat enjoyed its greatest successes, especially in the field of counterinsurgency. Subversive elements, domestic and foreign, had found it increasingly difficult to carry out clandestine operations within the country for any length of time; sooner or later the organization would be infiltrated and exposed. The resulting show trials—a favorite ploy of the government—would be highly embarrassing for any foreign power that might be involved.

During Nasser's fourteen-year dictatorship, Egypt became a virtual police state, with systematic surveillance of its citizens. So absolute had the power of the Directorate of General Intelligence become after the crushing defeat by Israel in 1967 that critics dubbed Egypt "the Intelligence State," and the repressive measures instituted as a result of the war seriously proscribed individual liberty.

In 1970, when Anwar el-Sadat assumed the presidency, he ameliorated the situation by decreeing a return to the rule of law: arbitrary arrests were forbidden, and such hated detention centers as Turah Prison were closed down. Political prisoners were released, and censorship of the media and the arts relaxed. But Sadat did not dismantle the nation's security apparatus; in fact his government remained in power thanks to the loyalty of the intelligence service to which the president himself owed his life. His successor, Mahmoud Sayed, saw no reason to curb its power, either, as long as he could rely on its support.

Ahmed Rahman, therefore, had the help of vast network of operatives to join the manhunt as he and his department worked around the clock to link the South American to some person or group within Egypt. He had been at his desk since seven a.m. and it was now lunchtime.

"I've received a handwritten note from the president asking what progress we've made, Uri," Rahman said. "He will expect an answer."

"You can tell him that I am making a fine recovery in spite of the doctor," replied Bar-Zeev, fingering the heavy bandaging around his ribs.

Rahman sighed and took a bite of his sandwich. The doctor had telephoned him when Bar-Zeev had insisted on leaving his room. The prognosis was that while the wound was deep, the knife had not touched any vital organs. Rest and a minimum of movement were advised. But Bar-Zeev had insisted that the doctor strap him up so that he could get back to work.

The Israeli's motivation for refusing to rest went beyond his sense of duty. He had a personal score to settle with the one-eyed man who had come so close to ending his life on a dusty Cairo street. He would not forget the face of his assailant—the image of the empty eye socket and the jagged pink scar kept coming back to him during the long night when he alternated between delirium and wakefulness. He knew that he had been singled out as the target of a carefully planned murder attempt. The fact that his attacker had identified him suggested to Bar-Zeev that either there was a leak in Egyptian intelligence or a Mossad operative had turned double agent. The one-eyed man must be found, not only to establish the link with Herrara but to determine if Israeli intelligence in Cairo had been infiltrated.

"As far as the president is concerned, our problem is merely a handful of lentils," continued Rahman. "Lentils. It is an old Arab proverb. It relates to the story of a man who committed adultery in the fields during harvest time. He was pursued by the woman's husband. As he ran away, he grabbed a fistful of lentils. When the villagers saw the man being chased, they apprehended him. 'Why are you running away?' they asked him. He replied, 'Because I have stolen this handful of lentils!' They rounded on the outraged husband, condemning him for his lack of charity, that a man could not have a handful of lentils at harvest time. The husband protested: "But you don't know what he has done. You see only the lentils.' It is always so. People always underestimate another person's problems."

"You never cease to amaze me, Ahmed. Here we are, two days away from the presidential visit. We're no nearer to solving this thing. I've been stuck like a pig in an alley. And you tell me stories about lentils."

"Enough, Uri. We are doing everything we humanly can. All our operatives have been questioned about the South American. The *muhbir*, our paid informers up and down the country, have each been interviewed. Airport staff, barbers, taxi drivers, students, embassy maintenance staffs, bartenders, hotel maids, businessmen. The *murshid*, the collaborators, people in positions of trust. The *amil*, police agents who have infiltrated every political group in the country. They could be killed if the target organizations uncovered them. They have all been contacted systematically, one by one. Believe me, we have left no stone unturned."

"But how can a one-eyed man with a scar down the side of his face be completely unknown to either of us?"

"We have to assume that he hasn't been involved in any high-profile activities up to now. Perhaps they have been saving him for something like this," replied Rahman.

"But a man like that just doesn't come out of nowhere. There must be something on him either here or in Jerusalem. If only we had a name . . ."

"I asked the Americans about him this morning. They don't know anything, either."

"The Americans?"

"Yes, the Secret Service. They were here earlier. They accused me of not keeping them fully informed. They insist that there is a much more serious threat to President Dunlap than we are admitting."

"What did you say?"

Rahman shrugged. "I told them the proverb about the lentils. They did not understand it, naturally. What else could I tell them? That someone's going to throw an atomic bomb at the fortieth president of the United States?"

"It would only end up in their newspapers." Bar-Zeev moved his position in the chair very gingerly so as not to put pressure on his left side.

"One thing is clear. The attempt on your life suggests to me that we are closer than we imagined. They are trying to slow us up." He paused for a moment before continuing. "Perhaps we are too blinkered in our approach, Uri. We are thinking in terms of a terrorist group's somehow getting hold of an atomic device and using it—presumably, for purposes of blackmail. Once the presidents arrive in Cairo, or Alexandria, or Aswan, the terrorists announce they have a bomb and will blow up the city unless their demands are met. But maybe there is no nuclear device at all. Have you considered that? Maybe this is some kind of elaborate hoax, designed to trick us into believing that weapons-grade material has fallen into the hands of a terrorist organization, when in reality nothing of the kind has happened. Do you see the ploy? We have been psychologically conditioned to believe such a device exists, so when the demands are made, we cave in to them."

"Do you believe they'd sacrifice Herrara simply as a decoy?"

"Why not? They've shown no concern for lives in the past when vital interests have been at stake. Why should they be any different now?"

"I'd like to believe you're right, Ahmed, but caution dictates otherwise. Let me test one of my thoughts on you. Suppose, God forbid, a group of terrorists did have an atomic device of some kind and their objective was the assassination of the presidents. Why not make the Oasis Hotel the target? It's isolated, so casualties would be limited and the danger of fallout confined. They'd have an exact fix on Dunlap's whereabouts for several hours. And not only would they be disposing of the presidents, they'd be hitting at American capitalism."

Rahman considered the hypothesis for several minutes. "No," he said finally, "it is not practical. Short of a full-scale military assault, it would be impossible to get anywhere near the hotel. My men have it sealed off. All aircraft have been ordered to avoid the area. We will be maintaining constant radar surveillance. Only our helicopters will be there. Striking across the desert overland—that, too, would be impossible. We have a battalion of men in three cordons around the place: one at the oasis perimeter, another one kilometer out, and a third five kilometers out. Not even a lizard could get through, let alone a group of heavily armed terrorists carrying a large bomb."

"What about a full military strike from Libya, in support of an internal terrorist group?"

"The only planes Libya has capable of penetrating our air defenses are the MiG-twenty-fives. As you know, they're all piloted by Russians, who take their orders only from Moscow. They would not leave the ground unless the Soviets were fully briefed. I can't imagine the Kremlin's taking the risk of setting off a world war for the pleasure of blowing up an American president in the middle of the Western Desert. It makes no sense."

"So what did you tell the crew-cut brigade?"

"The Americans? Nothing. I stonewalled—I believe that's their expression. But I know they were not convinced."

"Which means we have to find the one-eyed man," said Bar-Zeev.

"Find him out there?" Rahman said, gesturing at the window. "There are nine million people in this city. If he chose, a man could hide in Cairo until the return of the Prophet."

≈≈≈

Even in the heat of the day the street markets of Cairo were thronged with shoppers, and Mustafa Habib had to jostle his way through the moving wall of bodies. The pressure of each step on his branded foot still afforded him a measure of discomfort, but he hardly noticed it now. His main concern was to try to slip away from the bullnecked Gabal Marwan, who had been ordered by al-Rahid to escort him to his room and wait while he packed some belongings into a knapsack. He needed only a few minutes alone, but Marwan doggedly obeyed orders and did not let the new recruit out of his sight.

"Down here," said Habib, pointing into an alleyway that ran off Shari Gohar el Qaid, through the center of the spice bazaar. The passage was so narrow a man could touch both walls with hands outstretched, and it was further constricted by brightly colored sacks of spices set along benches in front of the stalls. The air trapped between the buildings was heavy with the aroma of cloves, cinnamon sticks, cardamom, anise, and ginger—all blending together in an intoxicating alchemy of delight. Stray cats brushed against the hessian sacks, noses held high, twitching at the agglomeration of smells, while the merchants patted the powdered spices into breast-shaped fantasies. They called to the black-robed women who passed, balancing their baskets on their heads, moving in stately procession down the shaded alley. A sweating laborer, bent double under a fifty-kilo sack of cumin, shouted hoarsely for a way to be cleared, and people pressed against the walls to allow him to stagger by.

"There is a coffeehouse here," said Habib, turning to Marwan as they reached the end of the bazaar. "My room is just up the way. Why don't you sit and wait for me here. They may wonder who you are."

Gabal Marwan frowned and shook his head. "I will go with you. Al-Rahid said I must remain with you at all times."

"As you will."

Al-Rahid had returned to the mausoleum in the City of the Dead shortly after noon. He had inquired about Habib's foot, and then called Marwan to a corner of the courtyard, where they whispered together for some time. Habib had tried to engage Salah Kader in conversation, but the tall young man seemed reluctant to talk with the one-eyed Libyan close by.

After a while al-Rahid had come back, sat down next to Habib, and begun questioning him closely about his childhood and schooling. Eventually, he had asked, "Have you ever fired a gun?"

"Yes," replied Habib.

"You have hunted?"

"Yes. I also took training at the National Guard center near my village before entering Al-Azhar."

Al-Rahid had seemed pleased by his answer. Finally, he had motioned to Marwan to join them.

"I want you to go with Habib to his room. You are to be with him at all times, in case his foot weakens and he has trouble walking. Do you understand?"

The instructions had been clear: Habib was to advise the doorkeeper that he had been called home for several days owing to an illness in the family. He was to pack warm clothes, sufficient to fill a knapsack al-Rahid had supplied. He was not to talk to anyone, nor act in a manner that would arouse comment or suspicion. Should anyone inquire, he expected to return in a week. Marwan was to be introduced as a cousin from his village who had brought him the urgent message to return home.

"Here." They stopped in front of a brass shop that occupied the ground floor of a three-story building. The blue paint—to ward off the evil eye—was flaking away from the facade, revealing the soft stone underneath. "My room is on the top floor. The entrance is at the side." Habib led the way around the corner and into the dank entrance hall. A toothless man in a striped galabia sat on a rickety chair by the door, enjoying the sunshine. On his lap was a ginger cat that looked almost as old as his master. The doorkeeper raised his hand in greeting when he recognized Habib, and listened without interest as the student explained why he was going away.

"You haven't been in your room for two nights," the old man complained.

"I stayed with my friends in Imbaba. My cousin Hamid has come to take me back to my village."

Habib and Marwan climbed the crumbling stone stairs to the top of the building. The room was small and dingy, furnished only with a bed, a chair, and an old, worm-eaten wooden chest. One naked bulb was suspended from the middle of the ceiling, and as soon as he switched it on, Habib knew that someone had been searching through his belongings, probably on Munir's orders. Nothing had been disturbed, but he felt the lingering presence of a stranger in his room. While Marwan waited in the doorway, he knelt in front of the chest. He took articles of clothing from the drawer, folding them neatly into the knapsack, all the while desperately thinking of some means of gaining a few moments alone, away from the cold, indifferent stare of his escort.

"It is done." He shut the drawer and glanced around the room. "That is all I need. Let me go to relieve myself, and then we can start back. The toilet is down on the next floor."

A couple of minutes in the foul-smelling bathroom gave Habib the time he needed. He scribbled a quick note on a piece of paper and wrapped it in a twenty-five-piaster bill. Marwan was waiting outside the door when he flushed the toilet and came out.

"I must give the old man baksheesh," Habib said as they walked down to the entrance hall. "He will expect it, or he won't look after my room while I'm away." At the door, he stuffed the folded money into the arthritic hand of the old man.

"May Allah be with you," the doorkeeper said, nodding.

"And with you." Without looking back, Habib guided Marwan into the street again. As they walked purposefully back up the alley of spices, it occurred to Habib that he didn't know whether the old man could read or not, let alone whether he would rouse himself sufficiently to get the note to Habib's immediate superior in the Mokhabarat.

≅≅≅

The object of the Mokhabarat's current concern, Saraj al-Rahid, had once more gone to ground in the City of the Dead. Mindful that the security services would be combing Cairo to find him, he posted Salah Kader outside the gate and told the children who played soccer in the street to warn of any stranger coming into the area. Alone in the mausoleum, he took the leather pouch from under his galabia. The legend that it contained a man's genitals was well known to him; in fact, he had encouraged the fiction and allowed it to grow and become embroidered in the telling. Such stories suited his purposes, since they inspired fear and respect in the minds of men. Nor had he lost his eye in a knife fight; that, too, was a canard he did nothing to dispel.

What the pouch actually contained was waterproof military maps relating to the coming operation. There were several large-scale charts, only one of which related to the target area—in the event he should be captured and the pouch seized by the police. None of them bore markings; al-Rahid had committed the coordinates to memory. In addition, there was a copy of the Islamic calendar with different figures circled in pencil; the significance of these numbers would not be apparent to the uninformed reader—they were not dates but encoded times for the various stages of the operation. The information on paper and in his head was all Saraj al-Rahid needed to carry out the plan.

Trained in guerrilla warfare as a noncommissioned officer in the Libyan army, he was familiar with the strategy and tactics of terrorist missions. He had so impressed his superiors with his ability to plan and execute clandestine operations behind enemy lines that he had been sent to Lebanon to act as liaison with the PLO in their strikes across the border into Israel. His real identity had never been known to the PLO command, a precaution the Libyans had taken to protect a valued operative. They knew that the Mossad had files on all activists and their advisers. In fact, the Mossad *did* have a file on al-Rahid, but it was under the name of Sami Gabr and the documentation made no reference to his having lost an eye.

While the romantic legend of how al-Rahid lost his eye might strike terror into his enemies and inspire awe among his comrades, the actual circumstances were more prosaic. After several brutally successful missions against Israeli targets, the Libyan had been ordered back to Benghazi to help set up what might be called a postgraduate school for terrorists. His students included members of the IRA, Italy's Red Brigades, the Japanese Red Army, and activists from various Latin American cells. It was at this secret camp that al-Rahid had met Juan Herrara.

Saraj al-Rahid held that the best way to prepare his students for action was to throw them immediately into combat conditions—a philosophy endorsed by those in command. The training in the camp was designed to prepare commandos for the toughest assignments. If they cracked during the exercises, they were summarily expelled; out in the field they would have died. So secret was this proving ground for fanatics that it had not been given a name, and it was said that those who survived its three-month course were equipped to do battle with the Devil himself.

Al-Rahid insisted on using live ammunition and explosives beginning with a recruit's first day of training. "You cannot teach a man to
keep his head down until he sincerely believes someone is about to blow
it off," he told his superior. Over the months, two men and a girl had
died from wounds sustained during maneuvers—a small price to pay, in
al-Rahid's mind, to battle-harden the rest against the chance of panick-
ing when exposed to the real threat of death.

The accident that robbed the Libyan of his eye had occurred on the
grenade range. Al-Rahid was giving instruction to a group of newcomers
on the handling of grenades. On his order to remove the firing pin, count
to three, and hurl the weapon with a straight-arm motion, one young
Palestinian suddenly froze with fear. Al-Rahid shouted to the others to
hit the ground while he lunged for the paralyzed boy in an attempt to
grab the grenade and throw it safely down the range. Just as he reached
the recruit, it exploded, killing the youth instantly. A piece of shrapnel
tore out al-Rahid's eye and opened up the left side of his face. He spent
the next two months in a darkened hospital room, fretting about the end
of his military career.

When they took the bandages off and he saw himself in the mirror
for the first time, he looked away in disgust. But when he noticed that
others did the same, he took a perverse pleasure in his appearance. He
refused to cover his empty eye socket with the patch the doctors offered
him. "Let my face be a map for those to follow on the road to liberty,"
he said contemptuously to the nurses who tried to persuade him to wear
it. He hated them for the way they averted their faces from him when
he passed in the corridor, and he sneered at his fellow patients who
could not look at his disfigurement without words of pity.

During his hospitalization he began to boast of his past successes,
like a general explaining his medals. Again and again he recounted his
part in the planning and execution of the Ma'alot massacre on May 15,
1974, when he sent a three-man team into Israel to hold twenty teen-
agers hostage for the release of fedayeen prisoners. All twenty children
were killed when Golda Meir refused to trade. Two years earlier al-
Rahid had supplied the submachine guns to the three Japanese who
opened fire on passengers at Lod Airport, killing twenty-six. He reveled
in these triumphs, and the more he brooded over the fact that his military
days were over, the more he trumpeted his past exploits.

But senior officers in the Libyan army had not forgotten him; they remembered his ruthless daring, his pathological need to see his orders carried out at whatever cost to himself or those around him. And when a request had come from President Jalil's office for a man to undertake an important mission inside Egypt—a man without any official government or military connection that could embarrass Libya if he were caught—they thought of Saraj al-Rahid, the former instructor who knew seventeen ways to kill a man with his bare hands.

When he was called in and offered the assignment, al-Rahid showed no emotion—only women showed emotion. But inwardly he swelled with pride. In spite of his deformity he could still serve a useful purpose. He would be in the army again, although without a uniform.

After a full briefing he had been smuggled into Egypt. There he made his way to Cairo, where he established contact with Professor Rashad Munir, his new commander. He had joined Wind of the Desert, enduring the initiation test with disdainful ease. When he had gained Munir's confidence, the professor had outlined the plan to him.

"From a military standpoint it cannot work," al-Rahid had said, shaking his head. "It is too big."

"It will work," Munir had replied, focusing his eyes on al-Rahid's empty socket like a challenge. "You are under my orders to make it work."

As the Libyan began to organize the logistics, based on the meticulous planning of Munir, he slowly began to believe it could work. Now, with the strike only a few days away, not even the Libyan army could convince him that it would not succeed. The death of Herrara and the need to recruit a newcomer at the eleventh hour had been a setback. But despite the young student's lack of training, al-Rahid believed Habib would be able to carry out his part of the operation. The student was the weak link, and al-Rahid recognized the need to watch him carefully.

He returned to the maps, smiling to himself as he recalled the global outcry against the Ma'alot operation. What would they say when Saraj al-Rahid, a man with only one eye, shook the entire world?

≈≈≈

That night, when Muhammad Ibrahim Helmy Street fell silent and work in the auto body shops had stopped, Professor Rashad Munir threaded his Peugeot through the skeletons of stripped cars in the darkened alley. When he was certain there was no one around, he entered the garage of Abdul Samy. Nothing appeared to have changed since his last visit four nights before—a good sign. His main preoccupation had been that the police might stumble onto the concealed laboratory before they were ready to move.

The guard, Jabir, was at his usual post at the entrance to the lab, although he seemed less relaxed tonight than he had been previously. It was as if the imminence of the operation had heightened the tension; a charged atmosphere pervaded the place, infecting everyone involved. The young man rose at the sound of the door, pistol in hand.

"It is I, Rashad Munir. All is well?"

"All is well, Sheikh. I will be glad to start."

"Soon, soon, Jabir. Open up, please."

Inside, the laboratory was quiet; gone was the sound of welding and the rasp of file on metal. Only the gray-bearded Dr. Nasif presided over the brightly lit room. He greeted Munir with a mixture of pride and obsequiousness.

"A thousand welcomes, Professor. May Allah give you peace."

"And to you, Dr. Nasif. You have good news for me, I trust?"

"I am happy to report that my work is complete, as you have ordered." The scientist rubbed his palms together in sycophantic expectation of approval.

"Let me see it."

Dr. Nasif waddled toward the workroom, smiling back at Munir with the air of a minor functionary leading a guest to a royal audience. He opened the door and stood back. In the center of the workroom, suspended by chains from a wooden cradle, was a large steel egg. Its curved surface had been sanded down to a dull matte finish to inhibit reflection, and it had been painted black. Several eyelets had been welded into the casing, top and bottom.

"Is it not beautiful?" murmured Nasif, like a father displaying a newborn son.

"Is it large enough?" asked Munir. The device was about two meters long and over a meter at its widest point.

Nasif let out a chuckle that gurgled in his throat. "A bomb this size will have the power of hundreds of tons of conventional explosives. It is not the size that counts. The amount of matter that was transformed into energy in the Hiroshima bomb weighed no more than a twenty-five-piaster coin."

"I am a man of God, Doctor. I know nothing of such matters. Explain to me simply, if you will, how it works."

"Ah, it is simplicity itself. The laws of physics are as beautiful as the words of the Koran."

"Indeed."

"In the core," began Dr. Nasif, tapping the metallic shell, "is a quantity of plutonium two-thirty-nine held in a beryllium casing the size of a large grapefruit, as I explained to you on your last visit. That core is surrounded with plastic explosive packed into a steel casing. All this is held by the outer shell. By detonating the explosive we compress the plutonium to a critical mass, which sets off the chain reaction. The whole process takes about one hundred millionth of a second from the moment of detonation."

"How is it detonated?"

"If you run your fingers over the outside casing, you will feel this seam here. Inside is a chamber. When the device is in position, this chamber will be opened and a timer will be inserted. It's in the other room. I will show it to you presently. The timer will be set to detonate the bomb at the precise moment you choose. The timer is wired to a miniature radio receiver tuned to the frequency you requested. A coded signal sent on that frequency will activate the timer immediately. In the same way, a differently coded signal will break the circuit and stop the timer, thus deactivating the bomb. I have made a note of the codes for you. I have also committed them to memory."

"You are certain the men will have no difficulty inserting the timer? Should it not be done now?"

"To do so would give us a live bomb. An accidental jolt could set it off. It is less dangerous this way."

"I understand. Is it safe to move now?"

"Perfectly. Because we had to hurry I was concerned we might produce an unstable device. We had little time to test the materials fully. But I'm convinced that we have overcome the problems. Your men should be able to transport it without fear."

"Should is not good enough, Doctor."

Nasif shrugged his shoulders and gestured apologetically to the makeshift laboratory. "These are hardly ideal conditions, Professor. One needs resources to manufacture a sophisticated weapon of this type. But my daughter and I have remained with it. Can we have more faith than that?"

"I put my trust in Allah, Dr. Nasif, not in the handiwork of man. Still, you have done a fine job. You understand what happens now?"

"Yes. The device will be crated later tonight. The other explosives are ready. Everything will be kept here under guard until tomorrow night, when all will be transported to the site. My daughter and I will also leave tomorrow night on our own, as you instructed."

"Good. You will be met at the airport on your arrival. I owe you my thanks, Doctor. The work you have done here may prove to be a turning point in the history of our country, Allah willing."

DAY SEVEN
FRIDAY, NOVEMBER 9

Ahmed Rahman buttoned his jacket against the cold morning air. An hour before sunup he had risen from his bed, abandoning all hope of sleep. Whenever he closed his eyes, the same images kept drumming against his lids: Bar-Zeev wounded, the Alexandrian fishermen sweating and shaking, the teasingly unformed features of a one-eyed man with a black beard. Rahman hunched his shoulders as he leaned over the stone parapet, gazing down on the inky Nile below him. The moonlight fractured on its swirling surface, splintering into thousands of dancing points of light. He had hoped that by walking the streets of Cairo he might draw some inspiration that would illuminate a mystery as opaque and unfathomable as the waters below him.

Rarely had Rahman been so frustrated. The president of the United States would be arriving at Cairo Airport at ten a.m. the following morning. Rahman's instinct, supported by every detail of evidence, told him that somewhere in the city were forces plotting an attempt on Dunlap's life. Yet with all the resources at his command he had been unable to do more than confirm his earliest suspicion that the threat was genuine. He recalled a village proverb: A small amount of luck is better than a lot of hard work. He had never subscribed to it before, but now he would gladly have traded the hundreds of man-hours put in by the Mokhabarat for just one tiny piece of luck that would unlock the door.

It had been less than a week since Juan Herrara's body had been pulled from the Nile, and yet he was reduced to waiting for a stroke of luck or for the conspirators, whoever they were, to make another move. The attack on Bar-Zeev had shown them to be well organized and well informed; the presence of the Israeli in Cairo was supposedly known only to the president, the minister of the interior, and Rahman's own immediate staff. Yet somehow the secret had leaked out and the result could have been calamitous for Egyptian-Israeli relations.

The damp morning air caused his arm to throb. He glanced up at the sky; the sun would be rising in about half an hour. He turned and began to walk slowly along the embankment. The street seemed strangely deserted, and for a moment he couldn't understand why. Then he realized: the sheep, they had all disappeared. It was Friday, the first day of *eid-il-adha,* "the Big Feast." Today the last of the red-marked sheep would be butchered to grace the tables of Muslims throughout the country.

Eid-il-adha. In his childhood the name had a magic ring; all year it was awaited with eager anticipation. His father had killed the sheep himself—a ceremony performed in the field beside the house after morning prayers. Every year when he was a boy, Rahman had listened to his father recount the story of Abraham and Isaac as he stroked the sacrificial sheep: how Allah had stayed the patriarch's hand at the last moment and provided a sheep for slaughter instead of his son. Rahman's father told the story in the same words every year, and although the boy knew it by heart, he was still moved by the drama of the telling.

His father would then dispatch the sheep with a quick, merciful thrust. Dipping his hand into the blood, he would lead his children to the front door of their home, where he made the sign showing to all that the Rahman family had kept the ritual. Tradition prescribed that one third of the beast be eaten by the family. The rest was to be distributed among the poor. Rahman remembered carrying portions of meat on a plaited reed tray for the beggars who congregated in the village square. While he was away, his father would dress the remaining carcass and prepare it for the midday meal, when the family would eat together, dipping *battawi* bread into the rich, meaty juices.

Rahman's mouth watered as he remembered the scene. After the meal, friends and relatives would come to the house to exchange greetings with his parents. Occasionally, after a bumper harvest, his father would distribute a few copper coins among the children, which they were allowed to spend on candy or rides at the small fair that visited the nearby town every year at feast time. A time of innocence, a time of uncomplicated pleasures. Why had he ever left the village?

Bars of pink began to cut across the gray of the sky, and a purplish haze hung over the river. Soon the muezzins would begin their call to morning prayers and a battery of cannons would fire a salvo to welcome in the feast day.

Rahman continued walking. He passed an old man squatting on the sidewalk under a tarpaulin. Next to him was a pot of boiling fat on a primus stove. Between his legs he held a battered tin pan filled with a paste of crushed fava beans, parsley, and spices. With great care the old man was molding the paste into walnut-sized patties, which he dropped into the boiling oil. He turned them over with a metal spoon, and when they were fried to a crisp on the outside, he took them out and stacked them in a small pyramid on a tin plate. The *tameya* would be sold to the men and boys emerging from the mosque after prayers. Rahman greeted the old man and received a smile and a salute in return.

At an intersection he glanced down one of the side streets running west from the Nile and saw a police car stopped in front of an apartment block, its blue light still flashing. A small knot of people had gathered outside. His curiosity aroused, he walked over to see what was happening. One of the police officers was making notes for a report in the car. The other, he assumed, was still inside the building.

"What's the matter?"

"Official business," replied the officer, not looking up. "Move along, please."

Amused, Rahman reached into his jacket for his identification card and held it out for the policeman to read. The officer quickly opened the door and stood to attention in front of him.

"My apologies, Colonel Rahman. I had no way of knowing."

"That's all right. Now, what's going on?"

"Night visitors, sir."

"Here?" The apartment house was only a few blocks from Rahman's own building.

"Yes, sir, I'm afraid so. An old woman was badly beaten. She's unconscious. We've called for an ambulance."

Rahman shook his head. The night visitors were becoming an increasingly serious problem in Cairo. The city's acute housing shortage had created a lucrative racket for gangs of thugs who terrorized defenseless tenants into signing over their leases. Desirable apartments in such fashionable areas as Dokki, Zamalek, and Garden City had become prime objectives, since a long-term lease was a valuable asset. A tenant prepared to surrender a lease might be able to command as much as twenty-five thousand pounds for it. Key money of this magnitude had attracted the attention of the Cairo underworld, and the night visitors were spawned.

Their methods were simple and brutal. Desirable properties would be watched to see which were occupied by vulnerable tenants—old women living alone were favorite targets. Then, late at night, there would be a knock at the door. When it was opened, several men would force their way in. The occupants would be threatened with physical violence unless they signed a legal document surrendering their lease in favor of a new tenant. Those who were too weak and too frightened to resist stood and watched while their furniture was carried out and dumped in the street. Those who fought back were beaten and often murdered. The next day, the lease would be sold, often through a cooperating lawyer, to a client willing to pay the exorbitant key money demanded. The police had tried on numerous occasions to put an end to the racket, but without success; as soon as they broke up one gang, another took its place.

The ambulance whined its way down the street and drew up behind the police car. Two stretcher-bearers hurried inside the building. A few moments later they emerged, carrying a woman whose gray hair was matted with blood.

"Animals," muttered Rahman. He turned to the policeman. "Who is the victim?"

"Her name is Amina Kader, aged fifty-eight. Lives with her son."

"Where is he?"

"The doorkeeper says he hasn't been around for some months."

"Anyone else who can look after her? A sister? A cousin?"

"All we know is the son. His name is Salah."

"I suggest you find him, then, and notify him of his mother's condition."

"Yes, sir."

Rahman watched the stretcher-bearers carry the old woman into the ambulance. When the presidential visit was over, he would concentrate on this growing cancer in Cairo.

The sun was up over the hills now. He decided there was nothing to be gained from wandering the streets, so he headed back to his own building, where the faithful Ismail Ali was waiting for him with the Mercedes.

"Well, Ismail, have you any news that will brighten the feast day for me?"

"We have questioned several one-eyed men, sir. Most of them are beggars. Some totally blind. We are no further ahead, I'm afraid." He handed Rahman an envelope. "From the president's office, sir. I was asked to hand it to you personally."

"Ah, yes." Rahman sighed. "I was wondering when I would be hearing from him again." He ran his finger along the flap to see if it had been opened since it was originally sealed. Then he held it up to the sun before tearing the envelope along one edge.

"As I thought," he said, folding the letter. "He wants to see me at nine o'clock this morning. Wait for me, Ismail, while I shave and change my shirt."

≈ ≈ ≈

The boom of the cannons heralding the start of *eid-il-adha* woke Uri Bar-Zeev from his sleep. A battery of howitzers loosed off a series of blank shells over the Nile, and the report echoed around the city, rattling windows in their frames. The last time he had awoken to the sound of a cannonade was Yom Kippur 1973, and now he went into a cold sweat that made his body prickle. He jumped out of bed and opened the window, trying to locate the guns. In the distance across the river, he could see a flash followed by a puff of smoke, and six seconds later he could hear the explosion. All of this in the name of God, he thought.

Bar-Zeev's mood had not been improved by being jolted from a shallow sleep by the guns of Bairam. Like Ahmed Rahman, he had spent the night wrestling with the fragments of a puzzle that refused to fit. They had everything in place except the one key piece that would lock it all together. They knew about the terrorist group they sought, the Libyan connection, the radioactive material, how it got into the country, even the face of the man presumed to be a leading member of the organization. And yet they did not know what was planned.

He picked up the phone and ordered breakfast in his room. As he sat on the balcony waiting for it, he began to reassess the known information. What if this had happened in Jerusalem? he asked himself. What would the Mossad have done? But then Jerusalem was not Cairo; it was only a tenth of the Egyptian capital's size, and so it was easier to monitor unusual movements there. Cairo was overwhelming. He wondered how Rahman managed to operate as efficiently as he did under the circumstances.

The sun had climbed to the height of the Cairo Tower, and to his left Bar-Zeev could make out the outline of the pyramids in the hazy distance. The Corniche road below his balcony, usually choked with honking cars, was relatively quiet, and several people were already out, strolling along the embankment in their best clothes, enjoying their day off from work. Out on the river, a number of feluccas were under sail, lazily floating downriver on the current, carrying families to picnic grounds outside the city. Friday, the Muslim Sabbath. Also the start of one of the most sacred of Muslim feasts, Rahman had told him. All government offices and most businesses and shops observed the holiday and would be closed for the next four days.

His strapped-up wound still pained him, and he shifted to a more comfortable position. In spite of the discomfort, it was healing well, and if at times he felt a little weak, he had to remind himself that at fifty-six he could be expected to be short-winded under the circumstances.

The guns had started again. They brought his mind back to 1973 and the Egyptian barrage along the entire length of the Suez Canal, the largest concentration of firepower since El Alamein. He could not let go of the obsessive memory: the surprise attack by the Egyptians on Yom Kippur, the holiest day in the Judaic calendar. It was that war, more than those before it or the terrorist atrocities since, that had turned Bar-Zeev irrevocably against the Arabs and led him to his uncompromising stand against the peace settlement.

But for the first time since leaving government service he was beginning to doubt his own principles. While he could see the dangers, his few days in Cairo—the enemy capital—had given him a new perspective on the problems of the Middle East. He acknowledged that the groundswell of a fundamentalist Muslim movement in Egypt would result in a new wave of anti-Semitism. Yet he could not see the experience of Iran being repeated in Egypt. The Egyptians, as Rahman had explained, were a different people. Western ideas were too much a part of the nation's psyche to be changed in a generation. The new Egypt was pragmatic, adventurous, and its leaders saw beyond the Levantine rim for the first time in history.

Bar-Zeev understood now why it was crucial for Israel to bolster and buttress the incumbent Egyptian government, and why he had been sent to Cairo against his will, in compliance with President Sayed's request. Israel's interests demanded a strong pro-Western government in Cairo. At the stroke of a pen the Jewish state had broken out of its encirclement; by declaring peace it had neutralized its strongest antagonist. Now, Bar-Zeev told himself, the destinies of Egypt and Israel are forged together. If there is a God, perhaps He understands the paradox: the country that invaded us as soon as our statehood was ratified by the United Nations, the nation whose leaders threatened to drive us into the sea, that sent the fedayeen to murder our children and massed tanks and planes against us in 1967, is now our friend. They could not negotiate with us until they had won a partial victory in 1973 to restore their self-respect, and now they are our trading partner, the recipient of our technological and economic know-how, and our ally against those who would still destroy us.

Bar-Zeev was cynical enough to appreciate the current political realities. He understood his own role in the scheme of things: it was essential that the presidential visit proceed without incident. The event was no mere diplomatic circus; the aid agreement that was to be signed would ensure that Egypt remained squarely in the American camp.

He looked at his watch; it was nine o'clock. In twenty-five hours' time, President Dunlap would be touching down at Cairo Airport.

There was a knock at the door. "Your breakfast, sir."

Bar-Zeev did not open up. "Just leave it outside. I'll get it in a moment." He waited for the sound of footsteps to die away down the corridor before turning the key in the lock.

≈≈≈

While Egypt rejoiced in the heady holiday atmosphere, in the presidential villa it was business as usual. Mahmoud Sayed sat at his desk, wearily reading through the terms of the agreement he would sign with President Dunlap on Monday. The burdens of statesmen were heavy; he would have liked to be in his summer house with his wife and his dog, enjoying the feast day along with the people. His face in repose belied the myriad posters that bedecked the city portraying a handsome, smiling leader, eyes full of warmth and understanding. Hours of briefings and mounds of official documents had left him tired and short-tempered.

When Ahmed Rahman knocked on the door, he was greeted by a curt "Come in," and there was none of the bonhomie that usually accompanied his weekly visits.

"Well, Ahmed? Have you dealt satisfactorily with the matter of the radioactive body?"

Rahman shifted uncomfortably. The strain was showing on his face; lack of sleep had etched deep, dark circles under his eyes. "We have made considerable progress, Excellency. I am happy to report that we may well have results by this afternoon. But I would be failing in my duty if I did not tell you that the danger continues to exist."

"First you tell me you will have results, and then you tell me the danger still exists. What am I to believe?" snapped the president. "We lost one war because we could not be honest with ourselves."

Rahman briefed Sayed, telling the president what he thought he ought to hear. The Egyptian leader sat listening to his explanations without a word. When Rahman had finished, he said, "You have given me the facts. Now I would like to hear your recommendations."

"I believe we can handle the situation, Excellency. However, I cannot give you a hundred percent guarantee."

"You are equivocating, Rahman." The president drummed his fingertips impatiently on the desktop.

"Excellency, I cannot but advise that the visit be postponed."

"That is impossible. I do not want even to entertain such a suggestion. Dunlap takes off in *Air Force One* in just over twelve hours. I will do nothing to prevent that from happening. Do you understand?"

"Yes, Excellency."

"Good. Now, it is up to you to work from that premise. What do you propose?"

"Under the circumstances I can only suggest we mount the tightest security screen we have ever used. But to do it, I must have your full co-operation, sir."

"First I would like to hear your plans in more detail, Ahmed."

The presidential tone had become less frosty, and Rahman sensed that Sayed had expected him to suggest postponing the visit and that his demeanor at the start of the interview reflected his annoyance before the fact. It occurred to him that the president no doubt had his own eyes and ears inside the Mokhabarat and probably knew exactly how the investigation was proceeding.

"Excellency, if any conventional means of assassination are attempted, I am convinced that we can counter them. Our American colleagues have gone over our initial plans in detail. They have offered us some useful suggestions, which we have incorporated. They complimented us on our thoroughness and appeared most impressed."

"The only compliments you need worry about are mine, Ahmed. It seems we are not dealing with conventional people here."

"We have taken every contingency into consideration in our planning. However, there are certain things that go beyond the realm of reason. If what these terrorists are preparing is an atomic device of some kind, we have no experience in dealing with a nuclear holocaust. But I don't believe they would be insane enough to plant such a bomb in Cairo."

"Perhaps our terrorist friends are taking a leaf out of the superpowers' book. One does not necessarily have to explode a nuclear weapon to inspire fear and respect among those who do not have such weapons," reflected Sayed.

"Our investigations have proved that sufficient uranium was brought into Egypt to make an atomic bomb. I can only act on the assumption that those who made it are not bluffing, Excellency. Even if it is only a blackmail attempt, we must assume that they will be ready to explode the device if their conditions are not met. At this point I can only believe that President Dunlap and yourself may well be the targets."

"If that is the case, then your job is much simpler. Instead of protecting the whole of Cairo, you need only worry about the two of us," said Sayed with a smile.

"All our efforts will be concentrated on making it impossible for anyone to get near you. A device of this kind would be quite large. A man could not conceal it under his coat. It presumably would have to be transported to a detonation point. And it would have to be set off when you were in the vicinity. So, Excellency, there is one way to neutralize the threat. Drastic, but necessary," said Rahman, pausing for dramatic effect.

"Well, Ahmed, don't expect me to guess."

"You must prohibit all vehicular traffic in Cairo for six hours prior to the American president's arrival and the ban must remain in force until you both have left the city. The same must be done in Alexandria and in Aswan. If nothing can move in the streets, the terrorists cannot deliver their bomb."

Sayed's eyebrow rose in a circumflex of disbelief. "My dear Ahmed, do you know what you're asking?"

"It is the only way, Excellency."

"But it's impossible. Our police cannot even control the traffic, let alone stop everything from moving."

"The army could be brought in. The broadcasts could begin immediately—on radio and television. No cars, trucks, wagons, carts—nothing must be on the streets after four a.m. tomorrow. Any parked vehicles to be towed away. Only police and military transport to be allowed on the roads."

"No, I cannot permit it. It's feast time. We cannot make prisoners of the people."

"I know it couldn't be enforced completely, but such an edict would keep all vehicles away from areas where the president and yourself will be visiting. We will have the manpower to search anyone who does venture onto the roads. Anyone trying to haul a bomb into the city could not escape such a dragnet."

"Why do you assume the bomb—if it exists, and I find that difficult to believe—why do you assume it will have to be moved? It may be lying in a cellar somewhere in the city, waiting to be detonated."

"You're correct, of course, Excellency. If the situation you describe is in fact the case, then the measures I am proposing will be of no use. But if there is a bomb, and if it does have to be moved from one point to another, my plan will make the task of the terrorists infinitely more difficult."

"Ahmed, I must tell you frankly that I cannot believe I am hearing this. The prospect of an atomic bomb in the hands of some demented terrorists is simply too frightening to contemplate. I know, I know. The evidence suggests we cannot be too careful. And if I hadn't been concerned, I would not have asked Jerusalem for Bar-Zeev. But to halt all traffic in the city because of such a farfetched possibility, with no firm proof—I cannot."

"Excellency, with the greatest respect, you must. It may be a useless gesture, that's true. On the other hand, it could be extremely important in thwarting whatever plans are being laid."

"And how will I explain the absence of cars on the road to President Dunlap?"

"With respect, sir, you can tell him it's a security measure to allow unimpeded passage through the city during his stay. He's probably been briefed about Cairo traffic. It's in all the guidebooks, after all. If you have to, tell him the truth. We are merely being prepared."

"It will cut down on the number of our people who will line the route for our motorcade," mused Sayed, doodling on a pad in front of him.

"Don't forget, sir, it is Bairam. The normal traffic flow will be smaller than usual. And we are only talking about fourteen hours or so. You and President Dunlap will be leaving for the Oasis Hotel late tomorrow afternoon."

"And you think it will work?"

"At least we will be in control, Excellency."

"All right, Ahmed." Sayed's voice was weary and resigned. "The people are to be told that cars will be banned from the streets in order for everyone to have a chance to see the motorcade. There will be no traffic jams anywhere near the route."

"Exactly, sir."

"Do what must be done, Ahmed. And if you turn up anything new, I am to be informed immediately." Sayed picked up the sheaf of papers in front of him and began to study them as if Rahman had already left the room. The intelligence chief nodded and began to move toward the door.

"Oh, by the way, Ahmed," the president called after him, "the Israeli, I understand he was attacked."

"Yes, Excellency, I regret to say."

"He is a guest in our country. You would be derelict in your duty should anything happen to him."

"It was a minor matter, Excellency. A mere flesh wound. He is a strong man."

"I need hardly remind you that his safety is almost as important to us as President Dunlap's. The diplomatic consequences of this incident might have been very grave. Has he been of assistance to you?"

It would have been simple for Ahmed Rahman to admit that Bar-Zeev had contributed much to the store of knowledge the Mokhabarat had amassed on the case. But to do so would have meant acknowledging a weakness in his own operation. Therefore, he murmured, "Our exchange of information has been mutually beneficial."

"Hmmm. Perhaps I should be grooming you for a diplomatic post, Ahmed. Maybe when this is all over . . ." President Sayed returned to his papers and did not look up again until Rahman had closed the door behind him.

≋≋≋

Tradition dictates that on the mornings of feast days Egyptian families pay homage at the tombs of their departed relatives. So it is that the nation's great celebrations begin in sadness, with the ritual wail of mourning rising from crowded cemeteries throughout the country as the living honor the dead.

The women arrive at the graveyards first, bringing sweets and fruit to distribute among the children and beggars who crowd outside the gates. The men offer prayers at the mosque, making their pilgrimage to the resting place of their ancestors at the end of the morning service. Some families invite a *qari* to recite the Fatiha, the opening verse from the Koran, at the tomb, in consideration of which the holy man receives gifts of food and a token payment of money.

Feast days are times of sadness and joy. The children wear their holiday best—bright primary colors that contrast with the somber stones and burial mounds. They run about the streets, laughing and shouting, collecting food and candy, while their elders exchange greetings with friends and relatives. The families linger among the tombs until the hour of the midday meal, when they return home.

On such occasions the population of the City of the Dead swells to the millions. Families swarm through the rubble-strewn streets from first light, and the ancient necropolis becomes very much a city of the living, vibrant with color and echoing with the wails of women and the shouts of the young. In midafternoon, when the crowds have gone, silence falls once more over the maze of tombs, and the wind blows sand over the debris the visitors have left behind.

For Saraj al-Rahid and the three disciples of Wind of the Desert, the sudden incursion of mourners into the City of the Dead was at once a problem and a welcome distraction. It meant that they had to leave their tomb for several hours—al-Rahid did not think it wise to remain there while the family who owned it was present. Temporarily evicted, they wandered the streets in relative safety, lost in the throngs of people. The Libyan took no chances, however. Knowing the police had his description and would be patrolling the necropolis, he had sacrificed his distinctive beard and donned a galabia with hood to hide the scar on his face. The empty eye socket was concealed behind a pair of dark glasses.

As soon as the women and children began to arrive from Cairo, he ordered Habib, Marwan, and Kader to mingle with the people in the streets. They were to move in pairs; he would accompany Mustafa Habib, the new recruit. Although there were no incidents as they roamed through the City of the Dead, the Libyan was relieved when the crowds of families returned home and the four conspirators were able to conceal themselves once more in the sanctuary of their tomb.

"What happens now?" asked Habib as they sat cross-legged in the cool sand of the vault, silent but for the droning of the flies that buzzed around their heads.

"We wait. Patience is the best ally of the warrior. Patience demolishes mountains," replied al-Rahid. The Libyan noted the young student's anxiety, which he ascribed to the impetuosity of his years. But Habib's thoughts were concentrated on the old doorkeeper; he wondered if his message had been delivered to the Mokhabarat.

The air in the tomb was stale. An inch of sunlight showed under the door at the top of the whitewashed steps, illuminating the dancing particles of dust. Kader and Marwan spoke in low voices, talking about their families and what they would be doing on this holiday.

They stopped suddenly when they heard a knock on the door. Al-Rahid motioned them to remain still and climbed the stairs. He opened the door a fraction. Habib craned his neck to see the face of a small boy who handed al-Rahid a piece of paper. The Libyan read it and said something to the boy, who ran off.

"We will be leaving here tonight," said al-Rahid, sitting down again. "Ten o'clock. You will take all your belongings with you. We shall not be returning here."

Kader and Marwan smiled at each other.

"Where are we going?" asked Habib.

"You will find out when we arrive. What you do not know, you will not be able to tell. It will be safer for all of us," replied the Libyan, and he took out a match and set fire to the paper. The four men watched as the flames reduced the message to a black ash.

≈≈≈

When he was depressed, Ahmed Rahman liked to pamper himself. Today, since his tailor would be on holiday and he could not be measured for a new suit, he had decided on a massage. In spite of the feast day, the Health Club at the Nile Hilton Hotel would still be open, and he had suggested that Uri Bar-Zeev join him there; afterward they could dine upstairs in the El Nil Rotisserie.

"There is nothing more we can do here except wait, Uri," he had said. "We are wearing ourselves out like this."

"I'll come with you, but a massage, no." The Israeli found Rahman's office at the ministry a dispiriting place to be. The grinding activity over the past few days had produced few tangible results, and the morale of the staff was low. Any excuse to escape the mounds of files and coffee-stained maps would be a welcome relief.

They made an incongruous pair—the large, stooping Rahman and the short, energetic Bar-Zeev—as they walked through El Tahrir Square to the Hilton. Gone was the usual turmoil in the streets: there were no buses and few cars; the downtown area was practically deserted.

"We are reduced to clutching at straws, Uri. We have no initiatives. We can only react." Rahman sighed, his black mustache accentuating his hangdog expression.

They walked along in contemplative silence.

Then Bar-Zeev spoke. "There was a report in the files circulated by Canadian intelligence. In April the International Atomic Energy Agency reported a shortfall in the inventory of spent fuel bundles at Pakistan's Candu reactor near Karachi. I've checked with Euratom and other agencies and that's the only recent loss or theft."

"Pakistan," repeated Rahman. "They've been trying to produce a nuclear device for some time. Didn't the Americans cut off aid when they tried to build a centrifuge to enrich uranium?"

"That's right. And the Canadians withdrew their technical assistance when the Pakistanis pushed ahead. That didn't stop them, though. They had decided to produce an Islamic bomb, whatever the consequences. When the Russians marched into Afghanistan and started making menacing gestures toward the Persian Gulf, it only strengthened that resolve. And of course at that point the Americans turned the aid tap back on."

"So what are you saying? That this so-called Islamic bomb has ended up here, in Egypt?"

"No. But its twin, perhaps." Bar-Zeev was turning over the possibilities in his mind. "There are problems with that theory, though. We know that Herrara made perhaps ten trips. But terrorists would need at least three tons of spent fuel to get the amount of plutonium needed to produce a bomb. Nobody could carry that much in one duffel bag. Besides, you need special equipment to transport radioactive material like that. Herrara would have had to have a death-wish to be near it at all."

"It sounds like you've just disproved your own theory."

"Maybe."

"Put yourself in their place, Uri. Could you have done it?"

Bar-Zeev thought for several minutes before answering slowly. "Well, apart from the expense of refining the plutonium from the fuel, the main hazard is radiation. Fuel bundles are usually kept under water, once they've been processed through the reactors, to allow the radioactive material to decay. To transport them with any degree of safety they would have to be left in an underwater bay for two or three years. But still they would need three or four tons of the stuff."

"Where would they get hold of the spent fuel?"

"They could only get it from a heavy-water reactor, such as Pakistan's Candu. You can't get it on the black market."

"Perhaps we caught them in the middle of their operation," suggested Rahman.

"But why would they expose themselves to the risk? They'd need three or four times the amount they've got. And they must have known the dangers."

"What is dangerous in industrial or social terms may be an acceptable risk to desperate men who are prepared to die for a cause."

"It doesn't feel right, Ahmed. There's something missing. Spent fuel contains only 0.4 percent by weight of plutonium. The Nagasaki bomb contained 1.3 kilograms. If they were making a bomb, they would know this. One man carrying that amount—it's not possible, forgetting about the radiation danger."

"Let us assume it is possible. What would their next step be?"

"They would have to isolate the plutonium from the other elements —uranium, chrome, molybdenum, and other metals."

"How would they do it?"

"By dissolving the rods in acid. It's a chemical process."

"Is it difficult?"

"No. As long as they took the necessary precautions."

"So the question is, how much plutonium do they have? Is there any way they could have obtained the amount necessary for a bomb with the rods they already have?"

Bar-Zeev shut his eyes and began to calculate. "There is only one possibility. If the fuel bundles had been pushed through the reactor ahead of schedule—say, six months instead of a year or eighteen months —there'd be a much greater concentration of plutonium left. You'd need someone on the inside, though. Someone who programmed the bundles through and then earmarked them, once they had ended up in the spent fuel bay. If they stayed under water for a couple of years, they'd still be dangerous, but they could be handled with the proper equipment."

"Supposing the theory is true. How does it help us?"

"Don't you see? Pakistan is a fundamentalist Islamic state. So is Libya. Right here in your own country there are any number of groups dedicated to the overthrow of Sayed. And why? They want to establish an Islamic state in Egypt."

"Yes, but the problem is that we have already thoroughly investigated all the known right-wing elements in Egypt. And we have found nothing."

"Then I suggest you keep looking."

"We shall, Uri, we shall," said Rahman. "Now, if you'll excuse me . . ." The strain of waiting had drained Rahman of his customary good humor. All he wanted now was a relaxing session on the masseur's table.

While Bar-Zeev sat impatiently in the reception area, flipping through newspapers, Rahman undressed in a curtained-off cubicle. The masseur invited him to lie face down on the table. He took the towel from Rahman's waist and began to soap his body. Steely fingers worked into his muscles, beginning with the toes and working upward, over his buttocks and along his spine to his neck. The combination of the soap and the powerful hands eased the tension from the Egyptian's body. He felt drowsy, and the world of terrorists and presidents seemed light-years away.

The masseur gave him a final tap on his back and asked him to sit upright. After lathering Rahman's hair, the man disappeared for a moment and returned with a bowl of warm water, which he poured over his client's head to rinse away the soap. There followed a succession of bowls, each cooler than the last, until the final ice-cold shower. Rahman returned to the locker room refreshed and alert. He weighed himself on the scales, shook his head in disbelief, and dried his body.

Bar-Zeev sat in a wicker chair reading the morning's edition of the *Egyptian Gazette,* Cairo's English language daily.

"What kind of a newspaper is this, Ahmed? All it seems to carry are stories about President Sayed. Even the social notes. Look at this: 'President Mahmoud Sayed yesterday received a telegram of congratulations on his recent speech to the People's Assembly from His Excellency Tawab Hashai Gowab, the ambassador of Turkey.' And here:

'President Mahmoud Sayed yesterday sent a cable to Indian Prime Minister Indiji Morsai to congratulate him on assuming the premiership.' It's just government propaganda."

"The newspaper is for the tourists, Uri. All very harmless." Rahman chuckled, adjusting his tie in the mirror. "If it makes you happier, they also printed an item the other day about Sayed's sending your own prime minister a telegram of congratulations on his birthday. You see, we play no favorites. Really, you should relax. Have a massage."

"I don't need a massage."

"Ah, of course, your wound. Or could it be that sign?" Rahman gestured to a discreet notice above the receptionist's head, next to the table of charges: GENTLEMEN WITH A CERTAIN AILMENT ARE REQUESTED NOT TO USE THE SAUNA AND MASSAGE FACILITIES.

" 'A certain ailment.' In my case, just the chance to catch it would be a fine thing," said the Israeli, laughing.

"Come, let me buy you a drink and dinner. Courtesy of the Egyptian taxpayer."

Upstairs in the El Nil Rotisserie, they were shown to a discreet corner table with a view over the Corniche and the river. Bar-Zeev glanced around the restaurant with a practiced eye as a red-jacketed waiter hovered over them, pencil poised expectantly for their drink order. All the other diners appeared to be American or European, apart from one lone Saudi who stared wistfully out at the string of lights along the Nile. The aroma of seared meat filled the air from a central grill, presided over by a histrionic chef who turned steaks and chops with a dramatic flourish of his tongs. His performance sent clouds of smoke up into a large copper hood above his head. His glistening face looked diabolical over the flames and the sizzling fat.

Bar-Zeev ordered a tomato-juice cocktail.

"Good idea. I'll have one, too," said Rahman, beaming at the waiter.

The two men gazed out of the window in silence until the waiter had withdrawn from earshot.

"I must admit that it gives me a tremendous sense of power to be able to stop all of Cairo's traffic, Uri. Imagine how it will be tomorrow. Not one car on the road. Nothing moving."

"It couldn't happen in Israel. Our drivers have too much chutzpah."

"Well, the broadcasts started this afternoon. We have also sent out sound trucks to warn the people. At midnight the police and the army will start setting up barriers at every major intersection. These will be manned throughout the period of the president's visit. Any car or truck or trailer approaching them will be ordered home and the driver's name will be taken. Not a wheel will move in this city from four o'clock tomorrow morning."

"One day I'll be able to tell my grandchildren that I met the man who stopped Cairo's traffic," Bar-Zeev remarked, laughing. *"Kol hakavod.* That's an old wartime expression; it means 'every respect.' "

"At least it will slow down our enemies if they are thinking of blowing up the presidents."

"It's brilliant, Ahmed."

"Praise indeed from the Mossad," Rahman said, smiling.

The waiter returned, pushing a trolley bristling with liqueur bottles, glasses, ice buckets, and containers of olives, sweet onions, and lemon twists. The two intelligence men watched in silence as he made an elaborate show of mixing their tomato-juice cocktails, pouring them into frosted tumblers with salt-crusted rims and garnishing the result with lemon wedges and celery sticks. A second waiter materialized at their table, offering a variety of breads and rolls from a huge wicker basket, while a third placed four brown ceramic dishes containing butter, pâté, *tahina,* and black olives on the table before them.

"Now I understand why there are revolutions," said Bar-Zeev. "Tell me, Ahmed. I'm used to tomato juice straight from the can—does it taste any better for all this upholstering?"

"Sometimes a little show is good for the constitution. My family was too poor ever to go to restaurants. I never ate in one until I went into government service. Even when I was in the army I never did. The idea of being waited on by someone else was inconceivable to me. You see, I've been spoiled by the West. When I was abroad, I got the taste for fine restaurants. Now I find the occasional dinner like this a treat. Especially before a major operation. It's part of my routine, you might say— a massage, a leisurely meal, and a good night's sleep. Look at Napoleon. He enjoyed his creature comforts before battle. An understandable weakness. I apologize if all of this makes you uncomfortable." Rahman gestured around the room.

"No, not at all," Bar-Zeev said quickly. "It's just a little rich for my blood. I'm too used to kibbutz life." He decided to change the subject. "Tell me, as one old spook to another, are you still using Nicosia now that the peace treaty has been signed?" (Nicosia, the capital of Cyprus, had for years been the center from which Egyptian intelligence controlled its operatives working in Israel. The city had also been used as a recruiting ground for new agents and as a rendezvous and drop point. The Israeli government had formally protested several times to the Cypriot authorities about such blatant espionage activities, but without success. For reasons of their own, the supposedly neutral Cypriots preferred to turn a blind eye to Egyptian activity on the island.)

As soon as Bar-Zeev had uttered the question, he regretted it. By voicing it he had committed two errors: he had let slip that the Mossad was not as well informed as it should be on the current state of Egyptian intelligence operations in Cyprus; and he had broken a tacit agreement between them: no probing for classified information.

A momentary cloud passed over Rahman's features. Bar-Zeev saw the change and added quickly, "No, I'm sorry. A stupid question. Forget I asked it."

The Egyptian laughed. "All those schools you went to, Uri, and no one ever gave you a course in small talk. What are you going to eat? I recommend the lamb chops. After all, this is what our feast is all about."

But the question had been asked, and it hung unanswered over them like an offensive smell. They ate their main course without speaking: Bar-Zeev angry with himself for an uncharacteristic slip; and Rahman wondering whether the Israeli was trying to catch him off guard with a calculated display of ignorance.

Over coffee, Rahman pulled out a note pad. "We should review the procedures for tomorrow, Uri."

"Fine," said the Israeli, happy to have a topic of discussion.

"I shall pick you up at your hotel at six-thirty a.m. We will drive through the city to make sure the prohibition on vehicles is effective. We will drive along the motorcade route for a final inspection. A control center has been set up at my ministry so we can monitor the president's arrival and the progress of the motorcade on closed-circuit television. Once that phase is over, we can then decide where to position ourselves."

Bar-Zeev nodded as Rahman glanced at his watch.

"It's coming up to ten o'clock. President Dunlap will be arriving in twelve hours' time. Come, I'll walk you back to the hotel. We both need a good night's sleep."

≈≈≈

On one wall of Professor Rashad Munir's library in his Zamalek home hung a small woolen tapestry with a passage from the Koran picked out in fine gold thread: "If my servants ask you about me, tell them I am near them; I fulfill the demands of those who turn to me in prayer." Seated at his desk facing this inscription, Munir vacillated between moods of apathy and the frenzied need to occupy his hands and mind. After morning prayers at the mosque, he had closeted himself with his books, eating nothing all day but a symbolic morsel of lamb. He had passed the hours rearranging his books and manuscripts on the shelves when the urge for action came upon him, or merely lying on his couch, fingering his prayer beads, when overtaken by lassitude.

Alone, in this frame of mind, Munir talked unselfconsciously to himself, as if he were conducting a dialectical debate to purge any doubts he might have about his faith or the crusade inspired by it. Tormented by his thoughts, he reached for the nearest book. He opened it at random, read a paragraph, and tossed it aside in disgust.

"Western historians falsify and distort Arab history to keep us a subjected people. They propagandize us to diminish our pride in our past," he declaimed at the walls. "Pride in our former greatness can inspire the new renaissance. Islam will prevail only when our people submit themselves to the will of God."

He began to pace the room, driven by energies he could not control, his mind racing feverishly over the details of the plan that would restore Egypt to the House of Peace. His robe swished angrily as he walked; he beat his clenched fist against his chest.

"Let the will of Allah triumph that I may smite the unbelievers and drive them from the land. Only then will the faithful cover the face of the earth."

He collapsed once more onto the couch, breathing heavily.

"Rest," he told himself. "You must rest mind and body." He reached

over to the television and switched on the set. The sound of a police
siren filled the room as the picture slowly came into focus. The inane
dialogue between two New York patrolmen had been translated into
Arabic subtitles at the bottom of the screen. Munir stared at it in
horror, and then, leaping to his feet with a roar, he wrenched the plug
from the wall.

"American trash on this, one of the most sacred days in the Islamic
calendar! What is wrong with this country? It is our own people who
do this thing. We dishonor ourselves. We degrade what is best in us."

He began pacing the room again, his lips flecked with spittle. His
anger fed on his words, and with a sudden movement he pushed the
television set off its stand. It hit the floor with the sound of smashing
milk bottles. He stared down at the wreckage but made no effort to
clear it up.

"We are eight hundred million believers"—he was speaking to the
broken TV as if it were the American president—"eight hundred million followers of Islam around the world. You talk of China; you talk
of the Catholic Church; but it is we Muslims whose time has come
again. We will be a light unto the world as once we were."

Munir slumped to the couch, exhausted by his rhetoric and a lack
of food. He looked at the clock on the mantel. It would soon be ten
o'clock. "They will be leaving the City of the Dead shortly," he said in
a whisper, and the thought gave him comfort.

He shut his eyes and allowed the feeling of weariness to take hold of
him. He felt himself hovering outside his body, being borne along
the margin of consciousness between wakefulness and sleep, back in
time to when he was a boy of thirteen, back to his hometown, Aswan.
In his mind's eye he could see a religious service in progress. It was
the fifteenth of the month of Sha'ban, when the fate of every man is
confirmed for the ensuing year. A procession moved through the streets;
children ran along in its wake. People sang and chanted, and loudspeak-
ers, hanging from the trees, blared out religious music. Inscriptions
from the Koran spelled out in lights were strung across the street leading
to the mosque. Running behind the procession, he tripped and grazed
his knee, but nothing could stop him from following the joyous line
of men to their house of worship.

The children waited with their mothers in the square, but since he was big for his age, he could pass for a young man. He crowded inside the dimly lit mosque and joined the men at prayer. The imam introduced a great religious leader from another land. The man seemed to radiate the light of the sun itself. He was very old, but his voice, thin and reedy as a pipe, reached the farthest corners of the place and floated up to echo around the vaulted dome. With the passage of years, Munir had all but forgotten the holy man's words, but his voice and his image remained, as did his final thought: "The true Muslim is he who will seek to make the world conform to the Islamic ideal, and not he who would conform to the world's."

Soon after that experience, Munir was asked by his father, a successful lawyer, what course he wished to pursue in life. There had been no hesitation in his reply: "I wish to go to Cairo, the Mother of the World, to attend Al-Azhar and become a holy man." His father tried to influence the young Rashad toward his own profession, or at least the civil service, but the boy was adamant and eventually got his wish. Once accepted at Al-Azhar, he was sent to live with his uncle, a wealthy doctor, whose home in Cairo he subsequently inherited.

The years that followed had been deeply satisfying for Rashad Munir. He and his uncle became close, and the aging doctor treated the boy as the son he never had. At Al-Azhar, Munir impressed his teachers as an unusually mature and highly intelligent young man, and his piety and observance was held up as a model to his fellow students. Despised by his peers as a result, Rashad retreated further into the ascetic life, withdrawing from all social activities and avoiding contact of any kind with women—even with his mother on his infrequent visits home to Aswan.

The year Munir graduated, his uncle developed a heart condition that confined him to the house. Fearing death, the old man turned more and more to Rashad for spiritual comfort. The young man would read the Koran to him, and the bedridden doctor slowly began to realize that his nephew had excluded everything from his own life except the path of the Prophet.

For a time Rashad would reply only in quotations from the Koran when spoken to, and his uncle would admonish him for his pride. "Humility, Rashad, that is the mark of the true holy man. You have to live in this world with others who do not share your single-minded pursuit of Islam." As a result of these conversations, uncle and nephew grew further apart, and Munir had been about to move out of the house in Zamalek when the old doctor died.

The death of his uncle was a great blow to him, and for a time he moved back to Aswan. But the call of Al-Azhar was too strong in him, and after six months he was back in Cairo as an assistant lecturer. The university, as the matrix of Islamic philosophy, became his life; and in the years that followed he established a reputation as one of the leading authorities on Islamic studies in the Arab world. He published several learned works, was frequently invited to lecture in Damascus, Oman, and Beirut, and his advice was sought by scholars around the world.

But in spite of his standing and his academic successes, Munir was not happy. Where once he had believed that the purity of Islamic thought was above political circumstance, events in the Middle East had proved to him that he could not ignore politics. He grew increasingly troubled by the westernization of his country, especially after the historic rapprochement with Israel and the establishment of close economic links with the United States. His study of history had taught him that these two happenings foreshadowed a new period of cultural domination for the Egyptian people. He resolved to fight against the threat of new colonial masters.

"The revolution against British domination began in 1919," he told a colleague. "It was fomented at Al-Azhar. The revolution against Jewish and American domination must also begin at Al-Azhar."

The sound of his prayer beads slipping from his fingers and hitting the wooden floor roused Munir from his reverie. He sat up and tried to recall what it was he had to do. Then he remembered. He looked at the clock, which showed five minutes before ten. He crossed to the telephone on his desk and leafed through his directory for the number of Oliver Simpson, his squash partner from the British embassy. After five attempts he made the connection.

"Simpson, here. Ah, yes, Professor. A little late, isn't it?"

"You must forgive me. Today is a feast day."

"Of course, of course. What can I do for you?" The voice exuded an alcoholic cheeriness.

"I wonder if it would be possible to change our squash time from our usual Sunday to the same time tomorrow for this week?"

"By all means, old boy. See you at the courts at ten tomorrow. Good night. Oh, and a happy—ah—feast day to you."

"Good night, Mr. Simpson."

Munir put the phone down and opened the French windows of his study onto the garden. He took out his prayer mat and unrolled it, and then removed his sandals. From the cupboard he took a large silver-plated bowl with a matching ewer of water and washed his hands and feet. When he had dried them on a towel, he sank to his knees and positioned the rug so that it pointed east to Mecca, along the same latitude that passed through the City of the Dead.

≈ ≈ ≈

While Rashad Munir recited the last prayers of the day in the comfort of his home, the conspirators under his command prepared to leave their refuge in the necropolis.

Saraj al-Rahid knelt on the sandy floor of the tomb and briefed his three men by candlelight. "This is a military operation. It is to be conducted as such. I am issuing you these watches, which have been synchronized. The timing is crucial." He spoke in a low, urgent tone; the prospect of action excited him, stimulating a thrill of expectation in his audience.

"We will leave here in exactly nine minutes. I will lead the way. We will walk for twelve minutes to a place where a truck is waiting. Habib, you will drive. Here is a license for you and registration for the vehicle. You, Kader, and you, Marwan, will ride in the back. When we arrive at our destination there will be two wooden crates to be loaded into the back of the truck. One of them will be heavy; it will require all four of us to lift it. It is to be loaded first. Habib, you will remain with me in the truck while we secure it under canvas. Kader and Marwan will return for the smaller one. Understand this well: there will be absolute silence during the entire process. I will direct you with hand signals. And when you load the crates onto the truck, I want to hear nothing but the sound of your breathing. Is that clear?"

The three men nodded, causing the shadows cast by the candle flame to dance over their faces.

"Good. Once the truck is loaded we will continue our journey. Habib, you will continue to drive. Kader will join us in the cab. Marwan, you will ride with the crates in the rear. If there is any trouble, any movement of the crates, you will rap on the window. You are to work as quickly as possible. The loading must be completed by five minutes past eleven. No delay is possible."

"Where are we going when we have loaded the crates?" asked Habib.

"You will find out when we get there," replied al-Rahid curtly. "It is time to go. May Allah be with you."

They moved like ghosts through the alleys of the City of the Dead, lit by the soft orange glow of a full moon already high in the clear night sky. The streets were deserted, apart from stray dogs that chased scuttling rats over mounds of garbage piled against the walls.

Beyond the necropolis, Habib could see the lights of Cairo shining green against the black velvet of the sky. The operation was about to begin, and he had to warn the Mokhabarat. But what could he tell them, even if he could get a message through? He had no details to convey. He knew nothing of the plan or where the strike would be made.

The truck was waiting, as al-Rahid had said, parked at the side of a mosque. Habib noted that it was an ancient Ford truck, thick with dust, its panels rusting. He memorized the license number as al-Rahid beckoned him angrily to climb into the cab. Kader and Marwan scrambled into the rear, throwing their knapsacks in ahead of them.

The Libyan handed Habib the ignition key. The engine turned over immediately; Habib was surprised to hear how well tuned it sounded.

"Drive along the Old Wall to Midan Ramses," said al-Rahid. "I'll direct you from there."

The truck bounced along the rutted dirt lane and onto the highway outside the wall. In a few minutes the City of the Dead was behind them and they were speeding along the empty road.

At Midan Ramses, al-Rahid directed Habib down Shari el Gumhuriya. Just past Opera Square they turned into Kasr el Nil. The traffic in the city's center slowed their progress, and al-Rahid cursed as he kept looking at his watch. A few minutes later, he ordered Habib to turn off into an alleyway.

"Stop here." The truck drew up outside a garage. The sign over the closed wooden doors read: ATELIER MÉCHANIQUE, ABDUL SAMY. Al-Rahid eased the door open and slipped out of the cab. The young intelligence agent watched as the Libyan slid the wooden doors apart to their full extent. Then al-Rahid motioned to Habib to back the truck into the empty bay. Once they were inside, he closed the doors again. The three men assembled in silence at the back of the truck, looking expectantly at the Libyan, who reached inside his galabia for a key to unlock the door of the private office. He pulled back the wall hanging and unlocked the inner door, indicating that they were to follow him. At the end of the passage Jabir, the guard, pistol in hand, nodded to them.

The laboratory had been stripped clean; there was no evidence to suggest what might have taken place there. In the center of the room under the neon lights stood the two unmarked wooden crates: one the size of a tea chest, the other large enough to house a bathtub. Leather straps had been attached to both cases for ease of handling. Al-Rahid motioned for each of them to take one corner. The larger of the two crates was unwieldy but not excessively heavy, and the four men were able to move it out through the corridor without difficulty. Habib noticed that all the doorways were unusually wide, as if they had been prepared for the dimensions of the crate they were carrying. Someone had done very careful planning.

They rested the crate on the floor at the back of the truck, and Marwan opened the doors and climbed aboard. At a signal from al-Rahid, they strained together and lifted the crate upward. Marwan grabbed a leather handle and pulled it inside. Al-Rahid waved his hand to position the crate as far back as possible. Then he pointed to Habib, who climbed up while Marwan and Kader returned for the smaller case.

Habib took a canvas cover and spread it over the crate with al-Rahid's help. They lashed the corners to cleats on the floor of the truck and tested to ensure the object could not move. The two others returned with the smaller crate, which they slid onto the truck and secured in a similar fashion. Jabir came out to watch the operation, and when it was completed he exchanged a few whispered words with al-Rahid. The Libyan took the pistol from him; the young man saluted, kissed him on both cheeks, and moved to the front of the garage to open the double doors.

Habib looked at his watch: it was two minutes past eleven. Al-Rahid herded them back into the truck: Marwan in the back; the three of them in front. The Libyan pointed at the ignition key, and Habib started the engine.

"Where now?" Habib asked when they were clear of the body shop.

"Take the Sixth of October Bridge to the west bank," said al-Rahid. "Then left on Shari el Giza. South to Highway Two, and keep going."

Habib knew the route. It was the main road through the Nile Valley —the only route connecting Cairo to Luxor.

"How far are we going?"

"We have enough fuel; that is all you have to worry about."

They drove in silence as the truck left the lights of Cairo behind and headed south along the Nile. The sprawling suburbs thinned out, giving way to the occasional village of whitewashed huts domed with beehive-shaped dovecotes, their roofs stacked with cotton-plant stalks. Beyond the villages the rice paddies and cotton fields stretched out into the desert, each neatly defined by a network of irrigation canals.

Al-Rahid placed the pistol on the dashboard in front of him and began rummaging in the glove compartment for a flashlight. For a moment Habib considered grabbing the gun and killing the Libyan. But he would have to shoot Kader, too, and then there would be Marwan to dispose of. Even as the thought passed through the young man's mind, al-Rahid picked up the pistol again and secreted it in his lap, covered by the folds of his galabia.

They were approaching the town of El Badrshein, and in the head-lights Habib could see a man in the center of the road holding up his hand.

"Police checkpoint," hissed the one-eyed man. "Slow down."

"What shall I say?"

"Nothing. Tell them to talk to Kader. He knows what to do."

The helmeted policeman, in drab olive-green, stepped to one side as the truck slowed to a stop. A second man holding a submachine gun sat in front of a small red-and-white-striped booth. Habib's heart began to pound. If he made any move to alert the policeman, he would break his cover; yet if he allowed the opportunity to pass, he might not get another.

He rolled down the window as the policeman approached. Suddenly, he felt the weight of al-Rahid's head on his shoulder; the Libyan was feigning sleep to hide the left side of his face from close inspection. The officer shone his light over the occupants of the cab.

"Papers?" he demanded in a voice that suggested he would rather be elsewhere.

"He has them," said Habib, gesturing at Kader.

With a grunt of annoyance the policeman ambled around to the other side of the truck. His partner remained seated, smoking a cigarette, indifferent to the proceedings.

Kader rolled down his window and handed down a sheaf of documents. The policeman shone his light on them and glanced at the stamps and signatures.

"It says you're transporting two electric generators to Beni Suef."

"They're in the back," said Kader. "Rush order."

The policeman turned his light on Kader's face and looked him over. "How come you're working on Bairam? It's a holiday."

"You don't have to tell me. We were supposed to make the trip yesterday, but the truck broke down. Now we just want to get home and spend the rest of it with our families."

"You're all from Beni Suef?"

"That's right."

"As long as you're not going back to Cairo. There's no traffic allowed on the streets from four a.m. tomorrow."

"No, we're staying in Beni Suef."

"Okay. You can go on." The policeman handed back the manifests and stepped back off the road.

"May Allah be with you," said Kader, rolling up the window.

Habib put the truck in gear and moved slowly away. He gave a sigh of relief, more for the fact that he had decided not to entrust his fate to the lackadaisical policeman than for their safe passage through the checkpoint.

A few hundred meters down the road, al-Rahid sat up and laughed humorlessly. "Fools. They didn't even look in the back. So much for discipline."

Fifteen kilometers south of El Badrshein, al-Rahid ordered Habib to slow down. He squinted out into the darkness, looking for a small dirt road. "There. In front, on the right. Turn down there."

The truck turned onto the unpaved road, which was partially concealed by a wall of reeds. They bumped over the uneven surface until the road ended in a clearing at the edge of the Nile. They were completely screened off from the highway and the neighboring fields by a tall line of reeds on both sides that grew down to the water's edge and rustled in a faint breeze.

From the sandy bank a small wooden dock extended out into the river. Moored at its farther end was a twin-engined seaplane with no discernible markings. Following al-Rahid's instructions, Habib backed the truck to the edge of the dock and turned off the motor. As they stepped down from the cabin, al-Rahid was greeted by a man who emerged from the shadow of the reeds. The two conferred together briefly; then the stranger returned to the shadows again.

"Who's he?" Habib asked Kader, who stood beside him waiting for instructions to unload.

"A friend. He brought the plane here. He'll take the truck out when we're finished."

"No talking," whispered al-Rahid as he came around to the back of the vehicle. "Get those crates unloaded and onto the seaplane. The large one first. There's a cargo bay at the back. The door is open. Hurry up. We're running behind schedule, thanks to that donkey of a policeman."

The four men hauled the heavier of the crates down the dock and lifted it into the cargo bay. Habib noticed that the rear passenger seat had been taken out to accommodate the two crates. While he and the Libyan tied the first one down, Kader and Marwan brought in the second. When the transfer was completed, al-Rahid signaled to the man on the bank, who climbed into the cab of the truck and drove off. Al-Rahid motioned the three young men forward to the pilot's cockpit and untied the ropes securing the seaplane to the dock.

Salah Kader slipped into the pilot's seat and began to check the instruments.

"I didn't know you could fly a plane," said Habib.

"There are many things you don't know, Mustafa. Now, please fasten your seat belt and be quiet."

Habib sat down next to Marwan behind the pilot and copilot and strapped himself in. The engines started with a roar, and al-Rahid slid into the seat next to Kader. He had to shout above the noise of the twin engines.

"Is everything all right?"

"There's not as much fuel as I'd like," Kader yelled back. "But we'll make it, all right. Hold on, I'll taxi her out."

Through the front window Habib could see the plane move ponderously away from the dock and turn out toward the center of the Nile. The silver reflection of the moon off the water provided excellent visibility. Kader maneuvered the plane into the current and turned its nose upstream.

"Get ready," he shouted. "Here we go."

The engines strained as he pulled back the throttle. Slowly the plane gathered speed, bouncing over the surface of the river like a flat stone. Soon they were airborne, and all Habib could see was the star-filled sky in front of them.

Kader banked the plane sharply right, a direction Habib knew would take them out over the Western Desert.

"Stay over the desert and keep low," al-Rahid said. "I don't want us showing up on any of those military radar screens." He pulled a map from the pouch inside his galabia. "The radar stations in the Western Desert are marked with a red X. Make sure we're below the dunes in relation to any one of them. I've marked the flight path here, in green."

Habib peered over the Libyan's shoulder, but his view was partially blocked. All he could see was a green line that zigzagged south.

Al-Rahid turned around in his seat. "You wanted to know where we are going, Habib? Now I can tell you. We have a very important appointment to keep. In Aswan."

DAY EIGHT
SATURDAY, NOVEMBER 10

For two hours the seaplane hugged the sandy terrain as it followed a drunken course south to avoid radar detection. At times Kader flew so low that the pontoons seemed to skim across the bluffs of sand. The weight in the belly of the plane made maneuvering difficult, and when Kader banked to alter course, it felt as if they would never straighten out of the turn.

The moon, which had lit their way for most of the journey, was down now, but its residual light provided the pilot with sufficient visibility to keep them from crashing into the sudden desert mountains. Kader looked at the map and then turned east. Directly ahead of him were the waters of Lake Nasser, the world's largest artificial lake.

Lake Nasser stretches five hundred kilometers south of the Aswan High Dam. From the air by day, it looks like a silver-blue dagger in the bosom of the Sahara. To create this vast body of Nile water, five thousand square kilometers of desert were flooded behind the Aswan High Dam, drowning many ancient monuments and displacing thousands of Nubian families from villages they had occupied for centuries. The flooding created archipelagoes of sand in the lake and an ever-changing coastline of hidden inlets and spits of land, odd promontories, and hunchbacked islands.

Once over the water, Salah Kader banked to the north. He held steady about seventy-five meters above the surface, which both he and al-Rahid seemed to be studying intently. Mustafa Habib, sitting behind them, could not make out any details; all he could see were tongues of water that probed into the low-lying, featureless desert, and islands like dark blots on the shimming face of the lake.

"Over there!" shouted al-Rahid, pointing to his right. As he said it, Habib could see twin beams of light rising from a point almost directly ahead.

"Prepare for landing," shouted Kader above the drone of the engines.

Habib braced himself as the water seemed to race up to meet the aircraft. The weight of the cargo caused the seaplane to hit the water and bounce off the surface. The tail veered dangerously around, and Kader fought the controls to keep the wing tips from dipping into the lake. Great arcs of spray scythed across the windows, obscuring their vision as the pilot slowed the plane down to taxiing speed and switched on his windshield wipers.

From ground level, the twin beams of light looked like massive pillars ahead, and Kader pointed the nose of the aircraft toward them. The source of the lights was a large hill of sand on an island that loomed black in front of them. As the seaplane approached the shoreline, the lights dipped and played on the water to guide it in. When they were about a hundred meters away from the island, Kader cut the motors and allowed the plane to float. He opened a hatch and dropped the anchor.

Al-Rahid unfastened his seat belt. "Come on. We must get the crates unloaded and get the plane out of here before the sun comes up." He squeezed through to the rear passenger compartment and opened the door. The cold night air made Habib shiver.

"Help me untie the crates," said Marwan, the only words he had uttered since they had left the City of the Dead.

The seaplane bobbed against its anchor as they moved about the compartment. Outside, the night was still. Habib could hear nothing but the gentle lapping of the water against the pontoons. The movement of the cargo in flight had tightened the securing ropes, making them difficult to undo.

As Habib worked at the knots he became aware of what sounded like a boat approaching; as it came nearer he could make out the rhythmic smack of water against the prow, but there was no noise whatsoever from the engine. Then he could see a large, low rubber craft, designed to carry cargo, silhouetted against the island. As it pulled alongside he noticed twin electric engines at the back and two men seated by them.

Al-Rahid saluted the two men, who returned his greeting.

"Let us move the large crate first," said the Libyan. "Marwan, Habib, help me get it to the doorway. You two down there, be ready to receive it. Kader, get down into the boat and give them some help."

The pilot, who had finished securing the plane, jumped into the boat while the three men on the aircraft strained to move the heavy case to the doorway. When it was in position, al-Rahid ordered them to inch it slowly forward until it began to tilt downward. The men in the boat were to grab it at that point and lower it into position.

Habib stood behind the crate, pushing against it with his shoulder. The wood scraped against the metal frame of the plane as the case was moved through the door. The weight of it caused the plane to dip precariously, and Habib could feel it slipping away from him. There were shouts of warning from the other side. In a moment, he knew, the crate would start sliding out of control into the lake.

He grabbed one of the leather straps and pulled back on it as hard as he could. For a moment it seemed the case had gathered too much momentum to be stopped; then suddenly it steadied. He looked across and saw Gabal Marwan straining against the strap on the opposite side.

"All right, they've got it now!" al-Rahid shouted. "Let it go— slowly, slowly. . . ."

With Habib and Marwan guiding the crate from above, the men in the boat were able to control it. Carefully, they lowered it into position in the center of the craft.

"Take it to shore and unload it," al-Rahid said. "Habib, go with them and help. Get the boat back here as quickly as possible. We still have this one to move."

Habib swung himself down onto the pontoon and stepped aboard the boat. As soon as he was seated, al-Rahid cast off and the rubber craft headed noiselessly back to the island. The trip took less than five minutes. The boat was beached on the sand, and the four of them—Habib, Kader, and the two men from the island—lifted the crate out and carried it to a canvas-topped shelter nearby. Then they returned to the seaplane, where the procedure was repeated with the smaller case.

When it was time for the boat to return to the island again, the two men pulled themselves up into the plane and al-Rahid and Marwan took their places on board the boat. They waved as al-Rahid put the engines in gear and the craft pulled away toward the island.

As they reached the beach, Habib heard the plane's engines firing. He could no longer see it in the dark, but a few moments later the silence of the lake and the desert was shattered by the roar of its takeoff. The drone of the engines quickly faded as the aircraft headed back out toward the desert, and the silence closed in once more. Habib was alone with three terrorists on an island in the middle of Lake Nasser. For the first time since he had joined Wind of the Desert, he felt frightened.

≋≋≋

Cleared of its morning traffic, Cairo had settled into an oppressive silence. Ahmed Rahman's embargo against vehicles on the roads had rendered the capital virtually noiseless and deserted. Gone was the habitual bustle and bedlam; cars, motorcycles, trucks, buses, and bicycles—all had been abandoned away from the city's center, leaving it as lifeless and eerie as a ghost town. The rising sun bathed the dusty facades of the buildings in an unnatural pinkish light, giving them the appearance of aged whores, overrouged and -powdered, slumbering before welcoming the first clients of the day.

Driving through the streets just before seven a.m., Rahman felt vaguely uneasy. The absence of noise imbued the scene with an ominous calm. I have killed the city, he thought. Nothing moves. He wondered if his sense of guilt had transmitted itself to the Israeli sitting next to him. All he could see was a few pedestrians moving cautiously along the sidewalks, as mystified by their mute city as he himself was. The car moved slowly by an old man seated atop a donkey cart who was arguing furiously with two guards at a barricade to let him pass. The policemen smiled amiably at him but ordered him back.

Ismail Ali turned the Mercedes into El Tahrir Square, usually the most congested area of the city; today it was empty and peaceful. Pigeons pecked at horse manure in the gutter, and the sun glinted on the hundreds of bottle caps studding the road. Small boys threw them under the wheels of cars on exceptionally hot summer days; the caps were pressed into the melting tarmac by thousands of tires, which had worn them to a polished silver sheen.

"I don't believe it, sir," said Ismail over his shoulder. "El Tahrir Square completely deserted."

"Your men have done an excellent job, Ahmed," said Bar-Zeev. "Frankly, when you suggested it I didn't think it could be done. But you've shut down the whole city."

"I don't think it could have been done if it hadn't been for the holiday," said Rahman. "Ismail, drive up to Talat Harb Square. There's a major roadblock there."

The silence had imposed a kind of deathly order on the city. Without its clamor, Cairo felt emasculated; the rhythm of its life was missing, as if its very heart had stopped.

"Pull up here, Ismail, by the cigarette kiosk. And turn off the engine."

Rahman got out of the Mercedes and stood in the middle of Kasr el Nil. He strained his ears to listen. Somewhere in an alley a dog was barking; a baby cried in a distant apartment; the wind scraped pieces of paper against the cracked sidewalks. Ordinarily, these sounds would be lost in the hubbub of car horns, screeching brakes, and shouting pedestrians. The citizens of Cairo had obeyed the injunction against driving to the point where they had kept themselves off the roads, too, it seemed. For all the activity there was to be seen, he might as well have been standing in the City of the Dead rather than on Cairo's choicest shopping street.

"What's the matter?" asked Bar-Zeev as Rahman got back into the car, frowning.

"I don't know. It's just a feeling. Very strange. It's not Cairo, that's all."

"At least you can hear yourself think."

"That's what worries me," said Rahman ruefully.

The six roads that converged at Talat Harb Square were closed off with waist-high metal barriers painted red and white. An armored personnel carrier was parked at the center of the square by the statue of Suleiman Pasha. Helmeted soldiers manned the checkpoint alongside members of the Cairo police force. A corporal with an automatic rifle on his shoulder waved down the Mercedes.

"Papers?" the soldier demanded curtly.

Rahman flashed his identification card. The corporal snapped to attention.

"Where is your commanding officer?" asked Rahman.

"Over there, sir. By the carrier."

"Open the door. I want to talk to him."

Rahman strode across the square, and Bar-Zeev had to break into a trot to catch up. The young lieutenant in command of the squad sat on the running board of the personnel carrier, studying a map of the city.

"Good morning, Lieutenant. I am Muhammad Ahmed Rahman, chief of Internal Security. This is Colonel Uri Bar-Zeev. What is the situation?"

The officer stood up and saluted. A professional soldier, thought Rahman. One of the new breed, battle-hardened in 1973. Confident, and proud of his uniform. "We've seen only two taxis, one private rental car driven by a tourist, and a few bicycles. They all claimed they hadn't heard of the ban on traffic today. Each vehicle was searched and the name of the driver taken. I have a list here if you'd like to see it."

"Nothing was found?"

"No, sir."

"What are your orders?"

"My orders are to stop any wheeled vehicle. It is to be parked in a side street, and the owner is to be instructed to return after six o'clock tonight to retrieve it. Once his name, address, and license number have been recorded, he is to be allowed to depart on foot."

"Good. You are in touch with your company headquarters?"

"Yes, sir. By radio."

"Have you had any reports from other parts of the city?"

"The situation is similar just about everywhere. In the Mouski area they're concerned about the movements of wagons and donkey carts, but nothing that can't be handled."

"Very good. You're doing a first-rate job, Lieutenant. Please pass on my compliments to the men."

"Thank you, sir. Sir? Are we allowed to know the reason for these maneuvers?"

"It is as you have been told. A security measure for the presidential visit."

"Do you think you can bottle up the streets like this all day?" asked Bar-Zeev as they made their way back to the car.

"I don't see why not. When I was a boy in my village, one of my jobs was to drive the birds from my father's chick-pea plants. My brother and I would beat little drums and run through the field shouting. When we had chased the birds away we could sit down in the shade, and if they came back we just had to beat the drum once to frighten them off. It's the same thing here, my dear Uri. Once we have cleared the streets it's easy to keep them that way. Provided there are enough men and enough barriers. We could not have done it without the army." And then he added, "It gives our soldiers something to do now they don't have to think about fighting Israelis." He gave Bar-Zeev a playful punch on the shoulder. "Come, let us check the motorcade route."

In contrast to the rest of the city, the streets through which the presidential motorcade would soon pass were alive with activity. Police and troops were busily moving crush barriers into place, parallel to the sidewalks. Workmen scrambled up ladders, hanging bunting and flags from lampposts and draping portraits of the two presidents over apartment balconies. Platoons of troops stood around, waiting to be deployed along the route. Transport trucks would be depositing them at intervals on the highway from the airport. They would be positioned ten paces apart, facing the road, along the first leg of the journey. But once the motorcade traversed Nasr City and entered the downtown area, the troops would be stationed shoulder to shoulder, facing inward toward the crowds so that they could watch for any potential threat.

Rahman noted with satisfaction that his own men had already begun the process of checking the buildings along the route. The whole security operation seemed to be running extraordinarily smoothly. And that worried him, too; the ease of the operation did not necessarily mean that it would be crowned with success.

≋≋≋

Mustafa Habib was awakened from a dead sleep by the whine of a mosquito in his ear. When it alighted on his cheek, he crushed the insect with the palm of his hand and rolled over in his sleeping bag. The soft sand under him gave way to accommodate the contours of his body. The thin canvas walls of the tent were bright with sunshine. He looked at his watch; it was almost ten o'clock. Next to him, Gabal Marwan slept on his back, mouth open and snoring loudly. Salah Kader was curled in a fetal position next to the tent flap.

Habib yawned and stretched. The atmosphere was hot and stuffy. He lay back staring at the roof of the tent, where tiny insects swarmed in patches. He tried to formulate a plan of action, going over in his mind the events of the previous night.

After the seaplane had taken off, Saraj al-Rahid had ordered them to move the crates under the cover of camouflaged netting, along with the rubber boat, to avoid detection from the air. Then he had called them together for a briefing.

"I want you to get as much sleep as you can now. We have long days ahead of us. You three take the large tent over there." He gestured at it with a flashlight. "I will sleep in the tent just behind us. Kader, take this light. We will unpack others for the rest of you.

"A word of warning. This island is infested with scorpions. These do not burn. Their sting is lethal. Do not walk around without boots on. Shake out your sleeping bag before you use it. Check your clothing and your boots before putting them on. We cannot afford to lose any of you, so take care. And get some rest."

Habib had not realized how exhausted he was until he had closed his eyes. Within minutes he had fallen into a dreamless sleep. . . .

He raised himself on his elbows. There was little point in lying awake thinking; he had no idea what he was going to do next. He reached for his boots beside his sleeping bag and, remembering the one-eyed man's warning, shook each of them vigorously in turn. He crawled out of his sleeping bag and slipped them on. He climbed carefully over the sleeping figures, quietly unzipped the tent flap, and stepped outside into the blinding morning.

The scene that greeted him was unlike anything he had ever witnessed before. Lake Nasser stretched away to the horizon in front of him, as majestic as an inland ocean; a gentle breeze moved the surface of the blue water, which sparkled silver in the sunlight. In the distance he could see the soft outlines of other islands. To his left, on what he assumed to be the eastern shore of the lake, a range of bald, rust-colored mountains rose sharply into the cloudless sky.

He could feel the warmth of the sand through his boots as he walked down to the water's edge and cupped his hands to drink. The lake water was lukewarm and silty to the taste; he spat it out. Scores of dragonflies hovered like tiny helicopters above the shoreline, darting over the water in search of food. Drowsy lizards sunned themselves on the rocks, gripping the rough surface with splayed claws. He thought he saw a scorpion —the color of translucent gold—scuttling into a crevice to escape the threat of his presence. He ran his tongue over his lips, already dry and chapped from the desert air.

A couple of meters from the shore was a wispy line of vegetation— papyrus reeds and an anemic brush known as *farum*. The fact that the plants grew in the water puzzled him until he realized that the level of the lake was at its height in November, following the annual flooding of the Nile. The bushes struggling for existence in the brackish water marked the natural boundary of the island.

The immensity of the sandscape, the great bowl of the sky, and the breadth of shining water accentuated his isolation. The fear he had felt the night before had turned to a numbing sense of apprehension. The tents behind him, the storage area covered with netting, the mysterious crates—all paled to insignificance against the vastness of the desert. What am I doing here? he kept asking himself. He turned away from the lake and looked back at the tents for a more human perspective.

The ground sloped up from the beach where he stood, culminating in a rocky hummock that would effectively conceal the camp from anyone approaching from the eastern bank. Other than the whiskery fringe of bushes around the waterline, there was no vegetation at all on the island, merely sand and rock baking in the sun. There was no shade from its pitiless rays, which the breeze did nothing to temper. Everything was the color of sand, even the tents and the equipment boxes, which blended with the environment. Habib knew there were hundreds of islands like this one in Lake Nasser, and countless bays, inlets, and submerged valleys. Despite the lack of natural cover, it was an ideal place to hide.

A crane glided over the crest of sand and settled into shallow water, where it took up a position waiting for fish. Habib was grateful for a sign of life. He kept his eyes on the bird, hoping to see it catch something. Despite the inhospitable terrain, there were living things here. He knew the lake to be rich in fish; farther up the coast there were trawlers. The fishermen set heavy nets to catch the giant Nile perch, which weighed up to two hundred kilos. A small trawler fleet was based at the settlement of New Harbor, under the shadow of the Aswan High Dam.

The Aswan High Dam! The thought came to him in a flash: Was that their target? He knew the dam lay to the north of the island, but he had no idea how far away it was.

He walked back to the camp, memorizing its layout. There was a third tent next to the one in which al-Rahid was sleeping. A makeshift antenna had been lashed to the pole. A radio set, he said to himself. Good. Beyond this tent was the supply depot, covered with canvas and secured by camouflage netting. Here the two wooden crates were stored along with toolboxes, rope, water bottles, military provisions, and metal-bound cases he suspected contained weapons and ammunition. Behind the boxes was the rubber boat, pulled up on its side. Next to it were two smaller dinghies with electric motors.

Habib knelt down in the sand for a closer look at the boxes, inspecting them for markings that might give him some idea of their contents. He was unaware of the figure approaching from behind.

"Allah be with you, Habib." The young intelligence man jumped nervously to his feet and found himself looking into the monocular face of al-Rahid.

"Enjoying the sights of our island, are you?"

≈≈≈

A blast of hot air filled the cabin of *Air Force One* as the flight engineer opened the fuselage door. The ground crew at Cairo Airport wheeled the ramp into place, and two Secret Service men took up their positions at either side.

"If you'd like to proceed, Mr. President, they're ready," said the press secretary.

H. Whitney Dunlap, fortieth president of the United States, tightened his face muscles into his world-famous smile and stepped out into the sunshine. The Egyptian military band on the tarmac immediately struck up "The Star-Spangled Banner," and Dunlap stood at attention on the top step, the wind blowing his hair, his wife, Sarah, at his side.

The anthem completed, Dunlap descended the stairs, to be embraced by Mahmoud Sayed, who planted the ritual kiss on both cheeks of the American leader. Dunlap maintained his unflinching smile throughout the ordeal.

"Welcome to Egypt, Mr. President," said Sayed, beaming. "Your presence in my country does us great honor."

"And I am honored by your hospitality," replied Dunlap, employing the phrase suggested for the occasion by an aide who had studied Egyptian etiquette. "May I present Mrs. Dunlap."

The dour woman in a severe summer dress held out a white-gloved hand. "Charmed, Mr. President."

"Madame."

A small girl in a powder-blue dress handed Mrs. Dunlap a large bouquet of roses, curtsied, and disappeared back into the knot of dignitaries assembled to greet the American president.

A great cheer rose from the crowds who thronged the observation deck of the main terminal. The two presidents turned and waved while photographers and film crews recorded the scene.

A host of other cameras, belonging to Egyptian intelligence, panned slowly over the crowds, feeding back their information on closed circuit to a central operations room set up in the Ministry of the Interior. The room had been fitted with a bank of fourteen monitor screens, each manned by an intelligence officer. These men were in radio contact with agents on the ground who mingled with the crowds at the airport. At the first sign of trouble a Mokhabarat operative would be immediately alerted. Other cameras would follow the motorcade's progress through the city, affording Rahman and his people uninterrupted surveillance of the entire drive.

"A very smart suit," said Rahman as he watched President Dunlap on the screen, inspecting the guard of honor. Bar-Zeev concentrated on a monitor showing the press pool, whose artillery of lenses was trained on the distinguished visitor. The inspection complete, Sayed escorted Dunlap to a dais draped with the flags of Egypt and the United States. In front of a bank of microphones Sayed began to deliver his official words of welcome.

"Anything happening?" asked Rahman as he turned away from the monitor to confer with an aide.

"Nothing, sir. Everything's normal. The president's just finished his speech of welcome."

Though he was outwardly calm, Rahman's heart was beating against his ribs, and telltale patches of damp were visible under the armpits of his jacket. Uri Bar-Zeev went from one monitor to the next, frowning in concentration, hands pressed into his pockets, causing his neck to disappear into his shoulders.

Sayed finished his address to dignified applause from the official party on the tarmac and ringing cheers and flag-waving from the observation deck. Dunlap stepped forward to reply. He had carefully committed his speech to memory to give the appearance of speaking off-the-cuff while avoiding any diplomatic pratfalls. His words were safe and solid—a description that might well fit the president himself: a former appellate-court judge from Little Rock, Arkansas, whose last-minute candidacy at a deadlocked party convention had catapulted him into the national limelight. His subsequent ascent to the highest office in the land owed much to the fact that a gossip columnist of *The Washington Post* had revealed that his opponent's wife was a hopeless alcoholic and was being dried out in an institution should her presence be required at the inauguration ceremony. That, coupled with Dunlap's ability to spout endless platitudes with an almost biblical sincerity, had swung the American people behind him and won him the presidency.

He was doing now what he could do best: investing well-worn phrases with openhearted candor. He offered fraternal greetings from the American people and pledged his administration's support in nurturing the growing bonds of friendship between the oldest civilization in the world and the newest. He paused after each phrase to allow his translator to repeat his words in Arabic, and not one of his audience could doubt that his sentiments came straight from the heart.

"Ahmed, do you see that?" Bar-Zeev pointed at the screen. "The man on the left there. Next to the old woman with the flag. He's carrying a paper bag and he keeps trying to push his way to the front."

"Ismail, have him taken out," ordered Rahman.

The aide had the message relayed to the officer in charge of surveillance on the spectators' terrace. Within minutes, two large agents could be seen shouldering their way through the crowd. They grabbed the confused-looking man by the arms and pulled him back into the mass of people until he disappeared from the screen. A couple of minutes later, Ismail's radio crackled.

"The suspect's bag contained his lunch, sir."

Dunlap finished his speech and waved to acknowledge the ensuing cheers. Finally, he gave his thumbs-up sign. (In his younger days a great admirer of Churchill, President Dunlap had adopted this gesture as the trademark he employed whenever he found himself at a public gathering where his audience was well disposed toward him.) Then Dunlap motioned to President Sayed to join him, and when he had grasped and raised the Egyptian's hand like a referee declaring the winner at a boxing match, the two men acknowledged the effusive chants of the crowd.

The band struck up a Sousa march; Sayed took his guest by the arm, and the two presidents walked to the waiting limousine with its plastic bulletproof dome—a last-minute concession to the anxious security men. When their wives had joined them in the car, the American ambassador and other invited guests had taken their places in those behind, and the gentlemen of the press had scrambled aboard the bus provided for them, the motorcade set off with its escort of motorcycle outriders for Cairo.

The progress of the motorcade was charted on the monitor screen as the line of vehicles moved briskly along the divided highway into the city at a constant speed of seventy kilometers an hour. As Rahman had predicted, the crowds were sparse along this section of the route: the ban on motor traffic had effectively kept the people in the city's center.

At Nasr City the column of cars rounded the traffic circle and turned right under the overpass without incident. Rahman exhaled deeply, the sense of relief apparent on his face; he had privately felt that if anything were to happen along the route, it would be here where the cars were forced to slow down. From this point on, the crowds became more dense, and in their enthusiasm they pressed forward against the line of troops. The young soldiers held their rifles across their chests to contain the shouting, flag-waving spectators. The flags and the tumultuous cheers were a spontaneous expression of warmth and friendliness from the people of Cairo toward a man they instinctively knew had the power to improve their meager lives with the stroke of a pen. The visit of the president of the United States signaled the beginning of an era of prosperity for all. Their hopes, their dreams found incarnation in the gray-haired man inside the plastic bubble who smiled back at them and pressed his thumb into the air.

President Sayed ordered the driver of the presidential car to slow to a crawl as the motorcade approached a vast throng of happy Cairenes in front of the main railway station. Men stood on the railings, climbing on each other's shoulders to wave photographs of the two leaders, while the crowd below chanted their names and clapped in unison. Mothers held their children above their heads for a sight of the two men who sat in air-conditioned comfort, receiving the adulation of the masses, each according to his self-image: Sayed, the father of his people; Dunlap, the vigilant judge smiling evenly through the histrionics of an alien culture.

"What the hell are they slowing down for?" asked Bar-Zeev.

"President Sayed is savoring the moment, Uri. He likes to bask in the love of his people."

No sooner had he spoken than the television monitor showed a man running straight down the middle of the road toward the presidential car. He was clutching something in his hands; Rahman couldn't make out what it was.

"Ismail, that man!" Before Rahman could issue an order, the man had run straight at the car. A motorcycle outrider swerved to head him off and collided with a crush barrier. Presidential bodyguards, both Egyptian and American, jumped from the following cars, but the man's sudden appearance had taken them by surprise. The nearest agent tackled him from behind just as the man hurled the object in his hands straight at the hood of the presidential limousine. The two bodies crashed to the ground as the driver of the car accelerated suddenly, throwing the occupants back in their seats. As the limousine roared away, a garland of roses hung from the American flag on its right fender.

The operations room, stunned into silence by the suddenness of the act, erupted in nervous laughter.

"Roses!" bellowed Rahman, collapsing into his chair. "The maniac risked his life to throw roses!" He threw his head back and allowed his anger and anxiety to dissipate in shoulder-wracking guffaws. "Well, he got his rose petals after all, didn't he, Ismail."

≅≅≅

For the convenience of its members, the Ghezira Sporting Club had had a television set installed in the bar so they need not interrupt their drinking should they wish to follow the American president's triumphal procession through the streets of Cairo. Oliver Simpson would have preferred to have his customary pink gin in the open air after his squash game with Rashad Munir, and he was surprised when the professor suggested they sit in the bar instead. The Egyptian had always made Simpson feel it was something of a concession for him to share a table with someone who partook of alcohol, let alone choose to sit in a roomful of drinkers. But today Munir had expressed a desire to watch the two heads of state.

Simpson, red-faced and still sweating from his shower, was somewhat piqued at having lost to Munir for the first time. He ascribed his opponent's uncharacteristic behavior to the unsportsmanlike braggadocio of a fellow who isn't used to winning. To show his unconcern he ordered himself a large pink gin and "a tonic water for my victorious partner."

"It is a tonic water, isn't it, old boy? When you get to my age, the memory's not as good as it used to be."

"It is tonic water," said Munir, his eyes riveted to the screen as the camera zoomed in for a close-up of the bloodless features of President Dunlap.

"Your nephew out there, is he?"

"My nephew?" Munir looked quizzically at the British diplomat.

"The one who wanted to meet Dunlap."

"Oh, yes. He stood in line from sunup this morning."

"Not a very imposing figure, wouldn't you say? I thought they liked their presidents tall. And rich. Not much character in the face, you know what I mean? Charisma, I believe the Yanks call it."

"I see no conviction in his eyes, Mr. Simpson. A leader must have conviction; otherwise, how can he lead?"

"It's the office, old boy, not the man. That's what all those people are out there for. Not Whitney Dunlap but the flag, the bald eagle, and the office of president of the United States. That's what those soldiers are protecting. That's why they closed down the city."

"The security is unprecedented. Never have I known this to happen in Cairo. There must be some reason."

"You know, I had the devil's own job getting here. Would you believe they wouldn't let my driver through? Diplomatic plates and all. Stopped the car and asked for my papers. I tell you, I had to talk to some police chap. I certainly put him straight about diplomatic immunity. Ah, here are the drinks. No, no, the gin's here." Simpson pointed in front of Munir, who pushed the glass away in disgust as the waiter placed it before him.

"Just my little joke, old boy. No offense." Simpson hadn't yet recovered from his defeat on the squash court.

"How did you get through the security blockade?" asked Munir casually.

"I told him I was part of the official reception delegation from the British embassy. He had me open the trunk before he'd let me pass."

"Were you?"

"Was I what?"

"Part of the official reception delegation."

"Good heavens, no. It's just how you carry it off with these fellows."

Simpson took an appreciative swig of his drink and then fished out a couple of ice cubes with his fingers and deposited them in the ashtray. "They always put in too much ice. Waters it down, you know."

"I'm no expert in these matters, but it would appear that the security precautions are unusually stringent. Would you not agree, Mr. Simpson?"

"You know the Yanks. All part of the show. Someone took a potshot at Dunlap a few months ago in Tennessee or somewhere. Bound to make them nervous."

"Surely they do not believe he would be assassinated here? We have too much to gain from his visit."

"There are always some lunatics who might try, Professor."

"I never know when you British are serious, Mr. Simpson. A man in your position would hear these things. If there are rumors—" Munir left the statement unfinished and took a sip of his tonic water.

"I suppose I get the inside track on most things."

"Then you have heard something?"

On the television screen, the two presidents were standing on the steps of Sayed's mansion; they turned briefly to the crowds for a final wave before disappearing inside the building.

"Gossip, my dear fellow, merely gossip. Surely a man of your standing wouldn't sully his ears with it. Leave the politics to us professionals. It's a dog-eat-dog world behind all the diplomatic trappings, I can tell you."

Munir sensed that the blustering Englishman would be pushed no further. Perhaps his very reticence was an attempt to make him seem more important than he was; or, if he did know something, he was prepared to conceal it behind his usual condescending prattle.

When Simpson suggested a second drink, Munir rose from the table. "If you will excuse me, it is time for my prayers."

"Certainly, old boy. Of course, I understand completely. Wish I were devout myself. Next Sunday, then, same time?"

"If Allah wills."

Oliver Simpson watched as Munir walked quickly through the tables and out of the bar onto the patio. He waited for several minutes to ensure the Egyptian was out of sight and then threw a bill on the table. He crossed to the bar and asked for the telephone, then took a small diary from his inside pocket and consulted a list of numbers.

"Damn telephones," he murmured on his third attempt at dialing. "Worse than London. Ah, at last . . . I'd like to speak to Mr. Sharif, please. Oliver Simpson, British embassy." He waited for Sharif to come to the phone. Simpson had dealt with his contact at the Ministry of the Interior on various embassy matters. And on these occasions, knowing Sharif to be a ranking officer in the Mokhabarat, the Englishman had indulged his penchant for intrigue by passing on cocktail-party gossip purely for the pleasure of appearing to know more than he did.

"Sharif? Simpson here. Yes, splendid weather. Sorry to trouble you on the holiday but thought I should let you know. That chap we were talking about last week. . . . Munir, the professor from Al-Azhar, yes. Just left him, actually. Terribly anxious to know about security for the president's visit. . . . That's right. Kept pressing me about any talk of an assassination attempt. Tried to be casual about it, but it seemed to me to be more than idle curiosity. Don't know what it's worth, but thought I'd tip you the wink. . . . Yes, Rashad Munir. Said he had to go for his prayers. . . . Not at all, old boy. We must get together soon. Glad to be of assistance. Good-bye."

Satisfied that he had done a good day's work and had stored up a credit for the future, Simpson returned to his table and signaled to the waiter to bring him another pink gin. "Not so much ice this time," he called across the crowded bar.

≈≈≈

There were few cars in the parking lot as Munir walked down the drive toward the main gate of the Ghezira Sporting Club. He turned left past the Zamalek police station and made his way home. His house would be deserted, since he had given his servants four days off for Bairam. After prayers he would pack a suitcase in preparation for his flight to Aswan at eight-thirty that night. He had originally planned to leave earlier, but when he had heard of the traffic ban, he had booked a later flight. The only means of getting to the airport while the ban was in force was by special buses leaving from the major hotels, for the benefit of tourists. Munir had no wish to have his movements known, so he had decided to wait until the ban was lifted before taking a taxi. The car would be left in his garage; parked in a public place, it might be noticed and provide a clue to his whereabouts.

There was still much to be accomplished before he could leave the city for the final stage of the operation, however. At one o'clock the head of the information division of Wind of the Desert would be meeting him at his house for a final briefing.

Munir's clandestine organization was much larger than any of its members, including al-Rahid, realized. Its leader took great pride in his ability to keep each cell separate and unaware of the others. That way, if any one branch should be infiltrated by the Mokhabarat, an informer could not destroy the entire movement. Munir was the only one who knew the structure of the organization, the interrelationship of its parts, and its active members. This information he kept in his head—nothing was written down—a mental feat well within the compass of a scholar who had memorized the complete Koran.

Wind of the Desert was divided into four main sections. The strike group was headed by the Libyan, Saraj al-Rahid. Its task was to execute operations planned by the organization. Although this unit was small by international terrorist standards, each man was a specialist and, apart from the newly inducted Mustafa Habib, had been extensively trained.

To the operations group fell the responsibility for logistical support; its members secured the supplies and transportation in support of the strike group. It was operations that had pulled off the biggest coup of all, by obtaining the nuclear fuel needed to build the bomb. Bar-Zeev's theory as to how they had done this was strikingly close to the truth.

Munir had planned it personally, years before. One of his most brilliant students at Al-Azhar had returned to his native Pakistan and, as an accomplished nuclear physicist, had found work at his country's first nuclear power plant. Munir had maintained close contact with the student, and the plan began to mature: he would arrange for the construction of an atomic bomb, using spent nuclear fuel stolen from the plant.

The plan had been worked out with two carefully screened technical advisers. They had quickly determined that it would be impossible to smuggle into Egypt the three or four tons of spent fuel needed to provide the necessary amount of plutonium. It was the Pakistani, by now working clandestinely on a bomb for his own country, who had provided the solution: program the fuel bundles through the reactor ahead of schedule. This meant a much higher concentration of plutonium in the rods, hence substantially less material would be needed for refinement. With the help of Herrara, the scheme had worked.

The political group was headed by Munir himself. It comprised a small coterie of academics who met at regular intervals, ostensibly to discuss the university curriculum. At their meetings they analyzed the political options open to Wind of the Desert, and they served as an unofficial board of directors for the organization.

The most efficient and far-reaching arm of the movement had proved to be the information group. The man in charge was Hussein Ayoub, who had for several years been with the Directorate of General Investigations, Egypt's equivalent of the FBI. Ayoub had long-standing contacts inside both the police force and the Mokhabarat, which still entrusted him with sensitive information. Through Ayoub and his network, Wind of the Desert had soon learned of the discovery of Juan Herrara's body and the subsequent investigation into his death. The information group was able to pass on the government's decision to call in Colonel Uri Bar-Zeev before the Israeli had landed in Cairo, and the corridor gossip around the Ministry of the Interior concerning the feud between Rahman and Bar-Zeev had provided a constant flow of information ever since.

Hussein Ayoub was strolling nonchalantly in front of the house when Munir arrived. Neither man acknowledged the other in public, and Munir walked quickly to his door. He left it unlocked and waited for Ayoub to let himself in.

"Allah be with you, Hussein. We stand on the threshold of a new dawn, my friend." In the presence of his subordinates Munir exuded the confidence of imminent victory.

"I have heard from al-Rahid. The pilot says the transfer went as planned. They are now on the island and ready to move."

"Excellent. What news from our friends in the Mokhabarat?"

"The presidents will be at the Oasis Hotel tonight. The talk around the ministry is that an attempt might be made on Dunlap's life there."

"Good. Do they know anything more of our plans?"

"They haven't found the laboratory. They think we have a bomb. They thought we were going to deliver it today. That's why they shut down the city. They are playing right into our hands. They create their own diversions for us."

"Allah is with us, Hussein. It is He who confounded our enemies. They know nothing of our target?"

"Nothing. They are merely reacting to events."

"I cannot thank you enough for the work you have done. Your intelligence has been invaluable to us. You will be rewarded, I assure you, Hussein."

"What I do is in the service of Islam," replied Ayoub. "May Allah bless our enterprise with success."

"It will be as He wills. I leave tonight. In two days we shall know."

≅≅≅

Mustafa Habib stood rooted in the sand, staring into the face of Saraj al-Rahid. Caught in the act of inspecting the material stored under the canvas shelter, he knew that if his explanation did not satisfy the Libyan, his life might end on that island wilderness.

"May Allah increase your well-being," he stammered.

"What are you doing in here?"

"I heard movement. I was checking."

"There is no one but us here."

Habib ran his palms over the cotton of his galabia. His tongue felt swollen in his mouth. If al-Rahid went for his knife, he would duck behind the boxes and grab a coil of rope to defend himself. He decided to take the initiative. "Perhaps you will tell me now what this is all about."

"You will be told soon enough."

"These rubber boats, the motors, the weapons. We are on a dangerous mission. We could be killed. I have a right to know."

"No one has a right to know anything until I choose to tell him," replied al-Rahid sharply. "We survive only if there is discipline. You will obey me. I have told you before, you ask too many questions for your own health."

Habib adopted a look of contrition. "I am sorry if I have displeased you. But to be ignorant is to be afraid. We have risked jail, perhaps death, to bring these crates from Cairo. Surely we have the right to know what they contain?"

"You have done good work so far," said al-Rahid, his tone softening. "I saw how you stopped the crate from falling into the lake last night. It would not hurt for you to know a little. It might strengthen your resolve. Come over here."

The Libyan placed his hand on top of the smaller of the two wooden crates. "In here are high-powered explosives that have been carefully prepared to do a special job for us. I will tell you precisely what that job is at a briefing tomorrow."

He reached over and patted the larger crate. "And this, my curious young friend," he added with the proprietary air of a man who has just acquired an expensive artifact, "is nothing less than an atomic bomb!"

Al-Rahid paused, relishing the shocked expression that slowly registered on Habib's face. "That's right. Last night you shared a plane with a nuclear device. Oh, I assure you it's perfectly safe. For the time being."

"What in Allah's name are we going to do with it?" Habib began to tremble uncontrollably.

"It is a message from Allah. We—Wind of the Desert—will deliver it. Tomorrow we will put the address on it. You are shaking, Habib. Fear is good. It will help keep you alive."

The young intelligence man stared wide-eyed at the nondescript-looking crate. It could have contained a piece of furniture.

"Come, it is time to eat," said al-Rahid. "Wake up the other two. We have much work to do today."

The four conspirators sat cross-legged on the sand under the shade of the camouflage nets, eating fava beans from tin plates. Habib kept his eyes on his food lest they betray the turmoil of his thoughts. *Nothing less than an atomic bomb* . . . Rashid's testing me, he said to himself. It's a bad joke. But the man is devoid of humor. And there was no mistaking the pride in his voice as he patted the packing case. . . . We are sitting here calmly eating breakfast next to an atomic bomb! Habib's stomach rebelled, and he felt the food rising in his throat. Terrorists with an atomic bomb! What are we going to do with it? What is this madness? Images of mushroom clouds over the desert, of cities leveled, their inhabitants dropping in the streets, flashed through his mind.

He stole a glance at the others, who ate in silence. His Mokhabarat training had not prepared him for anything like this. One thought hammered in his head: If I am to remain alive, I must show no fear, no emotion. I must be controlled.

"When we have eaten, we will begin preparations for our mission," said al-Rahid, wiping the back of his hand across his mouth.

A few minutes later, following al-Rahid's instructions, the four-man team broke open the case of Czech-made automatic rifles and caches of ammunition. They cleaned the rifles of their heavy grease and loaded the clips with cartridges. They fitted the electric motors to the dinghies, after oiling and testing them and filling the batteries with distilled water. They broke out night-combat fatigues and face blacking. They set up portable winches and laid out tools.

Around the middle of the afternoon, Kader and Marwan were instructed to uncrate two wet suits and scuba-diving equipment. Under al-Rahid's watchful eye they put on the gear and slipped into the lake to test it.

"Everything seems fine," said Kader as he emerged dripping from the water. "But the lake is full of sediment. It's like swimming in molten chocolate. I could see only a few centimeters in front of me. Are you sure we won't be able to use lights?"

"It is too risky," replied the Libyan. "You'll have to operate by touch. A light would be seen."

"It's not going to be easy," said Kader, unzipping his suit.

"It wasn't expected to be," said al-Rahid.

The team finished their work at sunset. The mosquitoes, inactive during the heat of the day, swarmed around them now and forced them to seek refuge inside the tents. Habib lay in his sleeping bag, thinking of what he had seen. The afternoon's activity had precluded any thoughts of what was to come. Now, reflecting on the events of the past days, he slowly came to an understanding of the operation in which he was involved. His mind recoiled from the thought, but it continued to hammer inside his brain. There could be no other explanation. Al-Rahid and his group were planning to blow up the Aswan High Dam! For what other reason would they transport a bomb into this godforsaken desert?

If they succeeded, billions of tons of water would flood the entire Nile Valley. Millions of people would be drowned, barrages swept away, whole towns wiped off the map. The torrents would destroy everything in their path: crops, animals, buildings, people. The Egypt he knew would cease to exist.

The man who had conceived the plan must be insane. Only a demented mind could will such a monstrous act. Then the realization came to Habib that he was the only person in a position to prevent this enormity. He alone stood between the conspirators and the destruction of his country. Somehow he must get a warning out. Paralyzed with fear, he lay back in his sleeping bag, the sweat standing out on his forehead despite the cold night air inside the tent. Marwan and Kader lay beside him, talking softly to each other. He turned his face away from them and pulled the sleeping bag over his head to shut out the terrible idea. Did they know what was about to happen? Should he warn them? If he did, they might take him to al-Rahid, and then his death would be certain. There was only one sure way to stop them: he must kill all three of them. Kill them all before they could kill him. He must wait for his moment and not arouse their suspicions. It was easy to say kill the three terrorists, but how? And when? Did he have the nerve to do it? Could he dispatch the three of them before one of them got him? Why had this burden been thrust upon him? Where was the Mokhabarat? It would be simpler if he just took his own life and abdicated all responsibility for what was about to happen. Incarcerated on this island of sand, he was now a prisoner of the information in his own head.

≅≅≅

Following H. Whitney Dunlap's triumphal entry into Cairo and his anodyne address from the balcony of the presidential palace for the benefit of the two hundred thousand Cairenes below (and a global audience of millions of television viewers), the American leader and his party were whisked south to the Oasis Hotel by helicopter. The president broke the ritual bottle of champagne on the great copper doors of Leamington's pleasure dome and declared it open before retiring with Mrs. Dunlap so that they might refresh themselves for the official banquet and the subsequent entertainment in the hotel's cabaret.

Rahman and Bar-Zeev had monitored the president's progress with grim satisfaction. They had changed the helicopter's flight plan at the last moment and had sent off several others, similarly marked, at varying times and on a variety of routes to act as decoys. Then they had availed themselves of the first flight out of the capital.

"If we are to be blown out of the sky, Uri," Rahman had said, "let me tell you it has been a pleasure and an experience to work with you."

"Likewise" was Bar-Zeev's laconic response.

The desert between Cairo and the Oasis Hotel bristled with the latest surveillance technology as well as missile batteries and an infantry battalion deployed along the fifty-kilometer corridor. Nothing could have moved on or above the desert without being observed and summarily destroyed at the press of a button.

"It is truly amazing that the health and safety of one man is more important to us than millions of people who die of flood, famine, and volcanic eruption every year," remarked Rahman as he and Bar-Zeev wandered the hotel grounds later that night.

"He's not a man," replied Uri. "He's an idea. A very powerful and persuasive idea."

Sounds from the cabaret drifted across the velvet night to where they stood, collars raised against the cold, gazing out at the desert. The sand gleamed like snow in the moonlight. A rifle bolt clicked in the darkness, revealing the presence of a guard. Bar-Zeev took out a pack of cigarettes and offered one to Rahman. He struck a match and cupped it in his hands, holding it out for the Egyptian, who bent and puffed until his cigarette was lit.

"What are these things, Uri? Don't tell me—you rolled them yourself from camel droppings."

"They're kibbutz issue. The cheapest on the market. You get a taste for them if you smoke them long enough. This is my last pack."

"Maybe soon you will be able to buy them in Cairo."

"Perhaps."

The music stopped and the audience in the nightclub applauded. Rahman looked up at the star-encrusted sky. The night was clear, and the distant points of light seemed closer in the desert.

"It is beautiful at night, is it not, Uri?"

"Yes, but the desert is a wasteland. I'm only impressed when I see things growing there. I shall never forget the words of Ben-Gurion when I was a young man. It was our duty, he said, to make the desert bloom. To grow roses and cotton out of rock and sand. That to me is beautiful."

"That's fine when you have the technology to turn the desert green, my friend. All that is best in us comes from here. Your people, my people—this was home to us once. Our tribes wandered here, looking for water and pasture for our sheep and goats. How did we manage to grow apart?"

"Jewish history, Ahmed, is five thousand years of warfare, migration, slavery, and more warfare. Once we had to flee from Egypt as slaves to found our first sovereign state. For the next thousand years we resisted the Assyrians, the Babylonians, the Egyptians, the Greeks, and the Romans, who finally conquered us. They destroyed our Temple and exiled us from Palestine. And now, despite dispersions, inquisitions, pogroms, and the Holocaust, we have returned. Through all our suffering we clung to the memory of our biblical homeland. Our dream is now a reality. In this jungle of a world of ours, only the strong survive. And history has shown me that the weak eventually become the strong."

Rahman flicked his cigarette into the sand. "What you say is true, but it is only part of a larger truth, Uri. My people, too, have suffered. We, too, have been subjugated. The Persians, the Greeks, the Romans, the Turks, the British—they have all left their scars on us. Have your people and mine learned nothing from our suffering? We share too much history to be enemies. We share our faith in the one true God; we revere the patriarchs—Moses, Isaac, and Jacob. Our moral code is the same. We are both Semitic peoples who believe in the sanctity of the family, the chastity of our women. Even our dietary laws are similar. Both our peoples seek peace, but when attacked we will defend ourselves with honor."

"What are you saying, Ahmed?"

"I don't know. Nothing. Everything. I will tell you from my heart, Uri. I did not want you to come here. When my president requested your government to send you to Cairo, I cursed your name. I have worked closely with you for a week now. I have sat at your bedside wondering whether you would live or die. I have seen the way your mind works, but I do not really understand you. Yet I cannot call you a stranger. It is as if—how can I put this?—as if a brother you have not seen since childhood has come home after many years' absence. You do not know him very well and you may not understand him, but your blood tells you there is a bond between you. That's how I have come to feel."

Uri Bar-Zeev stubbed out his cigarette and thrust his hands back into his pockets. "Thank you, Ahmed. In the past week, I've come to understand your people better and I've developed a great respect for you personally. We should have met at another time. There's too much blood soaked into the ground. My brother, Asher, was killed by snipers on a convoy to Jerusalem in 1948. My son, Yuval, was blown up by a land mine at El Arish in 1973. They were only defending what was rightfully ours. It's hard for me to love the Egyptians, Ahmed."

"Uri, what is there to be gained from living in the past? We must forget if we cannot forgive."

"It's difficult to forget, Ahmed, when I see copies of *Mein Kampf* in the bookstores of Cairo today."

Rahman placed a large hand on Bar-Zeev's shoulder. "Friendship is the beginning of peace, Uri. If there is more contact between us, perhaps one day the blood of Jews and Egyptians spilled in the wars between us will nourish the desert and make it bloom for all of us."

"Perhaps for our children, Ahmed. But our generation has seen too many wars."

DAY NINE
SUNDAY, NOVEMBER 11

At six-thirty in the morning, Rahman and Bar-Zeev climbed into the cockpit of their helicopter for the return flight to Cairo, where they would connect with a military transport to Alexandria. This would allow them two hours to make a final check of security arrangements before the arrival of the two presidents later in the morning. The sound of their engine brought Bill Leamington running from the hotel. He ducked under the slowly turning rotor blades and called up to the intelligence men.

"Hi! Good morning. I just wanted to thank you," he shouted. "Everything went off just great. The president's wild about the place." There were dark circles under his eyes from lack of sleep.

"We were here to protect your president, Mr. Leamington, not your hotel," Rahman shouted down to him. "Still, I am happy for you."

"I'd like you to have this." Leamington handed up a brown paper bag containing two bottles of champagne still cold from the fridge.

"Champagne, Uri." Rahman mimed a toast.

"A celebration now would be a bit premature, my friend."

"You guys off to Alexandria?"

"That's what you might call classified information, Mr. Leamington."

"I guess you'll be down in Aswan, too. I might see you there. I've got to fly down to settle some problems on the site. If you want to come back here as my personal guest tonight, I can fly you down in Venture's executive jet."

"Thank you, Mr. Leamington. Another time, perhaps," said Rahman. "Our pilot would like to take off now, so if you would kindly move back. . . ."

Bill waved as the helicopter lifted off; he stood watching as it veered out over the shimmering desert and was lost to sight in the low morning sun.

≅≅≅

Some eight hundred kilometers due south on an island of sand, Saraj al-Rahid checked his watch. He went into the radio tent, switched on the receiver, and set the dial at a prearranged frequency. At precisely four minutes past seven, the radio crackled the one-word signal JIHAD. He switched off the set immediately; that single word was sufficient to tell him that all was well and that the plan was to proceed on schedule. Any transmission longer than five seconds had been prohibited by Munir for fear of detection by radio operators at the military base near the Aswan High Dam.

The Libyan felt a flush of excitement; up until this moment he had taken no joy in the operation lest his enthusiasm tempt fate and the scheme be aborted. At last he had the green light—jihad, holy war against the infidel. The action was only eleven hours away; it was time to brief the men.

"Well, my young friend, your curiosity is about to be satisfied," he said to Mustafa Habib as he emerged from the radio tent. "Go fetch the other two—they're over at the supply area. I want everyone in my tent."

While he waited, al-Rahid opened his leather pouch and took out the waterproof maps. He spread one out in the middle of the tent floor and tossed the others into a corner. The men came in and sat cross-legged around the map as al-Rahid began to explain the details of the mission they were about to undertake.

"This is a map of the region we're operating in," he said. "Right now we're here—on an island near the eastern shore of Lake Nasser, thirty-eight kilometers south of the Aswan High Dam. As you can see, this is just one of hundreds of islands in the lake. It has no name—nor do any of the others—and it is almost impossible to find unless you know exactly where you're going. The only thing that distinguishes this one is its size and elevation. It's the largest in the area, which was one of the reasons we chose it.

"Our operation will begin just after the sun goes down tonight, at six o'clock. We will have only twelve hours in which to complete it, so every minute is precious. We must keep precisely to the schedule, for if we are not back here by the time the sun comes up tomorrow, we will be exposed, without cover, in the middle of the lake. If that happens, we're all dead. Is that understood?"

The three men nodded.

"Good. Now, I want each of you to commit this schedule to memory; nothing is to be written down. Just after six we will leave here in two boats. Each of you is to be armed. The bomb and the explosives will be uncrated beforehand and will be placed on the cargo boat, along with the scuba gear. I will be on that one with Habib. Kader, Marwan, you two will follow behind us in one of the smaller boats. Keep close— I don't want to run the risk of your being separated and lost out there. Because the moon will be out in the early part of the evening, it will be bright on the water, so you shouldn't have any difficulty keeping us in sight. On the other hand, because of the moonlight, the chances of our being spotted are greater."

"Spotted by whom?" Habib asked.

"There are fishermen on the lake. Also military patrol planes. We will keep to the eastern shore of the lake all the way up. It is mountainous and uninhabited. The fishing boats keep away from the rocks. The patrol planes usually swing down the center of the lake, so they are not likely to spot us. If we do come across any fishermen, Kadar and Marwan, you two are to detach yourselves and kill them. Your boat is powerful enough to catch anything we're likely to meet on the water. Your weapons are equipped with silencers. If you have to use them, make sure no one is left alive."

Al-Rahid returned his attention to the map and traced a finger along the jagged shoreline of the eastern bank. "Because of the weight of the bomb, we will not be able to make a great deal of speed, even with our heavy-duty motors. Electric engines don't have the same thrust as gasoline-powered ones. But we have had to sacrifice speed for silence. Sound carries long distances over water. The guards on the dam would hear conventional motors before we got within ten kilometers of them."

"Then the High Dam is our target?" Habib said.

"You will not speak until I tell you to," snapped al-Rahid. "Our speed will be about fifteen kilometers an hour. That means we will reach this point"—he stabbed a finger at the map—"at about eight-fifteen."

Habib looked at the chart and saw that the Libyan was indicating a fjordlike tongue of the lake that cut into the mountains about four kilometers below the High Dam.

"This will be our operations base for the night. It is an abandoned village. The fishermen don't come by here, and the mountains hide it from the soldiers at the dam. There will be two Jeeps waiting for us, one of them big enough to take the smaller bomb. I will ride in that one; Kader will drive. Habib will drive the other Jeep, with Marwan. The boat carrying the atomic device will be covered with a black tarpaulin and firmly secured before we leave."

"What if someone comes across it while we're gone?" This time it was Salah Kader who asked the question.

"There is no danger. The area is completely uninhabited and no one goes there. All right? From there, we will take the Jeeps overland for a distance of just over twenty kilometers. It will be a rough trip; there is no road, only the remnants of an old Bedouin goat trail. But it is necessary to get around the High Dam without attracting the attention of the military, which means driving through the mountains."

Habib was puzzled. If the High Dam was the target, why was al-Rahid going to such lengths to get around it? He refrained from putting the question, however.

The Libyan traced the overland route on the map with his finger. The Jeeps would pass well to the east of the small settlement of New Harbor, the collection of huts and sheds that served as the railhead and transshipment point for goods headed south to Abu Simbel and the Sudan. Then they would swing back toward the Nile, rejoining the river at a point three kilometers north of the High Dam, about halfway between it and the old Aswan Dam, built by the British in 1902.

"We have surveyed this area carefully," continued al-Rahid. "There is a point where we can bring the Jeeps to the riverbank. It is rocky terrain, but it can be managed. The motors won't be heard from the dam because the hills will absorb the sound. Also, we have made it our business to find out the times when the sluice gates are opened. The roar of the water on the north side of the dam effectively deadens all other sounds. We will reach this point at roughly half past nine. There will be two inflatable dinghies on the Jeeps, which, Marwan and Kader, you are to prepare immediately. The explosives will be loaded onto one. Kader, you will handle that boat. The rest of us will go in the other boat; you will follow us. Our target will be"—here he paused, looking into the faces of each of them in turn—"one of the underwater sluice gates of the old Aswan Dam."

Habib stole a glance at the other two men. Their eyes were shining and their lips were parted in a smile. As al-Rahid continued to outline the rest of the plan, he listened in growing disbelief. By the time the one-eyed Libyan had finished, Habib found himself shaking uncontrollably once more. What he had heard was the most audacious terrorist scheme ever undertaken, one that would, if it succeeded, have incalculable international repercussions. Either Munir and al-Rahid were raving lunatics, or he was caught up in a power play whose outcome could shake the world.

≅≅≅

The city of Aswan maintains the precocious air of a boom town. The industrial impetus created by the construction of the High Dam in the 1960s caused it to grow too large, too quickly. Badly planned and achitecturally without merit, Aswan stands at one of the world's most spectacular beauty spots. Here the majestic Nile, after meandering through the baking Nubian Desert, suddenly boils over a rocky cataract to fall, placid and untroubled again, on the fertile floodplain that extends outward along its banks as far as the Mediterranean.

For centuries, Egyptians regarded Aswan as the outpost of civilization. Beyond its limits there was only desert and, farther south, marauding tribes who roamed the dunes, warring mercilessly with each other when they were not attacking the caravans. Historically, the town was the last staging point for travelers heading south for the Sudan. The route is still marked by a chain of lighthouses on the high points of sand following the line of the river, each within sight of the next. At night, fires were lit on the roofs as beacons for the camel drivers.

The city itself lies on the eastern bank of the Nile. On the other side, great dunes of sand plunge steeply down to the rocks along the water's edge—a constant reminder of what this primordial landscape was like before man settled here. From these hills the Nile appears incredibly blue, but to the boatmen whose feluccas glide over it like huge white butterflies the water is inky black.

In its perpetual downward flight to the Mediterranean, the river shoulders its way through the granite and sandstone cliffs above Aswan and assaults the straits formed by Elephantine Island, whose tumble of sandstone boulders resembles a herd of bathing elephants. Below the island the jaws of rock open to allow the river a nobler girth on its 850-kilometer journey to the sea.

Aswan was the town of Rashad Munir's birth; here he felt closest to Allah, under a cloudless blue sky where the air was so pure a man could count the ridges of sand to the horizon. If Cairo was a city of dark secrets, ill-defined in the murky air, Aswan was a place of light where every contour was hard-edged and precise. In his lectures he often used the metaphor of the two cities to explain the dichotomy of the human soul: Aswan was the tranquil home of the philosopher, where perceptions were vivid and true; Cairo, the battleground of man against his baser nature.

Although Munir's parents were no longer living, he had retained his links with his birthplace. When it had become apparent that Aswan would be the focal point of his grand design, he had arranged for the purchase by proxy of a large, isolated villa on a hilltop overlooking the eastern bank of the Nile, just south of the city. The house with its walled garden was heavily guarded at all times; the local people were told that it belonged to a wealthy Saudi prince who entertained Western businessmen and Arab politicians in the winter months. Aswan was used to visiting celebrities who came there seeking anonymity. The former president, Anwar el-Sadat, had his own villa just outside the town; and until his death in 1957, the third Aga Khan had been an annual visitor, seeking relief from his painful rheumatism by having himself buried up to the neck in the warm desert sands. Even in death he returned to Aswan: his mausoleum stands white and gleaming, over-looking Elephantine Island. So, little attention was paid to Munir's villa by the townspeople; they were more interested in the movements of visiting movie stars who came to stay at the Old Cataract Hotel.

Rashad Munir did indeed resemble a Saudi potentate as he sat on the balcony of his villa looking down on the Nile rapids. To the south lay the old Aswan Dam and, beyond, a vast reservoir dominated by the Temple of Philae, newly raised from the water onto a small island.

It was Munir's custom here to dress in the flowing white robes of a Bedouin chieftain, complete with the traditional desert headdress—a costume that sat easily on him and gave him the outward trappings of authority. He sat cross-legged on a cushion, as did his guests, Dr. Nasif and Nasif's daughter, Leila. In front of them was a low table set with stuffed vine leaves and salad, the first course of their luncheon.

"All is in readiness, then?" inquired Dr. Nasif, between mouthfuls.

"It is," replied Munir. "I have been in brief radio contact with the island. The weapons arrived safely. We begin the operation tonight."

Nasif looked south toward the graceful buttresses of the old Aswan Dam. "Can it really work?" he asked. In spite of the shade of a large awning and cooling breezes off the river, beads of perspiration stood out on his forehead.

"It can if you have done your work correctly. The crucial factor will be the detonation at the old dam. It must take out one sluice gate only. It must not harm the superstructure of the dam."

"You need have no concern about that," replied Nasif. "Leila has carefully calculated the amount of explosives necessary. Correct, my dear?"

His daughter nodded but kept her eyes on her plate and did not speak.

"However, if you will permit me, there is something I do not understand," the bearded scientist continued. "There are—how many?—almost two hundred sluice gates on that dam. What will you achieve by blowing out one of them?"

"Attention, my dear Nasif. And credibility. Look at the lake behind the dam. At this time of year the water is at its highest level, somewhere between thirty and thirty-two meters. The flood occurs in midsummer.

By November the water has risen up to its maximum height. After that, the level drops steadily until the next flood. Now, that body of water is exerting tremendous pressure against the dam."

"Yes, I understand that," said Nasif.

"Then you will understand that if it is suddenly released, the water will rush through as if expelled from an enormous pressure hose."

"Yes, that's correct."

"Then imagine the impact tomorrow when we detonate the explosives. One sluice gate taken out. Water gushing through uncontrollably. And then the message that unless our demands are met, we will do the same thing at the High Dam—only there we will destroy the entire dam with a single device. Think of the force of water through that one sluice gate on the old dam, Doctor. Then imagine the weight of water behind the High Dam. The depth of the lake is one hundred and eighty-three meters, and the dam itself is more than three and a half kilometers long. The wall of water would pour down the Nile Valley like the Apocalypse. It would sweep away the old dam in a moment and wipe out Aswan. It would destroy everything in its path along the whole valley. Nothing would be left standing. Egypt would drown."

Nasif stirred uneasily on his cushion. "But why an atomic device? Surely what you describe is devastating enough, without adding the terror of a nuclear bomb as well?"

"My dear Nasif, for a scientist you are remarkably naive. How else could the High Dam be destroyed? It is too massive, too solidly built, to be damaged by any conventional explosive. We would have had to move in tens of thousands of tons of dynamite even to make a dent in it."

"But surely you don't really intend to do it? To unleash this dreadful weapon?"

"It would not be I who unleashed it, my good Doctor. Do you think I want to destroy the city of my birth and the country I love? The decision would be that of the president and his advisers. It would be they who brought down this calamity on our heads. The choice will be theirs: to relinquish power and set the people free, or to cling to it and destroy us all."

Munir placed his hands on his knees and leaned back to allow a servant to clear away the dishes. They were replaced by steaming plates of *fool mudhammas*. Munir attacked his hungrily, but across the table a troubled Dr. Nasif pushed the fava beans around his plate.

"Do you mean that if President Sayed doesn't accede to your demands, you will actually blow up the High Dam?" Nasif's voice betrayed his agitation. Out of the corner of his eye he could see that his daughter had stopped eating and was waiting for Munir's answer.

"Sayed will agree. What other option does he have? That is the beauty of my plan."

"But what if he does not?"

"He will. Doctor, do not be so concerned. The bomb will be armed when it is placed at the dam, correct?"

"Yes. As soon as they insert the timer."

"Therefore it will go off automatically at the preset hour unless we send an electronic signal from here switching off the timing mechanism."

"Correct."

"And a different signal will explode the device immediately?"

"Yes."

"Then, Doctor, you and your daughter have produced a weapon of great power, but one that is under our complete control. A weapon is useless unless we possess the will to use it when we have exhausted all other means. Sayed and Dunlap must be left in no doubt of our will and our determination. If they question our resolve, of course they will refuse our demands. But if they believe we are serious and committed, then they will understand they have no choice. For them to believe that, Doctor, we must believe it ourselves. We must be ready to detonate the bomb if our conditions are not met. For only then can we be secure in the knowledge that we shall never have to use it."

"But Professor, what if they are stubborn and try to bluff you?" Leila spoke for the first time during the meal.

Munir half turned to her, dominating the girl with his piercing stare. "Do you not remember your Koran?"

The girl nodded.

"Then you will recall the words of Noah when he spoke to Allah," said Munir. He closed his eyes and swayed slightly as he recited: " 'Lord, do not leave a single unbeliever in the land. If you spare them, they will mislead your servants and beget none but sinners and unbelievers. Forgive me, Lord, and forgive my parents and every true believer who seeks refuge in my house. Forgive all the faithful, men and women, and hasten the destruction of the wrongdoers.' " Munir opened his eyes. "And do you remember what Allah did then, Leila?"

The girl sat with her eyes fixed on the table. "He sent the Great Flood," she replied in a whisper. There was silence around the table, and the girl watched a fly settle on her plate. She did nothing to dislodge it.

≈≈≈

The Aswan Oberoi is regarded by members of the international jet set as one of the finest hotels in the world. It is located at the northern end of Elephantine Island, and its lavishly appointed rooms command a magnificent vista of the Nile and the encompassing desert. Nicole Honeyworth loved the place not only for its opulence and efficient service but also for its proximity to the river. Although she admired Bill Leamington's extravagant caravansary in the desert, the Oasis made her vaguely uneasy, situated as it was in the middle of thousands of square kilometers of sand and rock. The harmony of the immutable sand and the ever-changing river at Aswan appealed to something deep inside of her. The water had a soothing effect on her, a sentiment she did not experience at the Oasis.

Surrounded by the Nile on Elephantine Island, Nicole felt detached from civilization, especially since the only access to shore was by boat, a service provided by the hotel to ferry its clientele to and from the mainland. That narrow stretch of water was sufficient to ensure the isolation and privacy she craved.

Leamington had reserved a private bungalow on the western side of the hotel so that they could enjoy the sunset over Kitchener's Island. As she stood at the picture window, she could see the great lateen sails of the feluccas tacking upriver, their hulls low in the water, weighed down to the gunwales by the crowds of brightly dressed holiday makers on board. The sound of their singing and the accompanying drums carried across the Nile. At Kitchener's Island they would disembark to picnic among the exotic trees and plants of the botanical gardens, spreading out food under sycamore and camelfoot trees or strolling along avenues of dome palms. Young lovers would pluck blossoms from the acacia trees, and the girls would wear them in their hair. How Nicole envied them their carefree holiday mood.

Everything is so unspoiled here, she thought. Yet the beauty of it saddened her: the river, the purple bougainvillea and blood-red hibiscus cascading over the villa walls, the honey smell of the acacia trees, the birds, and the sunset. Across the water, set in the middle of a sand cliff, she could see the Tombs of the Nobles built by the princes of Upper Egypt more than four thousand years before. To spend eternity in such a place, she thought, with the Nile at one's feet, made death somehow less repellent.

She went outside and sat on a rock at the edge of the water, wishing that she could suspend herself in time as the princes of Upper Egypt had attempted to do. Her desire to hold onto that moment was as much motivated by her surroundings as by a subconscious need to postpone a looming confrontation. Now that the Oasis Hotel opening had passed, she had decided to talk to Bill about their relationship. The outcome of that conversation filled her with foreboding: without him, the years ahead looked bleak and meaningless. Yet the sleepless nights and the gnawing discontent she felt compelled her to speak. Not knowing was worse than swift disappointment.

Tears of frustration rose in her eyes. Why is he so stupid? she thought. How can a man who is so dynamic and successful in his career that presidents come to do him honor have a personal life that is one long history of failure? She knew the answer to her own question: because he was incapable of making an emotional commitment. He was prepared to gamble millions of dollars on the most ambitious construction projects, when other men would throw up their hands at the difficulties. But he wouldn't undertake marriage or father a child, even when the conditions were ideal. For three years she had lived with that knowledge. But she had not accepted it; rather, she had ignored it, instinctively feeling that the warmth of her love for him would in time make him understand that she was no threat to him or his ambition. But reluctantly she had come to realize that time would not change Bill Leamington; he wore his past wounds like campaign medals in some private emotional war. If he was unable to change, she was left with two choices: either she waited until he tired of her, or she walked away from him and started afresh somewhere else. She relished neither prospect.

Leamington was awake when she returned to the bungalow; he was sitting up in bed munching an apple. At his bedside was a wicker basket full of dates, oranges, pomegranates, and bananas, courtesy of the management.

"Hey, what do you think of this? A Red Delicious. The first apple I've had since I've been here. Now, that's what I call service."

Nicole crossed the room, sat down at the dressing table, and began to comb her red hair.

"I've got to tell our manager about this. . . . Hey, what's the matter?"

"Nothing. I was just out for a walk. It's sunset."

As she spoke, the room was suddenly shaken by the concussive boom of a howitzer on the eastern bank of the Nile, just south of the hotel. On Kitchener's Island the ibis rose in panic from their trees and circled about uncertainly.

"The guns of Bairam," Bill said, laughing. "Even here we can't get away from them. They'll have us up at six o'clock tomorrow, you'll see."

Another volley shook the room a few seconds later, to the growing consternation of the roosting ibis.

"How long do those damn guns go on?" asked Nicole, her frayed nerves responding to the noise much as the birds outside were doing.

"Till the feast is over, I guess—another day or so. Nicky, something's on your mind. It's not like you. You've been going around looking like somebody just died."

So you've noticed at last, she thought as she dragged the comb automatically through her hair. You've been so caught up with yourself and your hotels you hardly knew I was around.

"I'm just tired."

"Is it your time of the month?"

Men. They always blamed a woman's biological clock whenever she wasn't laughing and acting the adoring mate. "No, it is not my time of the month, Bill, as you so quaintly put it. It's us." She'd said it; she'd picked the plaster off the wound and now it was exposed. She caught his reflection in the mirror; he was staring at the ceiling with the expression of a small boy calculating how he might avoid a conversation he did not wish to have.

"Look, why don't we have an early dinner. You're probably hungry. I know I am."

"Screw dinner!" shouted Nicole, slamming the comb down on top of the dresser and wheeling around to face him. "You're right, something is on my mind. I'm unhappy, damned unhappy. I don't know where I'm going, and that makes me unhappy. Do you understand?"

"Okay. You're unhappy. Why are you unhappy?" His expression had become serious, almost solicitous.

"I told you. It's us. You and me. Is that so difficult to grasp?"

"No, but if you'd be more explicit . . ." He leaned his chin on his knees.

"I'm sick and tired of letting two women who might as well be dead determine what kind of a life we're going to have together."

"What do you mean?"

The vulnerable look on his face, which in other circumstances she had found so appealing, now began to irritate her.

The frustration of the past three years welled up inside of her, sharpening her speech. "You know damn well what I mean."

Leamington swung his legs out of bed and moved toward her as if to comfort her.

"No, don't touch me. I've got to say it. Please, just sit on the bed and listen to me."

"I'm listening."

"I love you, Bill, and I think in your own way you feel the same way about me. In any normal kind of relationship, when two people feel that way about each other over a period of time, they get married and have kids. But not us. Why? Because you allow yourself to be haunted by the ghosts of two rotten marriages. And now you hide behind them. And what's worse, you use them against me. No, don't interrupt me. I've been wanting to say this for a long time. I don't want to go on like this, Bill. And if that sounds like a cliché, I'm sorry. I think after three years it's time you made up your mind and decided where we're going. I've got to know, Bill, even if it means splitting up. But I can't go on trying to reach you with Katherine and Anesta in the way." She fought back her tears, turning her face to the mirror. The image of herself in the glass—the face strained and tired—made her all the more wretched. For the first time she could see what she would look like as an old woman.

"I just can't wait any longer," she ended, in a barely audible voice.

In the silence between them the guns continued to discharge their ceremonial salvos. The rhythmic chain of explosions that shook the room seemed to emphasize their isolation, the ominous rolling thunder of their own private battle.

"Well?" asked Nicole finally.

"What am I supposed to say?" Bill asked apologetically.

"Something. Anything."

He began hesitantly, searching for words that would calm her but avoid his own commitment. "I hear what you're saying. I'm not going to excuse myself by saying I've had a lot on my mind, but God knows I have. I need you, Nicky. All I ask is that you be patient for just a little while longer. You're right. My feeling about marriage has—well, I'm not very good at it. But I don't want to lose you. Will you let me think about it? No, I'm not procrastinating. I promise you I'll think about it. But I can't do it this minute. I've got to get over to the hotel site. I told them I'd be there before the end of the day. Look, why don't you come with me? It'll only be a couple of hours. Then we can come back and have a late dinner, and we can discuss it then. All right?"

It wasn't all right, but Nicole was too drained to argue. He was being evasive; yet in his very evasion he had come closer to facing the issue than he had ever done before. Another such outburst and he might well give in. She nodded and dabbed her eyes with a tissue.

"That's my girl. Now, go take a fast shower and put on a pair of slacks. It's going to be pretty chilly at the construction site."

≅≅≅

The television monitors set up in Alexandria's police headquarters showed a picture of the presidential limousine drawing up in front of Al-Montazah Palace, a former royal residence at the eastern tip of the city. Ahmed Rahman and Uri Bar-Zeev watched as the two heads of state, surrounded by their entourage, climbed the steps of the Byzantine summer retreat.

"That's it, then," said Rahman with a sigh of relief. Dunlap and Sayed would be safe in the sequestered palace set in a wooded garden high on a dune overlooking the Mediterranean. The two leaders would dine privately and rise early the next morning. *Air Force One* was scheduled to depart from Al-Nuzha airfield for the two-hour flight to Aswan at seven a.m.

"One day left, Ahmed," said Bar-Zeev. "All that remains now is to see them safely through Aswan."

"Do not tempt the evil eye, my friend. But I must confess I am feeling much better. The Aswan visit tomorrow will be very brief. The American president will spend no more than seven hours in the city, and most of the time he'll be on board the *Osiris*. He's scheduled to fly back home from Aswan at four o'clock tomorrow afternoon. Between you and me, Uri, I shall be happy to see him go."

"Why did he have to go to Aswan at all? He could have signed the agreement here."

"Politics, my dear Uri. Sayed must be seen to smile on the people of Upper Egypt in the presence of the American president as he has done here and in Cairo. It is a way of saying to the people there that our president understands their importance to the country. The High Dam has come in for a great deal of criticism in recent years, both inside Egypt and abroad. There are those who claim it was a monumental waste of money. That it has not delivered what it promised— unlimited electrical power, twenty-five percent more arable land, water for the farmers when they need it. And worse, they say that because the dam controls the Nile's flood, the soil along the valley has deteriorated, bilharzia has flourished, and the sardine industry at the Delta has been virtually destroyed. This is President Sayed's way of telling these critics that he supports the dam and does not accept these temporary setbacks."

"He could always blame it on the Soviet engineers," Bar-Zeev remarked, laughing.

"There are those who believe they are responsible," replied Rahman seriously.

"Well, even if the Aswan visit is to be brief, we aren't out of danger yet. And frankly, Ahmed, while I don't wish to be an alarmist, I have a bad feeling about tomorrow. Things have gone too smoothly up to now. I think the sooner we can get there and start reviewing the security plans, the better."

"I agree. I shall make immediate arrangements. How is your wound?"

"It's fine. A bit stiff, but no pain. I'll be all right."

"Good. I'll have the car brought around, then. Yes?"

Rahman was interrupted by Ismail Ali, who had just entered the operations room. "Excuse me, sir. I have just received a radio message from Cairo, and I thought you should hear it immediately."

"Well?"

"Sir, the call was from Selim Marzuk."

Marzuk worked in the political investigations section of the Mokhabarat. His specific area of operations was gathering intelligence on student unrest in Egypt's universities. Marzuk controlled the agents recruited on campuses throughout the country; his job had been created at the express instruction of President Sayed, who knew full well that any popular movement to overthrow him would begin in the universities.

"What did he want?"

"I'm not sure, sir, and neither was he. He had some information he said you might want to know. He could not evaluate its importance."

"Go on."

"He said he has a young agent"—Ismail referred to some notes in his hand—"a man named Mustafa Habib. Marzuk planted Habib at Al-Azhar with the usual instructions: to listen for seditious talk, to keep an eye on the Muslim Brotherhood—that sort of thing. Habib was to report anything he heard to Marzuk for evaluation."

Rahman was familiar with the practice. Many young Mokhabarat recruits got their start in the organization with similar assignments.

"What about it, Ismail? Get to the point."

"I'm trying to, sir, but you must have the background. Habib was given explicit instructions not to involve himself in anything dangerous, nor was he to try to infiltrate any suspicious groups he encountered. That is done only by more experienced operatives."

"I'm aware of the way we operate, Ismail."

"Yes, sir. Anyway, Habib filed routine reports to Marzuk until last Tuesday. He hasn't been heard from since. Until today, that is."

"What was the nature of his last report?"

"He told Marzuk he believed that one of the sheikhs at Al-Azhar was hinting at the need to establish an Islamic republic here. Along the lines of what's happened in Pakistan and Iran."

"What was the man's name?"

Ismail consulted his notes. "Munir. Rashad Munir. He's been there many years and is highly respected."

"They usually are. You say Marzuk got another message today?"

"Yes, sir. An old man delivered a note to headquarters in Cairo. Apparently it was written last Thursday."

"Thursday! Why did it take so long for us to receive it?"

"The old man was questioned about that. All he said was that he didn't know it was important."

Rahman groaned. A sense of time and urgency was one attribute his people did not possess. "All right. What did it say?"

"Very little. Only that Habib had been recruited into a terrorist cell by Munir and that it was about to launch an attack. There were three others besides himself. He gave their names. They were about to leave Cairo at that time."

"Where to?"

"He didn't say."

"What kind of attack? Against whom?"

"He didn't say that, either."

"Did he say anything more?"

"The note was written in haste. The old man he gave it to was the doorkeeper at the building where he lived. Marzuk had the room searched. Most of Habib's clothes were gone. He told the old man he was going home to his village with his cousin, but he isn't there and we can find no trace of him."

"What about the other names he gave us?"

"Unknown, except for one. A man named Kader. We were looking for him—his mother was recently attacked by the night visitors."

"Yes. I was there," Rahman said, struck by the coincidence. "Have we found him?"

"No. He hasn't been seen for some time. No one seems to know where he's gone."

"What about this Sheikh Munir? Have we found him?"

"Not yet. And there's something else about him."

"What's that?"

"Marzuk says someone in his division received a telephone call yesterday from a British diplomat. A man named Simpson. He plays squash with a university professor, named Munir, who had been asking him a lot of questions about President Dunlap's visit. About the route of the motorcade and so on."

"Why wasn't this reported to me?"

"It wasn't taken very seriously, sir. You know the British."

"Nevertheless, I should have been told. I will speak to Marzuk when I return to Cairo. Now, what is being done about Munir?"

"We have gone to his house. There was no one there, and a search revealed nothing. But we have a photograph of him and we have circulated it among all our staff. One of our people at Cairo Airport has reported that a man fitting his description was on the Egyptair flight last night to Aswan."

"Aswan!" Rahman and Bar-Zeev looked at each other in alarm.

"Yes, sir. But he couldn't identify him positively."

"Ismail, I want an immediate order put out. Munir is to be arrested on sight. Circulate his picture and his description to every police department in the country. The same for Habib and Kader. Alert Aswan especially. I want them found, and quickly. Tell our people to launch an intensive search. Roadblocks throughout Aswan, all drivers to show identification. Every hotel to be checked. The airport there is to be watched. I want the local garrison informed and street patrols mounted. And, Ismail—"

"Yes, sir?"

"Have my plane ready at the airport. We're leaving for Aswan immediately."

Rahman turned back to Bar-Zeev as Ismail hurried off to carry out his orders. "It looks as if your sixth sense has served you well, Uri. Whatever it is, it's going to happen in Aswan."

"Unfortunately the other side still holds the cards, my friend. They know what 'it' is going to be. We don't."

≈≈≈

The slap of the Nile water against the bow of the black rubber dinghy was the only sound Mustafa Habib could hear. Nervously fingering his automatic pistol, he sat in silence between Marwan and al-Rahid. The anonymous moon stood overhead, etching the dark outline of the second boat behind him, which was carrying Salah Kader and the explosives intended for the old Aswan Dam. The silvery light cast great shadows over the granite boulders on both shorelines, creating grotesque shapes that seemed to pursue them along the banks. They reminded Habib of the stories of jinns and the evil eye his grandmother used to tell him when he was a child, stories that tormented his dreams and made him scream in the night.

The cold night air cut through his black combat clothes, causing him to shiver. His face was blackened like those of the other conspirators, and all their equipment was black, a precaution against detection that made them look like messengers of death.

So far, al-Rahid's plan had proceeded on schedule. Following the trip down Lake Nasser, they had found the Jeeps waiting for them at the rendezvous point. The track through the mountains had been rough but negotiable, delivering them at a beachhead equidistant from the two dams. On this part of the river they moved more quickly, their speed augmented by a strong current that swirled around the boats in small whirlpools—an added turbulence created by the outflow from one of the twelve turbines of the High Dam, partially opened to regulate the water level.

A numbing sense of fear turned Habib's thoughts into a turmoil. Ever since he had learned the terrible dimensions of the plan, he had not been able to concentrate. He had tried to enumerate the courses of action open to him, but the enormity of the scheme overwhelmed him; caught in this evil vortex, he was carried along on its momentum, unable to act. By infiltrating Wind of the Desert he had gone beyond his brief, violating strict orders from his control at the Mokhabarat. His impetuous ambition had landed him in a situation from which there could be no turning back.

If he turned his pistol on Marwan and al-Rahid, killing them there, he would still have to face Kader. Was it not better to die with honor, protecting his country? But he had no wish to die. He would have to choose his moment. If he should declare his hand and be killed by the conspirators, nothing would be gained; his death would merely be the first of many. But each minute that passed brought the plan nearer to

implementation and lessened his chances of preventing a tragedy of
cosmic proportions. Why, of all the millions of people in Egypt, had
Allah singled him out for such a responsibility? He could find no answers
under the blind, indifferent moon.

Habib started at the touch of a hand on his shoulder. Gabal Marwan
held a finger to his lips and pointed straight ahead. Halfway up the bank
on an island was a cluster of mud-brick houses, set like fetid sugar cubes
among the granite rocks. That would be Biga, the first of the three Nubian villages they had to pass.

Al-Rahid steered the boat in toward the shore and moved into the
shadows cast by the rocks. The Libyan would have preferred a moon-
less night for the operation; now the light reflected off the water and
they could easily be spotted. But there had been no alternative. The
timing had been dictated by the American president's visit, and not even
Rashad Munir could make the moon stand still. Four pairs of eyes
watched the island as the boats moved quickly past it. From the direction of the houses Habib could hear the sound of drums and see the
orange light of a fire. A dance to celebrate Bairam, he told himself. The
whole village would be in attendance.

Biga slipped behind them, and the sound of the drums faded over the
water. The villages of Awad and Hasa were ahead. But the river was
beginning to broaden out into the lake formed by the old Aswan Dam.
They would be able to give those villages a wider berth. He saw al-
Rahid smile at Marwan; the two men relaxed their grip on their automatic weapons. Habib wished they had been spotted and there had been
shooting. The military garrison at the dam would have been alerted.

Al-Rahid steered a course between an archipelago of islands—some
large enough to support the villages of Awad and Hasa, others no more
than rocky outcrops. Behind them, Kader followed the same route.
When they had safely passed Hasa, Habib could see ahead of him the
towering silhouette of the Temple of Philae, its massive stone walls
dark against the sky. He knew that two kilometers beyond was the dam.

The ancient temple, newly raised to an island in the middle of the
lake, served as their landmark. From here, al-Rahid swung the boat toward the eastern bank, searching for the small cove that would provide
cover while they carried out their operation. As they skirted the temple,
Habib could see the dam directly ahead, a black line across the water

surmounted by a string of lights. A searchlight located at its midpoint played slowly back and forth across the surface of the water, while a second one, on the west bank, swept across the stonework to the opposite shore. During the briefing Habib had been told that there were machine-gun posts at both ends of the dam and that armed guards regularly patrolled the road across it. The terrorists' task was further complicated by a series of three antitorpedo nets that had been positioned in the lake behind the dam, originally as protection against an Israeli bombing attack. However, these did not extend all the way to the shore, and the plan was to go around them rather than attempt to cut a way through.

Al-Rahid located the cove and directed the dinghy toward it; he waved his arm at Kader, who followed his course. The inlet had been chosen with care. A rocky hill hid it from the guards on the dam, and a line of vegetation along the shore offered some protective cover. The area was rarely visited by local residents at night, although al-Rahid had warned the others to be on watch for workmen from a nearby hotel construction site who might be returning late to Aswan along an old goat trail. Al-Rahid's instructions, if anyone appeared, were to avoid detection if at all possible and to kill only as a last resort. If a witness had to be eliminated, his body was not to be left anywhere near the dam. The authorities must not be alerted prematurely.

The Libyan surveyed the shoreline along the cove and pointed the dinghy toward a spot on the north side where some *farum* bushes grew densely at the water's edge. Behind the bushes was a flat, rock-strewn strip of land, where he beached the boat. Kader pulled in beside them.

The four men stretched their legs briefly and inspected the area. Satisfied that it was deserted, al-Rahid turned to Kader and Marwan. "All right, get your suits on," he whispered. "We have to be finished here in an hour. Habib, you keep watch."

Habib climbed up on a boulder and positioned himself so that he could see the dam. Below him, Kader drew out the wet suits from the bottom of his boat and gave one to Marwan. The two men stripped off their night fatigues and quickly struggled into their diving gear. Al-Rahid was busy checking the explosives, which were packed in two black-vinyl knapsacks.

The three men were below him, their weapons laid aside as they went about the business at hand. He could kill Kader and Marwan with one burst and with luck have time to turn his gun on al-Rahid before the Libyan could reach for his own weapon. Habib's hand trembled as he reached down to his belt. Stealthily he drew the pistol out and held it between his knees. He calculated the distance between himself and the two terrorists at about fifteen meters. Al-Rahid stood at the third point of the triangle, some twenty meters away, but he was now partially obscured behind the boat. If Habib raised the pistol, he would have to fire immediately and duck behind the rocks. The steel of the grip was cold against his palm. No, it was too risky. They were all moving about now and would present a difficult target.

It occurred to Habib that if he could detonate the explosives by firing a shot into one of the knapsacks, this would kill al-Rahid and the explosion would bring help. He would have to retire farther out of range to avoid the splinters of flying rock, though. Then he remembered what Kader had told him: they were using slurry, a TNT-based product that did not deteriorate in water. Nor would it explode at the impact of a bullet; it required a firing mechanism. He recalled the delight with which Kader had explained the principle to him, as if he were describing a new camera: "The slurry is in these clear plastic tubes, just enough to do the job. No more, no less. We'll need forty-five kilograms." Kader had handed one of the hoselike tubes to Habib, who had gingerly turned it over in his hands. It was about fifty centimeters long.

"How do you set it off?" he had asked Kader.

"We'll use a preset timing device, housed in a waterproof case like the ones they use for underwater cameras." Kader had taken the cartridge back from Habib and undone the wire-twist tie at one end. "When we're about ready, we'll take off the ends of two of these cartridges, one from each bag. We'll insert some TNT primer and an electric blasting cap. Then we'll hook up the cartridge to the timer. When the hands reach the right position, *whoomp!* Beautiful, isn't it?"

Al-Rahid was now in the process of completing those final preparations. As Habib watched, he resealed the twist tie on the first cartridge, which was now primed and connected to the clock mechanism, and carefully placed it back in the vinyl bag. While Marwan fastened it, al-Rahid repeated the operation with the second package of explosives.

Habib knew that only one detonator was necessary to set off the blast, but they were taking no chances on a mechanical failure. Once the explosives were placed, a faulty detonator could ruin the entire operation.

Placing the explosives would be basically a simple operation. Kader and Marwan were to identify a target gate, dive to its base, and place the two bags as close to its center as possible. It was important that the explosives be set directly against the gate; in that way, the explosion would create a water hammer that would blow out the sluice with tremendous force.

Marwan picked up one of the bags and carried it to the water's edge, where he sat down and drew on his swim fins and face mask. Kader helped him on with a single air tank, adjusting the straps so that it rode on the right side of his back. He then assisted Marwan in strapping on the knapsack, which he placed adjacent to the air tank. When he was finished, Marwan was carrying almost forty kilograms of equipment. Once in the water, though, he wouldn't even notice the weight.

Al-Rahid helped Kader through the same procedure. When they were both ready, the two divers stood ankle-deep in the water, checking their regulators and pressure gauges. Then they carefully rigged a buddy line between them to ensure they would not lose their bearings and become separated in the murky water. A final check, a quick wave, and they moved out into the lake like two great black sea beasts. Habib, from his perch on the rock, watched them as they swam noiselessly toward the dam. He had missed his chance. Al-Rahid beckoned him down from the rocks.

"Now we wait," the Libyan whispered as Habib joined him on the beach. "They have forty-five minutes to plant the explosives and get back here. Help me hide the boats in those bushes. Then you stand watch behind that boulder over there and signal me if you hear or see anything suspicious."

"What if they're discovered?"

"We take one boat and head back upriver to the Jeeps as fast as possible. But don't worry. They won't be. Now get to it."

Out on the river, Kader and Marwan had just rounded the rocky headland that concealed the boats from the guards. The dam was directly in front of them, every detail clearly visible. Kader could see cars moving along the top of the kilometer-long structure—the dam provided Aswan's only bridge across the Nile—and armed soldiers on patrol.

The two divers were still at the surface and would remain there until they came within range of the searchlights. Rather than run the risk of losing their way underwater, especially with three torpedo nets to be negotiated, it had been decided to swim most of the way on the surface. This way they could conserve their air supply, since they were operating on only one tank apiece.

Kader pulled on the line for Marwan to stop, and the two men trod water as they studied the scene in front of them. The position of the torpedo nets was clearly marked by the large floats that supported them. The screens extended to within fifteen meters of the shore, closer than Kader would have liked. The risk of being seen by someone on the bank was not great, but was a factor nonetheless. He examined the pattern of the searchlights and noted that the shadows cast by the buttresses effectively concealed the eastern end of the dam from their beams. That would be the safest area to plant the explosives. The guards on the dam would hardly be alert, having no reason to suspect an attack. Yet it would take only one soldier spotting a trail of bubbles to set off an alarm that could destroy the plan.

Kader turned to Marwan and pointed to the eastern end of the dam; then he held up five fingers. The other man nodded. The fifth gate from the eastern shore would be the target. They swam toward it with easy strokes so as not to disturb the water.

As they approached the first torpedo net, they swung toward the shore. Kader examined the bank; there was no one to be seen. They edged around the screen, then negotiated the second one. The last screen was just ahead. Beyond it, the searchlights continued their sweep across the dam and the water behind it.

Kader pulled on the line and nodded to Marwan. The two men checked their wrist compasses and watches, and submerged.

The black, silty water of the Nile closed over them. Once under its surface, they could see virtually nothing. Only the strain on the line between them told Kader that Marwan was still beside him. He had to hold his compass right up to his face mask to check that he was heading in the right direction. The watch, which he wore on the same wrist, told him that they were ten minutes into the operation. It took them two minutes to skirt the last torpedo screen, a curtain of steel mesh one hundred meters from the face of the dam. Looking up, Kader could see points of luminescence on the surface of the water and then a bright shaft of probing light moving directly over them. He gave two quick pulls on the line, a signal to Marwan to dive deeper.

Kader didn't realize they had reached the dam until he ran into it. He groped his way along the slimy concrete facing until it gave way to riveted steel. He had found one of the sluice gates. With Marwan right behind him, he rose to the surface and cautiously poked his head out of the water. As he had expected, the shadows cast by the dam protected him from the lights. He looked toward the eastern end of the dam and counted the gates. They were at the fourth. The next one along was their target.

Resubmerging, he felt his way along the dam, Marwan close behind. When they reached the fifth gate, they dived together to the bottom. It was a deep dive, and Kader had to pause several times to clear his ears, pinching his nose through the mask and blowing. When he felt his ears pop, he continued down.

The water around them was now pitch-black, with no light at all penetrating from the surface. Kader felt his way down the steel gate, holding onto its chains to ensure that the current would not pull them away from the dam. He could feel the taut line behind him as Marwan followed him down.

Then they reached the bottom, their fins sinking into the muddy bed. Kader moved quickly, feeling his way to the edge of the steel gate. From there he worked his way back to what he calculated was approximately the center. Unstrapping the vinyl bag from his back, he deposited it at the base of the gate. Beside him, he could feel Marwan groping with his pack; then it was off and Marwan was thrusting it at him. Kader placed it beside his own lead-weighted bag. He wondered what was happening on the surface—had anyone spotted the bubbles and was the alarm even now being raised?

But there was no time to worry about that now. Checking to make sure the explosives were secure against the sluice gate, he gave four pulls on the line—the prearranged signal to Marwan that the job was completed and they were to surface. The ascent took almost two minutes, permitting their bodies to adapt to the changes in pressure. There was still another dive to come, and Kader could not risk an attack of the bends.

≋≋≋

The project office of Venture's Aswan Hotel was a large wooden shed perched on a rocky escarpment on the eastern bank of the Nile, over-looking the Temple of Philae. Inside, it was hot and stuffy; the windows were closed against the mosquitoes, and the Canadian project manager, Noel Barstairs, had added to the discomfort by chain-smoking French cigarettes. After three and a half hours of sitting on a hard-backed chair and listening to Barstairs and Leamington argue the merits of an engineer's report, Nicole was impatient and hungry. Leamington appeared to be oblivious to her as he pored over geological surveys and debated with the dour Barstairs.

"I can only repeat, Bill, if the hotel goes up as per the designs, I shall have to file a report with the building inspectors. All the evidence says it's putting too much pressure on the sandstone. That whole balcony's going to shear off. There's just no support."

The balcony in question was a large patio that was to extend out over the water of the reservoir behind the old dam—an exciting design feature that would give the hotel the appearance of a luxury yacht.

"Goddammit, man, we had the whole place surveyed. The structural engineers said it would be fine."

"But the geologists disagree. You can't afford to take the chance."

"What if we sank reinforced-concrete pillars into the rock face?"

"The weight is still too great."

"Okay, suppose we injected concrete into the rock face to stabilize it?"

"The water would in time erode the sandstone and you'd still have the same problem."

"Look, I hired you to *solve* my problems, not to play government watchdog," said Leamington.

The Aswan Hotel had given Venture International the most trouble of the three Egyptian projects. It was already three weeks behind schedule, and this new setback could scuttle the entire enterprise. Most of the problems arose from the site itself. Leamington himself had selected it, against the better judgment of his architects. Unwilling to admit that he had been wrong, he had ridden roughshod over any opposition to the hotel, determined that it would be built where and how he wanted it. He had insisted that this hotel must have a view to rival that of the Old Cataract Hotel, five kilometers downriver. The only comparable panorama was the one he had chosen: the Temple of Philae, recently raised by an Italian company above the floodwaters to an island behind the old Aswan Dam. He had already started negotiations with the government for a sound-and-light show he wanted to create, which would permit hotel guests sitting on the balcony at night to listen to voices from concealed speakers recreate the former glories of Upper Egypt while colored lights played across the twin pylons and colonnades of the twenty-three-hundred-year-old temple. This vista, combined with the rugged terrain, the view of the old dam, and the desert stretching along the western bank, made the site unique. After he had seen it, Leamington had refused to consider building anywhere else in the Aswan area.

As a result, the Aswan Hotel had progressed no further than a hole in the ground, a hole filled with heavy equipment and surrounded by several portable construction sheds that served at offices and storage huts. In its present state it was a depressing sight, and Nicole resented the hours they spent there.

Leamington was launching into another discussion about the possibility of floating derricks to provide additional support for the balcony. Nicole's stomach told her it was well past the dinner hour, and she was impatient to begin the discussion about their future together that Bill had promised her.

"Bill, I'm sorry to interrupt, but it's after ten o'clock. I'm sure Noel is tired, and so am I. Why don't we go back to the hotel for dinner? There's nothing you can do now, anyway."

Leamington looked at his watch. "Nicky, I'm sorry. You're absolutely right. Look, just let me finish up on this point and then we'll go."

"How long?"

"Twenty minutes. No more. Promise."

"All right. I'll wait outside. It's too hot in here."

"Okay, but don't go far. It can be treacherous walking around here at night, with all the rocks."

"I'll be fine."

Outside, it was fresh and cool. Nicole breathed in the sweet air to clear her head. Directly above her, the moon, like a newly minted silver coin, cast its sheen over the gray-and-pink boulders. The wind disturbed the surface of the water, each ripple phosphorescent under the stars. And in the center of the lake, on its rocky circle, stood the shrine to the moon goddess herself: Isis, the eternal woman, mother of all things, sister and wife to the sun.

Nicole gazed at the twin pylons, like great square breasts rising above the facade of the temple. A fitting monument to a moon goddess, she said to herself. She recalled an inscription she had read under a statue of the horned Isis: "I am that which is, has been, and shall be. My veil no one has lifted. The fruit I bore was the sun." Here, time seemed to stand still at the command of Isis. The rock, the water, and the limitless sands were imbued with her spirit. Nicole experienced a sudden impulse to utter a prayer to the goddess—not a prayer, really, more a supplication—to ask her help and her advice as one woman to another. The moon above her head seemed so close that everything else paled into insignificance.

She stood for several minutes looking out over the scene. Off to her right she noticed a goat trail, running along the hill in the direction of the dam. She remembered Bill's admonition, but she felt as if she had the protection of the goddess herself. Her way would be lit by the moon, and she wanted to see its effect on the facade of the temple.

As she picked her way along the track, she could see the sand dunes on the opposite shore rising white as icebergs out of the black Nile. The path began to wind steeply down the hillside. Below her was a cove set in the shadow of a wall of rock. She debated for a moment, then decided to continue down. She had the urge to touch the Nile water, as if she had to reassure herself that the river was real and that the moonlight had not conjured up a mysterious fantasy world.

≈≈≈

Kader and Marwan reappeared suddenly, like two great black fish rising out of the water. Al-Rahid and Habib stepped out of the shadows to meet them.

"Well, what happened? How did it go?" the Libyan whispered.

Kader paused for a moment to catch his breath. "Everything's ready. Nobody spotted us. The only problem was trying to work in total darkness. We had to do everything by touch. If it hadn't been for the line, we'd have lost contact."

"You're sure the explosives are properly positioned?"

"As sure as we can be. But we were working blind."

"All right. Get your gear into the boats. You might as well keep your wet suits on."

Marwan had already slipped off his fins and was walking toward the bushes where the rubber dinghies were concealed. Suddenly he dropped to the ground and pointed. The others reacted immediately. Habib looked in the direction Marwan had indicated. Someone was coming down the path, slipping noisily over the loose stones. He could see that al-Rahid, beside him, had drawn his automatic pistol.

Nicole knew it was time to turn back. The climb up the path would be much more difficult than the descent, and if Bill came out and didn't find her, he would be worried. But she had spotted some vegetation at the water's edge and wanted to take a few leaf samples for later identification.

Some of the bushes grew in the water, but there was a cluster on the shore just below her. She approached them and reached to pick a few sprigs. As she did so, her foot struck an object on the ground. Glancing down, she realized she had stumbled against a rubber boat. Before she could stoop to investigate, she was grabbed from behind and her mouth squeezed shut. She struggled to escape and tried to scream, but the man holding her was too strong.

"It's a woman!" whispered Marwan.

"Kill her," said al-Rahid. "We'll get rid of the body on one of the islands on our way back."

Nicole could feel one of Gabal Marwan's powerful hands tightening around her throat. In front of her she caught sight of the hideous face of a one-eyed man. She felt herself losing consciousness.

"Wait a minute." Salah Kader was suddenly beside the Libyan. "Why take any chances? Her body might be found, and our plans would be ruined. Why not take her back to the island with us? When it's all over, we can kill her if we have to."

Al-Rahid looked at the red-haired woman who struggled feebly in Marwan's grasp, and nodded.

"You may be right. But if she is missed, the alarm will be raised, anyway."

"Perhaps. But there will be no body, nothing to indicate violence," replied Kader. "She might just have slipped into the river and drowned. Or wandered off and become lost. Why jeopardize the plan with a needless killing?"

"All right, tie her up."

Nicole was vaguely conscious of a filthy rag being stuffed into her mouth and her hands and feet being trussed together with leather straps. Then she felt herself being lifted bodily and placed in the bottom of a rubber boat.

"Let's get started," ordered al-Rahid. "We've lost ten minutes already. We've got to be back on the other side of the High Dam by half past twelve at the latest."

DAY TEN
MONDAY, NOVEMBER 12

As the Jeep bounced blindly along the mountain track, al-Rahid could feel the pressure of Nicole's thigh pressed against his. She had been wedged between him and Habib, who was driving. Marwan and Kader followed in the second Jeep. At each jolt the girl whimpered through her gag, a sound that both infuriated the Libyan and inflamed him. The presence of a woman among them had created a new dynamic; somehow the single-minded purpose that welded the four men together had subtly changed. It would take all al-Rahid's authority to maintain discipline. He had seen how Marwan had eyed the frightened girl, how Habib kept turning to look at her as if concerned for her comfort. Al-Rahid himself was experiencing a growing sense of excitement, which he knew he must stifle.

"Keep your eyes on the track," he hissed at Habib. "We are losing time."

Al-Rahid's anger sprang from his own ambivalent thoughts about the red-haired woman next to him and, more, from his genuine concern about the feasibility of the next stage of the operation. When he had suggested that the plan was not workable, Munir had exploded in fury and accused him of a lack of faith. "If you believe, Allah the Almighty is your right hand"—such was the professor's practical advice, but it rested with al-Rahid to make the scheme work. Allah notwithstanding, the two

tired divers had to maneuver a ninety-kilogram bomb across four kilometers of open water and secure it to the back of the Aswan High Dam.

Kader and Marwan had undergone rigorous training in Libya to prepare themselves for this mission—weight lifting had built up their
muscles, and running, their lung power. But they were now asked to do
the work of three men—Juan Herrara was to have been a member of
the strike group—and al-Rahid wondered whether they could rise to the
occasion. Perhaps a gesture was called for—something to get their
adrenaline running. He considered slitting the girl's throat as soon as
they arrived back at the staging area on Lake Nasser. Just to heighten
their awareness of the perils they faced.

Not only was the swim they were about to embark upon hazardous,
but in their weakened condition they would be subject to cramps. The
base of operations was as close as they could get to the dam without
running the danger of encountering a military patrol. Al-Rahid had
dismissed the thought of delivering the bomb by boat; night fishing on
the lake by moonlight was a common local practice. And even if their
craft escaped notice, they might foul the nets stretched out across the
water. There was no alternative to the long swim. At least the divers
could conserve their energy by using the DPVs—meter-long, diver-
propelled vehicles shaped like small torpedoes, with a trigger mechanism to operate the battery-driven motors.

Habib negotiated the final hill, bringing the Jeep down to the small
sandy beach where the bomb and the rest of the equipment had been
left hidden under a black tarpaulin. As soon as they stopped, al-Rahid
jumped out and lifted Nicole bodily from the seat. He motioned to
Kader and Marwan to remove the tarpaulin. Underneath, the bomb
was sitting in the rubber boat like a ponderous black egg in a nest. As
soon as the tarpaulin was free he grabbed one corner and marched
Nicole a few paces down the beach and threw her to the ground; then
he spread the covering over her and weighted down the corners with
large water-blackened rocks.

"If she tries to move out of there, kill her," he whispered to Habib,
and handed him his knife.

As the young intelligence agent kept watch over the figure under the
tarpaulin, Kadar and Marwan began preparing the bomb for its final
journey down the lake. Al-Rahid rummaged in the boat for a plastic

roll. Unfurling it, he took out a black nylon air bag, which, when inflated to the correct pressure, would support the bomb in the water just below the surface. The bag was fitted with heavy-duty clips to secure it to the DPVs and to the bomb itself. In this fashion the two divers could propel the device underwater with a minimum of effort.

Kader and Marwan had conducted trials in freshwater lakes in Libya to determine the critical amount of air needed to provide sufficient buoyancy for the bomb. Too little and the device would sink to the bottom; too much and it would pop to the surface like a playful dolphin. While Kader laid out the air bag and clipped it to the DPVs, Marwan pulled fresh air tanks from the boat and tested the pressure gauges and regulators. For this swim he and Kader would each be wearing two tanks, and there was no room for error. Al-Rahid laid out a cylinder of oxygen on the sand and nodded to Kader. While the divers helped each other on with their equipment, the Libyan moved to the bomb and ran his fingertips over the casing. When he found a seam he gestured to Marwan to hand him his diving knife. Using the tip of the blade, he pried open a small hatch in the bomb's outer case. Reaching into his pouch, he took out a device the size of a transistor radio and placed it carefully in the hatch, securing it in a rubber clamp. Snapping the lid shut, he took a container of waterproof sealant from the bottom of the boat and, dipping his fingers in the tarry substance, smeared it around the seams. The atomic bomb was now armed.

The three men then lifted the bomb from the boat and set it gently down in the shallow water. Kader took the oxygen cylinder and attached it to the nozzle of the air bag. With an evil hiss the black nylon swelled out like the wings of a vampire. He then applied a pressure gauge to the valve and let some of the air out. When he was satisfied the bag was adequately inflated to support the weight of the bomb, the two divers slipped the bag over the device and clipped it to the eyelets on the casing. The bomb was ready for its lethal journey to the dam. Al-Rahid embraced the two men, who turned and waved to Habib. He saluted them in turn and watched as they pushed the bomb into deeper water, pulled their masks over their faces, and began to move away from shore, submerging as they went. The great egg-shaped bomb disappeared below the luminous surface of the lake, and all that remained visible was the tip of the air bag, like the back of a killer whale.

The thought occurred to Habib that now, as the Libyan concentrated on the launching of the bomb, was his chance to kill the unarmed al-Rahid. If Kader and Marwan were sufficiently out of range, he could use his pistol; or he could chance a swift attack with the knife al-Rahid had given him. A moaning sound from under the tarpaulin caused al-Rahid to divert his attention from the lake. He ran over to where Habib stood, and angrily rolled the stones away. Nicole raised herself to her knees, gasping for air and sobbing.

Al-Rahid raised his hand over his shoulder and brought it down with a crack across the girl's face. Nicole fell back in the sand, too stunned to utter a sound.

"Kill her if you want to," al-Rahid said, smiling, then looked back at the lake.

"She is as good as dead," whispered Habib. He looked at his watch. It was forty-three minutes past midnight. The divers had just over three and a half hours to complete the operation and return. At the final briefing, al-Rahid had stated that they would set out for the island at four-fifteen a.m. whether the divers were back or not. And Habib knew that al-Rahid, now in a triumphant mood, would not deviate one minute from his schedule for any errand of mercy.

≅ ≅ ≅

Two hours had passed since Bill Leamington had first become aware of Nicole's disappearance. It was shortly after midnight when he and Barstairs had finally emerged from the project office.

"She did say she was going to wait outside, didn't she, Noel?" said Leamington in surprise.

The area around the construction site was deserted except for two night watchmen who had been hired to keep an eye on the drilling equipment but had quickly mastered the art of sleeping in an upright position. When awakened, neither of them recalled seeing anyone. An ominous feeling of dread began to swell inside Leamington as he clambered over the rocks and shale to the crest of a sand hill overlooking the Temple of Philae. A trickle of sand and some small stones, dislodged by his steps, slid down a steep incline and plopped into the lake water. He called

Nicole's name several times, but the only answer was the echo of his own voice ricocheting off the rocks.

"Maybe she got tired and went back to the hotel," suggested Barstairs.

"It's miles," retorted Leamington impatiently.

"She could have flagged down a car on the road."

"Oh, for God's sake, man!" Leamington had the urge to hit the diffident Canadian.

"Sorry, just trying to help."

"Okay, I'll call the hotel."

Leamington waited tensely as the operator at the Oberoi buzzed the room. When there was no answer he asked them to page Nicole in the dining room and the bar.

"I'm sorry, sir, she doesn't reply," the operator announced finally.

"What the hell could have happened to her, Noel? She would have left me a message if she were going to wander off. She would have said something."

"She could have gotten lost. Twisted an ankle on the rocks."

"You really know how to comfort a guy, don't you, Noel? The first thing we've got to do is get help. A search party. She could be injured out there. Maybe even unconscious. How soon can you get some of our men out here?"

"I can send the watchmen into town with a truck and collect a dozen or so. But it'll take time."

"Why don't you phone them?"

"Egyptian construction workers don't have phones, Bill."

"Yeah, I can't even think straight. All right, tell them to get as many men as they can back here in an hour. Have we got flashlights?"

"Yes, plenty. But you know it's a holiday. They aren't going to be too happy about being yanked out here tonight."

"Offer them triple wages, goddammit. I'm going to keep looking. You wait here, and when they get back, split the men up into teams and send them out if I haven't found her."

By one o'clock Bill Leamington had combed an area within a four-hundred-meter radius of the project office. The exertion of climbing over rocks had made him sweat in spite of the cold night air. As he tripped and slid over the sandy surface, tricked by the moon into mistaking substance for shadow, he cursed Nicole for wandering off and himself for allowing her to do so.

Barstairs poured him a glass of Scotch when he returned, exhausted and dejected, to the project office. As he gulped it down, he heard the sound of a truck grinding up the construction road, its headlights leaping with each rut in the dirt surface. The watchmen had managed to enlist the services of their cousins and uncles—eleven in all—who willingly left the family hearth on Bairam at the promise of triple wages. Using one of the watchmen as interpreter, Leamington explained the situation to the men and issued each with a flashlight. He sent them out in two-man teams; if the girl was found, one member was to return to the office and one to remain with her. As they shuffled off to their allotted territories, Leamington could hear the men whispering among themselves.

"What are they saying?" he asked the watchman.

"They are saying that a woman should not be here at night. She will be a victim of the evil eye."

"Listen, you can tell those guys that I'm offering a reward of one hundred pounds cash money to the one who finds Miss Honeyworth. And then we'll see who believes in the evil eye."

The watchman put his hands to his mouth and leaned his head back. Facing each direction he repeated Leamington's offer like an incantation. Ghostly white galabias could be seen moving through the rocks with sudden determination.

"Money is a great spur, Mr. Leamington," said the watchman, "but we will need more men. Here there are as many rocks as there are stars in the sky. They cast long shadows. A man could walk right by your lady and not see her. Or the river may have claimed her. There are crocodiles here, you know. In the ancient times they would throw a young girl into the river to placate—"

"Noel! Get this man out of here before I throw *him* into the river," snapped the exasperated Leamington. Barstairs ushered the old man out of the office.

"Are there really crocodiles in the river?" asked Leamington when Barstairs returned.

"Not really. If there are, they're pretty small. I'd be more concerned about the jackals. If Nicole is out there somewhere, they could attack."

"Oh, my God," groaned Leamington, swigging another glass of Scotch. "Let's get back out there."

≅≅≅

The only reality for Salah Kader, sightless in the murky waters of Lake Nasser, was the gentle thrumming of the DPVs and the dark mass of the bomb, which moved inexorably below the surface toward its target. The momentum of the bomb carried him along behind it as if it had a will of its own and he was merely an appendage, an acolyte in its service, joined by an umbilical cord to its other attendant, Gabal Marwan.

All their months of training and preparation had come together now in this one act of skill and endurance: the delivery and setting of the atomic device at the spine of the Aswan High Dam. The reverence that Kader had felt toward his leader, Rashad Munir, was now transferred to the agent of the professor's revolutionary vision. He experienced an extraordinary sense of euphoria as he concentrated on the tiny sliver of green light from his compass. Every few minutes he would tug on his line—the signal to release the trigger mechanism to stop the propellers —and he would break the surface of the water for a visual fix on the dam. The gigantic stone shoulders of the dam dominated his line of sight. The awesome size of the structure—seventeen times as large as the great Pyramid of Cheops—dwarfed the rugged landscape around; next to it everything appeared puny and vulnerable. The dam seemed to defy time and stood like a cosmic creation rather than the work of mere men. He understood now why al-Rahid had said that only a nuclear explosion could destroy it.

The moon was down, and the surface of the lake was smooth as ice. A military vehicle moved along the service road above the sloping rock fill like a tiny insect against the massive paved wall. Kader waited until it was out of sight before signaling Marwan to start the engines again. Their plan was to maneuver the bomb to the right of one of the two jetties that protruded from the dam and secure it to the rocky face ten meters below the water level. They would anchor the nylon lines clipped to the bomb around the rocks and detach the DPVs for the return journey. His one concern was the possibility of fouling their air lines on the jagged granite as they worked in total darkness. Kader uttered a silent prayer to Allah to give him the strength to finish the job.

The defenses deployed around the Aswan High Dam are better suited to protecting it from aerial attack than to meeting the kind of threat now approaching silently below the surface of Lake Nasser. A major military base that protects Aswan Airport is located just west of the dam; SAM missile silos ring the area, alongside antiaircraft nests equipped with batteries of Russian ZSU-234s. In wartime, barrage balloons were sent up nightly as an added protection against a bombing attack, but that practice was ended with Anwar el-Sadat's peace initiative. Regular military patrols are carried out along the three-and-a-half-kilometer length of the dam, but their main purpose is to prevent infiltration of the power plant on the dam's north face by saboteurs seeking to put out of action any of the twelve 175-megawatt turbines that generate electricity for the entire Nile Valley. The threat of a terrorist attack on the structure had never been taken seriously by the High Dam Authority or the military planners. It would require tons of conventional explosives to make the slightest impression on the millions of tons of rock fill. So as Salah Kader and Gabal Marwan approached the High Dam, the security they had to contend with was minimal.

Kader surfaced for a final look. The dam was only fifty meters away. He could hear the roar of water through an open tunnel, and he could feel the pull of the current toward it. He steered the bomb away and signaled Marwan to dive. They moved slowly now, with Marwan in front, feeling his way, until they reached the mountain of rocks that extended from the floor of the lake. Groping along the granite protuberances, Kader found a suitable anchorage. He lashed the air bag to it and felt a tension on the line, as did Marwan. The two divers then swam under the bomb and secured two more lines from the base to the rocks. It took ten minutes for them to immobilize the great black egg. Kader checked his depth gauge: the bomb was exactly nine and a half meters below the surface—too deep to be seen in the muddy water and out of Geiger-counter range, yet shallow enough to receive the radio signals that would determine whether it would be detonated or not.

A final check and they unhooked the DPVs and pointed them back up the lake. Kader worked his way along the buddy line and grasped Marwan's hand in his. Now that their mission was over, they felt reluctant to leave.

≅ ≅ ≅

Aswan police headquarters was built by the British as a military post in the dying days of Empire. The moral rectitude of the former colonial masters was written into every line of the stockade—an uncompromising square of honey-colored stone that enclosed a central courtyard. The only concession to anything as unsoldierly as a pleasing design was the curve of the tall, arched windows set along the second story to catch the breeze off the river. The compound was further walled off by a wrought-iron fence on all four sides, which was painted green, as were the sentry boxes on both sides of the main gates. It was here that Ahmed Rahman and Uri Bar-Zeev had set up their operations center when they arrived in Aswan shortly after nine p.m. on Sunday.

Rahman had nipped a potential feud between the Aswan police and the military by insisting that the briefings take place at police headquarters, which was in the town, near the hotels, rather than at the army base five kilometers away along a winding desert road.

"Gentlemen," Rahman had begun, when the law and the army had finally agreed that they were wasting time arguing over the venue for the briefing, "Colonel Bar-Zeev of Israeli intelligence"—there were murmurs around the room at this, and chairs squeaked as the uniformed officials turned to take a better look at the interloper—"the colonel and I have checked the passenger lists of all commercial flights to Aswan over the past three days. Rashad Munir's name did not show up. This means either he has not flown here or he has used an assumed name. Or the manifests have not been scrupulously filled out by Egyptair staff. I am inclined to believe our man used a pseudonym. I have ordered a check on the whereabouts of all passengers on the lists and have had inquiries made among the taxi drivers and at the hotels and military checkpoints. Photographs of Munir have been circulated, and roadblocks have been set up at all access points to the city. I realize that the population of Aswan has swollen fourfold because of Bairam, which makes all our jobs more difficult. But I want Munir found.

"I need hardly tell you that the president of the United States will be arriving here tomorrow morning in the company of President Sayed. If Munir is in the city, he must be found before then. Are there any questions?"

"Colonel Rahman." An army captain stood up. "You mentioned that he may have accomplices here. Do you have any description of them?"

"No, I'm afraid we don't. All I know is that he could be with two young men. One of them is a Mokhabarat agent."

"You have no description of your own agent?" pressed the captain.

"Of course we have his description," flared Rahman, "but it is Munir I want you to find, not one of our operatives."

Following the briefing, Rahman and Bar-Zeev had been driven along the embankment to where the *Osiris* was moored. The entire area around the riverboat had been sealed off by armed police and troops. No one could approach within five hundred meters of it without a pass. Knots of curious sightseers stood on the sidewalk under the arcade of shops on the other side of the road. A young boy wearing a Charles Bronson T-shirt came too near one of the troops and was sent unceremoniously on his way with the aid of a rifle butt.

Below the river wall, the white vessel with its blue bowline was ablaze with light, rivaling the shimmering illuminations of the Oberoi Hotel across the river on Elephantine Island. On board, Rahman and Bar-Zeev had met the Egyptian manager, Hamed Sufy, who had conducted them on a stem-to-stern inspection of the German-built craft, operated by Hilton International.

"I understand the staff lives on board all the time?" Bar-Zeev asked.

"Yes, you may see their sleeping quarters if you wish. Some are asleep now."

"Have they all had security clearance?"

"Yes, Uri, it's been done," Rahman assured him. "Not only that, Mr. Sufy here has given the newer crew members leave for Bairam. Those on board have been with the boat for many years. They are all trusted hands."

As they disembarked from the *Osiris,* Rahman had paused for a moment on the quay and looked back at the floodlit craft with its twin blue-and-white funnels at the stern.

"A wonderful way to see Egypt, Uri. A nice, leisurely trip up the Nile. You and your wife must come and do it one day."

"If you only knew the travel tax we have to pay, Ahmed. Our government is very good at finding ways to tax us."

"You see the name there, *Osiris*. Do you know who Osiris was?"

"Listen, Ahmed, I don't even believe in my own God, let alone any of yours."

"I'm not trying to convert you, my friend. Osiris means 'many-eyed.' He was the lord of the underworld, ruler of the kingdom of ghosts, and god of death."

Bar-Zeev looked up at the freshly painted hull, glistening in the black water.

"It's true, Uri. Perhaps the company did not know this when they named their ships after Egyptian gods. I know of some local sailors who refused to sign on because of the name. Superstition is still very strong in this part of Egypt."

"Religion and superstition go hand in hand," replied Bar-Zeev as he began to climb the steps up to the embankment. "You and I are dealing with men, not stone idols."

"True, but the supernatural has a way of impinging upon reality. There are signs and coincidences that it does not pay to overlook. Laugh at me if you will."

By the time they returned to the police station, it was well after midnight. Cots had been prepared for the two intelligence men in adjoining rooms. Bar-Zeev suggested that they get some sleep.

"Tomorrow is going to be a difficult day. We shall need to be in top form."

"It is an occasion for a massage and a good meal, Uri, but I doubt if I will find either in Aswan at this hour. I'll leave word that we are to be called if there are any developments."

Shortly after three a.m., after tossing and turning on the hard, narrow cot for almost two hours, Ahmed Rahman drifted into a shallow, dream-plagued sleep. He had visions of Osiris, in the shape of an ox, battling his constant and implacable enemy, Set, the god of evil. As in the familiar myth, Set slew Osiris and hacked his body to pieces. Rahman groaned in his sleep and turned over to the wall at the same time that

Gabal Marwan and Salah Kader began their journey back from the Aswan High Dam.

≈≈≈

Along the rim of the Arabian Desert to the east of Lake Nasser, a purple light suggested that the sun would soon lift out of the sand for a new day. Mustafa Habib sat perched on a boulder, resting his chin on his knees. There was nothing to do but wait, and the waiting allowed him time to think. He had hardly exchanged a word with al-Rahid since the two divers had left. He had watched the Libyan pick up the semiconscious girl and literally throw her into the back of the Jeep, where she lay moaning for a while. Al-Rahid had climbed behind the rocks above Habib and kept him in view at all times.

A feeling of morbid depression overcame the young intelligence agent. He had failed the Mokhabarat, and worse, he had failed himself. By his indecision and inability to act he had put an entire nation in jeopardy. Because of his fear of death and his cowardice he had allowed two bombs to be planted at Egypt's most important strategic installations; and he had done nothing—nothing—to prevent it from happening. If it is Allah's will that Egypt be wiped off the face of the map, what can I, Mustafa Habib, do to stop it? he reasoned. But in his heart he knew that he had had the opportunity and he'd let it pass.

But what could he have done? It was obvious that the old doorkeeper in Cairo had not taken his message to his superiors, or he would have had some help by now. Could he be blamed for that? There had been no chance to sabotage the terrorists' equipment; al-Rahid had watched him too closely. At the checkpoint on the Cairo–Luxor road he could have been killed if he had alerted the military guard, and to what end? The gang would still have disappeared into the desert with their bomb. It was impossible for him to kill all three of them; therefore, was it not his duty to remain with them to assist in their capture and the arrest of the maniacal Rashad Munir?

"They're coming." The hoarse whisper in his ear made him start. He had not heard al-Rahid approaching behind him.

"Where?"

Al-Rahid pointed out across the dark surface of the inlet. For a moment he could see nothing but the black mirror of the lake. Then two heads became visible just above the surface, moving slowly toward the shore. Al-Rahid ran to the edge of the water, holding his genitals and rocking back and forth in excitement. As Habib watched, the two divers touched bottom with their feet, stood up like monstrous black fish, and waded the last few meters to the bank, where they pulled off their face masks and collapsed on the rocks, panting for breath.

"Well? What happened? Is it done?" demanded al-Rahid.

Salah Kader nodded. "It—is—done. All—ready."

For the first time since he had met him, Habib saw the Libyan smile. His thin face cracked in a demonic leer. "Excellent, excellent!" He hit his palm with his fist. "You two have accomplished a miracle. Come, you are tired, but we must get into the boats and return to the island before daybreak."

Wearily, the two divers stripped off their fins and air tanks and raised themselves to their feet.

"Habib, get everything into the boats. I will bring the girl."

Al-Rahid went to the Jeep and flung Nicole over his shoulder as if she were a sack of grain. He carried her to the bank and let her drop onto the duckboards at the bottom of the cargo boat.

Habib leaned over and stowed the scuba equipment under the seats, checking quickly to see if the girl was still breathing. "What about the Jeeps?" he asked quickly as al-Rahid stared at him, frowning.

"They will be picked up. Don't worry about them. Kader, you go in the cargo boat. Lie still and rest. Habib will handle the motor. Marwan, come with me."

They pushed the rubber boats out onto the lake, and as the first rays of the sun reddened the horizon, they were heading south to their island base.

≋≋≋

The rubber boats made better time on the return trip to the island, unimpeded by the weight of the bomb and the explosives. Even so, the sky was light and the sun an inverted bowl of fire on the horizon when al-Rahid and his group beached their craft and pulled them out of the water.

"I want all the equipment stowed under the camouflage netting," ordered al-Rahid. "Put the woman in my tent, Habib. I will deal with her later. We may need a hostage."

When all the paraphernalia had been concealed, al-Rahid gathered the three men around him.

"You have all performed very well tonight. You will look back on this day as the beginning of a new dawn. Allah will reward you for your endeavors. Now you will sleep. Our part is over. Relax and rest."

The Libyan watched as the men went wearily to their tent. Then he closed himself inside the radio tent and tuned in to Munir's wavelength to transmit a one-word message informing the professor that everything was in readiness.

In al-Rahid's tent, Nicole lay on the sand floor and tried to think clearly. Her wrists were chafed from the rope that bound her; her body was bruised, and her arms ached from being tied behind her back for so long. She had to keep fighting the reflex to choke on the dirty rag across her mouth.

She still had difficulty understanding what had happened to her. She had been seized by a gang of men—terrorists, perhaps? Somehow she had stumbled onto them in the middle of an operation. But what did they want with her? And what did they intend to do? She had kept her eyes open in the boat during the long trip back, and she knew they had to be on Lake Nasser. But where on the lake? And how could she possibly escape?

She was hungry and confused, but one thought kept pounding in her brain: her life was meaningless to these men. She had seen their faces. They were not likely to release her now. She had a terrifying vision of being murdered and left in a shallow grave on this godforsaken island. She told herself to remain calm and try to concentrate. There had to be a way out.

"Well, lady, are you comfortable?" The one-eyed man was standing in the door of the tent, staring down at her and speaking in fractured English. The empty eye socket and the facial scar made him even more hideous in daylight; now she knew she had seen the face before—on the day of the demonstration at the Oasis Hotel. She closed her eyes.

Al-Rahid was elated by the success of the mission. He wanted to celebrate, to enjoy some diversion. The red-haired woman in his tent offered such a possibility. Like all Arab males, he had grown up in the belief that women are basically creatures of passion who, left alone with a man, cannot long resist his advances. Western women, because of their liberated ways, are assumed to be even more inclined to the pleasures of the flesh than Arab girls. So he had resolved to be pleasant to his captive, offering her water and fruit and cajoling her until she lay joyously with him. By closing her eyes, however, Nicole had rejected him. Immediately, anger replaced anticipation in his mind. Once again a woman had turned away from him, revolted by the sight of his face. And just as he had successfully engineered one of the most daring military feats in history! How dare this whore treat him in such a fashion?

He reached out, grabbed Nicole by her long hair, and slapped her hard across the face. His voice was harsh and tight: "You do not close your eyes again. Do you understand? You will look on my face and you will learn to regard it as being as beautiful as the sun." Terrified, Nicole nodded.

Al-Rahid pulled the gag from her mouth, but Nicole was too frightened to scream. She cowered and stared wide-eyed at him.

"Repeat after me: I am a whore," he whispered into her ear, pulling her hair tightly back. "Say it."

"I am a whore," mumbled Nicole.

"Louder! A decadent Western whore."

"A decadent Western whore." Tears of pain smarted in her eyes, but she would not give him the satisfaction of seeing her cry.

Al-Rahid smiled. "As long as you know what you are, then you do not deserve to be treated like a decent Arab woman."

As she watched in horror, the Libyan unzipped the fly of the black cotton trousers he had worn for the operation and drew out his enlarging penis. "I was going to give you some fruit to suck on. Now you can suck on this instead."

He pulled her face toward him. Her nose was assailed by the smell of dried sweat and dirt. He pushed his penis against her lips. Disgusted, Nicole clenched her teeth and gagged. Al-Rahid pulled her head back, slapped her again, and threw her to the sand floor. His anger at the woman had now consumed him. She had become the symbol of all the females who had turned away from him in revulsion since the grenade accident that had cost him his eye.

"So you find that sickening? You find me so revolting? Then maybe you would prefer something else. Something even more suitable for a whore like you."

While Nicole whimpered in protest, al-Rahid grabbed her slacks at the waist and ripped the zipper open. He then pulled them off her, scratching her thighs. He tossed the slacks in a corner of the tent with the shoes she had been wearing. Underneath she wore only a pair of panties. Al-Rahid stared at her for several moments, taking in the long, slender legs and the whiteness of her lower body. Then he reached down and tore off the panties.

"There is only one way to treat a Western bitch."

In one move, he turned her over. Then, grabbing her hair again, he forced her to kneel, her hands still tied behind her. He stood behind her, put one hand in the middle of her back, and pushed her forward until her shoulders and cheek were pressed against the sand. Her glasses, dislodged by the sudden movement, fell near her head.

"If you move, I will kill you this moment, bitch."

He let her go. For a moment, Nicole felt nothing, although she could hear him moving behind her. Then she saw his trousers being thrown aside. A moment later, she felt him behind her, forcing her legs apart. She wanted to resist but was too weak and too frightened. She felt him place his hands on her buttocks, spreading the cheeks apart. The sudden sickening realization of what he intended to do made her cry out.

"For God's sake, no!"

"Silence!"

"Oh, my God, not that. Please, not that—"

Her words ended in a scream as he thrust himself into her rectum. Pain coursed through her body. The Libyan jabbed savagely at her, again and again. Nicole shook with agony and humiliation, her face driven into the sand by the bestial thrusts of the one-eyed man behind her. It seemed to her that the obscene rape lasted forever. There was nothing left in the world but a searing hurt and the brutal sounds from the creature behind her, using her like an animal. Mercifully, she lost consciousness.

≈≈≈

By eight a.m. the sun had risen high enough for the rocks around the perimeter of the Aswan Hotel construction site to cast deep shadows. Bill Leamington, gritty-eyed and weary from his all-night vigil, slumped in a folding chair outside the project office, sipping black coffee from a paper cup. His customary suntan had faded to an ash-gray and his growth of beard itched. There was blood on his trousers where he had fallen and barked his shins. His feet were swollen from clambering over the rocks all night, and he was hoarse from calling Nicole's name. Where was she? How could she have disappeared so completely? He did not believe that she had fallen into the lake; even if she had, she was a strong swimmer. As the night wore on, the need to find her had become more frantic, and as he jumped from boulder to boulder searching every cranny and crevice, he realized how much he needed her. Finally, in a state of near-exhaustion, he had returned to the construction site to rest for a while. The volunteers had long since abandoned the search and returned to their homes.

"We'll get up a new group and keep looking before the sun gets too high," Noel Barstairs said. "Why don't you put your head down for a while in the office?"

Leamington dismissed the idea with a wave of his hand. "Let's get the workmen on the site out there."

"It's the feast, remember? They won't be back here till tomorrow."

Leamington kicked at the ground in anger. "Something's wrong, Noel. I can feel it. She wouldn't just disappear like that. She's either had an accident and is lying out there, or somebody's snatched her."

"Perhaps it's time to call in the police."

"The Aswan police? You're kidding. They couldn't find the pyramids if they were standing on top of them."

"At least they could provide some manpower. And they've got helicopters."

"Helicopters! Of course! I must be getting punchy from the sun. I'm going to take the truck into town. The police chief owes me a favor. I gave him a bottle of bourbon. You can round up some workers and get them out there again."

Leamington raised himself painfully to his feet and threw the remainder of the coffee into the sand. "You got the keys?"

≅≅≅

The citizens of Aswan had taken to the streets early that morning in eager anticipation of the presidential visit. The streets were hung with bunting and the flags of the two nations, as well as portraits of the two leaders. Merchants had been up before dawn preparing their stalls, cooking in the streets. Young children, feverish with excitement, ran along the sidewalks, setting off firecrackers, which sounded like gunfire.

Ahmed Rahman was awakened shortly before seven by the activity in the streets. He called immediately for the duty officer, who had nothing to report. Rashad Munir had not been found. The men delegated to the inquiry would have to be pulled off the assignment in preparation for the arrival of the presidents in two hours' time.

Rahman reluctantly agreed but issued new orders designed to draw the security net tighter around the city. "No one is to be allowed into the airport without clearance, is that understood? I want the names recorded of everyone who goes out there, whatever the reason."

He rose from his cot and slipped into his trousers. "Have Colonel Bar-Zeev awakened and get us some breakfast. And bring me a map of the area, the largest scale you can find."

Bar-Zeev came into the room rubbing his eyes, to find Rahman poring over the map, looking less than his usual immaculate self.

"Good morning, Uri. There is no news, unfortunately."

"Good morning, Ahmed. I was lying awake thinking this morning. If our friends intend to employ their bomb here, the only means of delivery would be by water."

"Yes. I was just looking at the approaches here. The *Osiris* will sail to this body of water here, below Elephantine Island. There's no access from the south, so we must isolate the river for at least two kilometers to the north. I am ordering a complete ban on river traffic until the presidents are on dry land again."

The duty officer returned with an orderly who carried a tray of beans and bread and glasses of hot, sweet tea. Bar-Zeev waved away the food and lit a cigarette instead. Rahman instructed the duty officer to set a cordon of patrol boats, with armed troops aboard, at anchor in a line just north of El A'qab. Nothing must move on the river above that limit, not even the feluccas.

"But sir," protested the duty officer, "the felucca men are planning a sail-by in honor of the presidents. They have been given permission."

"I thought I made myself clear," shouted Rahman, his temper frayed from lack of sleep. "Nothing on the river except for police and military craft. And I want continuous helicopter surveillance over the *Osiris*."

"Yes, sir. What should the pilots be looking for?"

Rahman threw up his hands in exasperation. "How should I know? Can I tell the future? Just instruct them to keep their eyes open and to radio the bridge of the *Osiris* if they spot any unusual movement."

"Yes, sir."

"When is the chief expected?"

"He was planning to go directly to the airport to oversee arrangements there."

"All right, then, I will use his office in the meantime. Where is it?"

"Just down the corridor, sir. First door on the right."

"Good. Have some more tea sent in there. And more sugar this time."

"Yes, sir."

"Uri, I'm going to radio Cairo. You have a shave and join me when you're ready." Rahman turned back to the orderly, who stood at attention in the doorway. "Well move, man!"

Rahman had just sat down behind the desk in the police chief's office, when there was a knock on the door. "Come in."

Bill Leamington, red-eyed and tense, stepped into the room. The two men regarded each other in surprise for a silent moment. The only sound was the squeak of the overhead fan as the blades moved slowly around, circulating the warm air with no perceptible effect on the stuffiness of the office.

"Mr. Leamington! You said we might meet in Aswan, but I confess this is a surprise." Rahman took in at a glance Leamington's dusty, bloodstained trousers and his general appearance of exhaustion.

"Sit down; you look like I feel. Now, what do you want?"

"I was looking for the police chief."

"Unfortunately, he is not here. He has official business to attend to. Perhaps I might be of assistance?"

Leamington patted his pockets for a cigarette and, finding none, looked vaguely around the room. Rahman took a pack from his pocket and offered him one. Leamington leaned forward, and Rahman studied his face as he accepted a light. The American's hair was full of dust and his forehead was smeared with dirt where the sweat had dried.

Leamington drew on the cigarette, and the nicotine seemed to revive him. He launched into an explanation of the events of the past night, haltingly at first and then in a torrent of words as his concern for Nicole overrode his exhaustion. No longer the self-confident American, noted Rahman as he listened without interruption.

When Leamington had finished his narrative, the Egyptian drew a circle on the map in front of him. "I doubt very much that we are dealing with a criminal act, Mr. Leamington. The crime rate in Aswan is one of the lowest in Egypt. They are very proud of that. Your hotel site is an area where no one would go at night. I think it more likely that Miss Honeyworth has fallen or twisted an ankle and is lying out there somewhere, waiting for a search party to find her."

"I didn't come here to debate what happened to her. I came for help," replied Leamington, his old assurance returning. "I need the police."

Rahman pressed a buzzer on the desk in front of him. "Mr. Leamington, you're aware that the presidents are to arrive here very shortly. All our available men are needed to provide security. Later in the day, perhaps, when President Dunlap has left—"

"Nicole could be dead by then," observed Leamington. The emotion in his voice was unmistakable.

"My first concern is with the safety of the presidents," Rahman said gently.

"Okay, but what about a helicopter, then—just for a couple of hours?"

"I'm sorry. We have only two and they are on patrol. Rahman was genuinely apologetic. Before Leamington could speak again, the door opened and an aide entered the room.

"You will excuse us for a moment?" Rahman beckoned to the aide and conferred with him in Arabic. Finally he turned back to Leamington and smiled. "We can let you have one man."

"Thanks, that's a great help," replied Leamington scornfully.

"He is a sergeant and a veteran of the force. Abu Maraji, a Nubian. He was born in the valley and knows the area of your construction site like—what is your expression? Like the back of his hand. He is used to coordinating search parties for missing persons or escaped convicts."

"But what's the use of one man?"

"He will be able to help you find civilian volunteers. On such a day it might be difficult to collect such people, but I'm sure Venture International could make it worth their while."

"All right. Where is he?"

Rahman nodded to the aide, who saluted and left the office. A few moments later he returned with a tall, dark-skinned, dignified man whom he introduced to Rahman. The chief of Internal Security shook the man's hand and said a few words to him in Arabic. The tall man nodded and looked at Leamington.

"I would like you to meet Sergeant Maraji," Rahman said, introducing the Nubian. "I have told him to assist you in any way he can. He is at your disposal."

The tall, dark man in the gray uniform smiled. "My English no good. I know many people. We find your lady. Come."

Leamington looked doubtfully at Rahman, who smiled encouragingly. "Thanks," he said. Then: "I appreciate it. One day I'll return the favor."

Rahman nodded and watched them leave. Why do Americans always think in terms of favors? he wondered. He looked out of the window; in the inner courtyard a platoon of guards was lining up for inspection.

All this and a missing girl, too, said Rahman to himself. If she were president of the United States, it would be a different matter.

≈≈≈

Mustafa Habib lay in his sleeping bag under the glowing beige canvas. In spite of the heat he was shivering, and in his feverish state he called down every curse he knew upon his own head for his cowardice. He had heard the girl's screams, and yet again he had done nothing. His fellow conspirators slept the sleep of the dead beside him, but in spite of his fatigue, his guilt would not let him rest. He had tried to calm his anguish by self-deceiving sophistries, but he could no longer bear the dishonor he had brought upon himself. He had disgraced his family name, betrayed the trust of the Mokhabarat, and by omission committed treason against his homeland.

The arguments he had marshaled in his own defense for not obstructing Munir's master plan had shattered with each scream from the adjacent tent. Al-Rahid is torturing the woman, he thought as he tried to block out her cries for help. The mechanics of the operation had been abstract, involving cold military logic; but the sound of a woman in pain was real, and it had torn into his brain. When her cries stopped, Habib strained to hear if she was still alive. He pulled up the flap of the tent and shielded his eyes against the glare of the sun off the sand. He saw al-Rahid emerging from his tent with the girl slung over his shoulder, still bound but with the gag replaced over her mouth. She was naked from the waist down. It occurred to Habib that the Libyan would not have replaced the gag if she were dead.

"If you are going to whine, you can do it out of my hearing," he heard al-Rahid say as he carried the girl over to the radio tent and let her drop onto the sand; then he knelt down and rolled her inside. Habib dropped the flap as the Libyan turned and walked back to his own tent.

Habib began to shiver uncontrollably again. He could hear the girl moaning softly like a wounded animal, a sound that seemed to be for his ears alone, accusing him as his own conscience had done. He could also hear al-Rahid yawning and settling himself down to sleep. There was silence for a while; then the Libyan's nasal snore rose from his tent.

This would be his last opportunity to vindicate himself—to whiten his face before the judgment of cowardice had been irrevocably passed upon him. He sat up slowly, listening to the pounding of his heart. Marwan and Kader continued to breathe softly. He was conscious of his every movement; he slid his legs slowly and deliberately out of the sleeping bag and stood up. He opened the flap of the tent and backed out, watching the sleeping figures in case the sudden shaft of direct sunlight disturbed them.

Once outside the tent, he stood and listened. The hot sand burned his bare feet, but he hardly noticed it. All his senses at that moment were subservient to his hearing. He caught the sound of the girl moaning softly in the radio tent, the snores of al-Rahid under canvas close by, and the soft lapping of the water against the shore. Cautiously he made his way to the radio tent and peered inside.

Nicole lay on her side, her knees pulled up to her chin; her hands were still tied behind her back, and her bare legs showed traces of blood. The ground around her was also stained with blood. Her eyes were closed, and her face, contorted with pain, pressed into the sand. A gurgling sound emerged from her throat. Habib could not tell whether she was asleep or unconscious. He looked back to ensure that no one had been aroused, and then he entered the tent. He bent down over the pitiful figure of the girl and reached out, touching her arm.

Nicole opened her eyes and stared up into Habib's face. Immediately she cringed back in fear, terrified she would have to undergo more abuse.

"Don't be afraid. I'm a friend," Habib whispered urgently. "Don't make a sound. The others are asleep. I'm here to help you. Now, I'm going to take off your gag. If you scream, we are both dead. Do you understand?" Nicole nodded. As gently as he could, Habib withdrew the gag from her mouth; all the time she squinted at him shortsightedly. There was something in the man's eyes that told her he posed no threat to her. Her body was wracked with pain, but her mind quickly cleared.

"Who are you? Who are these men?" whispered Nicole as soon as the rag had been removed from her mouth.

"My name is Mustafa Habib. I am with Egyptian intelligence. Please don't talk, just listen."

As he worked on the ropes that bound her hands, Habib outlined the plan by which Wind of the Desert would hold the nation to ransom, and the details of the planting of the bomb at the High Dam.

"But that's incredible," gasped Nicole.

"You must believe it. It is vital you remember everything I have told you in case anything should happen to me."

Her hands now free, Nicole slid her legs around from under her. Suddenly she remembered her nakedness and instinctively tried to cover herself.

"Is there anything I can put on?" she whispered, drawing in her knees and pulling down her cotton blouse.

From a canvas bag behind the radio equipment Habib took out a spare pair of black night-combat trousers and tossed them to her. He turned his back as she rose painfully to her feet and slipped into them.

"What shall we do now?" whispered Nicole as she zipped up the fly and rolled the waistband over so the pants would not fall.

"I thought we would get one of the boats and escape. We can get to the High Dam and warn them what's happening."

"That will take hours. Is this radio working?"

"Yes. Al-Rahid used it when we got back."

"We can get a message through on it. I know how to operate one of these," Nicole said.

"But I don't know what frequency the military operates on here. It could take some time to find it, and by then we'd have awakened the others."

"I know the frequency of a radio near here. It's on a construction site near the old dam. Let me try to raise them."

"All right," said Habib doubtfully. "But just a couple of minutes. We can't take the chance of being caught."

Nicole moved stiffly to the radio and dialed Venture's Aswan frequency before snapping it on. Taking a deep breath, she spoke softly into the mike. "Calling Venture, Aswan. Venture, Aswan. Calling Bill Leamington. Come in, Bill. Over."

There was the sound of crackling and static on the set, but no response.

"Venture, Aswan. Come in Venture, Aswan. Over . . ."

≅ ≅ ≅

Bill Leamington was standing outside the project office with Sergeant Maraji, giving a final briefing to the men they had assembled. With Maraji's help and an added financial inducement from Venture, they had been able to press fifty men into service; a massive search of the area was about to begin. Leamington sipped coffee from a paper cup as Maraji translated the description of Nicole he had just given in English. The image of her filled his mind.

"Just a minute, Sergeant," he said as the officer finished. "I may have a picture of her in my briefcase to show them. Let me check; it's just inside."

He opened the door of the office and was momentarily stunned to hear Nicole's voice coming over the receiver.

"Bill, please hear me. Bill, come in. Please come in."

"Sergeant!" he shouted. "The radio! She's on it! Come here!"

Leamington ran to the set and switched on his microphone. "Nicole, it's Bill. I hear you. Where are you?"

"Bill! Oh, thank God. Bill, I'm being held prisoner. We're on an island somewhere in Lake Nasser. Do you know where we are?"

Leamington realized that the last question had been directed at someone with her. He looked at Maraji, who had joined him and was listening intently. Noel Barstairs had also come in and was standing behind them.

A male voice came on, speaking rapidly: "Listen carefully. We are on an island in Lake Nasser near the eastern bank, about thirty-eight kilometers south of the High Dam. It has no name, but it is the largest in the area. There's a big hummock in the center. We are camped at the south end. There is a plan to—" Suddenly the signal went dead.

"Hello. Nicole. Come in. Nicole, can you read me? Come in."

"It's no use, Bill," said Barstairs. "They've stopped transmitting."

"Do you know the island they're talking about?" Leamington addressed the question to Sergeant Maraji.

"Yes, I think. My people, they from that place. The island, I'm not sure. But I know about where. Fishermen on the lake, they know. I have friends. We get guide."

"Boats. Can we get boats?"

Maraji nodded. "At New Harbor. Plenty boats there. No problem."

Now that Nicole had been located, Bill Leamington was once again the battlefield captain he had been in Vietnam.

"All right. Since the police can't help, we'll go after her ourselves. Sergeant, find out how many of those men outside have had military training and know how to handle weapons. We'll need—let's say, six. Let the others go home. Noel, I assume we still have those rifles?" Leamington had ordered a small cache of weapons kept on the site to cope with any possible trouble.

"Yes. They're locked up in the shed next door."

"Get them out, and plenty of ammunition." Leamington thought for a moment. "Get some canteens, too, and tell the men Maraji picks to make sure they're full. Then get a truck around to the front and load the men into it. I want to leave here in five minutes." He turned back to Maraji. "Sergeant, do you want to alert your superiors about what's going on?"

"I telephone. All I say is the girl is at Lake Nasser and we go to her."

"All right. Get to it."

Hyperactivity born of exhaustion caused the adrenaline to flow through Leamington's veins. Eager to be under way, he would not allow himself to speculate on why the radio transmission had suddenly been cut off. The only thing that mattered was that Nicole was alive and more than anything else he wanted her restored to him.

≊ ≊ ≊

With a screech of rubber, *Air Force One* touched down on the heavily guarded runway at Aswan Airport. The guard of honor had been kept standing in the sun twenty minutes longer than the official timetable called for—a delay caused by the American president, whose constitution rebelled at having to rouse himself from bed while it was still dark outside.

Although Dunlap had invited the Egyptian president to accompany him to Aswan in *Air Force One,* the two men were spared the strain of continued diplomatic niceties by being placed at different ends of the aircraft, suitably screened off to preclude the possibility of any nonvoluntary meeting. Dunlap had napped most of the flight, and it was only when the pilot requested that all on board fasten their seat belts for the descent that he took any interest in the view from his window.

The blue artery of the Nile, fringed with green on both sides, wound its serpentine route through the flat brown desert. As the plane descended, the verdant line of cultivated land became focused into geometric plots extending out from the river to a distance of two kilometers, where they ended abruptly as if an invisible, razor-edged barrier stood between the fields and the desert. The sand stretched from the edge of the fertile valley to a range of low mountainlike ridges. Great rivers of sand appeared to course about the base of these mountains, an illusion caused by the flash floods during the rare rainstorms that wash through the wadis, depositing the sand in their wake.

"There's the High Dam, Sarah," remarked Dunlap to his wife as the jet banked for its final approach over Lake Nasser. "If we'd agreed to build it instead of the Russians, Egypt might still belong to the British."

He laughed at his own joke as he gazed down at the lake, with its profusion of islands whiskered about with pale-green shrubbery. It reminded him of Colorado. As the plane neared the ground, the president was able to make out small boats on the lake; others were drawn up on the islands near the western shore. He pointed to the ruins of Kashaba Temple just south of the dam, and off in the distance he could see a huge cloud of mist rising where water poured through an open sluice gate at the High Dam.

Air Force One came in low over the desert. On his port side Dunlap made out a military camp, protected by a double fence of barbed wire. The sand was crisscrossed with tank tracks between missile silos, camouflaged hangars, and great walls of sand enclosing huts and army billets. Then with a roar as the jets decelerated, the plane touched down on Aswan's sole airstrip, enclosed on all sides by desert. The only building to be seen was the rust-colored terminal with the word *Aswan* written laterally down its control tower.

"Here we go again," whispered Dunlap, flexing his facial muscles.

The ceremonies at the airport were mercifully brief, as a strong wind had suddenly sprung up. Fine particles of sand swept across the tarmac, making it difficult for the military band to read, let alone control, the score of "The Star-Spangled Banner." After the two anthems had been dutifully played, the presidents climbed into the air-conditioned cars awaiting them on the runway.

Ahmed Rahman and Uri Bar-Zeev watched the procedure from the control tower and then returned to their car, which would take them ahead of the presidential motorcade into Aswan to board the *Osiris*.

The road into Aswan from the airport runs first through a military zone, then through a bleak desert landscape where giant boulders and electrical pylons provide the only relief from the wilderness of sand. There were no crowds along this part of the route, and the cars made good time; it was only when the motorcade crossed the Nile over the old Aswan Dam and entered the city that the road became congested with cheering throngs. The embankment had been closed off, and thousands of people filled the pavement in front of the berth where the *Osiris* was docked.

When the cars appeared, a great shout went up and placards bearing pictures of the two presidents were waved. Sayed and Dunlap were escorted to the dais by the governor of Aswan, an unpopular man who was attempting to make political capital out of the situation to enhance his own prestige. After his overlong introductions, the two presidents each spoke briefly, to loud applause from the crowd. Then both men waved and disappeared down the ramp to the *Osiris*.

Rahman and Bar-Zeev had been watching from the ship's bridge. As soon as the presidential parties were on board, Rahman nodded to the captain to cast off and move out. As he did so, a wizened-looking man in a brown galabia and turban joined them on the bridge.

"Who's that?" Bar-Zeev whispered as the lines were untied and the cruise ship began to nudge away from its moorings into the Nile.

"He's the—what's the word in English? The pilot."

"Pilot? What for?"

"The river currents cause the bottom to shift constantly. One day there's a mud bank here; the next, it's moved over there. It's impossible to mark the channels. He can read the surface of the water and tell where the sandbars are. In difficult areas he'll take the wheel himself."

"Can he be trusted?"

"He's been doing this job for forty years. If not now, when?"

Satisfied that the *Osiris* was safely into the river and that the helicopter patrols were operational, Rahman and Bar-Zeev left the bridge.

"Nothing new on Munir?" the Israeli asked.

"No. He's not at a hotel, as far as we can ascertain. The police are now starting a house-by-house investigation, but that's a massive task. I've told the chief to radio us the minute he hears anything."

"I have a feeling we'll be hearing from him before the day is through," said Bar-Zeev. "Not to change the subject, but this is quite some boat."

They stood at the railing on the open top deck, where a small swimming pool was surrounded by lounge chairs. A canvas awning at one end of the deck provided shade against the blinding sun.

The two men stared out at the wind-sculpted dunes across the river.

"You say you are a farmer, Uri; then you will appreciate this. Before we built the High Dam, November used to be the month when the farmers sowed their seed. That was when the floodwater had retreated from the fields. I remember my father telling me that while the farmers believed in the teachings of the Prophet, they also followed the old country ways. A sort of insurance policy, you might say. I can still see my dear father lamenting over the first sheaf of corn he cut. You see, he was cutting the body of the corn god with his sickle. The corn god was Osiris, who introduced the cultivation of grain to Egypt."

"But now with the High Dam, no more corn gods, eh, Ahmed?" Bar-Zeev remarked, smiling.

"Science casting out the old superstitions. Is that how you see it, Uri?"

"We are growing roses and strawberries out of gravel—no dirt at all. That is science overcoming nature and ignorance."

"We can never overcome nature. It may surprise you—perhaps it will not—but I have read your Bible. And I will quote Ecclesiastes. 'To every thing there is a season, and a time to every purpose under the heaven: A time to be born, and a time to die; a time to plant, and a time to pluck up that which is planted.' "

"And a time to kill," added Bar-Zeev.

"Yes, and that, too. You are determined to keep my mind on my work, aren't you, Uri? Let's go down to the conference room."

The main lounge of the *Osiris* is decorated in cool shades of green and white. Large cane chairs with floral-patterned cushions provide the seating. A conference table had been set up in the room, large enough to accommodate the two presidents and their four advisers. Curtains had been drawn across the bank of windows. The working session was about to begin when Rahman and Bar-Zeev arrived.

Rahman drew the Egyptian president aside. "I would like to present Colonel Uri Bar-Zeev, Excellency. As you are aware, he has been assisting in the security arrangements surrounding this visit."

Sayed extended his hand and smiled broadly. After an almost imperceptible hesitation, Bar-Zeev took it.

"I wish to thank you for all the help you have provided Colonel Rahman," the Egyptian head of state said. "Tell me, how is your wound? I am terribly sorry this has happened."

"It no longer bothers me, Mr. President. We have chosen a dangerous profession," Bar-Zeev said, feeling his ribs through his shirt. "As for helping Colonel Rahman, I've done little, I'm afraid. Any success we have had has been a result of his work and that of his men."

"You are too modest, Colonel. But I am delighted to hear you say it nonetheless." He turned to Rahman. "Everything is under control?"

"As far as we can tell, Excellency. But I admit I will not feel comfortable until President Dunlap leaves."

"It will not be long. Now, if you'll excuse me, we must begin. It was a pleasure to meet you, Colonel Bar-Zeev."

The two intelligence men left the conference room and returned to the upper deck.

"What now?" asked Bar-Zeev.

"We wait. It's what we spend most of our lives doing, after all. Let's sit down and watch the river. And I will tell you more of our unscientific past, my friend."

≈≈≈

With Sergeant Abu Maraji's help, Bill Leamington had been able to organize and assemble the equipment and men he needed for the rescue attempt across Lake Nasser. He threatened and cajoled his way through every barrier and obstructive civil servant, spreading money like confetti where he felt it might expedite matters. A final obstacle had been the military: on special alert because of the presidential visit, the sentries at the entrance to the High Dam had been reluctant to allow Bill Leamington's truck to enter the area without special clearance, especially when they discovered armed men in the back.

It was only when Maraji hopped out of the cabin and embraced the startled guard, claiming him as a cousin, that they were permitted to pass, and then only under escort by an army Jeep carrying three soldiers with automatic weapons.

They had driven across the great curtain of the dam to New Harbor, the railhead shantytown at the head of Lake Nasser. There, following another argument with sentries, they had been permitted to drive through to the fishing docks. Maraji, with the cunning of a quartermaster, managed to requisition a number of boats. But he could not find the electric motors he wanted.

"We must have electric motors," he kept saying. "These motors, bad noise. They hear us. They wait in ambush, Meester Lem'ton." But none of the fishing vessels was equipped with electric motors.

"We'll just have to use regular outboards. When we get in range of the island, we'll row," said Leamington, desperate now as the minutes slipped by.

Maraji selected two boats normally used for night fishing, and the men prepared them for the journey up the lake.

The police sergeant disappeared for a while, and just as Leamington thought he had decided to give up on the enterprise, the Nubian emerged from one of the corrugated-iron-roofed huts arm in arm with a wiry-looking man of about thirty-five who, he told Leamington proudly, had been a commando in the Egyptian army.

"His name Raafat Shams. He fine guide. Good fisherman. Good fighter."

"All right, but does he know the island we're looking for?"

"He sure. It near east bank. Two, maybe three hours. But he say wait till night!"

As Maraji spoke, the Egyptian fisherman pointed toward the sun and indicated to Leamington they shouldn't leave in daylight.

"Tell him we can't wait, Sergeant. There are lives at stake."

Maraji spoke briefly to the fisherman.

"He say if go now, take longer. Have to hide behind islands. In case they see."

"Then that's the way it'll have to be. How long will it take?"

"He say four, maybe five hours."

"Then let's get going."

≋≋≋

Mustafa Habib lay staked out in the sand. He had been stripped of his clothes, and his wrists and ankles had been bound and secured to tent pegs driven deep into the ground. The sweat ran into his eyes, and behind his closed lids, the glaring sun burned red. His lips were dry and cracked, and his throat hurt when he tried to swallow; a pounding pain at the back of his skull created sea sounds in his ears. Caught hunched over the radio set, transmitting a message to Bill Leamington, he had been knocked unconscious by the butt of al-Rahid's revolver. The Libyan had switched off the radio before felling Nicole with a blow of his fist. He had stood over them trembling with fury, and Nicole had been certain that he would kill them both on the spot. Instead, he had marched out of the tent and returned shortly with Kader and Marwan. He had ordered the two terrorists to take the senseless body of Habib outside and spread-eagle him in the sand. Nicole could hear the sound of the stakes being beaten into the ground, as al-Rahid placed his foot on her hair. Holding her down this way, he began to interrogate her. Whom had they contacted? What had they said? What information had they given?

"We didn't get through," cried Nicole. "We didn't make contact. We weren't able to get a message out."

"Then who were you talking to?" demanded the Libyan.

"Nobody. He was sending out a general distress call. We hoped somebody would hear it."

Al-Rahid pressed down with his foot, exerting pressure on her hair. It felt as if it would come away from her scalp.

"You're lying."

"No, I swear!"

"I say you are lying, bitch. Habib was speaking in English. A distress call would have been in Arabic. Perhaps your friend outside will tell me."

When Habib regained consciousness he found himself immobilized on the ground. The three conspirators stood over him in such a way as to allow the sun to beat directly into his eyes.

"The girl has told us everything, Habib. What information did you transmit?" rasped al-Rahid.

Say nothing. Do not scream; do not cry out, Habib kept telling himself. You have proved you can bear pain. This is your punishment for dishonoring your name. Even if they kill you, say nothing.

"Perhaps it is time to offer him a drink, Gabal."

Marwan unscrewed the top of his canteen and poured out a few drops on Habib's chest in the declivity between his ribs. The intelligence agent lifted his head and strained against his bonds, but his tongue could not reach the water, which trickled down his side and dried in the hot sand.

"Answer my questions and you can have all the water you want," said al-Rahid.

Habib sank back and closed his eyes.

"We are wasting time," grumbled Marwan. "We have to find out who they spoke to."

"You are too impetuous, Gabal. We need some diversion. I have something more fitting for the occasion." Al-Rahid crossed to the camouflage netting, and from its shade he took out a small cardboard box. He walked back to the prostrate figure of Habib and opened the box for Kader and Marwan to inspect its contents. Inside was a large golden scorpion, which clawed frantically at the cardboard walls to escape.

"A fine specimen," al-Rahid said, grinning. "I found it in my tent this morning. I was going to keep it as a souvenir, but now we can recruit it into our service." The Libyan knocked the scorpion back into the box with the handle of his knife. "Do you know what is in this box, my treacherous friend?"

Habib opened his eyes the merest fraction.

"Kader, get me some string."

"Kill me now!" shouted Habib in desperation. "I will tell you nothing!"

"We shall see. Marwan, bring the girl here. I want her to see this."

Kader returned with the string, and al-Rahid cut off a meter's length. He fashioned a small noose with a slip knot and dropped it over the insect's tail. He drew the noose tight and lifted the squirming scorpion out of the box, holding it well in front of him. Marwan joined them, half carrying Nicole in his massive arms.

"Ah, the audience is all here," said the Libyan, smiling. Nicole stared in horror at the writhing scorpion, suspended by its tail and fighting to escape.

"Open your eyes, Habib." Al-Rahid's voice was gentle and soothing, as if he were talking to a child. "See the plaything I have for you."

When the young man did not respond, the one-eyed man kicked him viciously in the ribs. Habib cried out in pain and involuntarily opened his eyes. As soon as he caught sight of the scorpion, he arched his body away from it and turned his head.

"What is the matter? Don't you like this little fellow? You wear his emblem on your foot. Why do you turn away from him?"

"Don't torture the boy!" screamed Nicole.

Al-Rahid turned sharply to her. "It may be your turn next if he does not tell us what we want to know."

"Say nothing," croaked Habib.

"Tell me who you spoke to on the radio and he will go free."

"Say nothing," repeated Habib.

"I've already told you."

"And I say you are lying. Perhaps we should continue with our game."

The Libyan held the string over Habib's body, keeping it taut to ensure that the fatal tail was suspended. He lowered the tormented insect until it touched the intelligence agent's stomach. Habib ground his teeth to keep from screaming as he felt the spiky legs of the scorpion scuttling across his belly toward his genitals.

"Now, Mustafa, who did you contact?"

Habib shook his head.

"I said, who did you contact?"

Al-Rahid jerked the string back and held the scorpion above his victim's face. Slowly he lowered it. Nicole's eyes opened in panic as she watched the insect crawl across Habib's eyes and down his nose to his mouth. All the while, al-Rahid kept the tension on the string.

"I am not going to play this game much longer. Either you answer or you will know what it's like to be stung by a real scorpion."

Tears of anguish flooded Habib's eyes. He wanted to beg for mercy, to plead for his life; but he had forfeited his right to do so. The only way to efface the memory of his cowardice was to die with honor.

"You leave me no alternative, Mustafa." Al-Rahid sighed, lifting the scorpion from the young man's face. "Pity, I was beginning to like you."

"No!" screamed Nicole, but the Libyan had already let go of the string. The maddened insect dropped onto Habib's upper lip and struck instantaneously. The agent gave a cry and pressed his body upward, before falling back on the sand, damp with sweat.

"Just for your enlightenment, he will die in a few hours," said al-Rahid to the distraught Nicole. "He will go into convulsions and die in agony. If you do not tell us now, you will die beside him. Take her back to the tent, Kader. I'm sure she will be more cooperative now."

"Please, help him," pleaded Nicole as Kader dragged her away.

"What is he to you?" al-Rahid called after her.

"Nothing. But he tried to help me."

"Very touching."

"If I tell you, will you try to save him?" shouted Nicole.

"Put her inside the tent, Kader."

Nicole began to weep uncontrollably as she knelt inside the tent.

Al-Rahid pulled back the flap and stood over her. "Tell me now."

"What do you want to know?"

"Who is Mustafa Habib?"

"He told me he works for Egyptian intelligence," said Nicole in a tired, disembodied voice. The image of the boy writhing in the sun outside kept appearing before her eyes. "We were going to escape in one of the boats and warn the authorities at the dam about the bomb. I asked him to try the radio first. To talk to the man I work for."

"Leamington?"

"Yes."

"What did you tell him?"

"Nothing. We had just made contact when you found us. That's all. Now, please help him."

Al-Rahid laughed. "There is nothing I could do for him even if I wanted to."

"You bastard!" shouted Nicole. "You heartless, one-eyed bastard!"

Al-Rahid's face flushed momentarily. His scar stood out a livid red against his sallow complexion. He drew back his arm as if to strike her again. Instead, he placed his hand on her thigh and squeezed it suggestively. Nicole twisted away from him.

"Come in here and gag her, Kader," ordered the Libyan.

Marwan sat on a rock watching the body of Mustafa Habib twitch and shake as the poison worked its way through his system.

"It is time to eat," said al-Rahid. The brawny young terrorist reluctantly turned away and moved toward the provisions store.

"Was that wise?" asked Kader as he joined al-Rahid at the staked-out body; Habib's lips and eyelids were swollen, and a trickle of gummy saliva dribbled from his mouth.

"What else would you do with an informer? He worked for the pig Rahman. Forget about him." Al-Rahid turned away.

"What about the girl?"

"She claims they told Leamington nothing. They had no time. That may be true, maybe not. But we cannot take any chances. We'll set up a watch. On the hill behind us."

"Why don't we just move out?" asked Kader. "We've done what we came here to do."

"Two reasons. First, we would be exposed on the lake if we tried to move before dark. Second, the plane is coming back here tonight to pick us up. If we move, they will never find us."

Marwan came back with three plates of food. He handed them around and pulled loaves of stale bread from his pocket.

"We will have to stand watches in turn. Otherwise we could be surprised," said al-Rahid.

"What for?" grumbled Marwan. "We're in no danger."

"You will not contradict me!" shouted the Libyan. "I am in command here. We will take three-hour shifts. It is now just after ten. I will take the first watch. I will wake you, Marwan, at one. Kader, your watch will begin at four. You two, get some sleep. Make sure the girl is well tied before you go to your tent. I want no more trouble from her."

"What about Habib?" asked Kader. "Why not just put a bullet in his head?"

Al-Rahid looked over at the slowly dehydrating figure of the intelligence agent, groaning in the sand.

"Bullets make too much noise, and I would not sully my blade with his blood. Let Allah dispose of him as He will."

≈≈≈

Uri Bar-Zeev sat on a deck chair with his feet on the railing, enjoying the sensation of the sun on his face. Somehow the idea that a bunch of fanatics was running around the desert with an atomic bomb seemed an incongruous thought in this timeless landscape where the rhythm of life was dictated by the gentle movement of the river. Were it not for the hornetlike buzzing of the helicopters circling the ship at a respectful height and the possibility that they might suddenly be blown out of the water, this cruise on the Nile would be almost idyllic.

Ahmed Rahman stepped out onto the deck, emerging from the radio room, where he had been in communication with police headquarters ashore.

"Uri, there's something very strange. You remember I told you about the American Leamington's reporting his assistant missing this morning? Well, the local police sergeant I assigned to help him in the search telephoned the station a couple of hours ago. He told the duty officer they had located the girl."

"Good. One less thing to worry about."

"There's more to it. She radioed for help from an island in Lake Nasser."

"Radioed?"

"Yes. Apparently she was being held prisoner there."

"By whom?"

"She didn't say. The transmission was interrupted, and they couldn't raise that frequency again. There was someone with her—a man."

"What's being done about it?"

"Leamington and the sergeant have mounted a rescue expedition to find her. They left from New Harbor a short time ago with half a dozen armed men."

"Who would have a transmitter on an island in Lake Nasser? No one lives out there, do they?" asked Bar-Zeev.

"No. The place is uninhabited. . . ." Rahman's voice trailed off as he puckered his forehead in thought.

"You know, it occurs to me"—Bar-Zeev, too, was thinking—"there could be a connection."

"If the girl is being held on an island—" Before Rahman could finish his sentence, a tremendous explosion rolled out across the water, echoing down the valley.

"The Bairam guns again?" asked Bar-Zeev.

Rahman looked at his watch. "Not at this hour. Anyway, it came from upriver somewhere." He crossed the deck and shielded his eyes from the sun. The topography of Elephantine Island effectively obscured his view. "Let's check with the radio room."

The radio operator, wedged in his tiny room behind the bridge, had nothing to report.

"Raise one of the helicopters," ordered Rahman. "Tell the pilot to reconnoiter upriver as far as the first dam and report back."

The two intelligence men stood in the doorway while the orders were conveyed. Within two minutes, the excited voice of the helicopter pilot came crackling over the receiver. "Redwing One to base. Something's going on at the old dam. There's water pouring through one of the gates. I can see people on the dam running. It's coming through like a flood."

"Can you contact the military post at the dam?" Rahman asked the operator.

"Yes, sir." After he repeated the call sign a few times, an agitated voice came over the speaker.

Rahman bent down to the microphone. "This is Colonel Rahman of the Mokhabarat. Report, please."

"Colonel, we don't know much yet. There was a terrible explosion just a few moments ago. One of the sluice gates was completely blown out. We cannot say if there is any other damage."

"Ask him if there is any danger of the dam's collapsing," said Bar-Zeev.

"What about the dam? Will it hold?" shouted Rahman.

"We can't say yet, sir. The buttresses along the north side are all intact."

"Good. We are on the *Osiris*. Keep us informed." Rahman turned to Bar-Zeev. "What do you make of that, Uri?"

"If it were an atomic blast, it would have taken the whole dam and we wouldn't be standing here talking. The question is, have they set explosives along the length of the dam? Each blast would weaken the structure until it fell over like a child's building blocks."

"If the dam goes, the presidents are in grave danger. We had better order the boat to shore."

"No, wait. The danger could be greater if we do that. Think of Noah's Ark. Remember how he survived. If the dam breaks, it would be better to ride out the flood here in midstream. Tell the captain to head downriver as fast as possible. That water would rush out like a tidal wave. The force of it could carry us all the way to Cairo. But we're safer here than on land."

"But what if they're after the High Dam, too?"

"The water behind that curtain is a hundred and eighty-three meters deep?"

"Yes."

"Well, my friend, if they blow that up, we will know soon enough which of us is right on the question of the hereafter. In the meantime, let's advise the captain."

≅≅≅

As he stood on the balcony of his villa overlooking the now raging cataract, Rashad Munir's face was transformed by a beatific smile. The explosion at the old Aswan Dam and the roaring column of water gushing through the blown sluice gate were to him as moving an experience as if he were witnessing the return of the Prophet. His laughter came in short, sharp bursts as he scanned the Nile from the dam to the cataract and the point at which the river disappeared between two cliffs of sand on its way to Aswan.

"We did it!" He rubbed his hands together and then slapped Dr. Nasif hard on the back. "Allah be praised, Doctor, we did it! Look at that. Just look at it!" He flung his arms out at the torrential water cascading over the rocks below. Nasif and his daughter stared down in silence at the rampaging river, smashing white against the rocks.

"Leila, it was you who prepared the explosives for this dam, was it not? You are a true daughter of Islam. You have every right to be proud of her, Nasif. She has rendered a great service to Allah."

"I have always been proud of my daughter, Professor."

"Of course, of course. And now it is time for phase two of our holy mission. You will stay here. Please, relax and make yourself comfortable while I am away. It is time for me to talk with those godless men on their boat."

Gathering his robes about him, Munir swept off the balcony and through the villa. Outside the door, three cars were waiting in a line. Two were occupied by grim-looking men carrying automatic weapons. The middle car was empty, apart from the driver. Munir opened the door and climbed inside.

"It is our time now, Hanif," he said, touching the man on the shoulder. The cars pulled out of the drive and passed through the open gates.

The television station in Aswan sits on top of a barren sand hill southeast of the city; its red-and-white tower can be seen for miles around. The offices and studio at its base are housed in a bunkerlike building the same color as the surrounding sand. The gaunt fortress commands a view of the entire valley and, where the buildings along the embankment road do not obstruct the line of vision, of the river itself.

There is a military checkpoint on the winding road leading up to the station. A sentry on duty challenged Munir's cars as they approached. No sooner had he bent down at the window of the lead car demanding to see their pass than a burst of automatic fire killed him. Another guard offered token resistance at the entrance to the television station, but after a few shots were exchanged, Munir's men flushed out the military personnel and took command of the building. And, more important, Wind of the Desert assumed effective control of the transmitters.

Munir watched impassively as the station's employees were herded at gunpoint into the main lobby. When the operation was complete, he demanded that the manager identify himself. A short, balding man with bulging eyes stepped forward, his hands raised above his shoulders, showing great damp patches under his arms.

"I am Sheikh Rashad Munir, leader of Wind of the Desert. I have an important message for the *Osiris* and for all the people of Egypt. You are to arrange for my message to be broadcast throughout Egypt, and you will advise those infidels on the *Osiris* to be watching. I will give you thirty minutes to comply with my wishes. Otherwise you and all these good people will be dead."

"But Excellency," spluttered the terrified manager, "the technical requirements—we can't just break into the network. I have no authority."

"You will contact your people in Cairo. You will have them arrange it immediately. If my request is not followed to the letter, I shall have no alternative but to destroy the Aswan High Dam. You are aware of what happened at the old dam, I presume, so do not think this is an idle threat."

"Yes—yes, Excellency."

"Then make the arrangements. Oh, and you can advise the government at the same time that no attempt is to be made to storm this

station. Not only are all of you my hostages, but all the people of
Egypt, from Aswan to Alexandria, are in the hands of Allah. The day
of reckoning has come!"

≅≅≅

The *Osiris* rolled gently on the turbulent water, agitated by the uncon-
trolled outflow from the damaged sluice gate. Ahmed Rahman stood
in the doorway of the radio room listening to the voice of the TV station manager crackling over the loudspeaker above the operator's head.

"Get up and let me sit there," he ordered. "How do I talk to him?"

"You press this key here, sir," said the operator.

"Listen to me!" shouted Rahman into the microphone, as if the
volume of his voice better served to communicate with the distraught
station manager. "I am Colonel Rahman. You say he has an armed
force with him and they are in control of the building?"

"That's correct, Colonel."

"Where are you?"

"I am in my office. There's an armed man outside the door."

"Are you listening on headphones?"

"Yes, Colonel."

"Good. Just answer yes or no, then. Are there many of your own
people in the building with you?"

"Yes."

"Do the terrorists have anything other than the weapons they are
carrying?"

"No."

"Can you get Munir to speak with me?"

"No, Colonel. He says he will talk only to the president."

"You say he has threatened to blow up the High Dam if we try to
storm the building?"

"Yes."

"And that he wants to broadcast at eleven o'clock, and the lines
have been set up through Cairo?"

"Yes."

"I want you to remain calm. Do nothing to provoke these men,
do you understand that?"

"Yes, Colonel."

"Tell your staff to do exactly as they are told. We don't want any heroes. I am going to consult with President Sayed. I shall be gone for no more than five minutes. We will do everything in our power to make sure you and your people are not harmed. I will get back to you as soon as I can." Rahman flicked the key and ran his hand over his eyes.

"Uri, what do you think?"

"I think we have found our bomb," replied the Israeli glumly.

"Munir must be very sure of himself to allow that man to talk to us without monitoring him. That means the bomb must be in place. We have no choice but to do as he says."

"We can see the station from here," said Bar-Zeev. "That means that they will be able to spot any troop movements."

"There is no time to bring in tanks, anyway. Come, I must tell President Sayed. I wish I were not the bearer of such news."

The two intelligence men hurried along the deck to the lounge. The security men stepped aside to let them enter. The delegates around the conference table looked up, startled by the intrusion.

"Forgive me for interrupting, Excellency," said Rahman, "but we have an emergency. I must talk privately with you."

H. Whitney Dunlap read the alarm in the face of the Internal Security chief. He stood up.

"I was just about to suggest we have a break," he said, stretching. "Perhaps someone can show me the facilities."

As Dunlap left the lounge, Rahman steered Sayed urgently into a corner. The Egyptian president's irritation at being disturbed was evident in his manner, but he remained silent as Rahman began to speak. As he listened, his expression changed from one of anger to deep concern.

"He wants a nationwide television hookup?"

"Yes, Mr. President."

"And he's threatening to blow up the High Dam?"

"That's correct."

"Is the man mad? What kind of lunacy is that?"

Bar-Zeev intervened. "We've suspected an atomic device ever since that corpse was pulled out of the Nile. If Munir has it and it's in the vicinity of the dam, we have to play along with him."

Sayed nodded. "All right. I think we had better hear what the man has to say. Tell the military to stay clear of the station. Give him his national hookup. Is there a television on the ship?"

"Yes," Rahman said. "The captain has a portable set in his cabin."

"Have it brought in here. I want to see this man Munir."

"What about President Dunlap, Excellency?"

"He must be told, of course. I shall have to explain to him what is happening. You may go, Rahman You have my orders. I shall tell President Dunlap myself."

Rahman returned to the radio room and informed the station manager of the president's decision. Ten minutes later, the television set had been installed in the lounge of the *Osiris*. The two leaders and their advisers sat staring at the blank screen. Behind them stood Rahman, Bar-Zeev, and the security team that had been assigned to the ship to protect the two presidents. Suddenly, the triumphant face of Rashad Munir appeared in close-up on the screen in front of them. Without hesitation, he began to speak in classical Arabic.

"People of Egypt. It is Allah's will that I speak to you today from Aswan. I am Sheikh Rashad Munir of Al-Azhar. I have come to deliver a most important message in His name, blessed be He. I ask you to listen without fear to what I have to say, for Allah is great and good and will protect the righteous among you. It is His holy word that no harm shall come to you unless the evil that rests in the hearts of your leaders should force Him to act."

"What does he mean?" Bar-Zeev whispered. Rahman motioned him to silence.

"Allah's words, transmitted through me, are being heard this morning by two important men: President Dunlap of the United States and President Sayed of Egypt. They are meeting together on a ship in the Nile, here at Aswan. It is they who will have to make the decisions on those matters I am now going to lay before you. I know that they, like you, are listening to my voice. I would ask them to listen carefully, for I shall speak these words only once."

Sayed motioned to one of his aides to take notes. President Dunlap's translator kept up a constant whisper in his ear as Munir continued.

"The organization I am privileged to lead is called Wind of the

Desert. A short time ago, we were responsible for detonating a device that destroyed one of the sluice gates at the old Aswan Dam. The amount of explosives used was carefully calculated to achieve precisely the effect we desired. There are no more explosives at that dam."

Munir then switched to English.

"I wish to assure the American president that neither he nor the ship he is on is in any immediate danger. The damage from the explosion at the dam was minimal. But I also wish him to understand that unless President Sayed complies with the demands I shall be making shortly, the devastation in Egypt will be great. And all those on board the *Osiris* will be among the first to perish."

The figure on the screen switched back to Arabic while the men in the ship's lounge watched, transfixed.

"I have arranged to have an atomic device planted in close proximity to the Aswan High Dam. So that you will understand that this is not a trick, I shall tell you that plutonium for this device was obtained from spent nuclear fuel that our organization obtained from the Candu reactor in Pakistan. This material was brought into Egypt by sea, transported by a courier named Juan Herrara. All this information is known to the secret police. The device was assembled in Cairo by a nuclear physicist pledged to our cause. It was transported to Aswan by private plane and is now armed."

Rahman looked quizzically at Bar-Zeev. "Yes, it's possible," whispered the Israeli.

"This device has been set to explode at ten o'clock tonight unless I send a special electronic signal to counteract it. The code for that signal is known only to me. If anything should happen to me, therefore, there would be no way of stopping the explosion. If that should happen, the High Dam would be destroyed. I do not have to tell you the devastation that would cause, not only to Aswan but to all of Egypt.

"I wish there to be no misunderstanding. I do not desire this explosion to take place. But I am determined that it will unless the demands I shall make are met, and met promptly. People of Egypt, I ask you to understand what is happening. I am about to ask your leaders to restore the primacy of the one true faith in our country and to drive out the infidels. Egypt is still not free; we are once again under foreign domination. This time, we must resist. We must assert ourselves as a proud and dignified people. We must be masters of our own destiny, not the cultural and economic slaves of the West."

Dunlap shifted uneasily in his seat. He turned away from the screen to watch Sayed's reaction. The Egyptian leader was perspiring heavily, rubbing his hands up and down his thighs.

"President Sayed! Here is my message. Listen well and have your secretaries write down what I have to say.

"First, you and your entire cabinet must resign immediately and declare Egypt an Islamic republic again."

Rahman could see the blood drain from Sayed's face.

"Second, the People's Assembly must give immediate passage to legislation effecting the official union of Egypt and Libya into a single and indissoluble state.

"Third, President Abd Jalil of Libya is to be named president-for-life of the new union.

"Fourth, Libyan warplanes now standing by at airports near the border will be permitted to land at Cairo, Suez, Alexandria, and Aswan, and Egyptian officers in military bases in those cities will turn over command to Libyan officers on their arrival.

"Fifth, all air traffic in the Aswan area is to cease immediately until these demands have been met.

"Sixth, the presidents are to remain on board the *Osiris* and are to make no attempt to land.

"Seventh, my men and I are to be granted safe passage from this studio so that I may return home.

"Eighth, no attempt is to be made to locate the bomb."

Munir switched back to English.

"My final demand is addressed to President Dunlap. He is to give a public commitment that all American military and commercial personnel will be withdrawn from Egypt, that the agreement that is to be signed today will not be signed, that there will be no more American interference in Egyptian affairs, and that legislation will be introduced in the United States Congress prohibiting further American investment in this country."

"Does that mean what I think it means?" Bar-Zeev asked. Rahman nodded.

"If my demands are met, I will send the signal to prevent the atomic device from exploding. However, if my instructions are not carried out to the letter, I will detonate the bomb immediately. It is in my power to do so. There will be no compromises and no extension of the deadline. I am not prepared to negotiate with anyone. I have a villa near Aswan, where I am staying. I have a radio receiver there that will be monitored on this frequency. I am to be contacted only to be told of acceptance of my terms. I repeat, there will be no negotiating."

Munir switched once more to Arabic, his voice rising and falling in a hypnotic cadence.

"People of Egypt, do not fear. I act only in accordance with the will of Allah for the greater glory of our country. Allah will protect you and guide your leaders along the right path. Have faith."

The screen was suddenly blank again. A dreadful silence settled over the room. Suddenly it erupted in a babel of voices as everyone tried to speak at once.

"Why don't we bomb the bastard out of there!" cried an American aide.

"He's crazy, it's a bluff."

"The Libyans! I might have known it."

"Silence!" The voice of President Sayed roared above the pandemonium. "I want the room cleared. President Dunlap and I will discuss this alone. The rest of you go below. Remain calm and we will tell you of our decision."

≋ ≋ ≋

A stiffening breeze suddenly blew over Lake Nasser, sucking the water up into tiny, white-crested waves. The two fishing boats, their throttles wide open, appeared to move across the surface through a halo of spray. The water felt cool on Leamington's face, a welcome relief from the blazing heat of the sun. The expedition had been on the lake for almost three hours, and soon the engines would have to be cut. Exhilarated by the prospect of action, Leamington was impatient to arrive at the island; yet he was gripped by a morbid fear of what he might find there after so long a delay. Nicole's agitated cry for help kept ringing in his ears, and his apprehension warred with his anger, sharpening his hostility and awakening a long-buried appetite for vengeance. He could taste blood in his mouth, as if he knew that finding Nicole alive and safe would not be enough. The black, volcanic rage boiling inside him demanded the most primitive satisfaction of the hunter.

One part of him was alarmed by this need for revenge against those unknown men who had robbed him of Nicole, a sensation he had not known since his combat days in Vietnam. The unreasoning anger that consumed him encompassed not only those men but Nicole as well, for allowing herself to be snatched.

He realized that he had never before experienced such powerful emotions: in war he had not hated the enemy as he now hated Nicole's abductors, because it was his own life that had been at stake then. But now it was Nicole who might be killed, and he could not endure that prospect. It came to him that he loved her more deeply than he had cared to admit and to lose her would condemn him to a life of emptiness and regret.

A change in the sound of the motor brought him out of his reverie. Raafat Shams, the tough little fisherman they had taken on board at New Harbor, had eased in the throttle, and the fishing boat slowed in the water. Shams waved to Sergeant Maraji at the helm of the second boat to cut his engine. The two craft eased together and the helmsmen conferred.

"He say island that way," Maraji told Leamington, pointing up the lake. "About six, seven kilometers now. We shut down engines, row."

"That's a hell of a long way to row," protested Leamington.

"Wind behind us. We go fast. Use other islands for cover."

Leamington looked in the direction Maraji had indicated. The lake was stippled with small, bleak islands, tiny points of brown sand and rock rising from the water. They would effectively screen the boats from anyone watching for them from the big island.

"The radio broadcast said the camp was at the south end."

Maraji nodded. "We land north side. Go overland. Better chance, surprise."

The plan was dangerous, especially in broad daylight. If the gang holding Nicole was expecting them, they could walk right into an ambush. But they had no alternative other than to wait for nightfall, and Leamington could not bear any further delays. They would just have to protect themselves as best they could.

"All right. Break out the oars."

≈≈≈

Saraj al-Rahid stood at the highest point on the island, scanning the horizon with binoculars. There was nothing to be seen. The glare off the sand and the lake hurt his eye, causing it to water. He put down the field glasses and wiped his cheek with the back of his hand.

He thought he had heard the drone of an engine somewhere in the distance. But with the wind blowing so strongly, he couldn't be certain, and there was no sign of any movement on the water. Perhaps it was a fishing boat, he thought.

He glanced back at the campsite. Everything was still, except for Habib, who was writhing in the sun. Son of a dog, al-Rahid thought to himself. Suffer. You deserve all of it. He thought of the woman in the tent and felt a surge of excitement. It had been a long time since he had taken a female. Despite his anger, he had found her body highly pleasurable. He would avail himself of her white skin once more before disposing of her.

His watch told him his shift was almost over. Yawning, he got to his feet. The muscles in his back were stiff, and he was anxious to get out of the wind. He checked the horizon one more time and saw nothing. He brushed the sand from his knees and started down the hill to awaken Gabal Marwan.

≈≈≈

Summoned once more to the lounge of the *Osiris,* the presidential advisers filed in solemnly and took their places around the table. All eyes looked expectantly at Dunlap. It was apparent from the expression on the American president's face that the appalling implications of the drama had reduced him to a sullen anger. As he listened to the debate, he cursed himself for not having along military advisers instead of a raft of economists and lawyers. His eyes came to rest on the face of Uri Bar-Zeev. The Israelis had a proven record of dealing with Arab terrorists; perhaps his was the voice that should be heard. But to suggest it would be a diplomatic snub of the worst kind. Still, desperate remedies for desperate times . . .

"—so I think we—you should storm the villa." The voice belonged to Dunlap's foreign policy adviser. Rahman raised his hand to catch President Sayed's attention.

"Yes, Ahmed?"

"Excellency, if I may. With the greatest respect to our American friend, I think that would be an error. We have the villa under surveillance from a distance, of course. That is no problem, since Munir led us directly there from the television station. But we must believe what the man says. To launch an attack against his villa would precipitate the crisis before we're ready to deal with it.

"I have met men like Munir before. They have the instinct of the scorpion. They will destroy everything about them to realize their aims, even if they perish in the process. So when he threatens to detonate the bomb if we make any move against him, I must believe that."

"But what if there is no bomb?" countered another American voice. "What if it's just a gigantic bluff?"

"Then we might all survive," Rahman conceded. "But let me ask you this, sir. If this were New York City instead of Aswan, would you send in the Marines?"

"What would the consequences be if he set off such a bomb at the High Dam?" asked President Sayed.

"We have received a report by radio from the hydraulic engineers at the Ministry of Power, Excellency. They say there would be a tidal wave. There are forty-eight billion cubic meters of water behind the dam. Every city as far north as Cairo would be inundated. They cannot estimate the number of lives that would be lost, but it would be in the millions."

"My God," muttered President Dunlap.

"What are we to do?" asked Sayed, holding out his hands imploringly. "The man will not negotiate. You've tried to contact him, Ahmed?"

"Yes, sir. He will not talk to me."

"I cannot allow this catastrophe to befall my people," said Sayed resolutely. "But to hand over the country to Jalil—that, too, is unthinkable."

"You cannot do that," said Dunlap firmly.

Sayed spoke directly to the American president. "I have devoted my life to this country, trying to rebuild it after the years of war. I have worked ceaselessly to improve the lot of our people. And we have made great strides. With the conclusion of the agreement between our two countries, I felt we were on the verge of a breakthrough. Now this. If I capitulate, all that work will have been in vain. Jalil would plunge us back into the dark ages again. But if I don't accede to Munir's demands, this most ancient of nations will be destroyed by a madman. Mr. President, how would you resolve such a dilemma?"

Dunlap studied the anguished face of the Egyptian leader. "Of course, the decision on what must be done rests with you. I will abide by whatever you decide. However, I would be interested in hearing what Colonel Bar-Zeev has to say on the matter."

All eyes swiveled to the stocky figure of the Israeli, who was leaning against a pillar, hands in his pockets.

"Well, Colonel?" prompted President Sayed.

Bar-Zeev felt uncomfortable under the communal gaze. He could feel the suspicion of the Egyptian advisers as they waited for him to speak. He glanced quickly at Rahman, who nodded encouragingly. Slowly he took his hands from his pockets and laced his fingers across his chest.

"I am a guest in your country, Mr. President. A stranger, a former enemy. My government sent me here at your request to be of whatever help I could to you. Even if we were still at war I could not stand by and see your country destroyed—though there are those who still seek the destruction of mine."

"Colonel," interrupted President Dunlap, "we have little enough time. Enough of politics. The implications of what is happening here are global. It could mean a third world war."

"I am aware of that, sir. But we have, after all, until ten o'clock tonight, which gives us several hours yet. We could be strengthening our own position."

"What do you have in mind?" asked Sayed.

"To start with, Aswan, Luxor, and all the towns and villages along the Nile should be evacuated. That will minimize the potential loss of life if the dam is blown up, and there was nothing in Munir's condition to prevent you from doing that. Next, we should launch a search for the bomb at the High Dam—"

"But Munir said he would detonate it immediately if any such attempt was made," protested Sayed.

"Wait until dark," replied Bar-Zeev. "How can he monitor events at the High Dam that closely? Security is too tight there. And he can't see the High Dam from his villa, can he?"

"No," said Rahman. "He faces the First Cataract."

"All right. Begin a systematic search as soon as the sun is down."

"And if we find the bomb?" asked Sayed.

"I may be able to do something about it. Maybe. I am not inexperienced in this area," continued Bar-Zeev. "In any event, knowing that there is a bomb and whether or not we can deal with it will make your options clearer, Mr. President. Gentlemen, right now you have three options: give in, which seems to be your mood; call Munir's bluff and risk the destruction of your country; or find the bomb and disarm it. Option three at least gives us the initiative."

"But could you disarm the bomb if it's found?" asked President Dunlap.

"Frankly, I don't know," Bar-Zeev said. "It would depend on the type of bomb, its placement—many things. But because of the conditions under which it must have been made I suspect it's a relatively crude device. I believe I could handle it."

Dunlap looked across the table as Sayed. "This is your country and your decision, Mr. President," he said. "You must make the choice. I would point out to you only that if you do give in, you will save Egypt from an annihilating flood—but sentence her to destruction of a different and even more dangerous kind."

Everyone at the table turned to Sayed. The Egyptian president covered his eyes with his hands. Finally, he lifted his head and looked at the men about him. "Very well. We will proceed with Colonel Bar-Zeev's plan. But if the bomb cannot be found in time, I shall have to reserve judgment on Munir's ultimatum. You have until nine tonight to locate the device and disarm it."

There was a knock at the lounge door. Rahman left his seat and opened it. He returned a moment later, holding a message from the radio room. "Excellency, we must mobilize the military for a proper evacuation immediately. There is chaos in the streets of Aswan. People are fleeing the city. Already several children have been trampled."

Sayed shook his head sadly. "At all costs we must avoid panic. See to the evacuation of Aswan immediately, Ahmed. And of the other cities along the Nile."

≅≅≅

The two fishing boats moved slowly on a zigzag course across the lake, using the shelter of the chain of islands. Leamington stood by the mast of the leading vessel, shading his eyes against the glare. All he could hear was the rhythmic splash of the oars dipping into the choppy water, and the ghostly sound of the wind moaning across the sand.

"There!" Abu Maraji, at the prow of the fishing boat, was pointing down the lake. Bill Leamington shaded his eyes against the glare. "Shams say that is island."

To Leamington it was indistinguishable from the dozens they had already passed, except that it appeared to be larger and rose from the lake like a camel's hump.

"Are you sure?" asked Leamington excitedly.

"Yes. We go behind that island there," said Maraji, indicating a smaller rocky outcrop closer to them. "It hide us."

"Tell your men when we reach the island they are to make no noise," Leamingtor said. "No talking at all. Land the boats as quietly as possible. Then fan cut along the beach. No bunching together, in case they've spotted us. Tel! them to wait for my signal to move and then to follow me. If I do this"—he made a downward motion with his hand—"they're to flatten themselves on the ground immediately.

"This isn't going to be easy. There's very little natural cover, so we'll be almost completely exposed. Tell the men if any shooting starts, they're to return fire only when they see a target. No indiscriminate shooting. Understand? Remind them that these people are holding at least two hostages. Is all that clear?"

"Yes, sir. I tell them," said Maraji, saluting, pleased to be under orders again.

"Above all, no noise. Tell them to be especially careful when they're taking their guns and equipment from the boats."

"Yes, sir."

"Good. Thank you, Sergeant."

The boat inched out from behind the island and was briefly exposed again as Shams maneuvered them toward another rocky outcrop. The large island was clearly visible now. Leamington lowered himself in the boat so as not to present a target if their presence had been spotted.

≅≅≅

Saraj al-Rahid, his watch over, picked his way through ankle-deep sand to the tent where Gabal Marwan was sleeping. The Libyan paused for a moment, cocked an ear to the wind, and then proceeded, shielding his empty eye socket from the particles of sand blowing in the air. He passed the inert body of Habib and prodded it with his toe. There was no reaction; the intelligence agent lay bloated and still, his face barely recognizable, swollen as it was from hours of exposure to the sun and the scorpion's venom, which had killed him.

Al-Rahid spat on the staked-out body. He felt cheated that there was no longer any life in the traitor. Habib should have lived longer; death should have come with agonizing slowness, so the girl could have witnessed it before he took her again. Cursing, he strode to the tent where Kader and Marwan were sleeping and shook Marwan vigorously. The bullnecked man finally roused himself.

"Your watch," al-Rahid said. "Wake up!"

Wearily, Marwan crawled out of his bag. The long night on the lake had exhausted him, and he had not slept well; Habib's groans had kept him awake long after the Libyan had left to stand the first watch.

"Is it necessary?" he asked al-Rahid. "My eyes are like lead."

"Get up, weakling. If you fall asleep, I shall shoot you myself."

Grudgingly, Marwan picked up an automatic rifle and began to climb through the rocks to the top of the hill. Al-Rahid returned to his tent and stripped off the shirt he had been wearing. He thought briefly of visiting the girl, then decided he was too tired. She would refresh his awakening. He lay down on top of his sleeping bag, ignoring the flies that droned noisily about the tent. In a few minutes he was asleep. The wind freshened and whipped up the sand, driving it like grapeshot against the canvas.

Exposed on the top of the hill, Gabal Marwan protected his face from the stinging assault of the sandstorm. He looked out over the lake, but the glare of the sun off the water made it difficult to see. He glanced around the hilltop, seeking some shelter from the wind. A large pillar of sand, carved into a strange, vaguely menacing shape by the elements, appeared to offer some cover. Marwan made his way to it and crouched down behind it. The surface was warm from the sun and effectively shielded him from the stinging wind. He yawned and set down his weapon. He knew he should keep a constant watch, but a periodic glance at the lake would be sufficient. And he was very, very tired.

≅ ≅ ≅

Bill Leamington motioned the rowers to boat their oars and let the wind carry them to the shore. A few moments later, the prows of the two boats scraped against the shale and sand that formed the beach to the north of the island. The men were out of the boats immediately, fanning out as he had instructed. Leamington noted with satisfaction that they had indeed had military training and knew the rudiments of assault.

He scanned the hill in front of him. There was no sign of life. If this was the right island, then the camp would be on the other side. There was no way to reach it except by going over the top. He was not a religious man, but he uttered a silent prayer that the rocks above him were not thick with snipers. With a wave of his hand, he signaled the men to move ahead.

Sergeant Maraji and the fearless Raafat Shams led the way, acting as scouts. Leamington moved forward cautiously behind them, using the rocks and boulders for cover, as did the rest of the men. Slowly they made their way up the side of the hill.

As they approached the top, he saw Maraji freeze. The Nubian remained motionless for several minutes, then turned and carefully made his way back to Leamington, motioning to Shams to do the same.

"One man. Up there," he whispered when the three were together. "Sentry. He sleep."

"Armed?" Leamington asked.

"Yes." In a few words, Maraji explained the situation in Arabic to Shams. The fisherman spoke briefly in reply.

"He say he"—Maraji drew his hand graphically across his throat— "he have experience as commando." The fisherman grimly patted the knife he wore in his belt.

Leamington looked up the hill. They were almost at the crest. "Any others?"

"No. I look."

"All right. Tell him it must be absolutely silent."

Maraji passed the instructions to Shams, who merely smiled.

Leamington watched as the tough little fisherman carefully moved back through the rocks, making maximum use of the little cover they provided. He could tell by the way the man handled himself that he had done this sort of work before, and he wondered vaguely who the target was. Shams reached a conical pillar of sand near the hilltop and flattened himself against it.

"The man, he on other side," said Maraji.

The months of hard training under al-Rahid had refined one instinct above all in Gabal Marwan—the ability to sense danger and to react immediately to it. He was instantly awake and reaching for his gun as Shams's knife sliced through his jugular vein. He collapsed with a gurgle, his blood boiling out onto the rock-strewn ground.

≈≈≈

The crew of the *Osiris* lowered a rope ladder over the side so that Ahmed Rahman and Uri Bar-Zeev could disembark into a police cutter, which bobbed on the swell alongside the boat. Although their view of Aswan was obscured, they could hear the frenzy of the townspeople ashore in their efforts to flee to safety. On Elephantine Island the guests and staff of the Oberoi crowded onto the jetty, trying to force their way into the ferry that sat dangerously low in the water, weighed down by the crush already on board. Small boats, defying the police prohibition against river traffic, were making the crossing to the east bank loaded with families and their pathetic bundles of belongings.

"How are you coping in town?" asked Rahman of the police lieutenant piloting the cutter.

"It's like the end of the world, sir. There is no discipline. We haven't got enough men to handle the mob, even with the army. The governor is touring the streets with a loudspeaker, trying to keep the people calm, but it's no use. They all know of the broadcast. If they didn't hear it themselves, somebody told them."

As the launch rounded the *Osiris* and headed full speed for the land-ing stage, the force of the noise from the shore drowned out the sound of its powerful engines. Shouts, car horns, braying donkeys, women screaming—the symphony of a city in agony echoed off the sand hills. Somewhere in the distance the lament of an ambulance siren wailed above the din.

Uri Bar-Zeev looked back at the *Osiris,* lying uneasily at anchor in the middle of the Nile. The crew were leaning over the rails watching the activity on shore, worrying, no doubt, about their families. It had been President Sayed's express wish—a decision in which President Dunlap had concurred—that the *Osiris* return to Aswan. Both Bar-Zeev and Rahman had argued that this action would expose the two heads of state to greater danger should the High Dam be blown up, but Sayed had been adamant.

"I cannot have my people see me running like a coward from danger, leaving them to face the tragedy alone," he had said, and Dunlap had nodded his agreement. "I could never live with myself after such an act."

So the *Osiris,* by then well downriver from the town, had made its way back and had anchored below Elephantine Island. At that point, the decision had been made to send Rahman and Bar-Zeev ashore to super-vise the hunt for the bomb at the High Dam.

"Munir laid down the condition that President Dunlap and I were not to leave the *Osiris,*" Sayed had said, "but he made no mention of anyone else's doing so."

So the cutter had picked up the two intelligence men and headed for shore under the late afternoon sun. As it approached the eastern bank, the police lieutenant idled the motor.

The scene on the waterfront was one of pandemonium. Vehicles of every description, many of them piled with bedding and other household effects, choked the streets leading from the city. Soldiers and police with bullhorns shouted contradictory directions, which only added to the chaos. Some drivers had abandoned their cars in the middle of the thoroughfares, electing to flee the city on foot, and had thereby effec-tively blocked the escape routes for those behind. Rahman could see people running wildly in all directions, uncertain where to go or what to do, caught up in a frenzied, mindless scramble. Many were carrying prized possessions—a lamp, a chair, even pots and pans. Some appeared to be bearing trophies from looted shops.

"My God," said Bar-Zeev, standing beside Rahman. "What a sight."

As they watched, a gray-haired man in a white galabia was knocked to his knees by a group of running youths. He remained there as if frozen in prayer. No one stopped to help him.

"It's worse away from the waterfront," said the lieutenant. "When they fall in those narrow streets in the market area, they can't get up."

"It would take an entire battalion to bring order here," said Rahman.

"They tried moving in armored personnel carriers, sir, but civilians fought to climb on them. They were throwing money to the troops to take them out of the city."

"Where do they want to go?" asked Bar-Zeev.

"Anywhere. As long as it's high ground, away from the valley," replied the lieutenant.

As the three men stood in the launch watching the antlike movements of the terror-stricken citizens, they suddenly heard the sound of rifle shots.

"They're firing over the heads of the crowd," said Rahman. "To discourage looting. All that's going to do is stampede them like cattle."

"Shall I tie up here, sir?" asked the lieutenant.

Rahman surveyed the shore. The blind panic of the townspeople reminded him of the air raids at Ismailia during the wars. He looked across at Uri Bar-Zeev and wondered what the Israeli was thinking. Bar-Zeev was shaking his grizzled head. He, too, had seen the refugees of war, the uncomprehending fear in the eyes of women and children forced to flee their homes for reasons they would never understand.

"No," said Rahman thickly. "There is nothing we can do to help. If we land here, we won't be able to move. Our job is at the High Dam. Go upriver to the Cataract Hotel. Can we requisition a car there?"

"I'll radio ahead, sir."

Rahman turned to Bar-Zeev. "When we signed the peace treaty, Uri, I thought there would be no more of this."

Bar-Zeev sighed. "You can call me a cynic, Ahmed, but ink on a piece of paper doesn't change human nature. History is a prophet no one listens to. There'll always be men who will act out their sick dreams in the name of religion."

≈ ≈ ≈

Rashad Munir stood on the balcony of his villa watching the great copper gong of the sun slide into the western horizon. The wind carried the sound of the stricken city to him, a baying sound like the cry of a wounded animal.

"Out of pain comes redemption," he shouted, raising his arms. He was overcome by a mystical feeling of exaltation, as if he heard in the core of the sound a voice whispering to him of his own death and resurrection. He felt cleansed and imbued with an extraordinary calm that seemed to wrap him in light and render him invulnerable. His mind had never been so clear; the intensity of his purpose had burned away all extraneous thoughts, isolating his one consuming idea. Allah had prevailed. Egypt would rise again from the trough of degradation to follow the true faith, freed from the cancerous embrace of the infidel.

Summoned by Munir's triumphant cry, Dr. Nasif hesitated in the doorway, nervously rubbing his hands. Beads of perspiration stood out on his forehead, and tension made him gasp for breath. There had been no word from the *Osiris,* and the unbearable silence had left him weak and enervated.

"Pardon me, Professor, but what do you think is happening? When will they decide?"

Munir turned to him and smiled. "When Allah wills it, Doctor. Do not upset yourself. It will be as we have planned."

"But it has been hours now."

"And they still have five hours left. We stand at the crossroads of history, Doctor. Savor the moment. Events such as these are not decided at a snap of the fingers. That's why I gave them ample time. To allow Allah to speak to Sayed and guide him."

"But what if they refuse to meet your demands? Suppose they've escaped from the boat and gone inland? How can you be sure?"

"They are still on the boat. Where is your faith, Doctor?"

Nasif pressed his palms against his forehead. His tension had brought on an attack of migraine. "I never dreamed you'd actually use the bomb. If I had thought that, I never would have made it," he murmured, half to himself.

"We will not have to use the bomb, Doctor. We have already discussed this," replied Munir calmly. "Sayed will agree."

"What if he doesn't? He is a stubborn man."

"Doctor, you are beginning to try my patience. There is still plenty of time. Our demands will be met. If they aren't, then that, too, is Allah's will. It is for us to accept His holy purpose."

"But will you detonate the bomb?"

"If it is Allah's will. His people must be purified."

"Professor, I want to leave. I am not well."

"Leave, Nasif?" repeated Munir incredulously.

"I am a sick man. I want to go with my daughter." The rotund little scientist became agitated. The pounding in his head made his voice shrill. "You must let us go. If the bomb goes off—the blast, the radiation—we will all be killed. All of us!"

"You are wailing like a woman," said Munir. He placed his hands on the trembling shoulders of the doctor. "Control yourself, Nasif."

The doctor broke away and then suddenly dropped to his knees, sobbing. "You must let us go," he pleaded. "You cannot hold us here."

Munir bent down and gently raised the man to his feet. "We are all instruments of Allah. We are in His hands. You and your daughter cannot run from Allah. He is everywhere. You are part of His design. What you have begun you must finish. Now, you will go inside and sit down. When you have collected your thoughts, we will pray together."

Munir put his arm around Nasif and with great solicitude led the distracted little man back into the villa.

≈≈≈

It was a time of watching and waiting, for time had become an unpredictable weapon shared by both sides. Each measured its response to the drama by the angle of the sun in the afternoon sky. In half an hour it would disappear beneath the horizon. For Bill Leamington and the men positioned on the hill above al-Rahid's island camp, the wait seemed interminable; but the order to attack would not be given until the numerical strength of the kidnappers and the exact whereabouts of Nicole could be determined. Leamington did not want to risk her life with a premature assault.

The sight of the staked-out corpse of Mustafa Habib had checked Leamington's initial impulse to rush the camp. For two hours they had hidden motionless on the windy hilltop, waiting for a sign of life. Sergeant Maraji crawled over to where Leamington lay in the sand, supporting his binoculars on his elbows.

"Maybe they gone," whispered the Nubian.

"No, that man was a lookout," Leamington said, gesturing toward the body of Gabal Marwan. "They're down there, in those tents. The question is, how many?" But as the minutes ticked by, he began to doubt his own judgment. There had been no sight of Nicole, no movement of any kind, only the sand sliding over the rocks in the wind. Perhaps the camp was deserted and the sentry had been left to guard the equipment. If that was the case, they were wasting time. Yet, if Nicole was being held in one of those tents . . . He would have to make a decision soon.

Salah Kader sat up in his sleeping bag and stretched. He looked at his watch. It was after five o'clock. Gabal Marwan was supposed to have awakened him at four to begin his shift on the hill. It was not like Gabal to do any more than he had to. Kader's muscles still ached from the physical exertion of the previous night. He pulled himself wearily to his feet and shook out his boots before putting them on. Then he picked up his automatic rifle and pulled back the tent flap.

The sun hovered over the horizon, and he shielded his eyes as he glanced up at the hilltop; he could see nothing. Puzzled, he walked over to al-Rahid's tent. The one-eyed man was sleeping soundly; Kader had to shake him twice to rouse him.

"Where's Gabal?" he asked when the Libyan was awake.

"What time is it?"

"After five."

"He's up on the hill. Probably fell asleep. Go on up and kick him if he's snoring behind a rock."

"All right."

Kader left the tent and began the slow climb through the rocks to the top of the hill. Bill Leamington watched him approach and hastily weighed his options. The man would be on top of them in three or four minutes. They still didn't know where Nicole was or how many others were in the camp. But soon their presence would be known. The new guard would have to be killed. The question was, could he be dispatched silently, as the other had been?

Leamington motioned to Raafat Shams to position himself behind a large rock, and then patted his hip. Shams nodded. He was to use his knife again.

Kader paused in his climb to dig into his pocket and pull out a pack of cigarettes. He drew one out and casually lit it. As he did so, he carefully assessed the terrain in front of him. His instinct warned him of danger. Marwan's behavior was untypical, and the ominous stillness of the hilltop disturbed him. Something was not right. The sound of his approach would have awakened Marwan. He threw the match to one side and was just about to start upward again when he caught an almost imperceptible movement to the right of his field of vision. When he turned to look, there was nothing. But something had moved there, he was certain. And it was not like Marwan to play practical jokes. Someone else was on the island.

Slowly he turned around and began walking unhurriedly back to the tents. Al-Rahid had to be warned quickly.

"He's spotted us," whispered Leamington to Maraji. "He's going back to raise the alarm. Can you pick him off?"

"From here? Maybe. Maybe not. Too far."

"All right. Then we'll go in now. No indiscriminate firing—only when there's a target. You stay with me; we'll try to locate the girl. Signal the men. Let's go!"

Leamington moved out from behind the rock and began running down the hill; the rest of his men followed close behind, plunging down the slope. From the corner of his eye, Salah Kader caught the sudden movement, dropped to the ground, and immediately began firing. His opening burst hit one of Leamington's men, who screamed and went tumbling across the rocks. Al-Rahid came running from his tent and ducked behind one of the equipment boxes.

"Get him!" shouted Leamington.

Instantly the island echoed with gunfire as Leamington's men opened up with their rifles. But Salah Kader's automatic weapon kept the rescue team pinned down.

"Take cover!" shouted Leamington.

Al-Rahid quickly assessed the situation. There were at least half a dozen men on the hillside; Kader couldn't hold out for long, he had no spare ammunition. The Libyan crouched down behind the container for a moment, considering his course of action; then he raced for the radio tent.

"We can't waste time," Leamington was saying to Maraji. "If we get stuck here, we lose our advantage and they may kill Nicole."

"I get him," Maraji answered.

Leamington raised his head above the cover of the rock and began firing at the prone figure of Kader. As he did so, Maraji darted to the safety of another boulder, then another, working his way down the slope.

Kader saw the danger; he was about to be outflanked and would have to fall back. Where the devil was al-Rahid? Slowly, keeping his weapon trained on the hill in front of him, he began to wriggle backward.

In the fading light, Leamington kept firing at the retreating Kader. If he finds cover and it gets dark, he can hold us off for hours, he thought. There was only one thing to do. Leaping up, he started running down the hill directly toward Kader, his rifle blazing away in the general direction of the man. Maraji, seeing what was happening, broke from his cover and rushed in from another angle, firing as he slid down the sandy incline. A bullet from Leamington's rifle struck the rock by Kader's head, exploding shards of granite like a fragmentation grenade. A splinter lodged in Kader's cheek just as he had his sights trained on the tall, running figure of the American. Before he could recover his aim, Leamington and Maraji had gotten to within twenty meters of his position. The Nubian dropped to one knee and fired. The bullet struck Kader in the shoulder, the force of it spinning him around. A second shot tore into his back. He let the rifle fall and slumped into the sand.

Leamington barely paused when he reached the body. "He's dead," he shouted to Maraji. "Come on, let's find Nicole."

Saraj al-Rahid crouched over the bound-and-gagged figure of the girl in the radio tent as the battle waged outside. The shooting had stopped now, and he worked furiously at the leather straps that bound the girl's ankles. The moment he had seen the size of the attacking force, he had realized his only chance of survival was to use his hostage as a bargaining counter. Killing her now would serve no useful purpose, and her death would certainly ensure his own. But she could be his passport to safety. He had had no time to speculate on who the attackers were; because he had seen no uniforms on the hill, he knew only that they were not regular army.

When Nicole first heard the gunfire she had felt a surge of hope, but when the grim face of al-Rahid suddenly appeared over her, she was seized by a new terror.

"You are going to do me another favor," he whispered into her ear as he untied her. He raised her to her feet and gripped her arms behind her back. "In case you are thinking of breaking loose," he said as he placed the blade of his knife under her chin. Then he pushed her in front of him through the flap of the tent.

Leamington reached the encampment just as Nicole and al-Rahid emerged from the radio tent. He stopped short and held his hand up to prevent his men from firing.

Seeing Nicole sent a great wave of relief through him—even with the sight of the knife at her throat. She pulled forward as if to move toward him, but the restraining arm of al-Rahid choked her back. They stood in a frozen tableau looking at each other; between them lay the body of Habib. The only sound was the buzz of the flies settling on the blood-encrusted lips of the staked-out corpse.

"Let her go," demanded Leamington.

"You are in no position to give orders," shouted the Libyan. "If any one of you moves one step, I will cut her throat like a chicken's."

"Nobody's going to move," called Leamington. "Let the girl go."

"Only when we strike a bargain," replied al-Rahid.

"What do you want?"

"Her life for mine."

"Let her go and you have my word you can leave the island."

"Your word is not good enough. She remains with me. I take one of the boats. No one is to follow us. I will leave her on an island in the lake where you can find her. If you try to follow, I will feed her in pieces to the fish."

"No deal," Leamington shouted. "You can take me, but let her go." He threw his rifle onto the sand.

"One step nearer and your lady will look like me," replied al-Rahid, moving the blade of his knife up to the corner of Nicole's right eye. She moaned behind her gag, and Leamington stood as if his feet had taken root in the sand. The blood drained from Nicole's tearstained face, and she appeared about to faint. Al-Rahid began to move backward toward the shore, pressing the girl's body against him as a shield.

"Tell your men to pull out one of those boats from the supply area over there," barked the Libyan.

Leamington hesitated for a moment, then nodded. Sergeant Maraji beckoned to Raafat Shams, and the two men moved toward the boats. Al-Rahid's one good eye flicked between them and Leamington. He began to speak loudly in Arabic, addressing the other volunteers. Slowly they laid down their arms in the sand.

"For the last time, let her go," shouted Leamington. "I promise you can leave and we will stay here. You can take the radio."

"The girl is all I need," responded al-Rahid. "Start up the motor," he called to Shams and Maraji, who had placed the rubber boat in the water. The electric batteries purred to life.

Al-Rahid continued to back toward the shore. The boat was on his blind side, and he had to turn his head to see if everything was prepared for his escape. As he turned, Nicole felt his grip loosen slightly. Summoning all her strength, she twisted her body and wrenched herself free. As she did, Leamington lunged for his rifle.

"Nicole, duck!"

She threw herself to the ground, and Leamington opened fire. The bullets thudded into al-Rahid's body, spinning him one way and then the other as he staggered into the water. The shots sent birds screaming overhead as the Libyan fell face down in the milky-green water along the shore. In a blind fury Leamington kept firing at the body, which jerked with the impact of each shot, until Sergeant Maraji placed a comforting hand on his shoulder.

Leamington threw down the rifle and ran to Nicole, who was kneeling in the sand. He pulled the gag from her mouth, and she fell against him, sobbing uncontrollably.

It was several minutes before Nicole regained her composure. Sergeant Maraji took control of the men and ordered them to carry the corpses down to the shore. Leamington held Nicole in his arms.

"Don't try to talk, darling," he whispered as she tried frantically to warn him of the terrorists' plan.

"No, please, we must get help." Fighting for breath, she recounted what Habib had told her. Leamington listened with growing alarm.

"We've got to get this information back," he said when she had finished.

"The radio's in that tent over there," said Nicole.

Leamington helped her to her feet and supported her to the radio tent. When he knelt down in front of the apparatus, one look was enough to tell him the transmitter had been damaged beyond repair by stray bullets. "Christ," he muttered. He pulled back the tent flap. "Maraji! We've got to get back to Aswan as quickly as possible. The radio's broken. Get the men on the boats, fast!"

"What about the dead?" shouted the Nubian. "They kill two of our men."

"Have them put in one of the tents. We'll send the army out to get them. And hurry up. We've got to warn the people at the High Dam."

≈≈≈

Situated at the rim of the Aswan High Dam and dominating the skyline stands a gigantic monument to Soviet-Egyptian friendship. It rises eighty meters in the shape of a stylized lotus flower thrusting huge petals into the sky. This white stone structure was erected in the euphoric days of 1970 at the completion of the ten-year project—a project financed by Soviet aid and accomplished by Soviet technology. Today it symbolizes a different reality—an ironic reminder of the transience of political accord. These thoughts passed through Uri Bar-Zeev's mind as Ahmed Rahman drove along the desert approach road to the High Dam.

The Israeli could recite the dam's statistics by heart—3,600 meters long, 111 meters high above the Nile bed, 980 meters wide at the bottom, 40 meters wide at the top, its body composed of rock fill, sand, and clay—yet his theoretical knowledge of the structure, garnered over the years by the Mossad, had not prepared him for the visual impact of the site itself. It was one of the wonders of the modern world, an achievement more impressive to him than the pyramids.

The question was, where should they start looking for the bomb?

As they pulled onto the road running across the top of the dam, Bar-Zeev could see a company of soldiers, lined up and standing at attention, awaiting the order to commence the search. They got out of the car and sat down on the stone parapet beyond the sidewalk.

"What do you suggest we tell them?" said Rahman. "The sun's almost down. We'll be able to start in a few minutes." They had decided to wait until sunset to minimize the risk of Munir's discovering that a search was under way, in defiance of his demands.

Bar-Zeev shook his head in dismay. "Frankly, it could be anywhere. On the lake side of the dam, on the river side in a service gate, under water, in the power station—anywhere. Who knows? Depending on the yield, it could even be a kilometer away. Or even in Munir's villa."

Bar-Zeev's diffidence was interpreted by Rahman as a lack of concern, and he turned angrily on his colleague. "You are meant to be the expert, Colonel. Put yourself in their shoes. Where would you plant such a device?"

Bar-Zeev looked at him strangely for a moment. "I want to find it as much as you do, Ahmed. . . . What's that building over there—the ruin?" He pointed to a sand-colored structure on a small island near the western bank, behind which the sun was about to set.

"That is the Kashaba Temple, dedicated to the Nubian god Mandulis."

"Does anyone ever go there?"

"No, it is off limits. That is part of a military area."

"It should be searched."

"What do I tell the men to look for? How large is the bomb?"

"It could be any size from a suitcase to a small car. They'll know it when they find it. Lend me your binoculars a moment."

Bar-Zeev walked across the road and focused on the power station below to his right. Steel pylons supporting looping wire cable stretched across the northern face of the dam. The station itself was a large white shoe box of a building.

"Is the power station secure?" he asked Rahman.

"It would be impossible to smuggle a bomb in there, if that's what you mean."

"All right. We won't waste time on it, then. Send teams of men out on the lake side to search among the rocks. Have they got metal-detectors?"

"Yes."

"Good. The bomb's casing will probably be made of steel. What about divers?"

"Divers make routine inspections of the dam facing throughout the year. They have been called back on emergency duty."

"Have them work the lake side as well."

As Rahman went off to brief the waiting troops, Bar-Zeev sat once more on the parapet and stared down at the foaming water emerging from the turbines on the north side of the dam. When the Egyptian returned, he said, "You asked me to put myself in their shoes. Well, I don't think I would plant a bomb on this side."

"Why not?"

"Just look. The approaches to the dam from this side are too dangerous. See how those cliffs fall away? There's hardly a foothold there. And look at the river. It's a caldron. There's no way to transport a bomb against that current. If it were me, I'd come from the lake side. It's much easier to get at and less likely to attract attention."

They crossed the road and surveyed the area behind the dam once again. From the stone parapet a paved wall sloped at an angle of forty-five degrees down to a sandy service road. From this point the open rock fill descended into the lake. Jeeps were already moving along the service road as the troops spread out to begin the search. The blue of the sky had given way to a purple dusk, but all lights had been forbidden.

"Now that it's getting dark, we can get the presidents off the *Osiris*," said Bar-Zeev. "Our friend in his villa will never know."

"I've already tried," said Rahman, "but Sayed won't move. He says he will take his chances with his people. Dunlap has decided to remain with him."

"Politicians," muttered Bar-Zeev, thrusting his hands back in his pockets. He looked toward the great stone lotus, its whiteness standing out against the darkening sky.

"You don't think our friend might have hidden his bomb in that memorial to Egyptian-Soviet achievement, do you?" But before Rahman could reply he added, "No, probably not. I don't think he has much of a sense of humor."

≋≋≋

Rashad Munir, having completed his final prayers of the day, sat peacefully in a chair in the living room of his villa, reading from the Koran.

In front of him Dr. Nasif paced up and down, tormented by guilt and fear. Nasif's daughter, Leila, watched from the other side of the room.

"Please, Doctor, be good enough to sit down. Relax. Some coffee, perhaps?"

"Coffee!" exclaimed Nasif in a high-pitched, nasal voice. "How can you talk about coffee? There is less than three hours to go. We have heard nothing from Sayed. How can you sit there so calmly?"

"I have told you. All will be well."

The bearded scientist stamped his foot. "It will not! I can sense it. They are not going to give in."

"Then what will be, will be."

"No. I will not permit it. I did not volunteer my life, or my daughter's life, for this project. You asked us to build you a bomb, nothing more. I am not ready to die for some mad religious idea."

"Mad?" Munir snapped the Koran shut.

"No. Forgive me. I didn't mean that. I just meant—well, it is your fight, not ours. We have done our work. Please let us leave now, Professor. You don't need us anymore."

"Do you read the Koran, Dr. Nasif?"

"Sometimes. Not often," the scientist replied distractedly.

"You should do so more often. Its words are balm for the troubled mind. I was just reading from the chapter of Al-Imran. Allah might have spoken the words for you. Listen."

Munir opened the holy book again and began to read aloud.

" 'No one dies unless Allah permits. The term of every life is fixed. He that desires the reward of this world shall have it; and he that desires the reward of the life to come shall have it also. . . .

" 'Believers, do not follow the example of the infidels, who say of their brothers when they meet death abroad or in battle: "Had they stayed with us they would not have died, nor would they have been killed." Allah will cause them to regret their words. It is Allah who ordains life and death. He has knowledge of all your actions.

" 'If you should die or be slain in the cause of Allah, His forgiveness and His mercy would surely be better than all the riches they amass. If you should die or be slain, before Him you shall all be gathered.' "

Munir closed the book.

"His message is clear, my dear Doctor. You have nothing to fear. If we should die tonight, it is not death, merely a passage to enter Paradise and spend an eternity with Allah."

Dr. Nasif, his face twitching with the pain of his headache, stood staring at Munir. "That's fine for you," he said finally. "You believe. But I am a scientist. I beieve in empirical truth. I do not wish to take the risk."

"But there is no risk, Doctor. You will die when Allah so ordains. Not before."

"Nonetheless, I wish to leave with my daughter."

Munir looked over at Leila, who immediately cast her eyes to the floor. "No. I will hear no more about it," he said.

"Then I shall send the abort message myself and stop the timing device. I will not die by my own bomb."

"You will do no such thing," said Munir coldly. "Sit down."

"I'm not afraid of you. You cannot stop me. If you refuse to let us go, I shall send the message."

"You will sit down!"

Defiantly, Nasif strode across the room to the door. The radio set was in a small library adjacent to the living room. As the scientist reached the doorway, Munir put his hand into the folds of his robes and withdrew a pistol. Without a word, he aimed and fired. The bullet struck Nasif in the middle of the back. He grunted, lurched forward, and fell to the carpet. His daughter gave a small shriek and ran to his side; she cradled his body in her arms and began to rock it gently. She raised her tormented face to Munir, who leveled the pistol at her.

"Kill me! Kill me, too!" she screamed, and buried her face in her father's chest, sobbing violently.

"It is Allah's will, my dear. I am only His agent," replied Munir in a faraway voice as he put down the gun.

≈≈≈

The wind had dropped, but the cold steel of the desert air at night cut through Nicole's clothes as she clung shivering to Bill Leamington. The two fishing boats sped north up the lake; their crews, aware of the urgency of their mission, maintained a grim silence. Nicole had no desire to speak; she felt like a young girl again, wrapped in the comfort of

Bill's arms. There would be time for explanations later—if they were not blown out of the water before the authorities at the High Dam could be warned of the danger. Her ordeal had left her weak and dependent. Her body ached, but she would not allow herself to dwell on what had happened to her; she merely luxuriated in the warmth of Bill's arms around her and cried softly for the joy of just being alive and safe with Bill again.

For his part, Leamington was torn between his concern for Nicole, who desperately needed medical attention, and the terrible burden of the knowledge he had to impart. Yet he could not help feeling a thrill of excitement; he was intoxicated by the danger of it all and elated by the sheer physical sense of winning. If the bomb had gone off at that moment, he would have died a happy man. He had had to fight and kill for Nicole, and the challenge had, in a curious way, awoken a primeval power in him; with Nicole in his arms he felt invincible.

"Can't you make this thing go any faster?" he shouted to Maraji, at the tiller.

"We go top speed," grunted the Nubian.

"Take the boats to New Harbor. You and I and Miss Honeyworth will get a truck and go straight to the duty officer at the High Dam."

"There it is," replied Maraji.

Ahead of them, obliterating the first stars of the night, stretched the High Dam, a great curtain of rock, black against the deep purple of the sky.

≅≅≅

"Colonel, the men have completed their search of the Kashaba Temple. Nothing to report." The young army lieutenant stood at attention in front of Rahman and Bar-Zeev, awaiting new instructions.

"Very good, Lieutenant," said Rahman. "Take your group and join the search at the eastern end of the dam. Make sure every crevice is examined."

"Yes, sir."

"Time is running out, Uri," Rahman said, sighing.

Bar-Zeev sat on the parapet, his legs dangling over the side, watching the teams of soldiers working below. Bobbing flashlights and the chink of metal over rocks were the only indications of unusual activity along the darkened face of the dam. In the murky water, shafts of green light moved slowly, like enormous iridescent fish, as frogmen with underwater flashlights inspected the submerged wall of granite.

"President Sayed gave us until nine o'clock. It's almost that now."

"And what are you going to do?" asked Bar-Zeev irritably. "Stop looking?"

"The decision is the president's. We must tell him."

"We're not going to give in, Ahmed."

"Would you have Munir blow up the dam?" Rahman retorted angrily.

"Which alternative would be worse?"

"At least if we gave in we would all be alive. We are talking about a country. Forty million people. My people."

"We are talking of much more than that, Ahmed. We are talking of freedom. The right to live with respect," said Bar-Zeev. "This is the way my people have lived for centuries."

"The Masada complex may appeal to you, but we Egyptians have lived with tyrants before. We have survived," said Rahman, his voice rising in indignation. "We have outlived all our conquerors, and we will outlive—"

Before he could complete his sentence, a Jeep roared along the road and came to a screeching halt next to them. Ismail Ali jumped from the vehicle. "I've just come from the guard post at the eastern end of the dam, Colonel. Leamington, the American, is there. He says he knows of the bomb and must speak with the officer in charge. Do you want to see him?"

Rahman looked at Bar-Zeev. The two intelligence men leaped into the back of the Jeep. Ali wheeled it around in a screeching U-turn and accelerated back to the sentry post.

There was no time wasted on formalities. Leamington conveyed Nicole's information as the girl clung to him, nodding as the story unfolded.

"About ten meters below the surface, you say?" asked Rahman.

"That's what Habib told her, isn't that right, darling?"

Nicole nodded.

"Can you be more precise?" asked Bar-Zeev.

"I've told you all she knows," replied Leamington. "She's been through a pretty rough time."

"Please, my dear," continued Bar-Zeev, ignoring the American. "Please try to remember. Did he say anything more about the location?"

Nicole began to speak haltingly, as if each word caused her pain.

"He—Mustafa—he didn't say. He wasn't with them when they planted the bomb. All he told me—" She searched her mind, desperately trying to recall her hurried conversation with the young intelligence agent. "He said it was attached to the dam in ten meters of water— A jetty. Something about a jetty. East of the jetty. Does that help?"

"It certainly does!" exclaimed Rahman, smiling broadly. He slapped his thigh with excitement and punched Bar-Zeev lightly on the shoulder. "Ismail. Quick. Make contact with the divers. Have them concentrate on the face of the dam east of the first jetty, between eight and twelve meters down. I want everyone moved into that area now. Move!"

"Yes, sir."

"We have to break our radio blackout and get a message to the *Osiris*," said Rahman, turning to the Israeli. "Something to inform Sayed we're closing in. We need more time. But we mustn't alert Munir if he's monitoring. We'll have to risk it."

"Yes. Something that could be a routine military transmission," said Bar-Zeev. "A message that would not arouse his suspicions. We'll just have to hope that your president reads between the lines. Perhaps something like: 'Evacuation plan proceeding. Will be completed by 2130 hours.' He should understand that as a request for an extension of his deadline."

"Uri, you are worth your weight in gold," said Rahman. "We will try it." He turned back to Leamington. "We owe you a debt of gratitude, Mr. Leamington. You took a great risk by coming here. Now, I must ask you to leave. I advise you to get out of the area and keep to high ground. We are not out of danger yet."

Leamington looked down at Nicole, then back to the two intelligence men. "I'm going to send Nicole out with Sergeant Maraji. I'd like to stay. I may be of help to you."

"No!" cried Nicole sharply. "I'm not leaving without you."

"I can order you both to be taken out," said Rahman.

"Sure," said Leamington. "But you need all the men you've got. We've earned the right to be here. If the bomb's going off in an hour, as you say, I doubt if we could get far enough away for it to matter."

"As you wish," said Rahman. "Come, Uri, we must raise the *Osiris.*"

The reply to the message indicated that President Sayed fully understood its implication. "Proceed with evacuation," it said. "Advise status at 2130 precisely."

"Splendid!" said Rahman. "I think we have been cautious long enough. I want the searchlights brought to the jetty to help the divers. And I need a launch standing by for us."

"I'd like permission to accompany you, Colonel," said Leamington.

Rahman looked at Bar-Zeev, who shrugged. "As long as you don't get in the way."

By the time the police boat cast off, the section of the dam where the hunt had been concentrated was ablaze with light. Powerful beams strung out along the jetty played on the surface of the lake and the rocky slope of the dam. The underwater lights of the divers shimmered in wavy lines as they worked their way steadily along the rock face. Rahman's police launch nosed its way through a small flotilla of support vessels, standing by with reserve air tanks and emergency equipment. There was virtually no sound; the search was conducted in an eerie silence that invested the entire scene with the quality of a deadly dream. Nicole, still clinging to Leamington, experienced an extraordinary sense of serenity; the idea of imminent death held no more terror for her. In the past twenty-four hours she had come to understand that living in fear was worse than dying. Her only sensation was one of profound gratitude.

Sitting at the rear of the launch, Leamington took a keen interest in the activities of the search. He did not think of dying; nor was it false heroism that had compelled him to stay. The action on the island had honed his sense of survival; it had brought back to him the exhilaration of coming through the carnage of Vietnam, and he felt more alive now than at any time since the war. The risks he took daily in business were inconsequential compared to this. By returning to the High Dam he had chosen to commit himself to the fight, and he would not leave until the battle had been decided.

He looked at the two intelligence men and wondered what was going through their minds. They were an incongruous pair: the black-haired Egyptian with the luxuriant mustache, who towered over the short, ferretlike Israeli. He envied them their responsibility for the operation; at that moment he would have traded all of Venture International to be in command.

Uri Bar-Zeev held onto the gunwale of the launch as it rocked gently in the water. He recognized that the final act of the drama was now being played out under the floodlights on the vast stage of the lake. In the beginning he had been an unwilling extra brought in to swell the scene; but slowly, inexorably, he had been drawn into the center of the action.

He shook a cigarette from his pack and handed it to Rahman. He cupped his hands around the flaming match as the Egyptian leaned down for a light. Rahman's face had aged over the past few days, and since their arrival in Aswan his ready smile had rarely been in evidence. His forehead wore a perpetual frown. In each line Bar-Zeev could read the deep anxiety that troubled his friend's soul. The fate of Rahman's country hung on what would happen in the next few minutes. If they failed to find the bomb, Egypt would either be subjected to the will of a demented tyrant or wiped off the map. Either alternative was too terrible to contemplate. And there was so little time. He glanced surreptitiously at his watch; it was 9:18. Above them the sable sky glittered with tiny, impervious points of light.

Rahman flicked his half-smoked cigarette into the water. He turned to Bar-Zeev. His eyes were unnaturally large in the reflected beams of the searchlights. "Uri," he began, and he hesitated as if waiting for the right word. "I just want to say that if we—"

Suddenly there was a splash as a diver broke the surface thirty meters from their boat. The man tore the mask from his face and shouted.

"He's found it!" yelled Rahman. "He's found it, praise be to Allah!"

A spontaneous roar went up from the troops along the dam. Rahman ordered the pilot to move in closer to where the diver thrashed exultantly in the water. He looked at his watch: 9:20. He cupped his hands around his mouth and shouted to the diver, "What does it look like?"

"It's black, oval-shaped, like a large egg," replied the man.

"It'll have to be disarmed in the water," said Bar-Zeev excitedly. "We can't risk raising it. It might be unstable."

"Can you instruct the divers on how to disarm it?"

"No. I would have to see it. Have you got a spare suit? I'm going down."

"You? Have you ever dived?"

"No, but I am about to learn, Ahmed."

"This is a job for experts, Uri."

"Listen, and don't argue. There's no time left. Get the equipment and get a diver to explain the fundamentals to me. Radio Sayed to hold off."

"All right, Uri. We have diving equipment on board. I'll get one of the divers."

"I've done scuba-diving," said Leamington, coming forward. "I can tell you how."

As Bar-Zeev struggled into the wet suit, he listened attentively as the American gave him a crash course on how to handle himself underwater.

"The regulator is your source of air. It fits in the mouth—try it. Okay? Your mouth will feel dry down there. Don't worry about it; don't panic. Try to control your breathing; keep it slow and steady. Keep the regulator hose over your right shoulder, like this. If it pops out of your mouth, keep calm and reach over like so, grasp the hose, and pull the regulator back. Never waste time and energy trying to grab the mouthpiece.

"There's a cardinal rule among divers: never hold your breath. If you do, especially when you're coming up, the air in your lungs will expand and they'll explode. And that's that. Understand?"

"Never hold my breath. I understand."

"Sit here so we can get the tank on. It's heavy here, but you won't notice it in the water. Now, you'll have other divers with you, holding lights and the equipment you'll need."

"I'll probably just need a knife."

"Okay. You shouldn't have any trouble. If you do, tap on your tank three times. That's the signal for help."

"Three times."

"These holes in the mask are a purge valve. If you feel water seeping in, tilt your head forward, press the mask to your face with both hands, and blow through your nose until the mask is clear. Got that?"

"Yes, I think so. Like this?" Bar-Zeev held the mask to his face and did as Leamington had instructed.

"You've got it. Okay, we won't give you any weights. This vest is a buoyancy compensator; if you feel yourself sinking, use the oral inflator —this thing here—to blow some air in."

"Anything else?"

"A hell of a lot, but you haven't time to learn. Remember, you've got lots of help down there if you need it, so don't be frightened."

"I'm too old to get frightened, Mr. Leamington."

"Yeah. Well, anyway, when you're coming up, do it slowly. Watch your bubbles. Don't surface faster than they do."

"All right."

"That's all I can tell you for now. Here, let me help you adjust your mask. Is that comfortable? Okay. Sit on the edge of the boat—no, with your back to the water—now, hold your mask and just fall easily. . . ."

As Uri Bar-Zeev hit the surface with a splash, Ahmed Rahman returned from using the launch's radio. It was 9:37.

When the water closed over Bar-Zeev's head, he felt a momentary surge of panic. Then, reassuring hands touched him on both sides, stabilized him in the water, and began to guide him forward. He tested his fins and found them easy to use. Feeling more confident, he swam with the other divers toward the bomb.

There was no sound except for the steady pace of his own breathing. He was conscious of the bubbles of air frothing from his regulator and trailing away behind him as he moved through the water. The swim to the bomb was short; when he reached it he found several divers surrounding the black egg, treading water and focusing on it with their sealed-beam lights. He swam over to the device and inspected it closely. The diver's watch he had been given told him only twenty minutes remained until detonation.

A very professional job, he thought to himself as he examined the lethal egg. How is it armed? There had to be some kind of timing device. He ran his hands over the bomb's surface, feeling its cold smoothness. Where was the detonating mechanism? Surely they wouldn't have transported a live bomb from Cairo! The silty water obscured his vision, even at close range. He felt water seeping into his mask and paused for a moment to clear it as Leamington had instructed. He was surprised at how easy it was. He looked at his watch: 9:44.

His hands went back to the bomb, caressing it like a blind man reading braille. He worked his way around the black egg to the narrow end, which was wedged into the wall. He motioned to the other divers to move in and give him more light.

It was then his fingers found what he had been looking for. Some tarlike material on the bomb's surface. Sealant of some kind. He pulled his cork-handled knife from his leg sheath and tried to maneuver himself into a position where he could see; he had almost no room in which to work. He sprawled across the top of the bomb, beckoning to the divers to bring their lights in still closer. Peering down, he made out the square outline of the sealant. But he couldn't get at it. The bomb would have to be dislodged from the rock face. It was 9:47.

Pulling back, he dived under the bomb and used his knife to cut the nylon ropes holding the underside to the rocks. Then he gestured to two of the divers to take hold of the nuclear device and swing it away from the rock face so he could get in behind. The black egg swung loose and knocked against the sharp edges of the protruding rocks. An ominous dull thud reverberated through the water. It was 9:50.

Above the waterline all military personnel had been concentrated on the road across the dam. Only a small team of support staff waited on the rock face to aid the divers. The boats formed a semicircle around the critical area, and everyone waited, their eyes fixed on the snakelike beams of light glimmering below the surface.

Rahman gripped the side of the launch until his knuckles turned white. Drops of perspiration coursed down his face; his shirt was soaked in spite of the cold night air. At the other end of the radio link, President Sayed waited aboard the *Osiris,* delaying his transmission to Munir until he had word from the dam.

As the divers held the bomb steady, Bar-Zeev used his knife to scrape away the tarry sealant. Beneath it, his fingertips found the seam he had been looking for. Gently inserting the tip of his blade, he began to pry open the metal hatch. The blade snapped in his hand. Cursing, he waved the broken knife at a nearby diver, who immediately passed him a new one. Bar-Zeev let the old knife go, and it floated gently to the surface.

Leamington was the first to see the reflection of the blade as the abandoned knife bobbed on the water. He pointed to it and called to Rahman.

"Is he in trouble?" demanded Rahman.

"He's got help down there. He hasn't signaled."

Rahman looked feverishly at his watch: 9:54.

Bar-Zeev's face mask was fogging up and he could feel the pressure of the water in his ears, but he continued to work at the hatch, trying to lever it free. Under almost weightless conditions, this simple act demanded all his strength. Slowly the hatch began to yield. Air bubbles began to rise from the pocket inside the bomb. Suddenly, the metal flap swung lazily open. And there, sitting in its rubber housing, Bar-Zeev could see the timing device. It was 9:56.

He was about to wrench it free when a thought flashed through his mind: perhaps it was booby-trapped. He snatched the lamp from the nearest diver and peered into the metal pocket. He shone the light on his watch; there was no time for a proper inspection—the device was due to explode in three minutes. Gingerly, he placed his fingers around the timer, and with great deliberation he lifted it clear of the bomb.

≋≋≋

Rashad Munir stood on the balcony of his villa, staring south at the dark, rocky hills beyond which lay the High Dam. The rise of the land obscured his view of the structure, but he could see it in his mind's eye: a blasphemy in concrete and stone, as ponderous and overbearing as the Russians who had masterminded it. The Soviet technicians had treated the Egyptian laborers with contempt during its construction and had demonstrated their disdain for the local work force by segregating themselves in ugly apartment blocks, isolated in a special compound south of Aswan. The dam they left behind them was a vainglorious symbol of godless pride—a challenge to Allah, who, from the beginning of time, had ordained that the Nile should flood the valley to replenish the land. The Russian engineers had boasted that no act of God could destroy the dam they had built, but if Allah willed its destruction, as He had willed the Flood, then the mightiest efforts of man were no more than spiderwebs across the face of the land.

Munir could hear Leila Nasif moving about the room. He watched her as she placed a cushion gently under the head of her dead father. She moaned softly to herself, rocking to and fro as she knelt by his body. Munir glanced at the clock on the mantelpiece: 9:58. There had been no word from the *Osiris*. The girl raised her head, her eyes ablaze with hatred.

"Are you going to send the signal to stop the timer?" she demanded in a sharp voice.

Munir studied her for a moment but said nothing. He crossed the room to the mantelpiece and laid his revolver down beside the clock, which he picked up in both hands, staring at its face.

"Are you going to abort?" shouted Leila.

"No."

"Then we will all die! It will all have been for nothing!" screamed the girl.

"It is Allah's will," said Munir softly, his eyes mesmerized by the passage of the second hand around the clock face.

"Murderer! You are insane! You would kill all of Egypt!"

"It is not I, but President Sayed." Munir's voice was barely audible; he could have been talking to himself. As the seconds to ten o'clock ticked away, he dropped to his knees, facing east to Mecca. He clutched the clock to his chest, feeling the rhythm of time beating inside him. He closed his eyes and waited. Allah would come in fire and water to avenge Himself on the unbelievers. Out of the ashes a new Islamic republic would rise, purified and untainted by the hand of the infidels. A smile spread slowly across his face; he was ready. He began to recite the Fatiha.

"Murderer! Murderer! Murderer!" screamed Leila, blocking her ears against the sound of Munir's voice, and she collapsed, sobbing, across the body of her father.

Munir continued to pray, unaware of the girl, unaware that she had stopped crying. Instead, she was making little gasping sounds, which gradually became laughter—shrill, high-pitched laughter that cut through his concentration.

"Silence!" he roared, but Leila took no notice. By now she was howling hysterically.

"It is after ten o'clock. Where is the wrath of Allah?" she shouted triumphantly.

Munir looked down at the clock cradled in his arms. It read 10:02. He shook it vigorously and then cast it aside. "Impossible! Your father has bungled it!" He sprang to his feet and ran to the balcony. All was quiet in the valley below.

"Perhaps Allah has shown mercy to His people!" Leila shouted at him.

Munir whirled around. "You will send the signal to detonate!" he bellowed.

"I will not!"

Munir advanced toward her. Leila raised herself to her feet and backed away from him. His face was twisted with fury. "Then I shall do it myself." He turned and ran toward the radio.

Leila grabbed the pistol from the mantelpiece with both hands. "No!"

As Munir moved toward the radio in the library next door, Leila aimed at him and fired. The shot passed his head and smashed through a window. Munir stood up to his full height and faced the astonished girl. Slowly he approached her, his hands outstretched in supplication.

"Think of the Koran," said Leila, backing away from him. "Remember the Book of Al-Baqara. 'Believers, retaliation is decreed for you in bloodshed: a free man for a free man, a slave for a slave, and a female for a female.' My father was a free man."

Without another word, she squeezed the trigger. The bullet struck the advancing figure of Munir in the throat. He fell face down on the carpet, his blood spreading over the pile in a dark pool.

≋ ≋ ≋

"Excellency, it is my privilege as a loyal Egyptian subject to inform you that the bomb has been rendered harmless." Rahman's message over the radio to the *Osiris* was greeted with a great roar in the army command center at the High Dam. Tears welled up in Rahman's eyes as he spoke. When he had finished he took off the headphones and raised his arms to the assembled force. The room erupted in a carnival atmosphere of jubilation and relief. Leamington and Nicole laughingly embraced; the officers slapped each other on the back and shook hands; outside, along the dam, soldiers fired their rifles into the air in a spontaneous expression of victory.

Rahman raised his hands for silence. "Gentlemen, President Sayed and President Dunlap have asked me to convey their thanks and congratulations to you all. I have been instructed to tell you all that there will be a fitting and substantial recognition for your efforts here tonight. You will be interested to know that commando units of our army are at this moment storming Munir's villa."

The room reverberated with a loud cheer.

"We are beginning radio broadcasts immediately, advising the people that the danger is over and they are to return to their homes. The armed forces are securing the airports, and the president has called for a full alert along the Libyan border. The crisis is over." Beaming, he added, "It is an occasion for your champagne, but unfortunately all we have to offer is beer, Mr. Leamington. Good Egyptian beer."

"That'll do just fine," yelled Leamington.

"Speech! Speech!" called Ismail Ali from the ring of troops surrounding the intelligence chief.

Rahman looked at the circle of smiling faces. "I find it very difficult to express myself in words," he began. "My heart is so full. What does one say to those who have come to our country and risked their lives to save our people? Please, if you'll permit me—" His eyes wet with tears, Ahmed Rahman hugged Nicole and Leamington in turn. Then, looking around, he asked, "Uri? Where is Uri?"

Bar-Zeev stood at the periphery of the exultant crowd, leaning against a desk, his hands in his pockets, a faint smile on his lips. Rahman moved toward him, unashamed of the tears of gratitude that flowed down his cheeks.

He placed his large hands on the shoulders of the Israeli. "We have learned much together, my friend. About each other and about ourselves. Tonight you taught me what real courage is. Whether you like it or not, the blessing of Allah will follow you for the rest of your days. How will I ever thank you?"

Bar-Zeev opened his mouth to reply, but he had no words. The two men placed their arms around each other and stood in a long, silent embrace.

Outside, the black, silty water of the lake continued to gush through the turbines of the High Dam, generating the power to illuminate the eternal valley of the Nile.

____AUTHORS' NOTE____

Although *The Scorpion Sanction* is a work of fiction, we have made every possible effort to portray accurately the face and mood of Egypt as we found it while researching this book during late 1978 and early 1979. Many people in various cities helped to increase our understanding of this vibrant and dynamic society, too many to thank individually here. However, we would like to single out one man whose invaluable assistance and friendly guidance enabled us to see his land through the eyes of a native-born Egyptian who knows and loves his country: Mahmoud (Mike) Soliman of Cairo and Toronto.

In addition to numerous interviews conducted in Egypt and on both sides of the Atlantic, our research involved extensive reading on the history, politics, and sociology of Egypt and the Middle East, and a number of books contributed greatly to our knowledge and understanding of the region. Particularly useful were *Growing Up in an Egyptian Village* by Hamed Ammar (New York: Octagon Books, 1973); *In Seach of Identity* by Anwar el-Sadat (New York: Harper & Row, 1978); *The Israeli Secret Service* by Richard Deacon (London: Hamish Hamilton, 1977; New York: Taplinger Publishing Co., 1978); *The Mossad* by Dennis Eisenberg, Uri Dan, and Eli Landau (London: Paddington Press, 1978); *The Plumbat Affair* by Elaine Davenport, Paul Eddy, and Peter Gillman (London: Andre Deutsch, 1978; Philadelphia: J. B. Lippincott Co., 1978 [American edition entitled *Operation*

Plumbat]); *Students' Flora of Egypt* by Vivi Täckholm (Cairo: Cairo University, 1974); *Eternal Egypt* by Pierre Montet (London: Weidenfeld & Nicolson, 1964; New York: New American Library, 1968); *The Society of the Muslim Brothers* by Richard P. Mitchell (London and New York: Oxford University Press, 1969); *Kafr El-Elow: An Egyptian Village in Transition* by Hani Fakhouri (New York: Holt, Rinehart & Winston, 1972); *The Arab Mind* by Raphael Patai (New York: Charles Scribner's Sons, 1976); *Islam in Egypt Today* by Morroe Berger (Cambridge, England: Cambridge University Press, 1970); and *The Arab Secret Services* by Yaacov Caroz (London: Corgi Books, 1978). To all these authors, our thanks.

GORDON PAPE
TONY ASPLER
Toronto, September 1979